OF LOVE & RUIN

SANCTUARY OF THE LOST BOOK 1

LOU WILHAM & CHRISTIS CHRISTIE

Copyright © 2023 by Christis Christie & Lou Wilham

All rights reserved.

No part of this book may be reproduced in any form or by any electronic or mechanical means, including information storage and retrieval systems, without written permission from the author, except for the use of brief quotations in a book review.

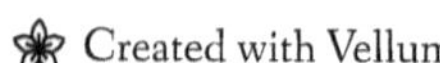 Created with Vellum

To the lost, the lonely, and the hurting who haven't found their place yet. May you find the family and love you're looking for. Always remember that family comes in all sizes, shapes, and colors, and sometimes the family we make is the best one of all.

Because family means no one gets left behind, left out, or forgotten.

Authors' Note

Please note that this book contains scenes depicting rape, suicidal ideation, eating disorders, and violence. We have done our best to handle these elements in a sensitive way, but if these issues could be considered triggering for you, please take care of yourself.

- Lou & Christis

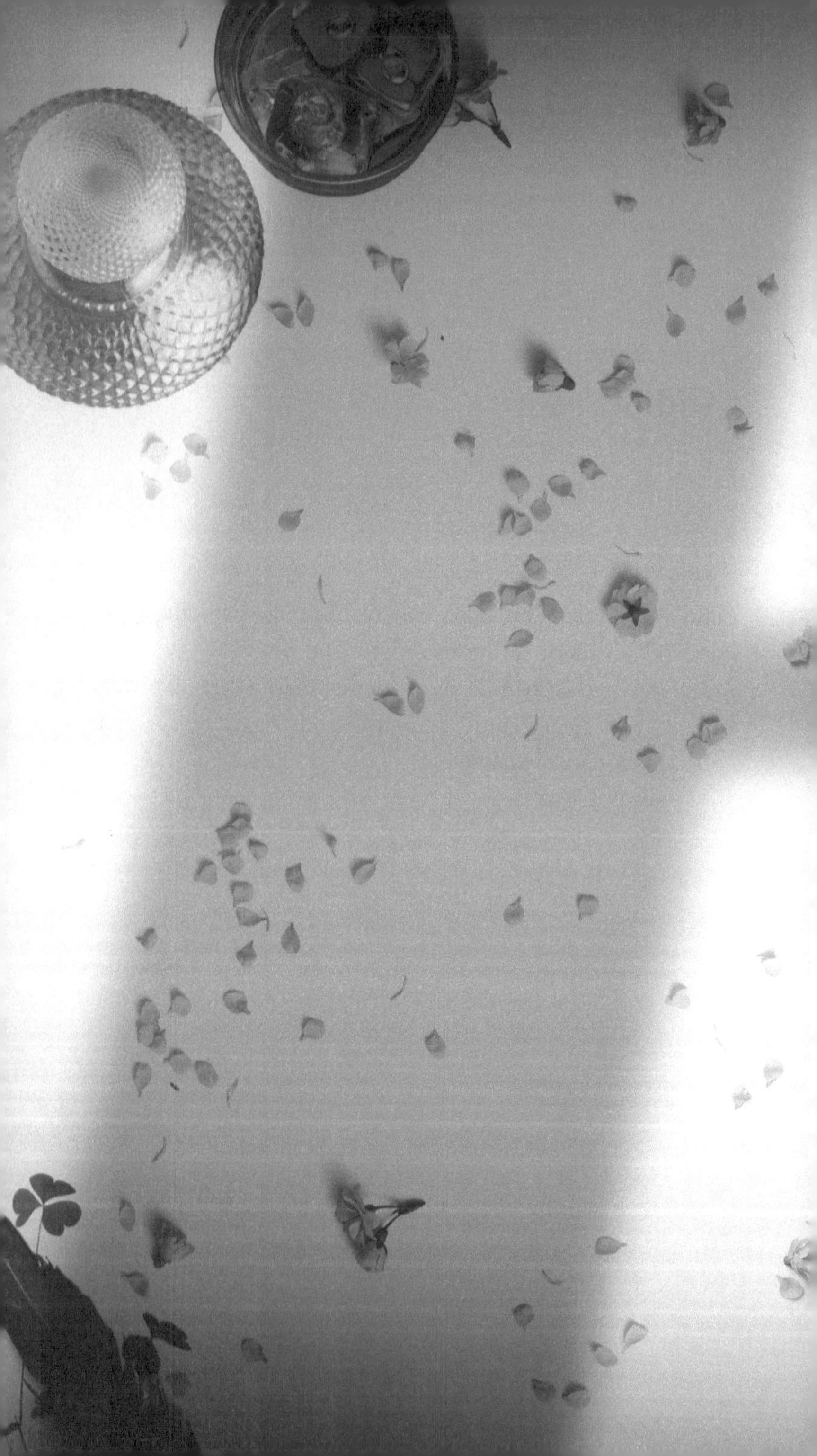

Prologue
Ander

Miami, Florida - June 2005

It was hotter than the pits of Acheron today, but the satisfaction of what was about to come helped to cool Ander like nothing else could.

Today, Ezequiel 'Zeke' Schields would get his due.

Exactly two years ago, Ander and Mab had moved to Miami following Ander's bright idea to open a world-class nightclub, catering to mortals and Underworlders alike. The location had been easy enough to settle on. The design already pictured perfectly in Ander's mind, and even the name had come to him without hesitation: Inferno. The one issue that had made itself prevalent on opening day—and every day since—was Zeke Schields, the owner of the nightclub across the street.

Eighteen months after signing the papers for the new location, Inferno had opened to a long line of excited Underworld residents and humans, all clambering to get in. When Zeke showed up, introducing himself, Ander thought he had come to welcome them to the neighborhood and perhaps offer a word of congratulations. Instead, he informed Ander that Inferno was little better than a trashy pimp's showroom and they would be out of business in two weeks.

Mab could barely restrain Ander from lighting Zeke's clothes on fire and dancing around his flaming body. Instead, he had settled for taking down the other nightclub by whatever means necessary.

Six months later, the two nightclubs were both still running strong but took every opportunity to undermine each other.

"You really didn't need to come," Mitchell, the health inspector, said for the second time since Ander met him outside of Element 79. He was badly balding, with sweat stains forming on his short-sleeved dress shirt and a tie that was clearly clipped on.

"No, I most certainly needed to be here." Ander wasn't missing this moment for anything. After all, he had to be certain that they *found* the rats he'd magically planted inside the club last week.

Ander tugged at the collar of his wine-colored velvet Louis Vuitton blazer. Over top of a white V-neck T-shirt and black skinny jeans, the blazer was definitely too much, and he was sweating profusely. Fortunately, unlike Mitchell-the-health-inspector, his sweating was not noticeable and a small snap of his fingers magicked it away for the second time since he arrived.

From his hairline, two elegant horns arched into the air, graceful like an antelope's, soft brown with light ridges. He had dusted them with gold glitter which sparkled in the bright Miami sunlight. To complete his look, Ander wore several rings on his fingers, a series of gold bands and sparkling gems.

He felt fierce, and it bolstered his confidence.

A white taxi van pulled up along the sidewalk. When the back passenger door opened violently, a little boy and girl who were *much* too old for the harnesses they wore launched themselves out onto the sidewalk. At the end of their leashes was none other than Zeke Schields. He climbed out over the fighting children. The little girl pinned the boy to the ground only for him to flip her and tangle the leashes even more.

On Zeke's back was a carrier, and a toddler flailed her limbs, crying most unhappily at being contained in the oversized BabyBjörn. Squinting at her, Ander realized there were a pair of pink wings—like they'd been ripped off of a flamingo—also flapping rapidly on her back.

The last to emerge from the van was a young boy, likely around nine or ten, who seemed to be the only Schields somewhat in control of himself at the moment. He was dressed in a light blue polo shirt and a dark navy button-up cardigan. Ander would have been shocked at the sight of the sweater if it weren't for the pair of brilliantly white wings gracing his back.

Ignis.

Created at the behest of King Indra, overlord of all Underworld, ignis were the soldiers that protected mortals from inanimi. Every magical creature in existence could find themselves being tracked down, questioned, and possibly imprisoned by the winged warriors for exposing themselves to humans. If they meant ill by their actions, the repercussions only got worse. They were obnoxiously tall, senselessly strong beings who were capable of drawing on an internal fire that made them perfect weapons.

Frack! Zeke Schields was a Guardian.

Made in the pits of Prometheus' forge, ignis were simply dropped to earth when they were needed, not born. Instead of creating them fully grown, Prometheus sent them to earth as infants. The Sanctum did not raise their own soldiers; instead, they left them with trusted humans to raise, train, and prepare for the position of being self-righteous pains in the ass.

It didn't change anything. *Couldn't* change anything. Ander wouldn't back down. No matter Schields' connection to the Sanctum.

The eldest wiggled an open candy bar in front of the toddler, calming her wailing for the moment, while Zeke attempted to untangle the two leashes, separating the middle children with his foot.

"Behave, you beasts!" Zeke grumbled at them, then eyed the health inspector with irritation. "Let's get this over with."

Schields handed the leash attached to the little girl over to his eldest child and dug a set of keys out of his skin-tight jeans. Stepping up to the front door to unlock it, he sent Ander a scathing look.

"This was you, wasn't it?" he hissed, shoving the door open dramatically. Ander merely shrugged and waved a hand before him, indicating that he was uncertain of what was going on. Schields only glared harder, then turned back to the oldest. "Stay out here with your sister. I can't do this with both the twins in here."

Schields and Mitchell-the-health-inspector then disappeared inside, leaving Ander and the two children outside.

Leaning against the hot brick wall, Ander gazed down at the boy holding the leash of his little sister, who was struggling against the restraint, attempting to get away with soft grunts of effort. "Le'go!" she growled.

The boy—clearly using his baby-ignis strength to help him—appeared to be holding her back with little effort.

"Cute pet you've got there," Ander said, not really certain what to do as he waited.

The boy frowned. "This is my sister." He sounded offended.

Ander smirked. "Are you sure? I have a puppy that I don't even treat this much like an animal." He nodded at the little girl, who'd accepted her defeat and was currently pulling a Lilo, lying face down on the sidewalk. "I think she's asking to be left to die."

Several emotions drifted over the boy's face, and Ander wondered what series of thoughts were going through his mind. Finally, he settled on asking, "You have a puppy? What kind?"

Ander blinked at the change of subject. "A teacup Pomeranian."

"What's its name?"

"*Her* name is Princess Monaco—Monnie, for short."

The small ignis grinned suddenly. "She's a princess."

"Yes, she is." And how. He'd only brought her home a little over a month ago, and already she ruled the roost. Mab was continually at him for his overindulgence of the animal. But he simply couldn't help himself.

The boy's smile faltered as his brows screwed up and another thought clearly came to him. "What did my Papa mean by '*this was you*'?" His bright hazel eyes, which bore a look of concern, shifted toward the door where his father and the inspector had disappeared, then returned to focus on Ander. Dark strands of fluffy hair fell to obscure his gaze, but that didn't seem to impede him. "Did you do something?"

Beneath the steady, inquisitive gaze of the young ignis, Ander nearly squirmed. "And if I did?" He felt haughty, saucy—defensive.

"Then that was very bad of you." His brow creased more, a look of near disappointment hitting his features. Though he was young, the soldier was there beneath the skin, just waiting to emerge. The suppressor of all social injustices.

"Maybe. Maybe not. Maybe it was warranted and deserved."

The boy was still frowning. "He's very stressed, you know. Daddy left for Syria last week, and we don't know when he'll be back. Papa has a hard time with the twins and Georgie all by himself."

He was eyeing Ander as if all of this were his doing and he'd heaped the stress down upon them. "Well, as unfortunate as that may all be, I have no control over whether your *Papa* is a good father or not."

The boy's face tightened in displeasure. "He's a good Papa!"

Ander lifted his hands up. "My apologies." Though, from what he'd seen, Zeke Schields was in way over his head with four children. Two of which were ignis, which meant a great deal of training and preparation for their future duties.

The life of a Guardian was a rigorous and difficult one. The Sanctum, from what Ander understood, expected a lot out of the couples raising their future soldiers to adulthood.

"Are you the one who owns the . . . the whorehouse across the street?"

Ander glared. *Of course Zeke would refer to it as such.*

"Nightclub," he corrected. "There may be whores, but no buying or selling. And yes, I am."

"Papa says you're his arch-nemesis. I'm not really sure what that means except that he has to *end you*."

Ander could only smirk in delight. "He does, does he?"

Clearly he had gotten under Schields' skin. That pleased him greatly.

The boy huffed and looked down at his sister, who was now poking at a bug crawling across the sidewalk in front of her, muttering her grievances to it. He must have decided she was fairly harmless at the moment, for his eyes drifted back up to Ander.

Or rather, Ander's head.

He squinted, then his face relaxed a little. "You have sparkly horns . . ." His gaze then fell to Ander's feet and shoes. "But no hooves." He met his eyes next. "What kind of Underworlder are you?"

Wouldn't he like to know? Wouldn't *Ander* like to know? "Some say I'm the devil."

He shook his head. "No, you're not the devil. You're too pretty." The little ignis then blushed, a charming shade that made his hazel eyes sparkle.

Ander chuckled, amused at the kid's reaction. "Too pretty to be the devil? What if that's the point?"

The boy shook his head. "No, there is no devil in Underworld. Just Hades, who the humans don't believe in anymore."

Oh, there were plenty of devils in Underworld. It simply depended on your definition of evil.

"I am half-muse, the other half no one knows for sure."

"Muse . . ." He fell silent then and looked to be in deep thought. "The muses live in . . . in . . . Hel . . . Hel—"

"Helicon. Yes. That is where I am from."

He nodded. "And do all muses have cool horns?"

Ander chuckled again and shook his head. "No, I am the only muse with horns. That's why they all think perhaps my father was a satyr."

"Oh. But satyrs are the servant race. Right?" He was a smart kid, it would seem. Schields had taught him well. Or maybe it was his partner, this unnamed "Daddy" who was responsible for all the schooling.

"Yes, they are."

"Oh."

"Mmm." Ander's eyes fell on the girl. "Your sister is eating that bug."

"Nox! NO!" The boy dropped down to fish his fingers into the girl's mouth. She began screeching, kicking and hitting at this invasion.

It was at this moment that Schields and the inspector stepped outside. Schields looked harried and upset, dark fury in his eyes as they landed on Ander. "I hope you're happy," he snarled. "I've been shut down for two weeks due to a *rodent* infestation." He handed the leash of the little boy to the eldest and then stooped to pick up the screeching little girl. "Is that a bug leg on your lip?!" He gasped in horror, plucking it from her mouth. "Seriously, you're seven years old. Whyyyyy?"

Ander watched the scene, dead positive he would never subject himself to the horror of having children.

Behind them, the inspector was stapling a notice on the door that the facility was closed until approval from the health board had been issued.

"It's a tragedy, really," Ander said, a smirk hitting the corner of his lips.

Schields whipped his head around to stare him down. "Don't think for one moment that I don't know you're behind this and that I won't find a way to destroy you. This will not be the end of me, Ruin."

"It's in the name darling: ruin. It's what I do best." Ask any life he'd touched in his three hundred years on the earth. Destruction and ruin were what followed in his wake. Even when he meant only the best.

Schields glared and then turned to say goodbye to the inspector. "Come, you hooligans, we're going home." The youngest boy cheered and darted for the street. His older brother just managed to stop him from careening out in front of the cab that was pulling up in front of the club.

Ander couldn't help himself as he saw Schields attempting to herd his children like a pack of wild cats into the taxi. "Schields, don't think of this as a loss for the club. Instead, think of it as a boon for your family. A chance to learn how to handle fatherhood."

Schields froze, his shoulders stiffening. Instead of responding, he finished getting the smaller children into the van before climbing in himself.

The eldest, who Ander had been conversing with, did turn though. There was a look of devastation and deep disappointment on his face. Slowly, he shook his head at Ander.

Ander didn't expect it, but he felt a wash of shame rising inside him.

Before he could apologize, Schields reached out of the van to grab the boy's arm and pull him up into the vehicle with him.

Just as the door shut, with one last view of bright white wings, Ander felt a twang of something deep and connected in his chest. Gasping, he raised his fingers to rub at the space right over his heart.

"Oh . . . fuck." Not waiting to watch the cab drive away,

Ander darted across the street without even looking and hurled himself through the front doors of Inferno. "Mab!" he shouted frantically. "*Mab!*" He screeched her name this time.

"What?!" Mab growled, stepping out of the back storage room behind the fine Brazilian cherry wood bar.

"We have to leave. Right now. Right *now*."

"What? Leave for where? I have to prep. We open in a few hours."

Ander raced over to her, slapping his hands down on the surface of the bar that had cost him thousands of dollars to buy, ship, and have installed. "Forget that. We're leaving Miami. I can't stay here."

Mab frowned in confusion. "What the hell do you mean? Ander, we just got our liquor license six months ago. Inferno is doing great. We're not leaving."

"But I think I've found him. *He's here in this city.*"

"Ander. Words that make sense, for the love of the gods, please."

"Erotes. The arrow. Ignis." He was panting, trying to catch his breath as anxiety filled him. "I think I just met my soulmate."

Mab chuckled darkly. "I don't care."

Ander blinked. "What?"

"You heard me. I don't care. We're not leaving."

"But—"

"No." With that, Mab turned and walked back into the storage room. The last thing she had to say on the matter was a rattling of wine bottles as she worked on stocking for that night's opening.

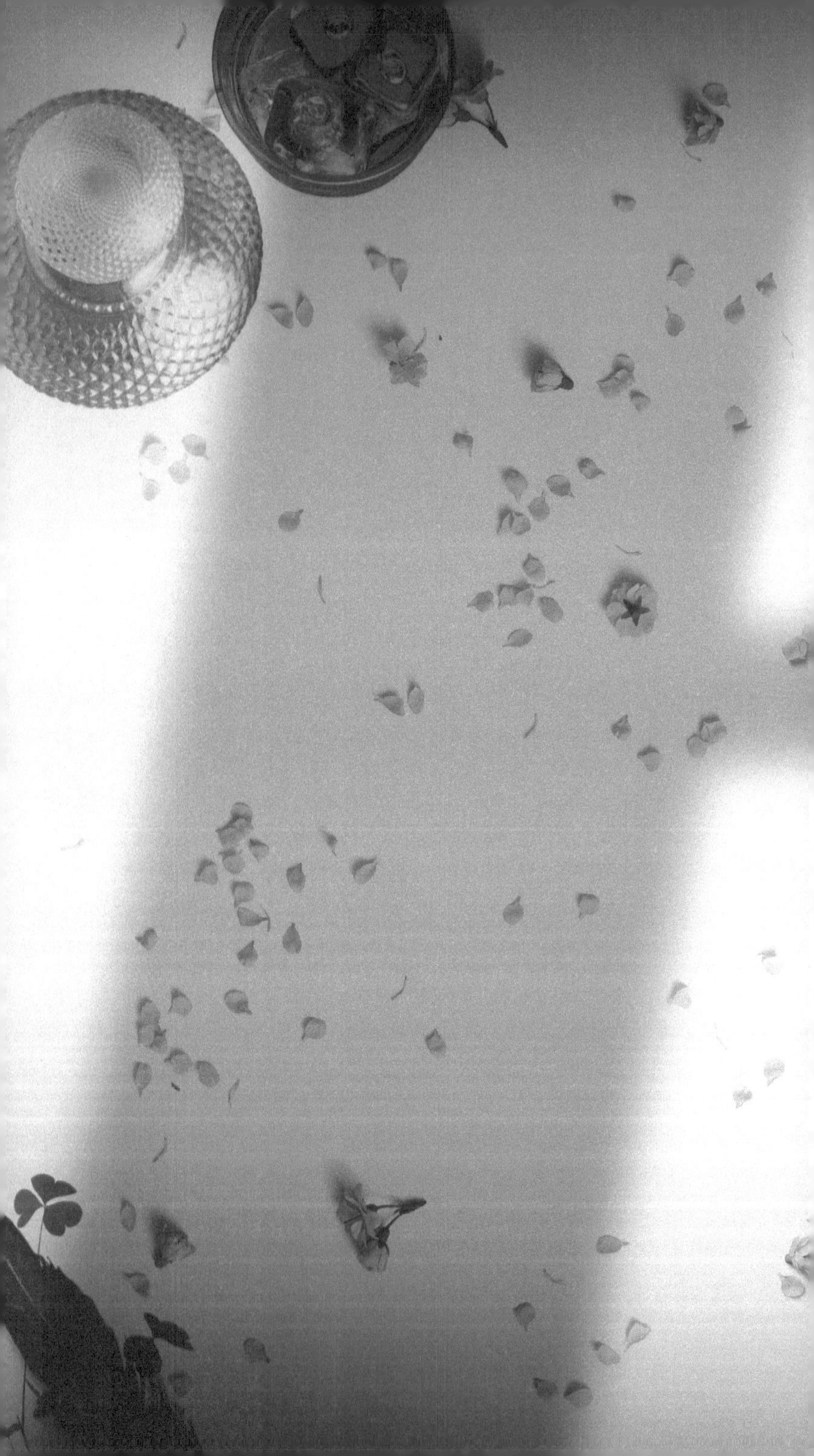

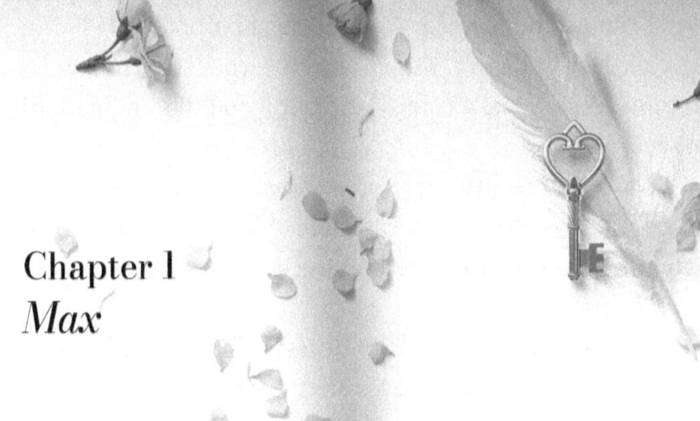

Chapter 1
Max

Miami, Florida - August 2018

The hair on Max's arms lifted, the skin below pimpling with gooseflesh as he and Nash walked beneath the air conditioning unit that adorned the entrance doors. It was the same all over Florida. Every store, restaurant, and even most residences had giant AC units bolted to the wall above the front door, as if the sudden blast of cool air could keep the heat at bay. It never did. All it served to do, in Max's honest opinion, was freeze the living daylights out of anyone as soon as they entered. Couple that with the unusually high body temperature of an ignis and you wound up with one very annoyed Max.

But it was an annoyance he could tamp down—bury—because there was a woman missing. Normally, that wouldn't have been enough to have the ignis investigating. Women went missing all the time in Miami. Usually, it was a matter for normie law enforcement. The difference here was that, after an unregistered normie stepped through a portal into Underworld in the neighborhood of Daisy Garcia, Daisy hadn't shown up to work the following morning. It could be a coincidence, or it could be an inanimi up to something.

"I told you to just wear your sweater," Nash said from beside him in the elevator, where Max could see Nash watching him rub at his arms in the reflection of the plated metal doors.

Max dropped his hands to his side, shifting on his feet. "You also told me I look like a ninety-year-old virgin in it."

"Yeah. So?" Nash tapped his fingers against his thigh while Max silently prayed that no one else would stop the elevator on their way up to Daisy Garcia's floor. He didn't want to share the tiny box with his brother, much less some mortal who he'd have to squeeze himself into a corner to protect his personal bubble from—his wings were already cramped. Gods he hated elevators. "That's never stopped you before."

It *had*, actually, but Max wasn't going to get into the way the twins' incessant teasing sometimes got to him. Not while they were on a job. He could grumble to his father over it later, when he had a practice sword in his hand and something to whack with it. Thankfully, the elevator dinged a moment later, ending the conversation. Max lifted his chin and stepped through the doors. He took a quick sweep of the hall Daisy Garcia's apartment was on—one could never be too careful—then gestured for Nash to follow him to apartment F.

It was down the end of the hall and probably had a stunning view of the strip. Another quick check to make sure no one was coming or going, and Max gestured for Nash to do his thing. His "thing" consisted of a little spellcraft done up by the folks at the Sanctum and left the door creaking open quietly. Nash stepped back, and Max pushed through.

The lights were out, but there was enough sunlight streaming in through the big bay windows to not need it. He'd decided to check Daisy's place in the middle of the day because it was a weekday and most people would be at work, but that didn't mean they could take any chances. So he did another cursory sweep to make sure there were no inanimi slinking about in the shadows before he motioned Nash in after him.

"I'll start in the bedroom," Nash volunteered and didn't wait for Max to give him the go-ahead before heading in that direction. Max huffed an annoyed breath and headed for the kitchen, where there was a little basket on the island full of Daisy Garcia's mail. It probably wouldn't help them at all, but it paid to be thorough.

He set aside a stack of bills—Daisy should really think about going paperless when she got back—and frowned as a shrill wolf whistle cut through the quiet hum of electricity. With an annoyed eye roll, Max bit back a groan. He knew he should have brought Nox, but she was busy with . . . *something*, he didn't rightly know what. And it was one of Quin's rare days off. So here he was with Nash. He supposed he could have brought Georgie, it was just an intel gathering mission, but he knew their Papa wouldn't have approved of that. She was still his "baby".

"Hey, Max! You gotta see this!"

"Nash, whatever you're doing, stop it," Max said, already halfway to the bedroom, curling his wings close to his body. Why did they make doorways so small in these places?

"How do you know I'm doing something?"

Max stepped into the bedroom to find his brother

digging about in Daisy Garcia's underwear drawer; his eyebrow twitched. "Nash."

Nash kept digging.

"Nash."

"Hm?"

"*Nash!*"

Nash jerked, whipping around with a pair of lacy white boyshorts hanging from his fingers, looking very much like a child who'd gotten caught with his hand in the cookie jar. "I was just looking to see if she had any receipts or love letters or—"

"Did you find anything?" Max felt his eyebrow twitch again; he was already developing a headache from this. He was definitely bringing Georgie next time, no matter what their Papa said.

"These." Nash grinned charmingly and held the underwear up to give Max a better view. "What do you think? Is this the kind of underwear Licia wears?"

"You have approximately three seconds to put those back and step away from that drawer before I write you up for misconduct and get you stuck with latrine duty, *again*." Max held up three fingers, lowering one and then two before Nash squeaked, dropped the underwear back into the drawer, and took a giant step back. "Good. Now go check her laptop. It's on the nightstand."

"You're really no fun when you're out on a mission," Nash grumbled, moving to retrieve the computer in question before dropping onto the bed with an impressive bounce. "I like you better when—"

"Don't care." Max shut the drawer Nash had been rifling through and went about checking the others. Nothing. Nothing. And more nothing. He scanned the top of the dresser: lipsticks, costume jewelry, and a tangle of different colored paper wristbands stuffed into a crystal dish like they were trophies. "Our girl likes the clubs."

"That's everyone in Miami." Nash shrugged, his fingers tapping loudly on the keyboard, then he seemed to realize who he was speaking to and added, "Well, except you and Quin, of course."

"I like the clubs."

A disbelieving grunt was his only response as Nash dove headfirst into his task, and Max moved on to check the bathroom. The only thing he found there was a shelf lined with enough Bath and Body Works lotions to keep the company running for the next five years.

"Anything?" he asked when he came back out.

"This might be something," Nash said hopefully, then spun the computer around so Max could see Daisy's Instagram. Picture upon picture of Daisy surrounded by a horde of other young people, their faces glossy with glitter or sweat, laughing with brightly colored drinks in their hands.

"What am I looking at?"

"This post"—Nash clicked to show a picture of Daisy with three other people, a glowing red wristband on each of their left wrists, their glasses raised—"is from the night before she went missing."

"Where was this taken?" Max asked, but even as he said it, his eyes drifted up to the location tag underneath Daisy's handle. "Inferno."

"Yu-*p*." Nash turned the computer back around so he could close out everything he'd been looking at and replace it where he'd found it.

His fingers skidded across the glass of his phone as Max called the sanctuary. Nox picked up on the second ring, which was suspicious since she was supposed to be *busy*, but he could grill her on that later. "What's up?"

Max bit his tongue to keep from laying into Nox about phone decorum on the official Sanctum lines for the third time this month. "I need everything we've got on Inferno."

"You mean the club across the way from Papa's?" Nox asked, and Max thought he could hear a potato chip bag crackle in the background. He cringed at the thought of crumbs all over their workstation again. Yeah, he was *definitely* putting the twins on clean-up duty next week.

"That's the one." He turned to see what Nash was doing. Nash's thumb flicked furiously over the screen of his phone, the blue light reflecting in his eyes as he scrolled through his own social media rapid fire. Swatting him, Max nodded toward the door. Nash's shoulders sagged, but he didn't fight any further as they did a quick sweep to make sure everything was exactly as they'd found it.

"It's owned by Ander Ruin and Mab Duchan."

"I want a workup on them too."

"All right." The bag crinkled again.

"You have twenty minutes." Max motioned to the door, then followed Nash back out into the hall and down to the elevator.

"Twenty minutes?! Max! That's not f—"

"I'm stopping for tacos on the way back. I'll bring you a quesadilla." Not that she deserved it, but Max thought better with food in his stomach, and it had always been the best incentive for the twins.

"Twenty minutes it is!"

Food sprawled around them on the meeting room table. Nox stuffed another too-big-bite of quesadilla into her mouth and clicked a button on the little remote to turn on the screen and start her presentation.

A quick call to Quin on the way back to the sanctuary had regrettably pulled him from his studio if the paint in his hair was anything to go by. But Max wasn't willing to wait to head to Inferno. Not if there was a chance that they might find Daisy Garcia still alive.

"Inferno opened about thirteen years ago," Nox said around a cheek full of cheese and tortilla. She had a picture of a building pulled up on the screen. It was a place Max knew well, had seen enough times when heading to his father's own club. "When Ander Ruin and Mab Duchan moved to Miami."

"I knew that." Max tapped his toe under the table, impatience making him jittery. "Tell me something I don't know."

"Okay, smarty pants," Nox sassed, swallowing her bite down with a loud gulping noise. "Ander Ruin and Mab Duchan—also known as Ruin and Blight—have quite the rap sheet. They party too hard. They piss off gods. And they generally cause havoc wherever they go. Ruin, being the crown prince of Helicon, has never really faced any lasting repercussions for his actions." She flicked to another slide of a beautiful copper-skinned man winking playfully at the camera and a brown-skinned woman tucked under his arm, looking thoroughly put out but also holding up a lazy peace sign. "Rumor says that he once pissed in Erotes' wine stores because the god of love hadn't invited him to a party."

"You know what Dad says about rumors," Quin mumbled into his nachos.

"That they all hold at least a kernel of truth?" Nash quipped.

"No, that's what *Papa* says."

"As I was saying," Nox huffed, flipping to the next slide, which was a picture of Ruin and Blight standing outside of Inferno, their hands lifted high and legs kicked back as they appeared to float in mid-air. "He's made quite the name for himself."

"Okay, what about Duchan? What's her deal?" Max crumpled the box for his tacos and tossed it into the bin in the corner over his shoulder.

"Two points!" Nash cheered.

"That had to be at least three." Quin was still looking at the picture of Blight and Ruin, his brow creased in the middle. Nox pushed a button, and the picture changed to one of just Blight, her white hair a halo of tight curls around her head and the light glinting off a set of three scars on her cheek that looked like nail marks.

"Fine, three." Nash pulled up something on his phone, and a second later, Max received a notification from the *Schields Scorecard* app on his own device that 3 points had been added to his ongoing tally.

"Well, the white hair isn't a style choice, for one. Duchan is a banshee." Nox took a long sip from her drink, the straw slurping loudly.

"Why isn't she in Sophelia then?" Quin had leaned forward in his chair as if to get a better look.

"They kicked her out." Nox shrugged. "Or at least, that's what the head of Sophelia says. But she wasn't born there, and from our records, Sophelia didn't actually pick her up until she was at least a hundred and fifty years old. So by that point—"

"She'd have been too used to life among mortals." Max

nodded. He knew what that could be like. They were all guilty of it—or maybe not guilty, maybe that wasn't the word. He shook off the thought. Either way, he knew how mortal life could get under a creature's skin and make them more human than creature eventually.

"Right. So there could have been any number of reasons why she left Sophelia." Nox clicked back to the picture of Blight and Ruin in front of Inferno. The joy on their faces . . . Max couldn't help but feel a little bad for everything that had gone down between his father and Ander back when Inferno first opened. But that was a matter for another time.

"What relationship do she and Ruin have?" Nash fiddled with what was left of his food, pushing the refried beans around the box.

"No idea. But Ruin's had a string of lovers, so I'd say they're just really good friends. I've uploaded a full workup of their histories to your tablets, but it was kind of a lot to put on the screen. Most of it's pretty trivial, nothing really that leads us to believe they might start abducting normies." Nox stuffed the last of her quesadilla into her mouth.

Max hummed, his eyes flicking over the report on his screen. She was right, there was nothing there that made it look like Ruin and Blight wanted anything more than a good time. But things—and people—changed. Max knew that better than most.

"What're you thinking?" Quin asked.

"I'm thinking we need to go to Inferno and at least have a conversation with these two—feel them out. Even if they have nothing to do with the disappearance, they might have seen something. It can't hurt to check." Max tapped his fingers on the screen, zooming in on a picture of Ander Ruin sitting on a plush velvet sofa, drink in hand. He looked exactly how Max remembered him from when he was ten. Ander had dazzled him with glittering horns and enough Disney knowledge to make a *Lilo and Stitch* reference. Beautiful. Effervescent. Gleaming with just enough easy charm to make Max's throat go dry now that he was remembering it. Max was in trouble.

Quin nodded.

There was a line around the block for Inferno. The roped off area was full of humans and inanimi alike. Humidity clung to the space between Max's wings, making him shift a little in his black shirt.

"Keep your glamour up," Max said to Quin over his shoulder as they made their way to the front of the line. He ignored the disgruntled grumbles from some of the other patrons. With a deep inhale, the heat of the air surrounding Max's wings shifted, wrapping tighter around him, warping the light like a mirage to better hide the massive white wings on his back.

"Why?" Nox asked in his ear over the comms. "Normies don't usually see them anyhow."

"Because neither Quin nor I want to deal with the paperwork associated with the bar brawl that two ignis walking into a known inanimi hangout might cause. Now tell me something that'll convince Ruin to talk to me." Normally, Max wouldn't bother. The ignis had the power and authority to make anyone talk to them at any time, but given the history between Ruin and the Schields family . . . Max wanted to make sure that this conversation ended on good terms. He didn't need Ruin getting it into his head to send a fleet of rats into Element 79 *again*.

"He likes pretty things." Nash sounded like he was smiling.

"And that is a reason he would talk to us . . . why?"

"Well, you're both very pretty," Nox teased, and Max heard Quin give an uncomfortable grunt behind him.

"You two are being particularly helpful this evening." Max sighed, rubbing at the bridge of his nose. The pressure behind his eyes from dealing with Nash at Daisy Garcia's apartment had only increased during the time it took Nox to brief them and he and Quin to suit up. Max reached for the pommel of one of his daggers and frowned when he felt nothing where it normally rested. Right. No weapons. They didn't want to appear threatening—not yet, at least.

"We try!" the twins cooed at the same time.

Max shook his head and turned his attention instead to the burly minotaur at the door. "We're here to speak to Ander Ruin and Mab Duchan."

"Yeah? Get in line. So are all of them." They snorted, lifting their chin to gesture to the long line behind Max and Quin.

Max pulled his wallet from his pocket, showing the minotaur his ignis identification. Usually they didn't need it because of the wings, but in situations such as these, it acted as the equivalent of any other law enforcement badge.

The minotaur's eyes widened, flicking to Quin and then back to Max. "I didn't mean—"

"We know you didn't." Max smiled, then shook his head and tucked the badge away. "Just let us inside, no harm done."

They nodded a little too quickly and motioned Max

and Quin through. "Ander's probably at the bar. And if not, Mab is always behind it."

"Thanks."

Heavy bass from Inferno's house music hit Max like a wall, and he had to take a minute to breathe. When he collected himself, he pushed through the throng of individuals with Quin and headed toward the bar. When they finally made it, Max looked over the heads of the mortals lining up for drinks to search behind the bar for Ruin or Duchan. They'd stand out, even among so many inanimi.

And that's when Max saw *him*. After thirteen long years.

Ander Ruin was dancing on one of the poles that had been bracketed into the ceiling, his hips rolling against the metal to the music, horns glinting in the low light. Max swallowed. His tongue had gone cottony and too big for his mouth. Yeah . . . he was *definitely* in trouble.

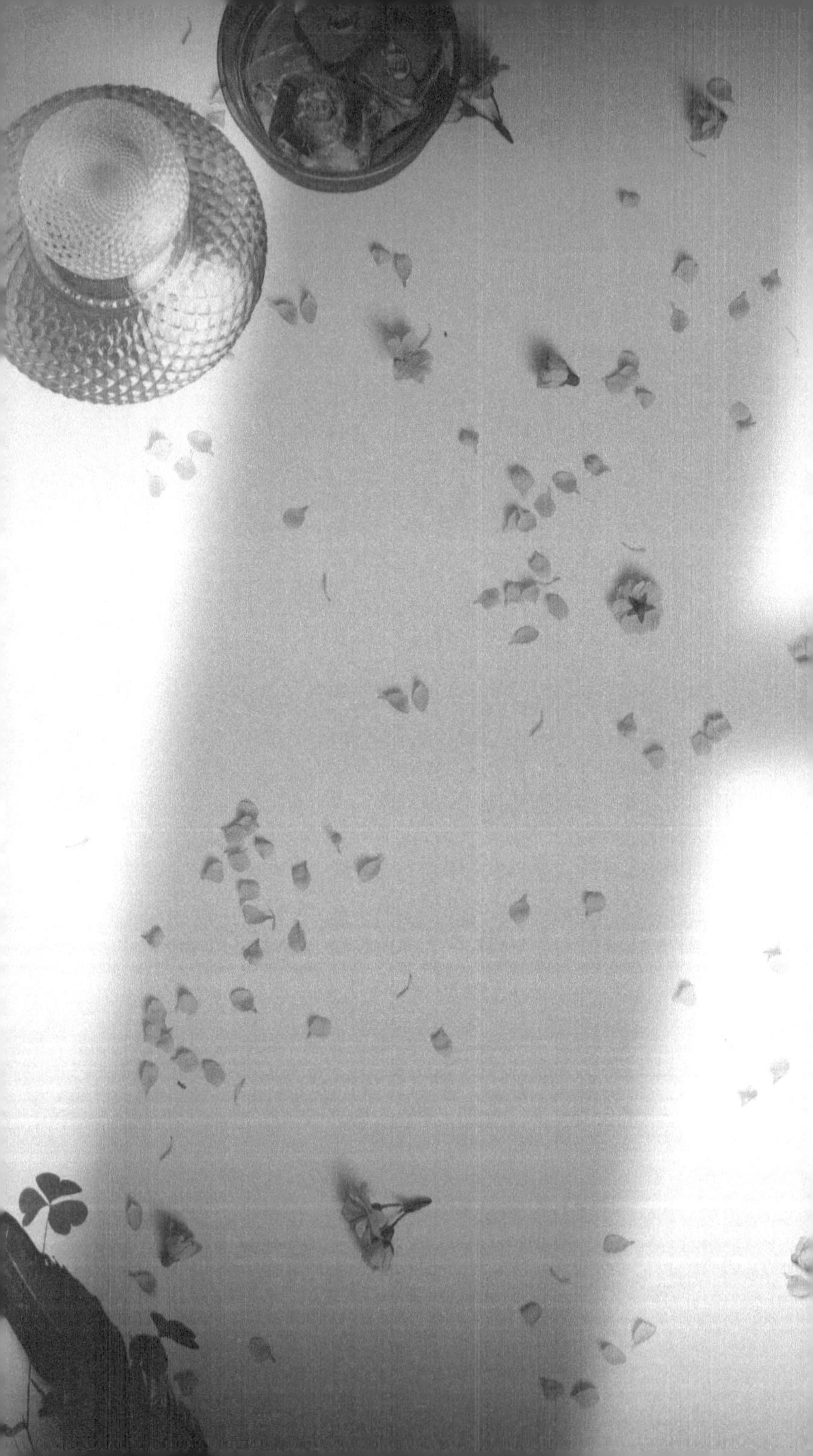

Chapter 2
Ander

The music hummed through Ander's body as he clung to the shiny copper pole that stretched all the way up to the vaulted ceiling, mounted on one of four three-by-three black platforms that stood at the corners of the main dance floor. Between each pole hung a copper cage connected to the floor by a matching ladder that led up to a hole in the center. In those cages, anyone could dance as they pleased without any concern of being touched or mauled.

Not that unrequested mauling was allowed in Inferno. Anyone accused of unsolicited touching was automatically banned. No ifs, ands, or buts. No reversals.

Ander grabbed onto the pole above his head and swung his body around, legs lifted in the air, most of the weight on his arms and torso. As his feet touched down on the third spin, he heard someone shout, "Excuse me, Your Highness?" over the music.

He leaned back so that he was viewing the club upside down and spun around on the pole until he came face to face with a pair of hazel eyes and black brows that made him halt in his twirl as a jolt of something powerful went straight to his midsection. "Gods, no, we don't use that title here."

While Ander *was* the son of Queen Aemiliana, the ruler of the muses in Helicon, he chose to forget that as much as possible. Ander had been born to an unwed Aemiliana who either didn't know who Ander's father was or refused to admit it. Ander was only half muse, the elegant horns protruding from his head a clear sign of it. It was better to just go on with his life here in the mortal realm and ignore his connections to the throne in Helicon.

Ander straightened up and turned around to face the male before him. A straight, aristocratic nose gave way to terribly kissable bow lips, a prominent chin, and an angular jaw a man could really sink his teeth into. He was absolutely beautiful, and Ander could feel the grin tugging at his lips and the itch to hold his fingers out and ask the other for a dance, even as something both familiar and foreign tightened within his chest.

"What can I do for you, handsome?" he asked, unable to tear his eyes away from the male's vaguely familiar face. Which proved beneficial as he caught the pink hue covering those wonderfully defined cheekbones.

If anyone was the perfect picture of what a highborn nobleman should look like, it was this one.

"We, uh . . . Well . . . Ander Ruin, right?" The male cleared his throat, shaking his head as if he needed to clear it of some cobwebs.

Ander could only watch and grin, wondering what had gotten under the poor thing's skin.

"We need to speak to you about a patron who visited your bar last night." Another male stepped forward, holding out a small black piece of leather with the Sanctum crest of two wings and a flame branded on its center in gold metal.

Where the first had the air of a highborn English aristocrat, this one looked like he'd come straight out of the heated sands of the middle east and was surely the prince of it all. He was lovely, in a way no man truly had a right to be. Straight, thick brows arched dramatically over a set of blue eyes that were crisp and clean as the blue sky. Lovely tanned skin stretched over high cheekbones, and a dusting of dark scruff accented his jaw, which only drew the eye even more prominently to his plush lips. Black, feathery hair fell into his eyes, shaved on the sides with only the swoop on the top. He was stylish but not annoyingly so.

And yet, despite how terribly pretty the second one was, it was the first that Ander's eyes drifted back to. "Ignis," he said calmly. Squinting a little, he saw through the shimmer of their glamour to the wings arching over their backs. Bright white on the first, pitch black on the second.

An angel and a devil.

Hopping off of the platform, Ander gazed up at the two of them, arching his head back. Ignis were annoyingly tall and broad-shouldered—built for battle. Ander trembled, not from fear but another dark, salacious emotion coursing through him.

"Y-yes." The first cleared his throat once more. "I'm Maximus, and this is my brother Quintus. We need to ask you a few questions about last night." His voice was lovely, not too deep but not too light. Soothing in a way that smoothed over Ander's body and comforted his soul. He wanted to bask in it.

Ander was staring. Blinking, he could only grin at himself and Maximus in turn. "Right, well, let's get away from the dance floor where it's a little quieter." With that, Ander walked closer to the side of the bar where a series of dark booths sat. Rich red velvet cushions curved around a dark cherry wood table and were backlit by LED flames rolling up the walls. "Now, what do you two fine gentlemen need to talk to me about?"

Quickly, Ander retraced his steps over the last week, and could think of nothing that he'd done that would bring the ignis down on him. At least nothing he could remember.

Maximus held out his phone so that Ander could look down at the screen. "This is Daisy Garcia. She was reported missing this morning. Her last known whereabouts were this club, last night. Do you recognize her?"

Ander studied the picture of the sweet looking girl but didn't recognize her. He shook his head. "Sorry, but she doesn't ring a bell."

"Are you certain?" Maximus frowned, and it brought out a terrible desire in Ander to feel his warm hands moving roughly over his body as he hoisted Ander up onto a table . . . counter . . . any hard surface would do really.

"Very, but let me ask my partner, Mab. She's usually working behind the bar, while I'm working *on* it." He winked at Maximus and then lifted his hand to twirl his fingers in the direction of the bar before giving a firm yank on the air.

The action magically grabbed Mab and pulled her swiftly across the bar toward them, knocking people out of the way without hesitation.

When she arrived before them, wobbling a little at her abrupt halt, there was a fierce look of fury on her features. "I told you to stop *doing* that! It's annoying, and performing magic in front of mortals is going to bring the ignis down on your head!"

Ander chuckled. "Funny you should say that." He waved his hand at the two ignis, Maximus gazing at him a little stunned and Quintus with a disapproving frown that did nothing for Ander's desires like his brother's had.

"She's right. You really shouldn't perform magic like that where humans can witness it. It raises too many questions," Maximus stated.

Ander waved his hand. "It's fine. They'll just all think she was hurrying through the club. Humans are far less observant than you give them credit for." He turned to Mab. "Meet Maximus and Quintus, two ignis here to see about one of our customers."

Mab turned quickly to peer at the two soldiers, concern marring her features. "What do you need to know?"

Maximus held his phone out to Mab. "Have you seen this human? She's gone missing, and this club was her last known whereabouts."

Mab studied the picture, her brow furrowed in contemplation. "Actually, I do remember her. She and her friends were getting really rowdy last night, and I had to cut them off when it seemed they were getting too drunk."

"Did you see her leave with anyone?" Maximus asked, and Ander watched the way his lips formed the words.

"No. Once I stopped serving them and signaled to Theranduil—our bouncer—to see them out, I moved on to other customers."

"Do you have security cameras on the premises?" His lips were moving once more and gave Ander just the smallest glimpse of straight white teeth and the tip of a pink tongue.

"Hm, wait . . . what?" Ander looked at the three sets of eyes staring at him and realized that last question had been posed to him. "Mm, yes. We have security cameras. I suppose you'd like to see footage from last night?"

Maximus nodded. "Yes, please."

Ander turned to Mab. "Why don't you take young Quintus here over to the bar and get him something to drink. I'll take Maximus to my office to show him the cameras." Before Mab could refuse, Ander wiggled a finger at the hazel-eyed ignis. "Follow me, darling."

Winding his way through the crowd, Ander headed for the staircase at the back of the bar, just behind the DJ booth, that led to his office in the mezzanine above the club. As he climbed the metal steps, he could feel the vibration of the ignis climbing behind him. Ander had to fight the desire to wiggle his bottom provocatively.

Ander unlocked his office door and flipped on the light as he stepped into the sultry den of sin that was his personal space here in the club. A big wooden desk with leather tufted sides sat in the middle of the room, a dark purple wingback chair set behind it. Above the desk hung a gold chandelier dripping with crystals that provided a luxurious feel to the lavish office. A deep navy chaise lounge was set beneath the two-way mirror overlooking the club.

He stepped up to a portrait of himself and Mab, swung it away from the wall on its hinges, and exposed the array of screens behind it showing off several areas in the club.

"What timeframe do you need to look at from last night?" When there was no response, Ander looked over his shoulder to see Maximus staring down at his desk, eyes wide and cheeks flushed with embarrassment. Following the ignis' eyes, Ander found what he was looking at: a selection of vibrators, lube, and condoms that were piled there. Ander laughed. "Once a month, we do a night called 'Sexy, But Safe' and give away toys and other sexual-related odds and ends. Proceeds go to the local Planned Parenthood. Those are some of this month's prize selections. You can have one . . . if you'd like."

The ignis shook his head and swiftly moved around the desk, putting as much distance between himself and the sex toys as he could. Coming to stand beside Ander, he shoved his hand into his black jeans, which caused them to stretch over the taught muscles of his hips and thighs.

"We're not certain what time she was here last night. It would actually be easier if you could provide us with your footage from open to close." His voice sounded rough, and the thought that perhaps there might be a hint of desire there made Ander's blood heat.

"That's going to take a moment to download. Do you have the time to sit and wait?" Ander purred the words, peering up at Maximus from beneath his lashes.

"I can wait." He glanced down, meeting Ander's gaze.

That abdominal hit from before seemed to shift and tighten in Ander's chest, and in response, his breath quickened just a fraction. He spun away from Maximus and rubbed lightly at the annoying sensation in his chest as he dropped gracefully into his chair. He opened his laptop to bring up the program that ran his security feed.

Ander grabbed a spare thumb drive from his drawer, connecting it to his laptop to begin the transfer of files. "For someone as pretty as you are, I've never seen you in here before." Ander slid a look over at the ignis, who stood just slightly beyond reach. Was he keeping his distance for safety?

"We have a family hangout . . ." He was blushing once more.

"Oh? Is this a private family hangout, or are others allowed to join?" Ander spun in his seat to face Maximus, schooling his features into a sultry look.

"It's open to anyone who wants to come." His cheeks were bright red, but there was a sparkle in his eyes that

Ander understood and recognized. He knew attraction when he saw it, and Maximus was certainly feeling it for him.

"Well, if you ever get tired of the same ol' hangout . . . you're always welcome at Inferno. Just give your name at the bar, the first few drinks are on me." Ander winked at him, then pulled the thumb drive out of the USB port when his computer dinged its completion. Standing, he closed the distance between himself and Maximus. "Or if you ever need someone to spice up the other place, you know where to find me." He held out the thumb drive.

Maximus, still blushing brightly, accepted it, their fingers connecting and sending a tingle straight up Ander's arm. Their eyes met, and Ander was breathless, getting swept away in a sea of hazel. Warmth filled him, and he almost took another step closer, wanting to be rid of any distance between them. Wanting to feel the firm muscle of the ignis beneath his hands. Needing to know what those bow-shaped lips tasted like.

"My number," Max whispered.

"Huh?" Ander rasped.

"I'll give you my number, in case you think of anything else—about the case," he was quick to add.

The spell broken, Ander stepped back. "Of course. For the case."

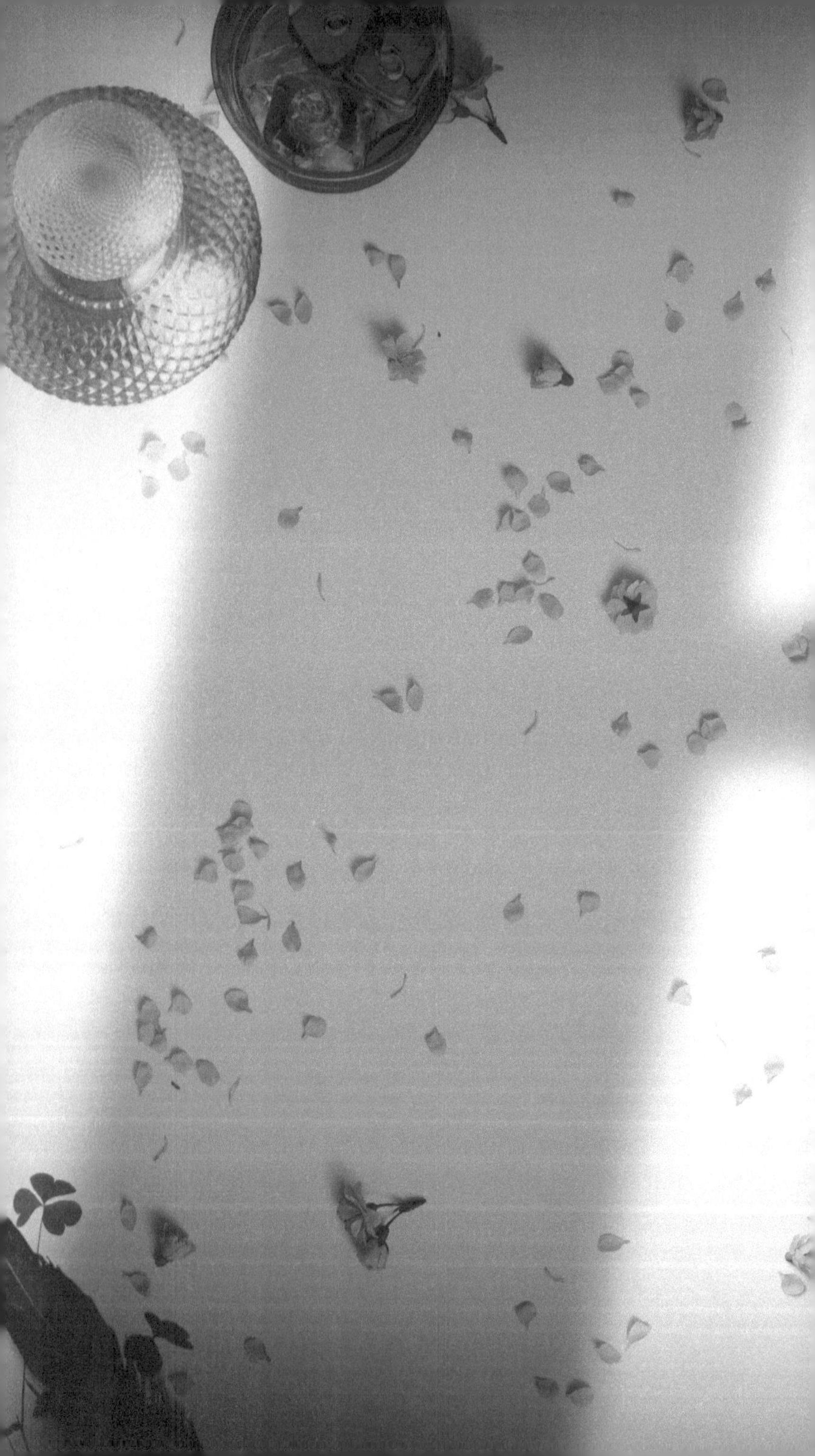

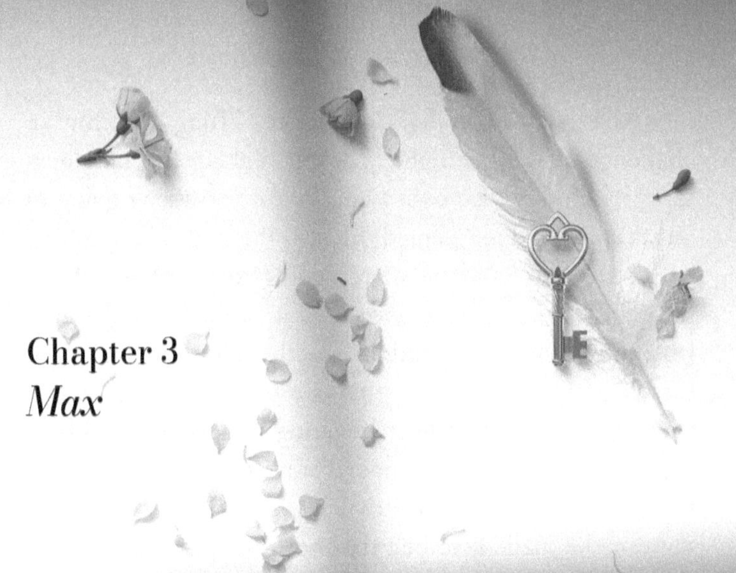

Chapter 3
Max

"I'm going to the training room," Max said on his way out of the office that was the Schields family command center, where Nash and Nox were already looking over the footage from the thumb drive Ruin provided. "You can head out, I don't need a sparring buddy."

Quin followed behind Max without a word.

"Really, Q, today was supposed to be your day off. Go home and take a nap. Or finish whatever you were working on. Or—" Max stopped at the expression that greeted him when he turned back to face Quin on the threshold of the training room. His brother, for as rarely as he spoke to people outside of their family, had the ability to say a thousand words with just one look. And what his face was saying right then was that he was judging Max. Hard. "I just need to clear my head, okay?"

"Okay." Quin shrugged, brushing past him to head for the racks of training weapons along the wall and retrieve a set of bo staffs before throwing one at Max.

Max caught it easily, a frown settling onto his face. "I'm serious, Quin, go home."

Quin fell into a fighting stance, lifting his chin in challenge, and Max sighed, defeat making his shoulders sag. His brother—his own twin, in a way—wasn't going to let this drop. He seemed to see there was something bothering Max, and he wasn't going to walk away from him. It would've been sweet if it weren't so damned frustrating. But he couldn't exactly tell Quin that the reason he needed to train this late in the evening was to work off the sizzle of heat lingering under his skin like a brand everywhere that Ander Ruin's eyes had touched— which was *everywhere*. Or that he hoped to be so tired by the time he made it to bed that he'd just pass out and not dream at all. No. Quin was already judging him, Max couldn't tell him all *that*.

"Fine. But you asked for it." Max laughed, spreading his feet to ground himself, and with a deep inhale, he spread the fire from his core out to his hands where it caught quickly on the metal of the bo before he made the first move. They traded blows, their bos smacking loudly against each other as they circled one another on the mats. Quin had the upper hand with this weapon, but Max was lighter on his feet from all those years of dance their Papa had dragged him to as a child.

Still, they sparred in silence, and Max almost thought maybe he'd gotten away with it. Maybe Quin wouldn't ask. But then he got a good swipe in at Max's legs, dropping him onto his ass on the mat. While Max was laying there, looking up at the ceiling, his brother came to hover over him. "What's bothering you about the case?"

Max groaned, smacking his head back against the mat. "It's nothing."

"It's not nothing." Quin dropped down beside him, setting a bottle of water on Max's stomach. It threatened to roll off with every deep inhale Max drew in, so he grabbed it and pushed himself up to sit.

"It just . . . doesn't feel right." Max threw his head back to take a deep swig from the water bottle.

Quin looked like he wanted to say something, his thick brows pulled together to crease his forehead. He let out a huff, shaking his head to clear it, and asked, "What doesn't feel right?"

"The whole thing! We're . . . we're looking in the wrong direction." Of that Max was certain. He might not know anything else, but he did know that. He could feel it deep in his gut, and his gut had never led him astray before. "Daisy may have been at Inferno the night she went missing, but Ruin and Blight have nothing to do with her disappearance. It's either coincidence—"

"There is no such thing as coincidence."

"—or a setup." Max frowned down at his boots, the water bottle dangling from his fingers.

"There's no evidence to suggest that." Quin's tone was reasonable, but his lips were pursed, still holding back whatever else it was that he wanted to say. It'd probably be better if he just spit it out so they could have whatever argument they were going to have and get it over with.

"I feel it in my gut." Throwing himself to his feet, Max started pacing across the mat.

"In your gut, or somewhere . . . a bit lower?" When Max whipped around to glare at Quin, he had one brow raised in question.

"Excuse me?" Max asked through his teeth.

"You heard me."

"That's not what this is." But already Max could feel heat crawling up his neck and across his cheeks as he remembered Ander sitting behind his desk, his legs gracefully crossed, and the soft, warm light of the chandelier shining down on him just so. Ander had looked like a king—no, a god. And Max had wanted nothing more than to fall to his knees and worship at his feet. Max shook himself and repeated, "That's not what this is."

Quin was still staring at him, his bright blue eyes narrowed like every thought that had just flitted through Max's mind had played out on his face for all the world to see. It probably had; Max was terrible at hiding his emotions. But Quin had always been the best of them, and instead of calling Max on his shit like the twins, Georgie, and even their parents might have, Quin just nodded. "Well, how about instead of following your intestines, you follow the evidence? Like we've been trained to do."

"Right." Max nodded, lifting one hand to run it down his face, and let out a long, slow breath. "Right."

"Good talk." Quin signed the words with deft motions, a clear indication that he'd exceeded his word quota for the day, then rose to his feet, patted Max on the shoulder, and took their bos back to the storage rack without a backward glance.

Max sucked in another slow breath and decided it was probably time he headed to bed. There would be plenty of time tomorrow to wallow.

The following morning rose too bright and too early, Miami's relentless sun streaming in between the blackout curtains on Max's windows to burn his eyelids, drawing out a groan as he buried his face further into his pillows. He didn't usually mind, but last night's restless sleep lingered as an ache in every muscle of his body. He'd kicked the blankets off at some point, too hot for his skin, and the heavy comforter he usually slept under now lay in a crumpled heap at the foot of the bed, a black ball of purring fur curled up on top of it looking quite content.

"Good morning, Hester," Max mumbled, scrubbing at his face as he reached for his phone where it had been buried under his pillows at some point when he fell asleep. "Where's Lady PurrPurr?"

The fluffy white monstrosity that was Lady PurrPurr answered by poking her head out of where she'd buried herself in the comforter with a delighted *mrroow*.

"Good morning to you too, Lady." Max huffed. With a tap, the screen of his phone lit up, and he had to squint to check the time as he'd turned the brightness all the way down the night before. "So early." It wasn't really, it was just about ten, and he had a training session with the ignis younglings in about an hour, but it *felt* earlier than that. "All right you two, scat. I need to put the blankets back on the bed."

The two cats just peered at him as he rolled off the edge of the bed, not moving from the safety of their little nest. He gave one corner a tug and felt Lady PurrPurr dig her claws into the blanket and the bed beneath, unwilling to move from the warmth she'd found there.

"Are you serious with this right now, Lady? I'm not in the mood."

Lady PurrPurr hissed, taking a swipe at his hand from where she'd hidden herself entirely in a sea of blue, just a single jagged white ear poking out. It was the one with the little cut in it from when she'd been a stray, and it flicked in annoyance.

"You know what? Fine. Keep it." Tossing the corner

he'd had in between his fingers over Lady PurrPurr's ear, he stood up to stretch, his back arching. Someone knocked on the door, and Max grabbed a shirt from the floor. It was rumpled, the sides still unzipped from where he'd taken it off a couple nights ago and not cared to put it away correctly. Stumbling over his discarded boots, he slipped his head through the hole and wrapped the back flap under his wings and around his waist to zip at the sides before he yanked open the door.

"Oh good. You're up." His Papa greeted him with a wide smile and a mug of coffee. "Dad told me to tell you that he made breakfast. It's in the oven for whenever you're ready."

"Thanks, Papa." Max took the mug, grateful for the heat of it in his morning-chilled fingers. "Am I the last one awake?"

"Mhm. The twins didn't come home last night. They said they were going over footage. And Quin wanted to get an early start at the studio before he needed to be over to the sanctuary for work. I've got everyone's shopping list, is there anything you need?"

"No." Max shook his head, taking a sip of the scalding coffee and letting it warm him all the way down to his stomach. It was nice. But it couldn't burn away the lingering traces of dreams from the night before. Clearly, he hadn't sparred enough.

Zeke nodded but lingered in the door, his eyes staring thoughtfully down into his own mug. Colt had switched him to decaf a couple of months ago, and Zeke still wasn't happy about it, but the doctors had said his blood pressure was through the roof. And with all the stress at the club . . . Well, something had to give. "Nash said you're digging into Ander Ruin."

"Of course he did." Max gripped the mug in his hand tighter. It wasn't exactly against the rules to share case information with their families, but Max didn't think this particular case needed to be discussed with their Papa, especially given his and Ander's shared history. He didn't want them to appear biased just because Inferno and Element 79 had been at war for well over a decade.

"You're going to get him for what he did to that girl, aren't you?" Zeke looked up, his brown eyes narrowed.

"If he did this, Papa, we will. But I don't . . ." Max chewed on the inside of his cheek in thought. He had to be careful how he said this; he didn't want to send his Papa off into one of his dramatic fits. "I don't know that he did this."

"What're you talking about?" Zeke's fingers had tightened around his own mug.

"There's no reason to believe he'd hurt a mortal." Max lifted his chin, meeting his Papa's eyes without flinching. If Zeke wanted to be angry with someone, it could be with Max. "He's never done anything to hurt one before, and I know you don't like him—"

"Don't like him?" Zeke snorted. "He's my nemesis."

Sucking in a deep breath, Max forced himself not to roll his eyes at the dramatics behind that statement. They were club owners, not superheroes. "Regardless, we can't be seen to be carrying out a vendetta. You know that. If he did this, I'll make him pay for it," he promised, earnest and needing his Papa to understand. "But I'm going to follow the evidence."

"Of course, Maxxy." Zeke's shoulders sagged a little, and he reached out to grab Max by the back of the head, pulling him into a one armed hug. Max went willingly, his free arm wrapping around his Papa's middle.

"Besides, he can't be all bad, right?" Max mumbled against the soft material of Zeke's robe.

Zeke clicked his tongue, pulling back to meet Max's gaze. "He's the worst. Don't be taken in by him just because he's pretty."

"What? I'd never!"

"Of course not." Zeke chucked him under the chin with his knuckles.

"What does that mean?"

"Just like your father." Zeke shook his head, whirling on his heel, the robe flowing out around him like a cloak. "Better hurry up, you know how those chicks get when you're late."

"Crap!" Max drank the last of his coffee in one quick gulp and turned back to get ready. His Papa was right, the ignis younglings were unbearable when he was late for their training sessions. He'd have time to think about Ander Ruin later.

"And then . . . And then . . ." the little girl said, her pale blue wings flapping behind her like a baby blue jay about to take flight. Floriane, or Flo as she preferred, was the youngest of the lot, barely even old enough to hold a training sword, and she'd latched onto Max the moment he'd walked through the door. Her little arms wrapped tight around his leg as he made his way across the training room to inspect his students' progress.

"And then what?" Max prompted, moving to correct the stance of a boy named Fidel. "Feet wider, if you keep them that close, it'll be too easy to knock you off your balance."

Fidel nodded, his shoes making a loud squeak as he scuffed them against the mats.

"Much better." Max hummed approvingly and earned a wide, gap-toothed smile for his troubles. He had a class of five this month, smaller than usual, but no less rambunctious or tiring. "And then what, Flo?"

"And then . . ." Flo puffed out her chubby brown cheeks, then let the air out, deflating. "I forgot."

"That's 'cause you took too long, stupid," Ardelis said, her tone sharp. She was the oldest and seemed to think this class was for babies, which always put her in a bad mood when her Guardian dropped her off. Although, to be honest, Max had never seen her in a good mood. She was a perpetually grumpy child. Max wasn't sure how much of that was to do with her home life. Most Guardians had a tendency to treat their charges like tools, soldiers, a thing rather than a person, no matter what age they were. It was only Colton Schields, really, who seemed to think they should be treated as family, children. With that in mind, it was hard to be too harsh with her.

"I'm not stupid!" Flo growled, her wings flaring out behind her.

"Yes you are. You're just a stupid little baby who doesn't know anything!"

"Ardelis, we don't call people stupid." Max crossed his arms, fixing her with a look of disappointment. "Apologize."

"But I—"

"Apologize. And then I want you to run laps." Carefully pulling Flo from his leg, Max pushed her to stand in front of Ardelis to accept her apology. Ardelis huffed, throwing down her practice sword. "That's an extra two."

"Ugh! Fine." Ardelis turned to Flo, holding out her

hand. "I'm sorry for calling you stupid, Flo. That wasn't nice. And I know better," she said like she was reciting lines from memory, which she was because they went through this at least once a day. "I promise to do better."

"You're forgiven!" Flo threw herself at Ardelis, tackling the bigger girl in a tight hug and only letting her go when Max grabbed her by the waist and hauled her off so Ardelis could climb to her feet. Ardelis was stiff as she rose, clearly uncomfortable with the physical affection. Most of the younglings were. Flo was different: she was still fairly young, and she'd been a part of Max's class for several months now and had gotten used to the care Max showed them. While the others still railed against it. Not that Max could blame them; Guardians weren't *supposed* to show affection for their charges. The younglings weren't *children*, they were warriors in training.

One quick nod sent Ardelis on her first lap around the training room as he sat a wriggling Flo down.

A prickle at the back of his neck told Max he was being watched, and he turned to find Nox leaning against the doorframe to the training room, smirking. "Something you need, Nox?"

"You need to come look at this." Nox lifted her chin to gesture to something behind her, and Max carefully extracted Flo from where she'd attached herself to his leg again. "Nash can show you, I'll sit with your class."

Max nodded, holding out a wriggling Flo to her before making his way toward the Schields family command center, where Nash was sitting in front of a wall of screens, his fingers flying over the keyboard. "Nox said you guys found something on the footage?"

"Yeah." Nash picked up a bent can that looked to be some kind of energy drink and took a gulp from it while his mouse moved to pull up the footage on the big screen in the center. Once it was there, he hit play. "This is about an hour before Duchan cut them off and sent them home."

Blueberry pancakes turned sour in Max's stomach as he watched Daisy Garcia grind against Ruin. Her hips pressed back hard into his as his hands moved to brush down along her waist.

"Looks like Ruin was lying when he said he didn't know who Daisy was."

"Yeah," Max said, forcing the word past a suddenly tight throat. "Looks like."

"Do you want me to call Quin? I think he's out at the training fields with Dad and Georgie."

"No. I'll go down there." Better to get the I-told-you-so out of the way. "Finish going over this footage and then go home and get some sleep. You two need your rest. I'll have Georgie and dad take over my class."

"Aye, aye, Captain!" Nash gave him a salute that looked like it might be jittery from caffeine, and Max moved to pat his brother on the shoulder before making his way out of the command center to hunt down Quin.

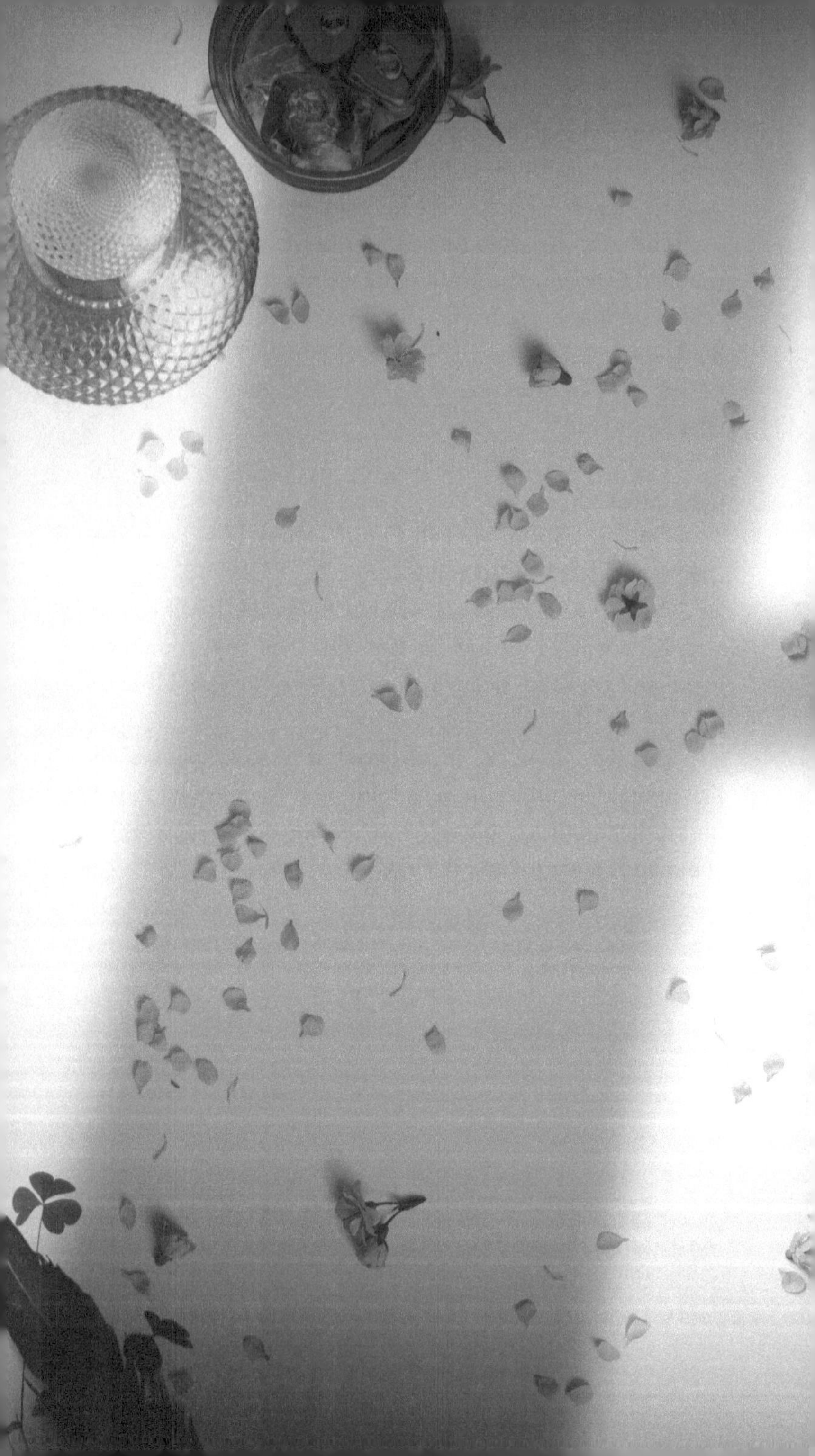

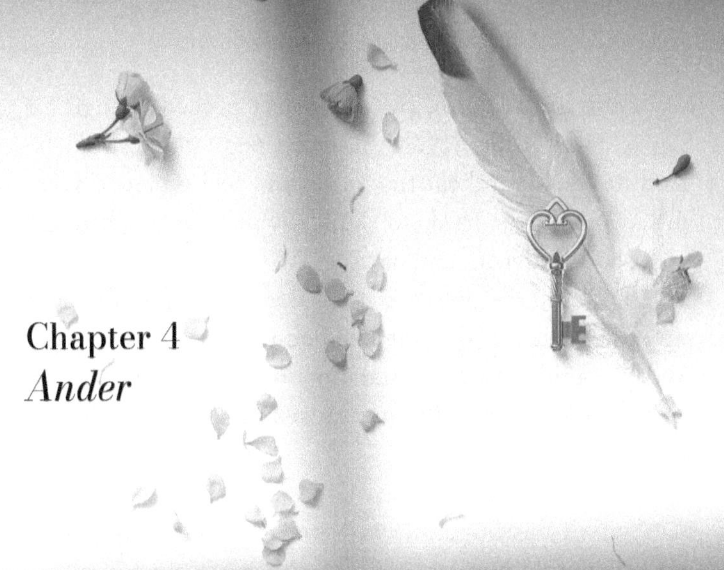

Chapter 4
Ander

Ander had taken his phone out half a dozen times to send a flirty text to the beautiful ignis who'd walked into his club the night before. Each time, something held him back.

Now he sat in his office, staring down at the white screen of his phone with the new contact drawn up. *Maximus (Hazel-Eyes).*

His thumb hovered over the button reading Message, threatening to press it and let him dive into a whole new experience. Ander's heart wrenched within his chest, making his breath hitch, but instead of Message his finger hit the button on the side, returning the screen to blackness. He lifted a hand to rub at his chest where a dull ache had settled, and something niggled at the back of his mind like a tiny bit of fluff on the tip of an eyelash. Blurry, unrecognizable, but there.

Maybe he'd wait one more day, then he wouldn't appear so desperate.

The music from below filtered in through his open door, making him feel like he was down in the club rather than up in his office. It was early yet, and while people were beginning to stream in, Inferno wasn't packed enough for him to take up his regular place amongst them. Still, he liked to be able to hear the music and feel a part of what he'd worked so hard to build while he worked on paperwork, ordering, and payroll.

He sensed the presence in his doorway before the light rap of knuckles on the frame announced him. Looking up, Ander found Maximus standing there, tall and broad, gazing back at him with an unreadable expression on his face.

The ache in his chest gave a spasm.

Ander's lips tipped up in a smile of their own accord, not listening to him or his desire to remain aloof at all. "I didn't expect to see you back here so soon. Did you come for that drink I offered?"

"No." His response was curt. "I have more questions for you concerning Daisy Garcia."

"I'm starting to get jealous that you're always speaking about another woman in my presence." Ander grinned. "I already told you, I didn't see her that night."

"That's the thing, Mister Ruin." Maximus ducked a little through the door so that his wings would clear the opening and strode across the office toward him. Behind Maximus, the other ignis, whom he'd referred to as his brother, waited in the doorway, arms crossed over his chest. "The footage proves otherwise."

Ander frowned, peering between the two of them and their very serious faces. "What do you mean?" He'd barely gotten the words out of his mouth before there was a phone in his face, and security footage of him grinding with Daisy Garcia on the dance floor played out.

"Do you honestly expect me to believe you don't remember dancing with her?" Maximus peered down at him, his brows creased in a pensive, stern manner. Ander thought perhaps he was meant to be intimidating.

It did take Ander's breath away, but not in a terrified manner.

"Yes," he said simply. "I do." A little chuckle slipped out as he leaned back in his chair. "Do you know how many people I dance with on a nightly basis?"

Max frowned. "Her backside was in your groin."

"So?" Ander quirked a brow at him, his gaze flitting back and forth between his eyes. Did that notion bother the ignis? "I dance. I get familiar. I flirt and I tease. I get customers' blood pumping and their lust brimming, and in the end, it sends them back to the bar to get more drinks. I barely look at faces, I interact with so many people in an evening." He settled back in his chair more comfortably, folding his arms across the expensive linen dress shirt covering his chest. "I may have danced with Daisy Garcia, but I don't remember her. And that's the truth."

There was a troubled look on Maximus' face. Ander couldn't help but wonder if it was to do with the case or if he was disturbed Ander could get fresh with so many people in a night that he forgot faces. His dancing was fun, light-hearted flirting that meant nothing and was used purely to drum up sales. It was part of his nightly duties and it meant nothing.

"You have to admit it seems suspicious."

"Very suspicious," Quintus parroted behind Maximus.

Ander leaned over so he could look past hazel-eyes to the other ignis. "I am sorry to disappoint your vivid imaginations, but I had nothing to do with that girl beyond a quick bump and grind on the dance floor." He sat back in his chair once more and crossed one leg over the other, his black boots gleaming in the chandelier light.

"Now, if there's nothing else, I have things to get to tonight."

His skin prickled, and beneath the flesh scurried little beetles of anxiety, stirring up feelings of disappointment in his gut.

Maximus nodded. "Same as before, if you remember anything else—"

"I have your number," Ander finished for him. Something in his chest throbbed and tightened, sinking more deeply into him.

The ache in Ander's chest didn't seem to want to go away. It kept him up all through the night, no matter what spells he worked on himself. It throbbed all the rest of the next day, and no amount of alcohol made it fade entirely. He made it through one more sleepless night of fitfully tossing and turning only to sit up in bed as the bright sunlight outside streamed in through his window and declare to the empty room that he was going to do something about it.

Monnie, who was asleep on the spare pillow, had twitched her ears and whined in disapproval at having been woken up.

Doing something, of course, involved dragging Mab along with him, which she wasn't exactly pleased about on their day off. But he didn't feel like doing this alone.

"Andy, what the *hell* is this?" Mab stood on the dock in the midst of the Everglades, staring at the houseboat floating on the swampy waters. "You told me we were going to the Olsen twins' house-warming party!"

"Gods, Mab, everyone knows the Olsen twins would

never be caught dead in Florida, let alone on a houseboat." His fingers pressed over the pain in his chest, the skin beneath his linen shirt damp from the humidity.

"What is going on?" The annoyance in her eyes nearly glowed.

"Patience." Ander leaned over so he could rap on one of the windows. "Vejovis. Excuse me, are you in there? Oy!"

"Vejovis?" Mab's brow furrowed. "Wasn't he thrown out of Olympia for messing around with immortality magic for mortals? And then executed by Indra for continuing to do his experiments?"

Ander huffed. "Don't be ridiculous. The guy brought medicine to the human world, and once he was finished with his life's work, he hid away in his retirement."

"In a swamp in *Miami*?"

"Everyone comes to Florida when they retire."

Mab huffed, crossing her arms over her chest and tapping her foot on the dock. "Take me out of here. Now."

"Not yet, just wait."

"He's clearly not home, Andy. Let's go."

"Mab, I *need* this. If I have one more sleep—"

"Who are you and what are you doing here?" an irritated voice interrupted their squabbling from inside the depths of the houseboat.

Spinning around, Ander peered through one of the windows. "My name is Ander, Crown Prince of Helicon, and I am in deep need of your help."

A face suddenly appeared in the window, golden eyes peering out at Ander. "Queen Aemiliana's bastard son?"

Ander glared back at him, his hip jutting out as he crossed his arms defensively, his tone short. "Yes, that one."

Vejovis disappeared from view, then after a moment of silence, the front door to the houseboat swung open, and a puff of smoke and the scent of incense greeted them. "Well, come in then."

Ander and Mab shared a look, one of confusion, refusal, and insistence. Knowing that Mab wouldn't go in unless he did, Ander stepped over the small wooden ramp leading from the dock to the boat and disappeared inside.

The interior of the houseboat was dark and damp—a true representation of the swamp it sat in. Plants lined the walls in pots, baskets, and any other bucket Vejovis managed to find and hang up. From the ceiling, herbs hung upside down, drying out. The floor was littered with dead leaves and grasses. Ander felt more outdoors than when he had actually been outside.

Vejovis sat on a plush ottoman beside a round coffee table made from a tree stump and a round sheet of glass. On the opposite side of the coffee table sat two more ottomans, which Ander guessed they were meant to sit on as well.

Mab followed them apprehensively, her nose curled up in disfavor as she claimed her spot beside Ander. Her white afro of curls seemed stark against the dark, natural colors of the houseboat.

"So, son of Helicon, what can I do for you today? Trouble with one of your lovers? Do you need a performance enhancer, perhaps?"

"*Excuse* me?" Ander gasped, offense ricocheting within him only to settle in his shoulders, which he straightened, and his jaw, which he clenched and angled upward. "That is *hardly* the issue here." He contemplated leaving. Maybe it wasn't worth dealing with someone who'd assume *that* of him right off the bat. Beside him, Mab didn't even attempt to hide her cackle of delight. Ander shot her a glare before continuing. "I'm having chest pains that keep me up at night, and nothing I've done has been able to take them away. I'm exhausted and need your help."

"Chest pains?" Mab growled. "Since when have you been having *chest pains?!*"

Ander motioned for her to be silent, looking to the god before him instead of responding to her question.

Vejovis nodded and stood, waving Ander toward him. Standing himself, Ander moved toward where the god indicated, then suffered through the prodding and mauling of his hands as he examined his chest and back. He felt it when Vejovis placed his hand over his heart and sent a heavy pulse of magic through him. It shook him down to the soles of his feet then echoed back up through him.

"What did you just do?" Ander wheezed.

"That was not me," Vejovis responded. "That was the pulse of your amare bond."

Ander laughed shortly. "What? No." He hadn't been around Zeke Schields' little brat. He'd made certain to stay clear of the Guardian and his offspring since that fateful day outside Element 79. He preferred to snap in and out of the club just to make sure there were no more run-ins with *that* particular ignis. And he would never forget how it felt to run into his soulmate for the very first time. That sharp snap of recognition as the bond had locked into place. He hadn't experienced that since.

Vejovis nodded. "Absolutely, yes. The bond has been set."

"Amare bond? Is that—?" Mab asked.

"Yes, he's trying to say that I've met my soulmate, the one chosen for me by Erotes' arrow. It's the official term for being arrow-bound to someone."

Mab eyed him, reminding him that he hadn't gone into much detail with her after Erotes had shot an arrow into a descending ignis for each of them that night in Berlin. It had seemed in their best interests to just forget it had happened and avoid ignis at all costs.

Ander laughed once more, shaking his head in denial. "There's no way this is from my amare bond. I haven't come in contact with anyone who—" A set of hazel eyes in a small face peered up at him. Dark bangs ruffling in the wind and falling into a gaze that became disappointed with the way Ander had treated his father. That same face morphed into a handsome young man with a firm chin, now looking at him with hazel eyes asking if he'd kidnapped a young woman. "Oh . . . shit."

Ander sat down quickly, feeling lightheaded as the houseboat spun around him.

"Andy?" Mab sounded far away, distant. Trapped beneath a wave of disbelief and uncertainty that washed through him. "Are you okay?"

"Maximus," he whispered. "It's Maximus." This was terrible. He couldn't possibly be arrow-bound to the ignis currently investigating him for such a heinous crime. "But it doesn't make sense! I know what the amare bond feels like! I felt it snap into place thirteen years ago. If this is the same one . . . how come I didn't feel that this time?" Ander stared over at Vejovis.

"I would assume that first meeting was when your bond was officially locked into place. Now you have simply woken it back up."

"How do I make it go away?" he blurted out. "I will pay you whatever you want if you will just remove the bond."

Vejovis was shaking his head. "No."

"No? Why?! I came here for your help. Money is no object!"

"Even if I wanted your money, it wouldn't matter what you could offer me. An amare bond cannot be broken."

"Then how do I make the pain go away?"

"Easy. Now that your soulmate has been found, acceptance and consummation of the bond."

A shudder coursed through Ander as he momentarily imagined just what *that* would be like. "I don't think it's going to be quite that easy."

"If you refuse, then the pain will remain."

Standing, Ander huffed. "Thank you for a great deal of nothing." He turned to leave but found an invisible wall holding him in place.

"There is the small matter of my payment."

"Payment? I thought you didn't want my money!"

"For this, I do."

"For what? For an insignificant act of palm reading?" Ander wanted to break through the barrier and hurry out, but instead, he pulled a wad of cash out of his pocket and tossed it down on the coffee table. "Thank you for a great deal of nothing."

With the money on the table, the barrier disappeared, and Ander was able to escape the heat and humidity of the houseboat for the only slightly lesser humidity of the outdoors. Taking deep breaths that in no way helped to steady him, Ander jammed a hand through his hair.

"I *told* you we should have left Miami thirteen years ago! But nooooo, you needed to stay!" he said to Mab as she came up behind him.

"Yes, I did. We had just opened our bar and settled here. We weren't going to run away just because you're afraid of your soulmate."

Hurt rolled through him, making his throat constrict and his breathing run shallow. "A soulmate who can't love me back." A soulmate who would end up being just one more person in the long list of people in Ander's life who hadn't been able to love him. Who'd been unable to find something in him good enough to stick around for and accept.

"Andy—"

Ander held up his hand, silencing her. He then twirled his hand, creating a swirling vortex behind her, and used magic to push her through it. She'd be fine; she'd wind up back at her place, far away from him.

As for Ander, he had every intention of ignoring the fact that this was his day off and was going to go to Inferno and get so drunk, he forgot who and what he was.

There were lips on his neck and hands in his hair. They weren't the lips or the hands that Ander wanted, but for the moment, they would do. Behind him, the brick wall of Inferno's exterior dug into his back and buttocks, making him long for the gentle bite of a lover's firm hand.

Drinks at Inferno had spiraled into shots, which had cascaded into cocktail after cocktail, until he and the young lady he'd begun flirting with at the bar were playing a drinking game with a $750 bottle of scotch.

He and Shanna—Shealyn—Shondalonda-something-or-other had left the bar arm in arm, giggling and flirting and whispering naughty suggestions into each other's ears. Now, they were leaned up against the exterior of the building, waiting for a cab to arrive.

Ander didn't particularly desire the girl whose name he was far too drunk to remember. However, there was a deep, aching void within him that could not seem to be filled with alcohol and which he was hoping her sloppy kisses and wandering hands would be able to take away.

So far, that was not working either.

"You're very pretty, Ander," the girl murmured, peering up at him through painted lashes.

"You're very pretty too, my dear." This wrung a giggle out of her.

"So, your place? Or mine?"

If he thought really hard, Ander could just picture the place that he lived, yet his drunken brain didn't seem to want to contribute the street name or a house number. His legs were also beginning to turn into the sort of jelly that was not meant for standing upright.

"I think we need to get you home."

The woman—possibly named Stacey—grinned and cooed. "Take me away."

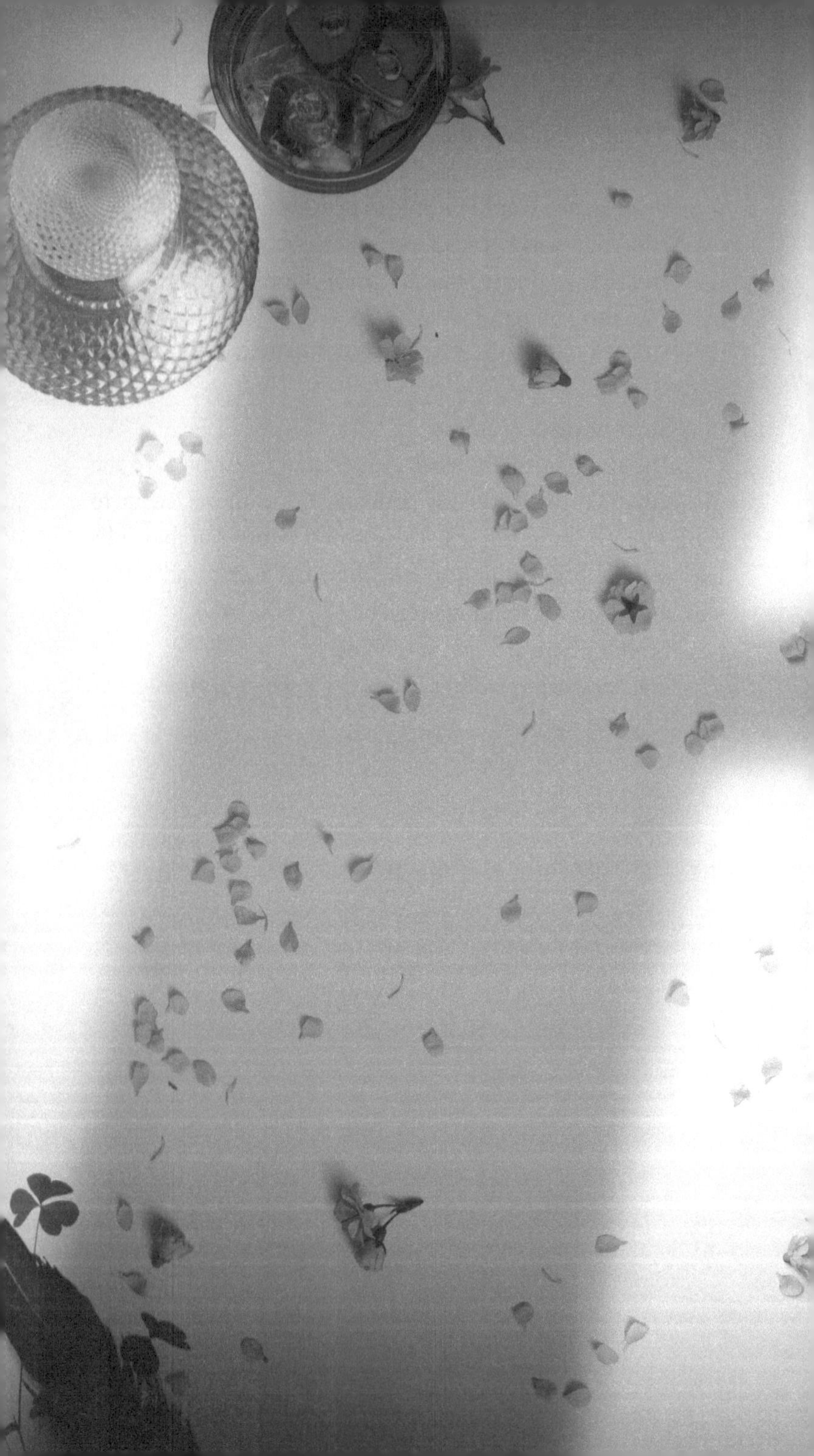

Chapter 5
Max

The *one thing* Max did not want was to feel his phone vibrate in his pocket while on his run, or to pull it out to find a text from Nox that simply said: *we've got another one.*

He didn't need her to expand upon that or to explain herself. He *knew*. This was number four, how could he *not* know at this point? He was swimming in a sea of missing women, and every time he thought about one of them, it turned his stomach. Max bent over, clutching his knees to suck in a deep breath, his wings fluttering slightly with each inhale, hoping to regain some control over his racing mind. It didn't do much, but at least it kept him from throwing up on the sidewalk.

When he'd breathed through the worst of the nausea, he straightened and adjusted his course. There was no time to run home and shower, he'd just have to use the facilities at the sanctuary.

You're the boss, applesauce. (҂•̀ᴗ•́)҂

Scoffing, Max got back to his run. His T-shirt was soaked by the time he reached the sanctuary, but the exercise cleared his head. Peace settled into his bones, letting him focus for perhaps the first time in days. He should have known that wouldn't last.

Max scrubbed at his hair with a towel as he made his way to the Schields team command center and found Nox looking over footage on the big screen. Quin stood behind her with his arms crossed over his chest. They both turned to look at Max when he entered. Nox almost looked apologetic, Quin looked . . . like he wanted to say "I told you so" *again*. Blast.

"What is it?" Max asked, only half wanting an answer.

"Katlyn James was a regular at Inferno," Nox said, pulling up Katlyn's social media feed, each little square photo backlit by the neon flames that decorated the walls of Inferno.

"That doesn't mean any—"

Nox pushed a button on her keyboard, and the screen shifted to footage from one of the neighboring buildings. Ruin and Katlyn James were making out in the alley between Inferno and the restaurant next door, their bodies melded together against the coarse brick wall.

"*Fuck*," Max hissed, running his hands through his still wet hair. "When was this taken?"

"About one thirty in the morning. I've got another angle of them getting into a cab together right after. Do you want to see it?" Nox didn't mean to sound smug, Max knew that. But she was proud of her bit of detective work, and it was *good* work, he'd give her that. It just wasn't exactly what he wanted to see after his last encounter with

Ruin left him raw and aching. Still, credit where credit was due.

"No. Good work, Nox. But no."

"And there's something else."

"Something else?" Max's stomach churned.

Another fatal click-clack of the keyboard, and a file popped up, an old sepia-toned picture of Ander Ruin, horns hidden by a glamour, standing very close to a dainty blond woman, his arms wrapped loose and relaxed around her waist as she leaned into him. "This is Estelle Corbyn. She was Ruin's fiancé back in the 1830s. Before the news of their engagement could even come out, Estelle killed herself by jumping into the Thames."

Max inhaled sharply, his fingers tightening into fists at his sides. "Does it say—" He cleared his throat when the words came out a little too high. "Does it say why? Did it have anything to do with Ruin?"

"Unclear. We just know that it happened, and for months after, Ruin went on a bender. He practically drank England dry and exposed himself to everyone in his wake, horns out."

He was grieving, Max wanted to say, but he didn't know that for certain. There was no way to know anything for certain. "Is there anything else?"

"I'll keep digging."

Max nodded, lifted his chin, and met Quin's gaze. Quin was watching him in that way only siblings could. "Not a word, Quin."

Quin raised both brows in question.

"Not a single word." Max growled, lifting the towel to his head to finish drying his hair, leaving it in a mess of curls before he turned on his heel to get ready.

"You didn't even say anything," Nox said, but whatever

Quin's reply, he didn't hear it as he slammed the locker room door behind himself.

Inferno wasn't open to the public yet when they arrived, but the door was unlocked, likely to not hinder Mab and Ander as they went in and out preparing for the evening. Mab was behind the bar, her white head bent over where it looked like she was cutting up lemons.

"The hell do you two want?" Mab asked, lifting her head to fix them with a hard glare, her fingers curled tight around the little paring knife in her hand.

"Is Ruin here?" Max sighed, hating how he could feel Mab's eyes flicking over him like a brand. She was angry, and she had every right to be. They were there to take her best friend in on charges of kidnapping a mortal, after all. And yet, still, Max didn't feel like it fit. The clues pointed to Ruin, but something felt wrong about the entire thing. His jaw clenched around the words, not wanting to hear Quin's opinion on the matter again.

"And what if he is?" Her dark eyes narrowed on them. Max felt Quin shift beside him, readying for a fight.

"Just answer the question, Duchan. Or we'll have to charge you with obstructing an investigation." He held a hand up to keep Quin from advancing. If they could prevent any damage to the bar, that'd be best; he didn't want to add that to the reasons Ruin hated him. *Not that it matters*, he tried to remind himself, but the thought didn't hold much weight.

"I'd like to see you—"

"Mab, let's not give these nice ignis any more trouble

than we've already caused them," Ruin's voice broke through the standoff, a strained smile tugging up one side of his mouth. He stuffed his hands into his pockets, his posture forced into something relaxed and languid that didn't seem to fit the narrowed tightness of his eyes. Max's fingers twitched to reach for him. To do *what*, he wasn't sure, but he wanted to reach out anyway.

"Ander Ruin, crown prince of Helicon, you're under arrest for suspicion of kidnapping," Max said, clearing his throat of all of the other things he wanted to say that sounded suspiciously like *I'm sorry*. He pulled the cuffs from his belt and made his way over to Ander.

"Kidnapping? Really?" Ander asked, but he held his wrists out, not even bothering to fight. "Now, normally . . . handcuffs are *definitely* my thing." Ander lifted his shackled wrists, giving Mab a little wave and making them clank together. Mab's response was to mime gagging. "But I have to say, this isn't how I imagined us using them, darling."

Max felt heat crawl up his neck and into the tips of his ears at the images *that* particular comment elicited. He gave the cuffs a little unnecessary yank to hide the awkwardness. "It'd be in your best interest for you to cooperate."

"Anything for you, handsome." Ander cocked his head, his smile growing a little more.

A huff, and Max's gaze flicked back to Quin, who was watching them with an amused tilt to his head. Jerk.

"Need a hand?" Quin asked via sign language, his eyes tilted up in that expression that would have been a smile if he weren't swallowing it down.

"Let's just go," Max grumbled, leading them back out onto the street.

Max shut the door to the interrogation room behind him and turned to his glaring brother. Quin was leaning against the wall opposite, his gaze fixed on the man now locked in the room beyond.

"You can't lead the interrogation," Quin said by way of greeting.

"And why can't I?" Max tilted his head back, his brows pinching together in what their Papa had affectionately nicknamed his "serious business" face. It didn't work on anyone inside of the family, but Max wasn't above trying.

"You know," Ander called, his voice sounding over the mic in the room, "far be it for me to kink-shame anyone, but voyeurism isn't normally my thing."

Max choked on his own spit, his face turning so red, he could feel the heat from it on his neck.

"I think you know why." Quin raised one brow, a clear challenge. Would Max do what he knew he should do and hand over the interrogation to his very capable brother? Or would he keep trying to prove that he could be objective when he clearly—

"As the leader of this team, I am handling this interrogation," Max said, hating himself as soon as the words left him. He didn't like pulling rank, he never did. Not because he hadn't earned his position as the team lead —he had. He'd worked his ass off for it. But this was his family, and it always felt weird to tell one of his siblings to do something they didn't agree with. It might have been easier if he were the leader of *any* of the other ignis teams—

they weren't all related like his was—but he wasn't, he was the leader of the Schields team.

"Fine." Quin's jaw clenched, his eyes narrowing, but he didn't say anything more to argue against Max's orders. "But I'm not going to sit in there and watch him make a fool out of you."

No, you'll sit out here *and watch me make a fool of myself,* Max didn't say. He nodded and headed back into the room to a delighted crow from Ruin.

"Ah, there you are, darling. I was beginning to get oh so lonely in here." He pouted, poking his bottom lip out as he stretched back in the chair, the red shirt he was wearing riding up a little to show off spectacularly defined ab muscles. "Will your brother not be joining us for this bit?"

"No." Max clenched his teeth, taking a deep breath as he lowered himself into his chair and forced his gaze away from Ruin's stomach.

"Oh? So it's just going to be the two of us in here? And he *is* going to watch?" His eyes drifted to the two-way mirror that Quin stood hidden behind. "Kinky," Ruin purred, one hand lifting to twirl a bit of hair around his finger, the motion drawing the shirt up another inch.

"We need to know about Katlyn James—"

"Katlyn who now?"

"The girl you were with last night. The one from the club."

"Oh! Was that her name?" Ruin hummed thoughtfully. "So it wasn't Shealyn after all," he said mostly to himself, giving the hair curled around his finger a little tug before he let it go. "Ah well, what about her?"

"She's missing."

"Yes, I assumed that." Ruin held up his shackled wrists, making them clank loudly.

Max folded his fingers together in front of him on the table, resisting the urge to crack his knuckles in nervousness. "We have footage of you . . . having relations with her in the alley beside the club."

"You know you can say sex, darling," Ruin cooed, his eyes gleaming as he licked his dry lips. "Anyway, what about it? I've had *relations* with a lot of people."

"There's also footage of you two getting into a cab together afterward. That's the last record we have of Miss James." Max forced himself to look at Ruin's face, to watch for any tells, not because if he let his eyes move even a fraction, he'd be distracted by all of the skin on display. Not at all.

"Well, I had to see her home, that's the gentlemanly thing to do. She was quite drunk." Ruin shrugged, his shoulder muscles rolling beneath the skin. Gods, maybe Quin was right, maybe Max should have let him do this.

"So, you just took her home?" Max pressed, sitting up a little straighter. "And then what?"

"And then I snapped myself home and slept it off on my couch. The bed was too far away, and Monnie was lying right in the middle of it. It's really very tricky to get her to move once she's gone to bed."

"Aside from your dog, did anyone see you once you'd gone home?" All Max needed was one witness, one person to corroborate Ruin's alibi, and this could all be over. He could let Ruin go back to his club, and Max and Quin could move on to other suspects. More *likely* suspects, in Max's mind.

"No. I live alone, and I didn't go up through the lobby." Ruin leaned back further in his chair, the front legs lifting from the floor as he made himself perfectly comfortable. How could someone make a creaking metal folding chair look like a throne? Max didn't understand it.

"Right." Max cleared his throat, lifting his hands from the table as he stood. "Well, we're going to have to hold you for a bit then, just until we can corroborate your story."

Ruin tilted his head to the side, his eyes raking over Max like a physical caress. "You'll have to go by and feed my dog."

"I'm sorry, what?"

"Monnie, my dog. You don't want her to starve, do you?" Ruin raised a questioning brow, but his lips had ticked up at the corners like he already knew the answer.

"I . . ." Biting at the inside of his cheek, Max looked back to the glass window in the door. Quin was on the other side, his eyes narrowed. Screw it. "No. I don't. You won't mind if we search your place while we're there, will you?"

"Of course not. What's mine is yours, handsome. Just don't go digging around in the chest on the right side of my closet . . . or do. Your choice." Ruin winked, and Max only had a moment to flounder before Quin came in to see Ruin to his cell.

"With me," Max said to Nash on his way out of the sanctuary, not looking back as Ruin purred a goodbye. Nash scrambled from his chair, and they were off.

Ruin's condo was in one of those ridiculously lavish high-rises. The kind of place that their Papa had owned before he'd stalked Colt Schields in the grocery store and settled down with five children. The helpful man at the front desk gave them Ruin's floor after Max flashed an empty wallet that was charmed to show whatever ID he needed at the moment, and Max and Nash rode the elevator all the way up to the penthouse.

"So, what are we looking for?" Nash asked as they fanned out in the spacious living room.

"Anything any of our missing women might have left behind. And a dog. Ruin wants us to feed his—" Max was cut off by a soft yipping and the sounds of nails click-clacking on the marble floors.

"Wait . . . *that's* his dog?" Nash asked, biting back a laugh.

Max squatted down to the tiny cotton ball and held out his hand to let her sniff him. "Guess so." He smiled a little when Monnie licked his knuckles. "Get back to digging around, I'll find her food."

Nash took one last lingering look at Max as he bent to scoop up the little dog before shrugging and going off to investigate the bedroom. Which is where he *always* started. They were going to have to have a talk about that.

"Let's go find your food, Miss Monnie," Max cooed softly to the dog, heading into the kitchen. The kibble was in a pretty little glass container with Monnie's name written on it next to her bowls. Max was just pouring some when he heard Nash let out a cackle of delight. "Whatever you found, put it back!"

"Not a snowball's chance in hell, big brother. Come look at this man's sex toy collection!" Nash whistled. "I mean, he told you to look, didn't he?"

"Actually, he told me not to." Max made his way into the bedroom, the heat of embarrassment already prickling at his neck.

"Yeah, but Max, I mean . . ." Nash gestured to the chest that it looked like he was on the verge of just dumping onto the bed so he could go snooping. "I'm honestly a little jealous."

"Of his toy collection?" Max asked, moving to swat Nash away and start putting everything back.

"Dude. No. Of the fact that he's clearly good in bed and he wants you."

"He does not. He just likes embarrassing me." The chest clapped shut before Max could look any of the toys in the face, and he moved to return it to the closet.

"Yeah, okay. Whatever you say, man." Nash sounded like he was rolling his eyes, but Max was done with this conversation. So *beyond* done with it.

"Just go look through his computer and let's get out of here. I've got other work to do."

"*Fine,*" Nash whined.

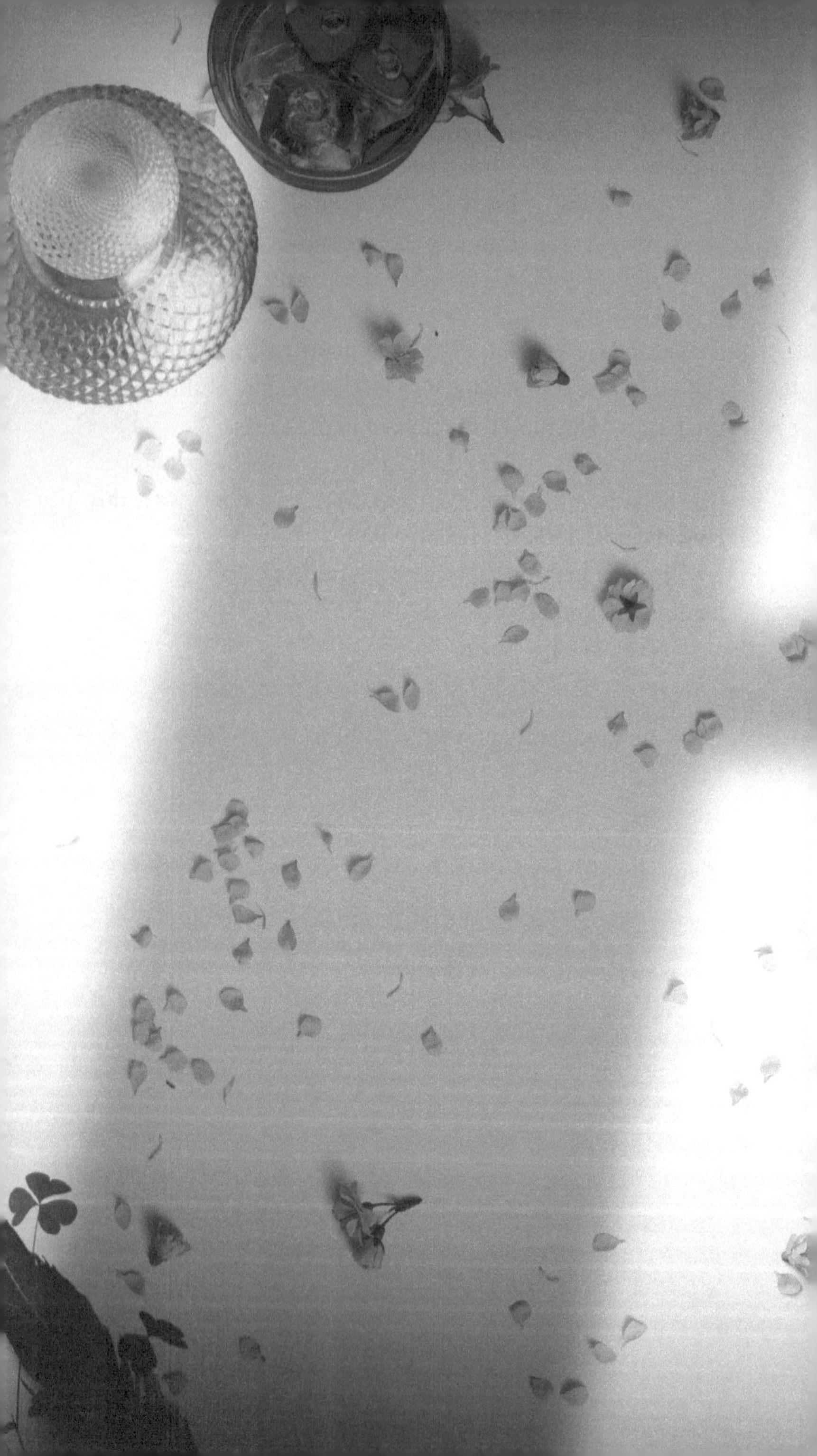

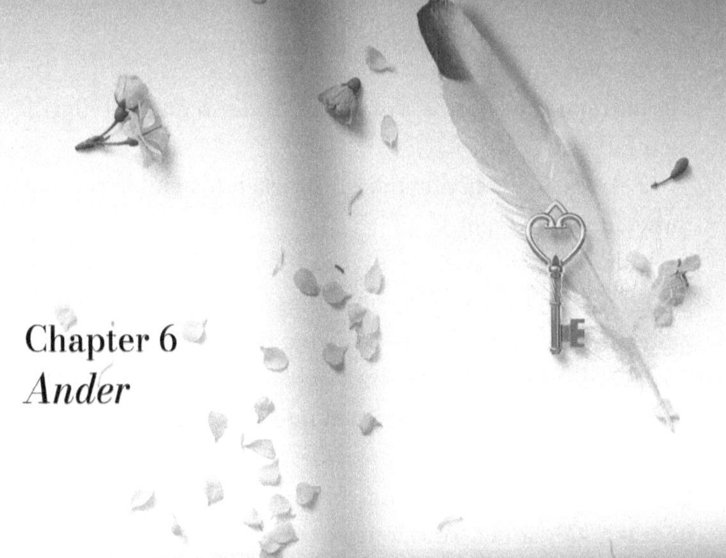

Chapter 6
Ander

Hearing Maximus' voice in his club so soon after realizing he was his soulmate had felt like a horse kick straight to his sternum. Mab getting into an argument with the ignis hadn't helped the situation either. As Ander came down from his office to find the tall, dark, and serious ignis in his bar, he realized he'd never seen anything so beautiful in all his life.

Now here he was.

In prison.

Or a holding cell in the Feugo City sanctuary. This sanctuary was an in-between. From the outside, which sat on a back street in Miami, it was nothing but an old brick wall with a locked gate. However, once the gate had been opened and Ander was dragged through it, he found himself in Underworld, within the control and ever-watchful eye of the Sanctum.

Once the interrogation was over, Quintus had brought him to this cell. There had been a shared look between the brothers that Ander had not missed. The scowling Quintus wanted to keep Maximus and Ander apart. That was clear.

His outright distaste and distrust of Ander reminded him of their father.

Zeke Schields had managed to teach his children *some* things, it would seem.

Ander sighed frustratedly and threw an arm over his eyes. The bed he was lying on was essentially a cement slab built into the wall. A thin mattress that reminded him of cardboard sat on top. His back ached. His head hurt. The chill in the cell was starting to get into his bones.

He wanted a more comfortable bed. He wanted a large bottle of vodka to drown out the fact his soulmate thought he was a kidnapper. And he wanted something to eat. He'd had coffee and a single grape for breakfast, and that had been the extent of it for the day.

While his eating habits weren't great on the best of days, even Ander needed to put something substantial into his belly on occasion.

As if to reinforce his current thoughts, Ander's stomach rumbled. He sat up quickly, dropping his feet to the floor as he spun around. "Hello, is there anyone out there?"

There was silence until a wispy voice from a few cells down rasped, "I'm here."

The words, though innocent enough, sent a thrill through him, followed by an echo of severe cold and a breathless sensation. *Mermaid.* While tales told of sirens calling men to their doom, it was actually mermaids who did, and if this one was locked up, Ander assumed another croc hunter in the swamps had gone missing.

"While I appreciate the response, I really don't think you can help me."

"Suit yourself."

Ander walked to the bars, curling his fingers around them. He pressed his forehead to the cool metal, his horns clinking against the rods, and looked down the hall as best he could toward the guard station. There was no one there. Huffing, Ander chewed on his lip.

These cells were specifically made to hold magical beings inside, but he couldn't help but wonder just how good they actually were. Most things didn't seem up to tackling his particular brand of muse magic. Snapping his fingers, Ander quickly teleported to the front doors of the sanctuary. He heard someone at the front desk sputtered a confused "What the—?" at the sudden appearance of a being in front of them before pushing through the doors. Stepping through the Feugo portal, Ander found himself back on the streets of Miami.

Smirking, he walked around the corner to the small deli. Fortunately, its Open sign still glowed in the window. Inside, he walked straight up to the counter and ordered the largest charcuterie board he could, with the best meats, cheeses, olives, and pickles. Once it was packaged and handed back to him, Ander returned to the sanctuary entrance, summoning a bottle of wine from his own stores before crossing through the gate and back into the sanctuary itself.

As he walked through the front door, a young woman with bright green eyes, bronze skin, and gorgeous dark hair cascading down her back halted and stared at him. Slowly, her eyes widened as her mouth fell open.

"But . . . you were just in your cell. How—*How* are you out here?!"

Ander shrugged. "I snapped myself out?"

"But that's not—that's not possible," she stuttered. "They're magic-blocking. We keep warlocks and elves and everyone else locked inside without any trouble." She looked dazed, as if at any point she might ask if this were real life.

An ignis with white-and-brown-speckled wings blinked at him in confusion from the reception desk.

"I don't know what to tell you, cupcake. But I snapped myself out of there without any issue. Guess your magic-prevention wards have failed you. Charcuterie?" He lifted the plastic tray of food up to show her.

She was still eyeing him with a great deal of confusion. "But . . ." The girl looked back in the direction of the cells, then turned her gaze on him once more. "If you were able to leave, why did you come *back*?"

"Well, I would have looked even more guilty if I just *left*. But I was hungry." Ander shrugged, then strolled on by, heading through the doors that led to the holding cells.

An angry looking Quintus was waiting for him on the other side of the doors. It was clear he had been searching Ander's cell, wondering how he'd left.

"Nox!" Quintus grunted, referring to the young woman who was following behind Ander. "Why did you let him out of his cell?!"

"She didn't, Oh Growly One," Ander replied for her. Tucking the bottle of wine under his arm, he snapped his fingers and reappeared suddenly in his cell. "I let myself out." He winked at the blue-eyed ignis.

Waving his hand in the air, Ander summoned a plush chair for himself and sat down in it, then called forth a small table. Spreading out his feast, he found Quintus and Nox staring at him, dismay, confusion, and—on Quintus' part—fury written on their faces. Nox, Ander noted, seemed a touch impressed.

"You can't just come and go as you please." Quintus seemed quite ruffled at this obvious breaking of protocol.

Ander couldn't help but wonder if it was rigid rules and regulations that kept the straightlaced, tightly wound fella held together.

"Well, buttercup, it appears that's exactly what I've done." Ander grinned brightly, feeling a little zing of delight pass through him. It felt truly wonderful to know that he was here of his own volition and not because he was trapped. He would stay because otherwise it would cause more problems for himself and likely Mab. But the knowledge that he could leave at any point certainly helped. "Now . . . my offer of charcuterie still stands."

Nox laughed, brightly and without concern for the glare Quintus was giving her. "I'll take you up on that!" She moved to grab a stool from the guard station and pulled it up next to his cell.

Smiling, Ander resituated himself near the bars so that Nox was able to reach her hand through them and take what she wished from the board.

Ander's first priority was getting the wine bottle uncorked, and he did so with flare, tossing the cork over his shoulder.

"Is that wine?" Quintus was frowning again. "You can't have wine in there."

"Oh, give it a rest Quin, what's it going to hurt? He's already left once . . . At this point, just be happy he's still here."

Ander chuckled and winked at Nox. "Plus, you really need to stop fretting so much. All the frowning is going to give you terrible wrinkles, and that would be a great shame on such a beautiful face."

Quintus shifted uncomfortably and signed something to Nox, to which she gave a nod and another quick sign of her own, then he turned to go and sit down at the guard station, arms folded across his chest.

"Have I offended him?"

Nox shook her head, biting into a piece of cheese. "He gets uncomfortable when strangers comment on his looks, or speak to him in general, really."

"Ah." Ander gazed down the hall at the ignis, then looked back at Nox. "How do you fit into this whole thing? You're human." He could tell because there wasn't a stitch of magic coming off her, and she bore no wings on her back.

"Quin and Max are my brothers. Our parents raised me and my twin, Nash, to help out in the best way normies can in the Sanctum. Tech and information gathering. Well, outside of being a Guardian and raising a brood of younglings."

Ander sipped his wine from the bottle. "Oh, so you're the one who's been ferreting through my security footage and finding videos of me making out with missing girls that make me look guilty AF."

Nox plucked up a piece of pepperoni. "I only find what proof is there. You're the dirty bastard macking out with ladies in an alley." She pointed a manicured finger at him, eyes narrowed.

"It wasn't an alley, it was the street. I would never." He would. He had. He likely would again.

Nox laughed, eyes brightening. "Sorry, in the street."

"Thank you." Ander straightened his shirt, then popped an olive into his mouth. "Your brother . . ."

Nox pointed over her shoulder at Quintus in question.

Ander shook his head. "Maximus."

"What about him?"

"Is he . . . seeing anyone?"

Nox's lips twitched. But before she could speak,

Quintus piped up from down the hall. "Max's personal relationships are none of the suspect's business."

"Is he always like this?" Ander asked.

"Quin is particular about the rules," she said, then leaned forward to whisper, "but I'm not."

Ander grinned. "So?" he encouraged.

"Max isn't seeing anyone right now." Her eyes squinted at him, studying him. "Why? Are you interested in my big brother, Mister Ruin?"

Ander settled back in his chair, draping one leg over the knee of the other and letting his expensive Italian leather shoe bounce in the air. "Let's say that I am . . . curious."

"Bi-curious?" Nox grinned.

"Pan-curious." He winked at her once more. "Curious only as it comes to your brother. I've understood myself since the early days. Does Maximus—"

"Dates guys. Exclusively."

Ander nodded, drumming his fingers on the neck of the wine bottle. That got one potential hurdle out of the way. "Have there been many?"

"Well . . . that depends on your idea of many. I mean, I've seen your history." Nox smirked. "I don't think there are a lot of people who could live up to your idea of many."

He lifted one of his hands, waving it in front of him palm-up. "I've lived a long and eventful life."

"But no, there haven't been many, even by normal people standards. Just a couple of other ignis that didn't really go anywhere."

"Nox, that's enough. The suspect really doesn't need to know any of this," Quintus chimed in once more.

"Excuse me. For one, my name is Ander, and you will address me as such. And two, I am an innocent muse whose privacy and personal life you have all been through with a fine-toothed comb. I think I deserve a little dirt in return." He huffed and slouched in his chair a little more. "Am I able to have a phone call? Or is it only the human cops that give their suspects that decency?"

"No . . . we can give you a phone call."

From his place at the station, Quintus grunted at this response. Ignoring him, Nox reached into her pocket and pulled out her phone. Unlocking it, she handed it to Ander through the bars. Taking it, Ander quickly dialed Mab's number.

When at last she picked up, Ander's foot was bouncing all the more.

"Hello?"

"Mabbers!"

"Andy! Are you okay? What have those bastards done to you?"

"I'm fine, Mab. Just in a dirty, cold cell."

"Do you want me to contact your mother? She can get you—"

"No! No . . . please, not yet. The last thing I want her to hear is that I've been brought in under suspicion of kidnapping mortals."

"Well, she could tell those jackasses that there's no way in human hell you'd have done it."

Ander sighed and rubbed at his forehead. "Well, I didn't. So they're not going to find anything and will have to let me go soon anyway. Can you just hold down the fort for me until this mess is all cleared up?"

"Of course, Andy. I've got Inferno covered."

"Thanks, doll. Love you."

"Love you too."

Ander hung up and handed the phone back to Nox. "Thanks."

The young woman nodded. "Was that your girlfriend?"

Ander chuckled. "Gods, no. That was my sister."

The door to the holding cell area suddenly swung open and Maximus strode through, a halo of white light surrounding him that had Ander's eyes squinting and his heart palpitating erratically. At least until he realized it wasn't some holy sign from Venus herself but the main hall light shining behind him.

"Let him out," Maximus declared.

Quintus rushed to his feet and was at his brother's side in a flash. "Wait. What do you mean?"

"There was nothing at his apartment linking him to the missing girls. No evidence of any kind. All we have is the video. It's not enough to hold him."

Ander's lips slipped into a self-satisfied smirk. "And there won't *be* any evidence, because I didn't do anything wrong."

"Max," Quintus growled softly. "He's our best suspect, we can't just let him go."

"We can. And we have to." At this, Ander stood, brushing himself off and righting his clothes smugly. "But not before we place a tracking cuff on him."

Ander froze. "Say what?" As he reached out to grasp one of the bars, Ander peered through at Maximus. Looking at him was like looking at a too-bright light. When he managed to pull his eyes away, the image of the ignis seemed burned into his retinas.

Instead of responding, the pretty boy wonder stepped up to the cell, grabbed the hand holding onto the bar, pulled it through, then clamped a wide gold band around his wrist. As it locked into place with a deafening finality, a blue light glowed around it before dulling to a light hum.

"What the actual *fuck?*" Ander declared, a furious sense of rage washing through him.

"I'm sorry." And he did look sorry. "But we have to make sure you can't leave the city. This cuff will track your movements and contain you to within one hundred feet of your home and business. You're a flight risk until we can prove absolutely that you had nothing to do with this."

A crushing weight settled itself on top of Ander. The cold metal of the cuff slowly warmed against his skin, reminding him of another band that had similarly kept him hostage. His breathing hitched as his heart began to trip along at an alarming rate. There were a million little beetles crawling beneath his skin once more, and Ander wished to tear through his flesh to free them.

It had been over one hundred and fifty years since the horrors of Acheron, and the memories had faded, but they never went away. Nothing would ever fully wipe away the stain of those years on his heart and mind.

"So you're only releasing me to a slightly bigger prison," Ander hissed.

Maximus appeared to blanch a little. "You're free to go to work and return to your daily life."

"As long as my daily life takes place in the vicinity of my *home* or my *business*." He was shaking, the weight of the cuff on his wrist beginning to make him sick to his stomach, and he knew what little of the charcuterie board he had managed to eat was definitely going to come up. "Very well, Maximus *Schields*, do let me know when you've finally realized I'm an innocent man and you care to *free* me of this hideous piece of trash."

Lifting his hand up before him, Ander kept his eyes on Maximus as he snapped and teleported himself from the cell and back to his own apartment.

He barely made it to the bathroom before he was sick.

Over the course of the next few hours, he did everything within his power to remove the cuff. In the end, it was futile. Which left him curled up on his sofa, mascara tracks down his cheeks and Monnie cuddled up in his arms, licking the salt from his chin.

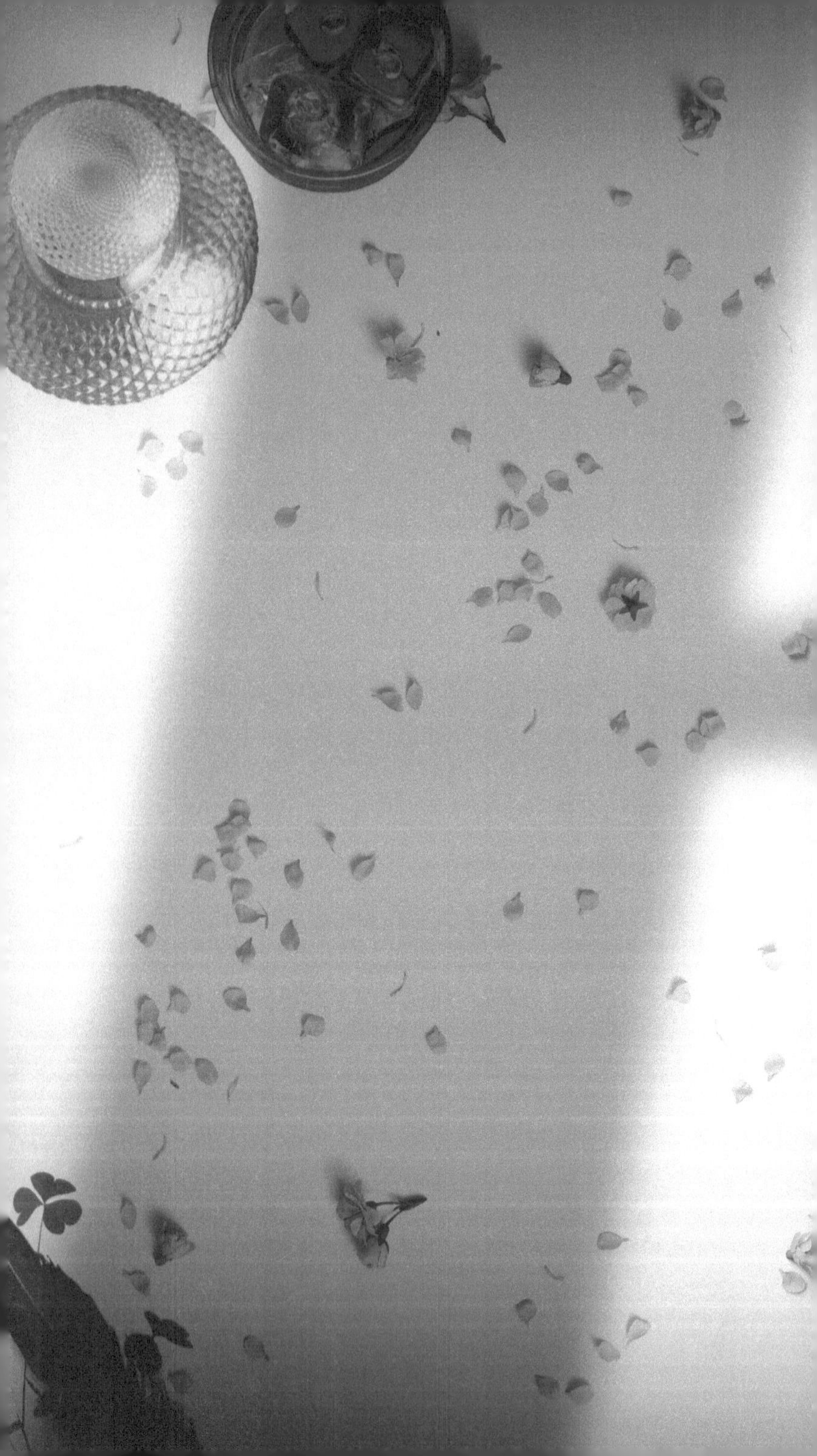

Chapter 7
Mab

"I don't need you to come and look after me, Mabbers. I'm fine," Ander assured from the other side of the phone.

Mab wasn't listening to him, and not just because her focus was taken up by the fruit she was currently slicing behind the bar. She'd stopped listening to him when he said things like that a very long time ago because usually he was either wrong or trying to cover up the fact that he very much did need someone there but didn't want to bother anyone. He wasn't bothering her, she knew he knew that, but she also knew he had a complex about being too much for people, and even all these years later, she suspected he was still waiting for the other shoe to drop with her at times like this. Waiting for her to just get tired of all of it and walk away. She wasn't going to. She'd never walk away from him. But there were some insecurities that not even a couple hundred years of friendship could shut up.

"I didn't exactly ask, Andy." Mab rubbed at the space between her eyebrows with her fingers where a headache was quickly forming, and frowning at the stickiness on her fingers. This was a complete and total shit show. How had things gotten this out of hand? It just didn't even make sense why the evidence was pointing to Inferno and Ander. Why every woman who'd been taken had come from their clientele.

"But the club—"

"The club will be fine under Parker's management. That's what we hired them for, isn't it?" She really needed to take some painkillers for this damn headache before it turned into a full-blown migraine, or she'd be no use to anyone, least of all Ander, who needed his sister to be strong for him. Damn it.

"Fine." Ander let out a long breath, and she could imagine him sinking farther under the blankets he'd piled himself in, hoping to disappear under them.

"I'll bring dinner with me, and I can make cocktails for you once I'm there. We'll watch *Golden Girls* and make a night of it, doesn't that sound nice?" It sounded nice to Mab, who hadn't had a proper girls-night-in in what felt like a decade. They'd both been too busy with the club lately. Maybe this was what they needed to remind them to slow down. Not that Mab appreciated the ignis coming into their life and throwing it into the proverbial woodchipper, but it would at least give Ander an excuse to take some much-needed time off. Mab wasn't going to express that sentiment out loud, though; Ander would pitch the biggest bitch ever about it if she did.

"Yeah. Nice," Ander mumbled.

"Well don't sound so enthused, you'll give me a complex." Mab rolled her eyes. The bell over the front door rang, drawing Mab's attention from where she was stocking the bar, and her jaw clenched at the sight of the two ignis walking in like they owned the place—*again*. Perfect. "I'll call you back, Andy. Tweedle Dee and Tweedle Dum are here again."

She didn't wait for an answer before she hung up on him and turned her attention to the two males making their way toward the bar.

"Miss Duchan," Maximus said, moving to lean against the bar, what could have been considered an amiable smile on his face. Mab wasn't fooled.

"Mab." She moved to work on another orange, her fingers sticky from the pulp. "My name is Mab. Use it or get the hell out of here."

"Mab," Maximus amended, his smile twitching a little on his lips, like he was uncomfortable with the confrontation. Too bad. "Would you mind getting us your employment records and schedules for the last month?"

"Are you really asking?" The knife cut through the orange, hitting the cutting board with a hard *clap* that she didn't even try to muffle, and she raised her brows until they hit the loose white curls that framed her face. The scratch marks on her cheek burned, a reminder of what the very first lawmen she'd faced down had done to her. But she waited, stood her ground, watching as Maximus shifted his weight around, his brother a steady presence beside him that seemed to be trying to glare Mab into submission. Let him try; she'd faced down scarier.

"Not really." Maximus sighed, running a hand through his hair. She hadn't ever seen the ignis so ruffled. He looked like he'd maybe slept in his clothes, and there were dark circles under his eyes. He was a pitiful sight to behold, but she wasn't going to start feeling sympathy for him now. Because if he was bad off, Ander was worse.

"Didn't think so." Mab sat down the knife and reached for a wet rag to clean her hands. "Wait here."

She left them there, heading up the steps to Ander's office to print out the information they'd need. At least they were looking at other suspects, she supposed. But she couldn't see anyone in their bar doing this. She was on her way back down the stairs, her soft-soled boots silent against the steps, when she heard the two males talking. She stopped to listen. Eavesdropping might be rude, but so was locking up her best friend, so screw the rules of propriety.

"Another one," Maxmimus murmured, his face lit a sickly blue color by the phone screen he had his head ducked over. "While we had Ruin in custody."

"Maybe he has a partner." The brother shrugged, throwing suspicion around like people did beads on Mardi Gras. Asshole. "Duchan?"

"No. It doesn't feel right." Maximus shook his head, dark curls falling into his eyes as he locked his phone and put it away. She supposed she could see what Ander saw in him. He was handsome in that gross, Superman kind of way. She kind of wanted to punch him in the nose just to ruin it, but then Ander would be pissed at her, and she didn't need that on top of everything else right now.

The brother must have shot Maximus a look that Mab couldn't see, because Maximus huffed and asked, "What? Are you going to accuse me of wanting to sleep with her too?"

Well. Isn't that an interesting development? Mab's lips twitched into what threatened to be a smirk. Ander would enjoy that. It might be the only thing that could pull him from his funk, actually. Thank the gods for Mab being a petty bitch and eavesdropping. She made a point to let the rest of her steps land loudly on the metal stairs, and the pair quickly shut up.

The file folder with the records they wanted hit the bar

with a *slap*, and Mab came back around to glare at them again. They both were at least two heads taller than her, but that didn't mean she couldn't eye them like inept jackasses.

"That is our employee records and scheduling for the last six months. We don't have a high turnover rate, so if you find anyone that looks suspicious, I can call them in, and you can chat with them."

"Thank you," Maximus said, trying for a smile, but it didn't quite work considering the circumstances. All it did was make her want to punch him a little more. He reached to take the folder, and Mab smacked her hand down on it to keep him from sliding it off the counter.

"Don't thank me," Mab said, her voice dipping into a raspy growl very close to her banshee wail. A threat. "Fix this shit. Find who actually did it and get that cuff off Ander. He's innocent, and all you've managed to do is dredge up some spectacularly traumatic bullshit which he doesn't deserve to have to relive. You get this son of a bitch, you free my friend, and you stay the fuck out of my bar. Are we clear?"

"I didn't—" Maximus took in a deep breath, his jaw clenching around whatever words he was trying to sort through.

"Frankly, I don't care what you didn't or did. I care about the fact that my best friend, the only person who's ever given a damn about me, is upset. So like I said, Wonderboy, fix this shit and stay away from us. Have I made myself clear?" Mab cut her eyes to the brother, narrowing them on him when she found him glaring back at her. "That counts double for you, Stink Eye."

"Understood," the brother said, dipping his head forward in what might have been a sign of respect.

"Good. Now get the fuck out of my hair. I've got a bar to

get ready for open and a brother to look after." Mab slid the folder closer with a hard push that would have sent it to the floor if it weren't for Maximus' quick reflexes. She didn't watch them leave, just dipped her head back to working on cutting citrus for the evening.

The door opened and closed, letting the ignis out, and letting Micah, one of their floor guys, in.

"What was that all about?" Micah asked, making his way behind the bar to help Mab prep. She was glad at least one of their workers had been available to come in early; it would make things easier. It would've been better if it had been Parker, but they'd be there eventually, and then Mab could take off.

"Just two assholes with their heads up their own asses," Mab grunted, sliding the cutting board over to Micah. "Can you finish this up so I can check if anything needs restocking in the fridge?"

"Sure, boss." Micah gave a little salute and turned to wash his hands at the sink. "They've been in here a lot lately."

"Yeah, they think Ander's kidnapping those women." Mab snorted, heading into the walk-in fridge behind the bar to check the stock of beers and ciders for when someone didn't want tap. She grabbed a couple of cases to stock the fridge under the bar and came back out. "Which is obviously ridiculous."

"Obviously," Micah agreed readily. "So what'd they want then? Proof that it was him?"

"Nah." Mab shook her head, squatting down to fill the little fridge. "Employment records and schedules. I think the one with the white wings thinks it's someone else who works here. Which is a bit of a relief, as it means he's not looking to peg this on Andy, but still . . . Why would someone hunt for girls in their place of work? That's just stupid."

"Yeah, super stupid," Micah mumbled.

"Parker will be here soon. When they get here, I'm heading out to spend the evening with Andy. Let me know if those two dipshits return. Just shoot me a text, and I'll come back as soon as I can to handle them."

"All right." Micah shot her a smile and went back to work.

It was a couple hours before Mab finally got away from Inferno to head over to Ander's, but she didn't show up empty handed, and she thought that counted for something. Without bothering to knock, she used her key to barge right in, then called, "Andy! I've brought all your favorites."

She held up the reusable grocery bag, smirking at Ander peeking over the back of the couch. "What favorites?"

"Vodka, froyo, me, *aaand*," she said, dragging out the word, "some fresh gossip. Which do you want first?"

"Do I have to choose?" Ander reached out, opening and closing his hands at her, and she handed over a spoon and a small container of frozen yogurt before moving to the bar cart to make him a drink.

"No. Because I'm amazing like that."

"You are," he nodded around his spoon. "So, gossip?"

"Ah, yes. Our two favorite birdbrains were at Inferno this afternoon. And as I was strategically *not* eavesdropping"—Ander cut her a look that called her a liar, and she shrugged it off—"I heard that your lordy-love apparently wants to sleep with you."

Ander gasped loudly, nearly choking on the frozen yogurt in his mouth. "Way to bury the lead, Mabbers!"

"I didn't bury it." She huffed, holding out a drink to him, which he took to sip from. "Besides, I thought we hated him now."

Ander shrugged, burying himself further in his drink. Mab didn't press him. She'd get her answers eventually, she always did.

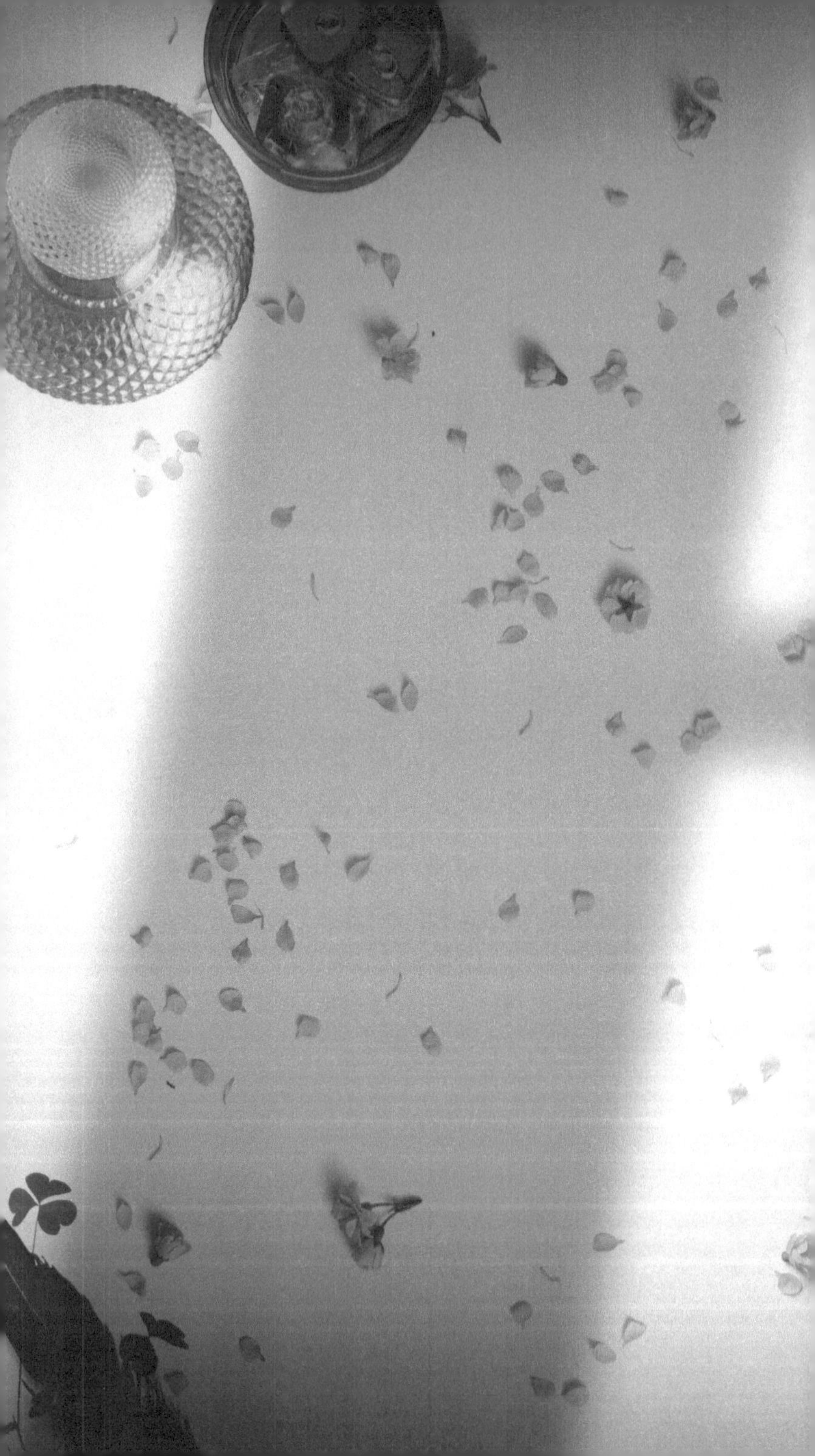

Chapter 8
Max

"Spectacularly traumatic bullshit" was what Duchan had called whatever Ruin was currently dealing with. If he were honest, Max had known it to some extent. He'd seen the way Ruin's skin paled a fraction and his eyes had gone wide and frightened, more caged and injured animal than cornered killer. The expressions were similar, yes, but there was a subtle difference. And Max had seen that look on Quin's face enough over the years to know what it meant even before Duchan said those words. Something had happened to Ruin in the past, and the cuff was a trigger for those memories.

It left Max feeling . . . horrendous. His stomach was in knots. There was a ringing in his ears. And even though he'd gone home and tried to sleep, all he'd been able to do was imagine Ruin's face over and over as he slapped the cuff on him. Quin may have not realized what it meant—he'd never seen his own trigger response— but Max remembered those first few years after Quin came to the Schields family so vividly that he could call up almost any given day as if it were yesterday. He'd watched his brother close himself off from anything and everything, hyperventilate, look but not see the world around him as his mind took him back to places that none of them would ever truly understand. And he'd done all that he could for Quin at the time. Talked him through it. Reminded him he was safe and loved. Kept others from invading further on his space until Quin had control again.

He couldn't do those things for Ruin, though, because he wasn't Ruin's brother. Or his friend, or his *anything*, really—however much he realized he might want to be after a quick chat with Nox where his sister told him all about her conversation with their wayward prisoner. What he could do was prove that Ruin didn't do this awful thing and free an innocent man. Because he was innocent, whatever the current evidence might say, however much he might irritate Quin.

After tossing and turning for a good hour, Max pulled on a fresh shirt, jeans, and one of his comfiest sweaters before he headed back to the sanctuary to run the tapes again. They were missing something, and he was going to figure out what it was.

The sanctuary was empty apart from a small skeleton crew. Lights turned down low. Noise muffled by stillness. It was the most quiet these halls would likely ever see, and Max wished he could relish it. But he was too busy thinking about what he might find when he looked through the footage Ruin provided again.

He tugged the sleeves of his cardigan down over his knuckles, braced his elbows on the desk, perched his chin in his hands, and hit Play.

Nox and Nash had just been looking for the victims, which meant they weren't looking at everyone else in the bar. Yawning into his wrist, he sped the video up a little to look through the night that Daisy Garcia had gone missing.

Inferno was packed, wall-to-wall people, and so many of them had come into contact with Daisy. It could have been any of them, really. But no . . . he was looking for someone who stayed on the periphery. Someone who maybe hadn't even spoken to the group of rowdy club-goers but had been watching them. Max's eyes scanned the scene. Then he found him: a blond man walking around the bar—No. He was making a circuit around the group, circling them like a shark would a bloody seal. He was being careful not to draw attention to himself, dancing to the music and occasionally making conversation with other people. If Max hadn't been looking for that exact behavior, he would have missed it entirely.

He pulled that feed onto one of the smaller monitors and put a pin on the man, making it easier to follow him in the footage, then pulled up some of the other nights when women had gone missing. Each one was the same. Max was able to find the man, pin him with their software, and watch as he made the same circuit, over and over again, around the victims, waiting for them to leave the bar or get kicked out before following a minute or two behind. Long enough that people wouldn't think much of it, short enough that the victims would still be loading into their car on the curb or stumbling down the block once he exited.

"Got you, you son of a bitch." Max sat up a little straighter, zooming in on one of the screens to try to get a better look at the man's face. He seemed to know where the cameras were, confirming Max's suspicion that he was an Inferno employee, keeping himself carefully turned away from them at all times so that they wouldn't catch his face. But as he made his way to the bar and sat, Max glanced at the mirror behind the shelves and saw the man's face reflected there.

Pulling his phone from his pocket, he called Nox.

"Hi?" Nox asked, her voice foggy with sleep.

"How do I enhance the footage on our system again?" Tapping on the keyboard, Max frowned at the screen. He didn't want to chance doing it wrong and screwing up all the work he'd just put in.

"Maxxy, I love you, but do you know what time it is?"

He didn't, actually. He didn't even know what time he'd left their house and come down to the sanctuary to work. Papa hadn't been home, which meant he was at Element, but that wasn't really saying much as Papa would be at work any time from eight in the evening to four in the morning.

"I found our guy," he said instead of answering, because out of all of them, Nox would be the most likely to respect what that meant. She seemed to be the only one in the Schields family that didn't think Ruin was a horrible person on principle—or because of evidence—aside from Max.

"Ugh." Max could hear her moving around on the other side of the connection, likely throwing her blankets off and grabbing clothes. "Just give me, like, a half hour, all right?"

"Okay." He could do that. What was a half hour? Nothing, really. "I'll have coffee ready for you when you get here."

"You're a prince," Nox muttered sarcastically and hung up, leaving Max to get a good look at exactly what time it was: 3 a.m. She'd probably just gotten to sleep herself if she and Nash had gone out for drinks after work. He was definitely going to be grabbing the good coffee for her.

The pot was done brewing by the time Nox made it down to the sanctuary. Max knew better than to say a word as he pressed the mug into her hands and they headed back to their command center. The sanctuary was unusually quiet at this time of night. They switched off doing overnight shifts when teams weren't working on cases, keeping the place on a skeleton crew during times when most creatures would be at home in bed, even the night-dwelling ones. So no one was there to bar their way or ask inconvenient questions as Max pulled the wheelie chair in front of Nox's screens out for her and pointed to the bit of footage he wanted enhanced without a word.

She gulped down half of the mug before she set it down, hissing as the heat scalded her throat, then got to work. Her well-manicured nails click-clacked against the keyboard as she isolated the frame he wanted to get a better look at, zoomed in, and ran noise-canceling software over it. The whole process took a total of five minutes—her coffee hadn't even cooled by the time she finished.

"Holy shit," Nox muttered, clicking a button to zoom in a little closer on the face—no, *faces* in the mirror behind the bar. There were two of them, sitting side by side on the creature's shoulders. Long teeth poked its chin where they extended past its bottom lip. A mane of tangled hair pulled back from the visage of a wild beast. "Is that what I think it is?"

"Yeah. It is." Max rubbed at his temples with a sigh. A demogorgon. Right under their noses, and he and Quin hadn't even noticed it.

"Quin is gonna be pissed." She picked up her mug and chugged the rest of the coffee. When she'd lowered it back to the table, she asked, "Can I tell him?" with smugness curling at the corners of her mouth.

Max narrowed his eyes on her and leaned forward to get a better look at the face in the mirror. "Did any of the staff IDs throw up a red flag?"

"Not that we noticed." Nox shook her head, running her hand through her thick brown hair.

Of course they wouldn't. If a demogorgon was looking to hide amongst other inanimi, it wouldn't want them finding out what it was. Especially at a bar that served normies.

"I want you to run through the schedules again, see who had nights off that corresponded with the disappearances. I'll go put another pot of coffee on and call Quin. We need to get this guy off the streets before he takes anyone else." He rubbed at the back of his neck where an ache had settled. Gods, how could they have been so far off base?

"Are you going to tell Quin you told him so?"

"*Nox.*"

"Right. Cross-referencing schedules. Don't mind me." She turned back to the screens, and Max pulled out his phone to call his brother, already wishing this day were over.

Micah Brown—their new demogorgon friend—had a very human address in Miami. Which wasn't all that surprising, lots of inanimi did. They linked their human address to places in Feugo to make it easier to go back and forth, and lived near a known portal. But they liked to have a place where they could receive things like magazine subscriptions, and take out. Not that Max could hold that against them, he liked those things too.

What he could hold against Micah Brown was how the demogorgon seemed to be living in one of the more luxurious condo complexes that Miami had to offer. Two floors down from Ander Ruin, in fact, but Max didn't mention that. This meant that it either had been very good at investing or that it was making money somewhere on the side, because it wasn't even management at Inferno.

Micah also wasn't the demogorgon's real name. Micah Brown had been a mortal boy who won the lottery some years back and settled in Miami to spend his considerable wealth the way only the truly flippant could: on boats, booze, and women. Then he'd suddenly gotten a job at Inferno? Which would have been tip-off enough if they'd run the records for the other employees like Max had wanted to do. But *someone* had insisted they focus their efforts on only people who had been seen with the victims, and Max wasn't naming any names, but he was definitely going to be mad at Quin for the foreseeable future about this.

Max's hand tightened around the pommel of his sword, his heart beating hard against his chest as he raised his other hand to knock on Micah Brown's door. There was crashing on the other side, then a noise like a vacuum nozzle catching on a blanket, and Max didn't wait for an answer before he broke the door down.

The unstable portal Micah had opened was in the middle of the living room, and it was sucking in anything and everything that weighed less than ten pounds. Micah was in front of it, its human face melted away to show off a lizard-like face and fangs dripping with venom. It lunged for the portal, intent on escape, but Max's dagger buried itself deep in its calf, pinning it to the couch.

With a quick motion over his shoulder, Quin fanned out, circling the edges of the living room as Max advanced on the creature that was lashing out with all that it had. Its considerable musculature made it a danger to both of them. An arm turned into a tentacle, and Max had just enough time to duck before it could knock him clear off his feet or wrap around his neck or whatever Micah had been planning. He felt the sting of one sharp edge leave a cut on his forehead, blood already dribbling down into his eye.

Max rolled to his feet, grabbed the second dagger from his belt, and hurled it at the creature's torso with enough force to embed it into Micah's fur-lined midsection. It thrashed again, with a roar of fury, and swung for Max, giving Quin enough time to get up behind it and knock it unconscious with his staff. The portal shut a second later, and Max and Quin were able to get the creature cuffed, forcing it back to a form that was almost human.

"Well, that was fun." Max laughed a little, rubbing the back of his wrist over his forehead to clear away some of the blood that was still dripping down into his eyes.

Quin grunted.

Getting Micah back to the sanctuary was easy enough with the creature unconscious. Quin shackled the demogorgon to a chair in the interrogation room, and Max went off to have his wounds tended to by one of the medics while they waited for Micah to wake up. It didn't take long; the creature was roaring and furious within the hour.

Max and Quin moved to sit in the chairs on the other side of the table from Micah Brown. The creature tilted its head, a serpent's tongue peeking out between its lips to scent the air. "Took you long enough."

"Where are the missing girls?" Max asked, his hands laid out flat on the table in front of them, posture forced into something like relaxed to keep the creature from seeing how close he was to grabbing it by the collar and forcing it to answer. The sooner they got this done with, the sooner he could go and apologize to Ander.

"You won't find them." Micah laughed, and the sound had an echo to it, as if coming from two separate people. But it was just the demogorgon dropping its glamour enough to let Max know that it had a second head hidden under its human disguise. "They're dead."

Max fought hard to hide his flinch, but he felt Quin stiffen further beside him. "How many were there? Do you have names?"

"Fuck. I don't know. Twenty? Fifty? What's it matter in the end? They're just humans. Barely even a blip on the radar, their lives are so short."

Max waited, his gaze hard on the creature in front of him.

"What's it to you, or any other immortal, if I take a couple for food?" Micah shrugged, rolling its head from one side to the other to stretch out its neck. "He was right, you ignis really are a bunch of idiots."

"He who?"

"My boss." Micah curled its lips back from its teeth, the smile stretching inhumanly far up its face to reveal more pointed teeth than Max thought he ever wanted to see again.

"You weren't working alone." They had suspected that whoever it was had a partner, but Max hadn't thought there would be a "boss". That made it sound like some kind of underground crime ring. Like maybe it wasn't just one inanimi getting a taste for human blood. "Give us his name, and we might be able to get your execution stayed."

There was no guarantee, not if Micah had killed as many people as it hinted at. But Max was willing to bargain for answers. There had been an increase in crimes against mortals in the last few years, and while they had never seemed connected, Max had always wondered . . .

"Don't know. Just know that he goes by Timoros."

"Timoros." Max wrinkled his nose. It was the first they were hearing of the name, but that didn't mean anything. "And he's the . . ."

"The one in charge." Micah leaned back farther in its chair, unbothered by the thought that it was rolling over on its boss. Max supposed crime didn't exactly engender loyalty. "He's got all you little ignis chasing your tails."

Or maybe it just wanted to rub in their faces how much smarter this Timoros was than they were. Either way, Max could use this.

"I see." Max nodded. "Is there anything else you can tell us about him?"

"You guarantee I won't be executed and you can protect me from him, and I'll tell you everything." Micah leaned forward, baring yet more teeth somehow. "I won't give you anything else before I see the paperwork for all that."

"Of course. We want you to trust us." Max offered him a smile in return and patted Quin on the shoulder lightly.

"Why don't you show our guest back to his cell, and I'll get started on all that?"

"You're not really going to let this bastard live?" Quin signed, his brows lifted and his movements sharp.

"Let me handle it," Max said, fingers working slow and tired over the words, then nodded to their prisoner again. "Go on."

With a frown, Quin rose and escorted Micah out of the interrogation room. Colt Schields was waiting on the other side of the door, and when it opened, he smiled at Max, who had just stood to stretch out his back. With a groan, he eyed his father.

"Come to scold me for not seeing it sooner?" Max asked, heading out of the room and down the hall to his small office off of their command center. He had at least a foot of paperwork to look over because of this mess. Colt followed behind.

"No. I came to congratulate you on a job well done. That was a pretty big win for you all, I'm impressed." Colt was smiling, Max could hear it in his voice, and the pride made something warm curl up in Max's stomach. It always felt nice when their dad told him he'd done a good job, but the feeling soured when he stepped around the desk and saw the tracking cuff request form.

"Shit." He dropped into his chair with a graceless slump.

"What?" Colt moved to sit in one of the chairs. The office was cramped, barely enough room for Max's desk, his chair, and the two on the other side. He couldn't even walk around the desk to sit behind it without turning sideways, but he didn't mind. He liked the enclosed feeling, and besides, that left more room for the command center, which was where he spent most of his time anyway.

Looking up at his father, Max shot him a sheepish grin. "You wouldn't happen to know what I can get a guy to apologize for slapping a tracking cuff on him and wrongfully accusing him of kidnapping, would you?"

Colt's lips twitched a little, and he coughed over a laugh into his fist. Max had seen the gesture enough times when his Dad was dealing with his Papa to recognize it for what it was. Colt was making fun of him. "Depends. Is this just an 'I'm sorry' gift, or is it an 'I'd like to try dating' gift?"

"Who told?" Max narrowed his eyes.

"A father has his ways." Colt waved his hand, as if that could brush off the suspicion Max was ready to throw Nox's way. It couldn't, they both knew that, but if this turned out okay, he might buy her a thank you gift instead of yelling at her. "I'd say, get a nice bottle of wine and some flowers. That always works on your Papa."

Max huffed, scrubbing at his face and accidentally brushing over the scab on his forehead. "Right. Any recommendations?"

"Oh, I might have a few." Colt winked, then leaned over to grab a Post-it from Max's desk and scratch some wine names onto it.

"Thanks, Dad, you're a lifesaver."

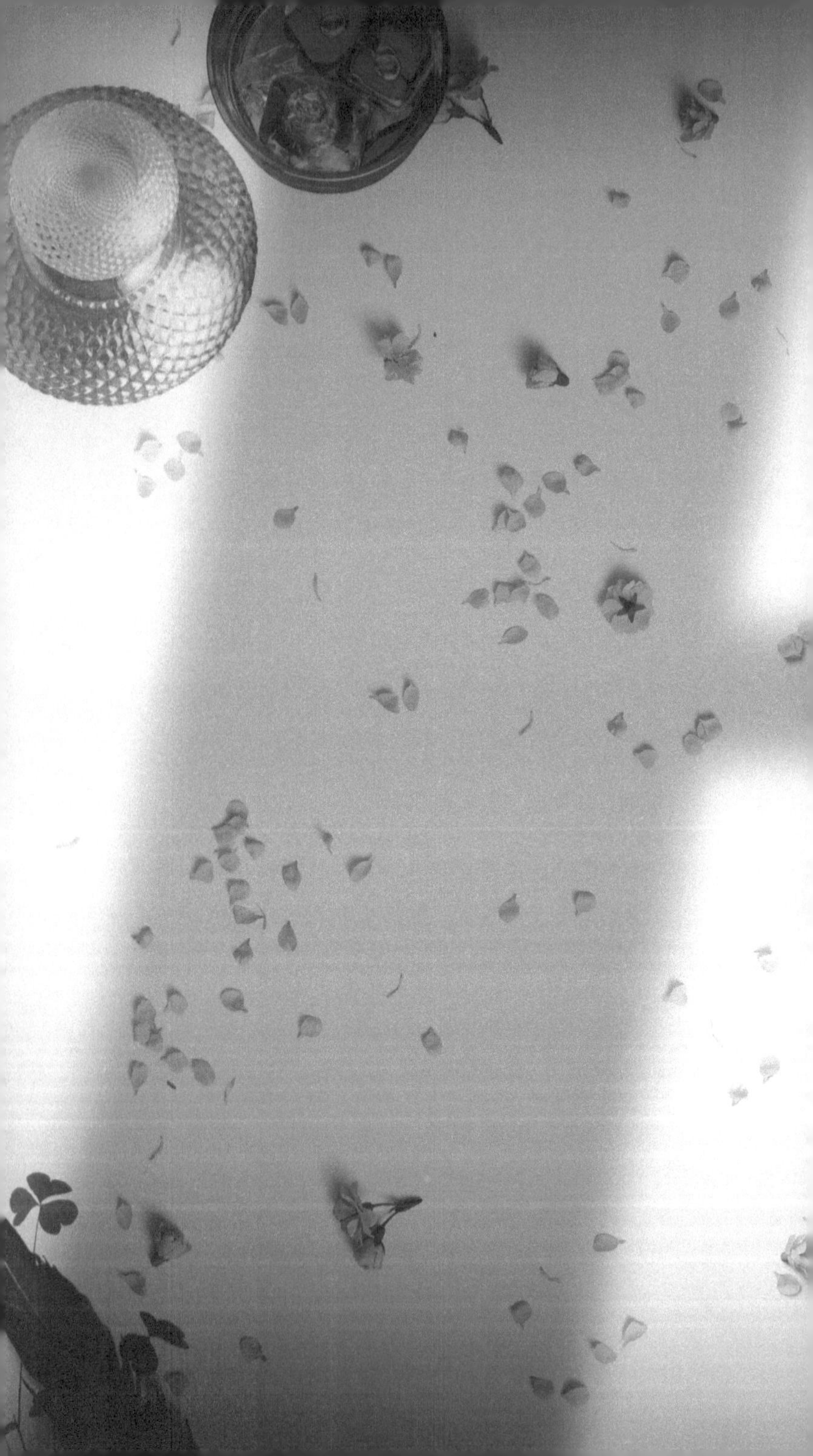

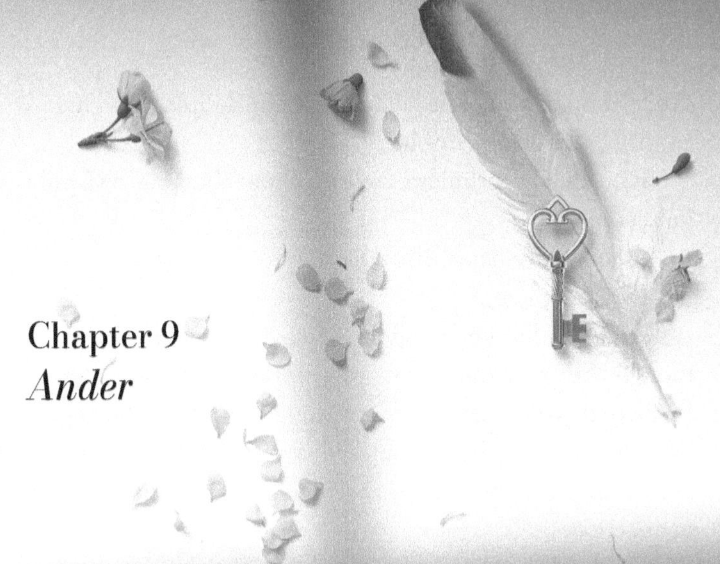

Chapter 9
Ander

Mab stayed all night, mainly because they hadn't gone to bed until the sun was coming up. By the time they'd finally had their fill of Blanche, Rose, Dorothy, and Sophia, there had been no point in Mab returning to her place, so they crawled into Ander's giant bed together to sleep most of the morning away.

It was well after lunch when they woke up, and while Ander offered to magic them in some food, Mab settled for going home instead. She claimed she needed new clothes and her own solitude for a while. Ander showered and then dressed in a pair of satin lounge pants before plopping himself back down on the couch beneath a fluffy blanket.

The blanket wasn't so much to combat the chill of his AC but to add an extra layer of comfort that blocked out the heavy metal cuff surrounding his wrist.

Ander wasn't technically confined to his condo, and he could have continued to go in to work, but there had been something crippling about the tracker the minute Maximus slapped it around his wrist. He hated the weakness it dredged up in him. The feelings of being helpless and not in control of his own life or body.

His already turbulent feelings about the ignis had only increased.

I thought we hated him now.

Did they?

Ander didn't know what he felt. Devastated. Betrayed, though he had no right to expect anything. Horny. Saddened. Confused. Anxiety ridden. And all the while, the pain in his chest from the amare bond increased—demanding that he accept the bond and consummate the connection.

But how could he? How could he possibly accept that he was arrow-bound to an ignis that could never love him back? That saw him as a villainous inanimi who was out to kidnap mortals for who knew what sort of nefarious purposes.

Ander's hands lifted to brush over the horns rising from the top of his head, then wrapped around them, tugging on the solid pieces and pulling his head forward. He didn't blame Max. Ander couldn't even pass for normal in Underworld. His own people had always seen him as an abomination. A half-breed whose other half was a *satyr*. Of all the lowly things his mother could have possibly chosen to intertwine with.

His own grandfather had seen him as a blight against this world. Why shouldn't Maximus?

Ander could see the way he was spiraling. Yet there didn't seem to be a way to stop it. Mab's visit had only temporarily pulled him out of the dungeons of his own creation. This morning, he'd placed himself right back in the cell.

He could feel the heat of Acheron on his skin, smell the

faint tang of sulfur in the air from the pits of Tartarus and the scratch of pumice stone beneath his feet once more. The back of his neck prickled with awareness, fear tightened his esophagus, and dread twisted up his stomach.

It had been one hundred and fifty-six years since regaining his freedom from that hell, but in this moment, it felt like yesterday.

Ander didn't know that he would ever be free of the ghosts of those days. From the monster who had overshadowed his life and stolen something precious from him. Orcus, god of punishment, right hand to Hades. To Ander, he had been Enrique. His love. Until that love soured, and Enrique effectively cut Ander off from everyone he cared about. He had separated him from his mother. Separated him from Mab. He'd blinded Ander to his manipulations. To his gaslighting. Made Ander think he deserved the mental, emotional, sexual, and physical abuse doled out by Enrqiue on a daily basis. And trapped him there in Acheron. Bound by aeternus rings that kept him from leaving no matter how hard he tried.

Ander had fought against it in the end, and when that hadn't been enough, he'd willed himself to die. Dying had been a better option than staying there, bound to *him* for all eternity.

The cuff made him feel trapped, effectively transporting him back to that place. To hell.

He needed to escape the memories. To run from the doubts that thoughts of Acheron and Enrique filled him to the brim with. Could he ever love again? *Should* he ever love again? The love spell he cast on Venus and Erotes had been to take his own judgment out of it. But how was he supposed to trust the process? Look where it had landed him. Could he even find it within himself to fully trust a lover again? Was it possible to open himself up to such vulnerabilities once more?

The sudden and unexpected sound of someone knocking at his door rang a startled squawk out of Ander that was not a proud moment for the half-muse. Embarrassed at himself, he flung the blanket off agitatedly and stomped to the foyer, where he wrenched the door open without even checking through the peephole first.

Maximus stood on the other side. Gray jeans, white boatneck shirt, sage-green knit cardigan, and tan loafers graced the firm body of the ignis, giving him the appearance of a sexy kindergarten teacher. His bright white wings filled up the space of the hallway behind him. In his hands, there was a bottle of expensive looking wine and a bouquet of exotic flowers.

Ander crossed his arms over his bare chest—which drew Maximus' gaze downward—and leaned against the door jam.

"What?" he snapped, not feeling particularly accommodating. Even if the flowers and wine did tug at his curiosity and the sight of Maximus in his preppy clothes made something else stir with curiosity too.

"I, um . . ." Maximus seemed dazed, his hazel eyes caught somewhere between Ander's collarbone and crossed arms. The ignis unconsciously licked his lips.

"My face is up here," Ander pointed out, lifting his hand to wave at his face.

Maximus blinked, his eyes rising to meet Ander's, and a bright flush swept from his throat all the way up to his hairline. "Sorry, I . . . can I come in?"

Ander grumbled but stepped back, sweeping a hand out toward the rest of the condo. "Why not, you've already taken liberties with my body, why not my home?"

He could see Maximus' lips open, the ignis wanting to say something in response, perhaps rebuttal. But he must have decided otherwise because his lips closed, and he swept past Ander, taking up *so* much space with his body, his scent, and his overpowering presence that it made the ache in Ander's chest pang with regret and recognition.

As he rubbed at the throb in his breastbone, Ander slammed the door shut and followed the ignis in.

Monnie came prancing into the kitchen where the ignis now stood, somehow seeming even larger in the open space. Ander expected her to begin yipping territorially, protective of her home and of her master. Instead, she scurried over to Maximus, her nails clicking on the marble, hopped up onto his foot, and began pawing at his pant leg to be lifted up.

Ander blinked in irritation. "Tiny traitor," he grumbled under his breath as he watched Maximus set the flowers and wine aside and stoop to pick up the palm-sized ball of fluff.

He didn't want to admit how watching the large male with his tiny dog did something to his heart and his loins. Instead: "Why are you *here?*" he snipped.

"Right." Maximus blushed again, as if remembering finally he had something he was meant to do. "I came to remove the cuff. We found the actual culprit—"

"Oh, you mean I *didn't* kidnap several of my own customers? *Shocking.*" The amount of sarcasm in his tone was enough to carry them both away. Ander wished he'd been able to add even more to it. "Well, get on with it then." He stepped forward, invading Maximus' space so he could steal Monnie from his clutches and hold her to his chest with one hand while he held out his other with the cuff.

"I just . . ." Maximus dug into his pocket, pulling out a set of keys, which he fumbled with almost nervously. "I wanted to say that . . . well, I *need* you to know that I never thought it was you." His strong fingers closed around Ander's wrist, turning the cuff to the latch. It sent a tingle of pleasure up Ander's arm and straight down into his toes, making them curl against the marble of his kitchen floor.

"You could have fooled me."

Maximus looked up from the cuff, his eyes wide and earnest. "I didn't. I could feel it—but Quin wouldn't let me follow my intestines, and there was all this pressure to follow procedure. But I knew it in my bones it wasn't—I just . . ." His rambling finally came to a stop, and both hands fell to clasp Ander's, holding it firmly yet gently between them. "I did everything I could to prove it wasn't you because I knew it couldn't be."

Flustered, Ander looked away from the intense gaze of the ignis, hating how his heart betrayed him by *thump, thump, thump*ing away speedily in his chest. "I don't know why you're talking about your intestines, but could you please just take the cuff off?" His tone had softened, a blockage of undefined emotion lodged just around his vocal cords.

"Sorry," Maximus whispered, then returned to the cuff.

When the click sounded and the severe metal popped off, releasing his skin, the crushing weight at last lifted from Ander's shoulders. Sighing gratefully, he fell back against the island and let his body finally relax. Burying his face in Monnie's fur, he took a moment to center himself, hating the fact that he felt like he could cry. When he was ready, he turned to set the white fluff ball on the island countertop and faced Maximus.

As he rubbed the tender flesh of his wrist, Ander glanced at the wine and flowers, then back up at Maximus.

Reminded that the items were there, the ignis hurriedly picked them up, and held them out to Ander.

"I wanted to say I'm sorry. Truly sorry that I had to cuff you. Mab said that it drudged up some truly awful memories for you, and I hate that something I did caused that." Silently, Ander cursed Mab for spilling the beans. "I thought . . . actually, when I talked to my dad, *he* thought, maybe these would help show my remorse?" Maximus finished at last, giving the bouquet a little rustle.

Ander sighed and reached out to take them from him. The wine he slid into his undercounter wine cabinet, and the flowers he magicked quickly into a vase of water with the flourish of his hand. "Very sweet of your dad," he muttered. Though, there was something a little bit adorable about the fact Maximus had sought advice from his father. "I'm assuming the non-Zeke one?"

"Yeah," Maximus chuckled nervously.

Ander rearranged the flowers a little, a thumb brushing over the silken petal of an orchid. The lad had chosen expensive florals, he would give him that. "So, who was the actual culprit in the end?"

Maximus was silent for a second before responding. "Micah Brown."

A string of curses spilled from between Ander's lips. "What?" He stared Maximus down.

"He's a demogorgon and was kidnapping the girls to be sold into the food trade. Supplying other demogorgons in Underworld."

Ander cursed once more. "I need a drink. What are you having?" How could he have missed the fact that one of his own staff was a demogorgon? He was sure there were a few innocents amongst those monsters out there somewhere, but so far in his long life, he had yet to meet one.

"Oh . . . uh, beer?"

Ander eyed him for a second, shaking his head. "Martini it is." This was not a beer household.

Ander crossed over to his wet bar that sat halfway between the open-concept dining room and living room. Making the martinis from pure muscle memory, he let his mind wander, trying to recall if there had been signs from Micah that he missed. "You're absolutely positive it was Micah?"

"He confessed."

Ander jumped, Maximus' voice coming from much closer to him than he'd expected. Turning around, he handed one of the glasses to the other male. "I hope you like them dirty." He didn't mean to purr the last word, it simply came out that way.

Maximus blushed and took the glass from him. Sipping at it, he made a face, then sipped again. "It's good," he rasped.

Ander couldn't help but chuckle a little. Sipping his own, he moved back to the island and pulled out a stool to sit down. Maximus followed, like an eager puppy, unsure what to do with himself besides follow the lead of his new master holding the treats.

Maximus faced him on his own stool, knees spread wide, heels on the bottom rung, elbow of the hand holding his drink resting on the counter. Ander could tell he was attempting to look cool, relaxed—at ease. Maximus looked anything but. There was a nervous energy about him that was quite endearing to Ander. It made him loathe the way the pang in his chest only increased, demanding that Ander lean over and seal his lips with a kiss.

Clearing his throat, Ander gulped down half of his

drink. "So, what you're telling me is, I've had a demogorgon right under my nose for months now and never realized."

"Don't feel bad, it happens to most. They're really good at hid—"

"No. Not for me. Glamours and magical masks don't typically work on me." Ander frowned, hating that Micah had slipped one by him. "I can assure you, it will never happen again."

Each person or creature entering his employ from here on out would be subjected to a thorough scan. No more mortals coming to Inferno would be caught in a deadly trap. He would see to it.

Maximus reached out, his hand resting on Ander's knee, his thumb brushing lightly over the silk material there. "I believe you." His hand squeezed lightly.

A flood of heat filled Ander, making his body hum with desire and his throat go dry. He wanted to push Maximus back against the counter and ravish his mouth until they were both moaning uncontrollably. He wanted to peel those jeans off his body, spin him around, and bend him over the cool marble of the island. Watch his wings spread out wide in the open space of his kitchen while he took him until he cried out in pleasure.

The fantasy was interrupted by a shrill ring. Maximus pulled back and fished his phone out of a tight back pocket.

Ander downed the rest of his martini, hoping to douse the fire within him. It wasn't enough. Not to quell the need or to silence the images of Maximus grinding against his counter. Sweating, Ander brushed a hand through his hair, forcing it all back over his head.

He slipped off his stool as Maximus began talking to someone on the other end of the phone. Moving to the wet bar, Ander mixed himself another drink, shaking his frustrations out on the cocktail.

"I've got to go," Maximus announced from the kitchen.

Ander turned to face him and lifted a brow in question.

"Micah's dead." A series of emotions played over Maximus' face that Ander wasn't able to decipher yet. A part of him wanted to learn what they all meant. "Maybe this is presumptuous of me . . . and if it's a no, then just tell me. I can stomach it, I swear. And I'll completely understand—"

"Maximus," Ander interrupted. "Your point."

The ignis cleared his throat and nodded. "Can I, maybe, get a raincheck on the drink?" He pointed to his unfinished martini on the counter.

Ander stared at the martini, the toothpick of olives resting so innocuously against the rim of the glass. Should he? His body screamed yes. The steady, painful pang of the amare bond intensified the screaming. Maybe he should do it. Try to hammer one out with the ignis. Consummate the bond just to get it to shut up and deal with the consequences later.

Another part of him, a quiet but steady voice in the back of his mind, whispered no. That this ignis hadn't earned the right to his time or his body. That males who ignited pain within him did not deserve access.

Was his apology real? How was Ander to know for sure? He'd seen false promises and apologies before. Had been gaslit into believing *he* was at fault for the wrongs done to him.

He looked up at the ignis, the throbbing in his chest tightening and pulling. Trying to draw him closer to Maximus.

"Fine. But—" He held up his hand to stop Maximus,

whose face had brightened with hope and joy. "You will have one shot, and only one, to prove you deserve it. So don't mess up again, Maximus."

The ignis nodded quickly, a small, happy smile slipping over his lips despite the chastisement. "Understood. Absolutely." He shoved his phone into his back pocket, stepped toward Ander, then halted. He seemed confused about how to say goodbye.

Helping him out, Ander moved over to the door and opened it up. "Go, you've got work to do."

Maximus nodded and walked to the now open door. But he fetched up once more as he reached Ander. "And it's Max, if you would like. Only my commanders call me Maximus." He shifted a little, appearing nervous.

"Max it is." The name rolled off his tongue, soft and seductive. It coiled around Ander's loins and made his fingers itch to skim over the male's body.

It appeared to have the same effect on Maximus, because his cheeks flushed and his eyes glistened with heat.

There were no further words shared between them, however. The ignis stepped out into the hall, and Ander soundly closed the door behind him.

"Interesting houseguest you were entertaining," a voice rang out behind him.

Spinning around, his heart pounding in fear, Ander found Indra leaning against his island counter, holding Monnie in one hand and finishing off Max's martini with the other.

"What the *hell*?!"

Indra winked at him and set the empty martini glass down. "What are your plans for this evening? I want to hit up that burlesque stripper bar." The king of the gods was a close friend of Ander's mother and had interceded on her behalf when Ander's grandfather had attempted to kill his shameful, bastard grandson for the third time.

For some reason, after that, King Indra had taken a special interest in Ander.

Ander stomped down on the growl of annoyance that wanted to slip out of him at the sight of the king of the gods making himself at home in his condo.

"Of course, Your Majesty."

"Surely after all this time, Ander . . . just Indra."

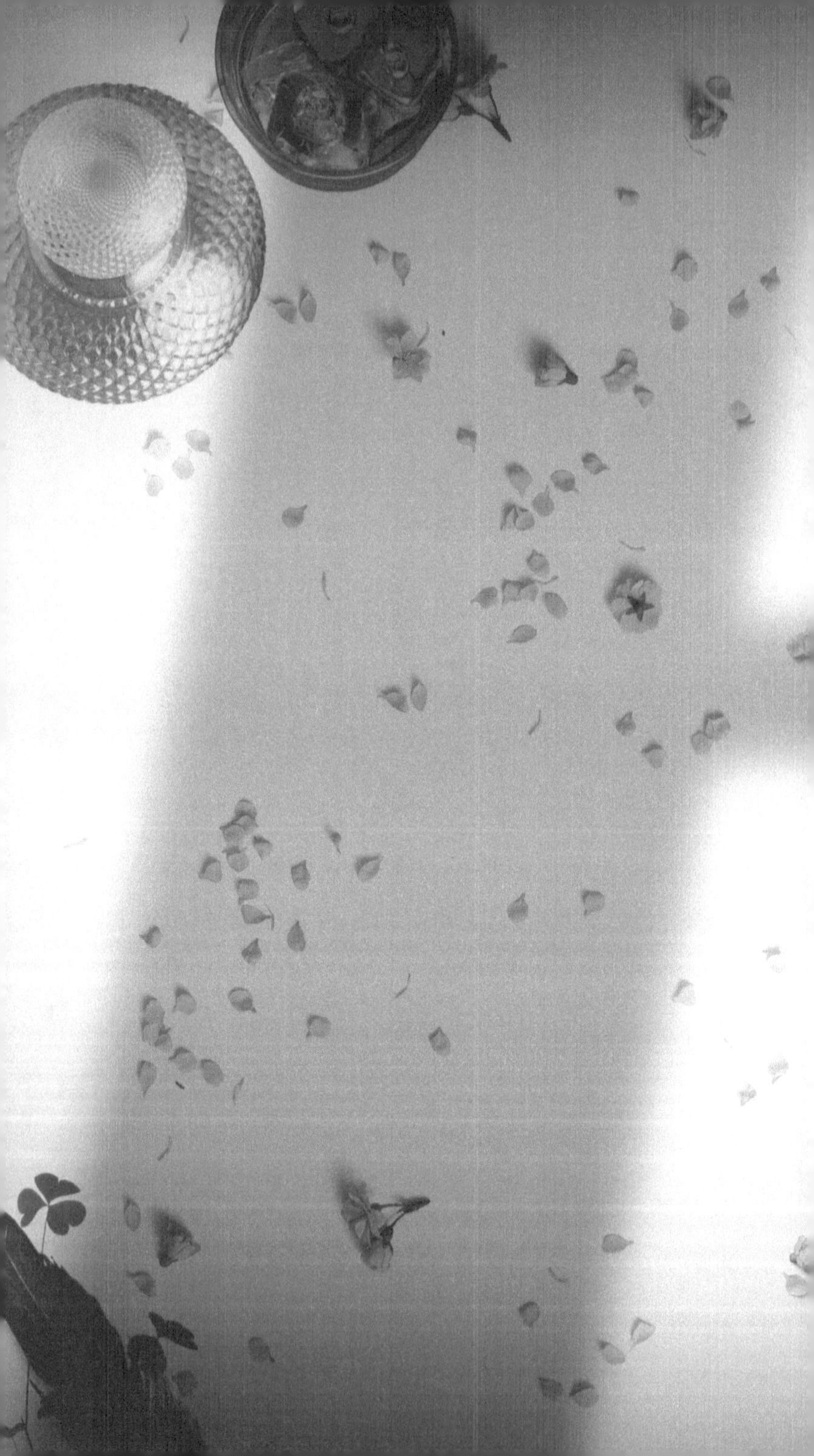

Chapter 10
Quin

Quin ended the call and slid his phone back into his pocket. He stared at the body of their suspect, its throat a mangled mess, blood coating the front of it and dripping into a large puddle on the floor. This was a disaster, and even worse, it happened on his watch. Galeo would have his head and likely run Max through the ringer at the same time.

"Yowzas! That . . . is not what I was expecting to see," Nash groaned from behind him. "Really regretting those burritos with extra salsa right about now."

Quin shot him a silencing look. "I need you and Nox to run all the footage from around this cell for the last hour. Retrace every step that led up to the moment where Brown was killed. I need to know *exactly* what took place before he died."

"Sure thing." Nash pulled his phone out to call his twin, telling her to meet him at their desk as he disappeared around the corner.

Quin stepped into the holding cell and slowly made his way around the body, careful not to step into the blood pool and contaminate the evidence. His eyes swept over every inch of the corpse, looking for any detail that might help him understand what had happened. Bending down by the chair, he noticed the ballpoint pen sitting below its dangling fingers, the tip of it caked in blood and bits of flesh.

The murder weapon, if he wasn't mistaken.

"Quintus! Status report!"

Quin looked up to see Captain Galeo standing just outside the cell looking less than pleased. The head of the Feugo City Sanctuary answered only to the Princeps in Rome and was a stern, no-nonsense ignis. He worked them hard and expected the best from those within his command. Failure was not an option with Galeo, and praise was hard earned and rare, especially for the Schields family, whom he saw as abominations for the way they had been raised.

"Micah Brown was brought in this morning by Maximus and myself under suspicion of kidnapping and selling young human women in the underground food trade. The demogorgon rolled over on its boss, Timoros, we brought it in here, and it was found dead fifteen minutes ago."

"Suicide or homicide?"

"Trying to sort that out now, sir."

Galeo nodded. "I want your findings on that within the hour."

"Of course, Captain." Quin sighed, watching him walk away, his blue wings underlined with white feathers proud and strong on his back.

Standing, Quin followed in the direction Nash had disappeared. If Captain Galeo was expecting information in the next hour, Quin was going to need to stay on top of the twins. Quin didn't need to give him another reason to come down hard on their team. He really hoped Max got back soon. It was always easier to rein them in when Max was there to help contain them.

The twins were bickering when he stepped into the room, Nox demanding that Nash return her mouse, and Nash arguing that he didn't have her mouse, he had his. Quin grumbled and, stepping up, grabbed ahold of each of their heads, turning them away from each other, and back to their screens.

"Enough. Galeo wants to know what happened. Bring up the footage of Brown's cell fifteen minutes before it was found."

Nash swatted his hand away. "Not cool, man, the hair is not to be touched." He smoothed his hair back down.

"Just bring up the footage, Nash." Still grumbling, Nash did as he was ordered and pulled up the camera feed to show the current image of Brown sagging dead in the chair in its cell. "Nox, bring up the hallway footage from outside its cell for the same timestamp."

Together, the twins rewound the two camera angles, taking it back in time to see Micah Brown stabbing its own throat out with the pen. Both of them hissed and looked away at first before returning their gazes to the screen.

"Keep going back, I need to see what brought this on." Leaning in over his younger siblings' shoulders, he peered at the screen. "Stop! Right there, who is that?"

The twins both paused their footage, showing off the face of Cyprian, another ignis with blue and teal wings. *What the hell was he doing there?* Cyprian was supposed to be on duty in Feugo City itself.

"Can you bring it up to when Cyprian first approached? I need audio as well as visual."

Nox tapped away on her keyboard, and soon, they were

watching Cyprian walk down the hall and stop before Micah Brown's cell. The conversation was quick.

"I heard you're the worthless demogorgon who admitted to taking those girls."

"What's it to you if I am?"

Cyprian leaned in closer to the cell. "According to his sin shall a man be punished."

Quin watched the other ignis turn, a pen falling from somewhere on his person as he did so, then he walked down the hallway and out of the frame. Without hesitation, Brown stooped to pick up the pen, sat back down in its chair, and began to violently stab itself repeatedly in the neck until there was nothing left but a gaping hole and its hands fell lifeless at its sides.

While Quin watched every detail without blinking, the twins hissed and winced. "Gods of Olympia! Why would anyone kill themselves that way?" Nox moaned.

"Why would it kill itself at all?" Quin asked instead. Max had promised Brown it wouldn't be executed if it gave up the name of its boss. Why had a few words about punishment from Cyprian driven the demogorgon to suicide?

"Hey, what'd I miss?" Max was suddenly in the room, looking both winded and shocked.

"Come here." Quin waved him over. "Play the footage again." He tapped Nash on the shoulder.

The twins quickly reversed the feed and let their older brothers watch the conversation between Cyprian and Brown once more, then the hurried and painful death that followed.

"Well that is . . . odd," Max muttered.

"Very," Quin replied. Looking at Max, he frowned. Leaning in, he sniffed, his heightened senses picking up on a scent that was strange for Max. "Have you been drinking?" he signed to keep it between the two of them, his words in sharp, pointed bursts of movement.

"I don't want to talk about it," Max signed back.

Quin frowned more. Max barely drank. It just wasn't something he bothered with much. For him to have had alcohol in the middle of the afternoon was not only a foreign concept, it was concerning. Quin turned to face him so that he could have a better conversation with him in ASL.

"I know you feel you owe him an apology, but you don't have to get into things that aren't like you just to make him feel good."

"I was being polite." Max's hands moved with snappy motions, indicating irritation.

"There is being polite and then there is doing things that aren't like you just to make someone else happy. Don't fall into that trap for some guy, not again."

"You two know we can understand you, right?" Nox asked, the twins both turned around in their computer chairs, watching their older brothers converse silently.

Max sighed roughly. "Let's go talk to Cyprian."

Quin followed him, as he always did. He couldn't make Max's decisions for him, and he wouldn't. But he didn't want to see his brother hurt over some playboy again. Ander Ruin didn't give off the vibe of someone who was looking to settle down and start a family. Not with the string of lovers he'd left in his wake.

Cyprian was in the training room when they tracked him down, a pair of daggers in his hands as he fought against a set of swinging axes hanging from the ceiling.

"Cyprian, we need to talk," Max called out from the sidelines.

Quin came to stand beside him, his arms crossed over his chest and his black raven-esque wings tucked firmly against his back.

Crypian ducked, sliding the daggers into their hilts at his thighs, then rolled across the floor, out of the way of the swinging axes. Popping back up in front of the two of them, he looked between the Schields brothers, appearing completely at ease. "What's going on?"

"Why were you down in the holding cells speaking to Micah Brown?" Max asked.

"I heard we had a scumbag demogorgon on site and wanted to see for myself."

"Are you aware that the demogorgon killed itself with a pen you dropped shortly after you left it?"

Cyprian showed neither surprise nor former knowledge. "I'd like to say that's unfortunate, but Underworld and Earth are better off without it."

"So you were not aware, then, that it killed itself with a pen *you* dropped?"

"No, I was not." His face was passive, showing no emotion.

"Are you certain?" Quin asked, stepping closer.

"Very." Cyprian met his stare, unblinking.

"So you didn't drop the pen on purpose?" Max pressed.

"No, I did not. Now, if you'll excuse me, I have training to finish." He turned and walked back out to the swinging axes.

"I don't like it," Quin muttered to Max. "Something seems off. I've got this feeling—"

"In your intestines?" Max clipped back.

Staring at his brother, Quin suddenly wished Max were still at Ruin's place rather than here mouthing off.

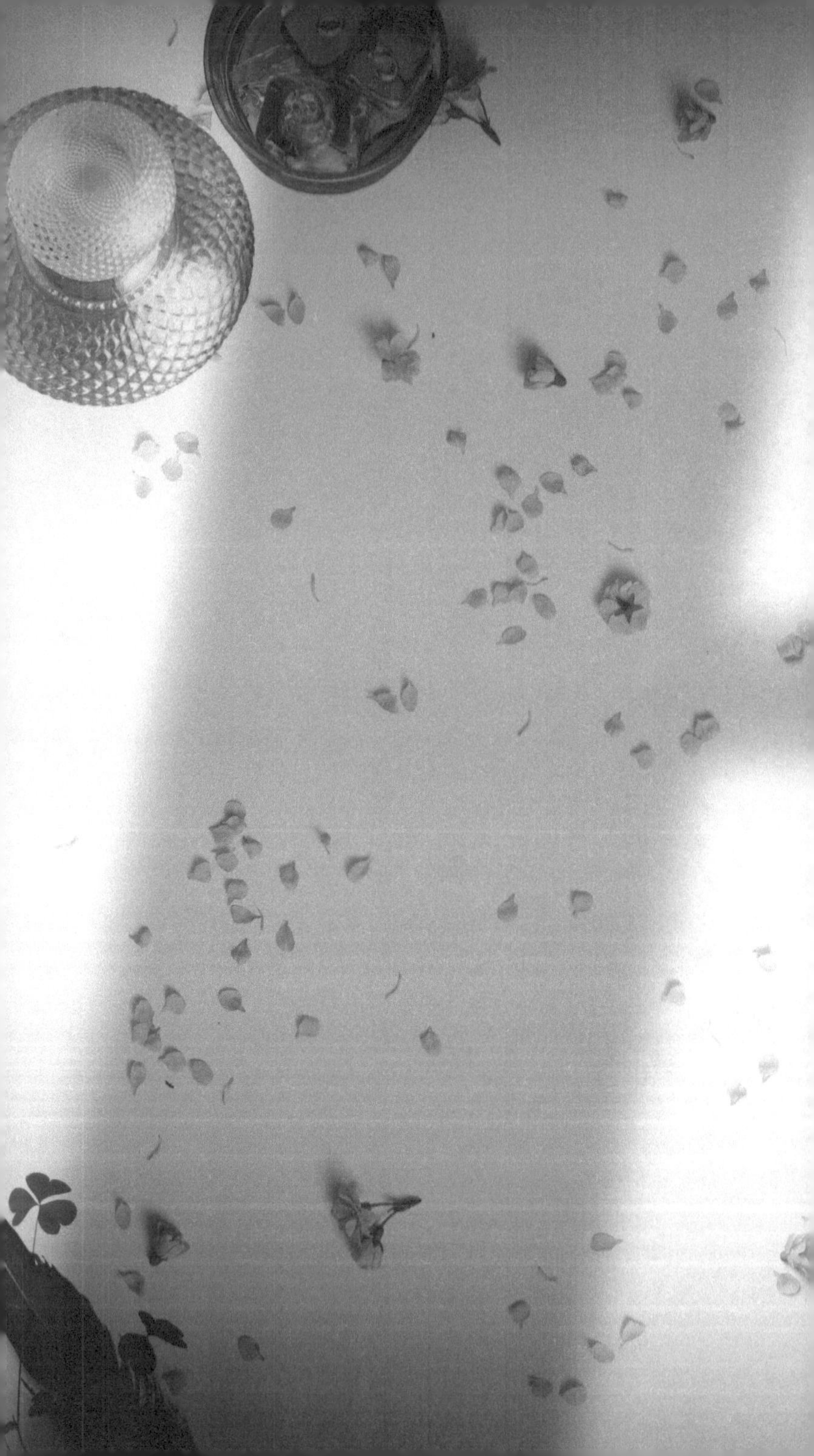

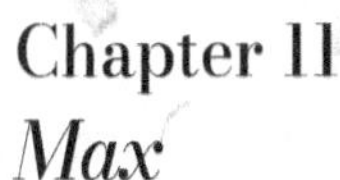

Chapter 11
Max

Quin wasn't wrong, the whole thing with Micah Brown did feel off. It wasn't just that people didn't normally commit suicide by stabbing themselves repeatedly in the neck with a pen, although that was strange enough to set off any number of alarms in Max's mind. It was also that Cyprian wasn't even supposed to be in the sanctuary that day, yet he'd come back just to spit in Micah's face, which would normally hint at something personal. If ignis were able to hold grudges, Max would think there had been something like that between them, but everyone knew they couldn't.

Then there was the way he said what he'd said. Cyprian wasn't as young as Quin and Max, but he wasn't as old as some of the other ignis, like their captain. The syntax hadn't been modern, and it sounded almost scripted. Couple that with Micah's almost immediate reaction and . . . well, it just didn't feel right. Which was something coming from a male who specialized in what normies considered to be mythical.

Unfortunately, as Quin had pointed out when they were investigating Ander, they had to go where the evidence led, and at the moment, the evidence led to suicide. So, when they met with Captain Galeo the next day, Max was already prepared for what his answer would be.

"From the evidence we've been able to gather, it looks like the suspect committed suicide," Max said, even as his stomach turned with it. It wasn't right. He knew it wasn't. Quin knew it wasn't. The twins knew it wasn't. Max would bet his last set of Mickey ears that if he had their father look over all of it, he'd say the same thing. But Colton Schields wasn't their captain, Galeo was. And Galeo wanted answers. Definitive ones. Not gut feelings.

"Good, then we'll consider this case closed." Galeo nodded, sandy-colored hair falling into his eyes as he dipped his head to sign off on the report that Quin had written up.

"However," Max said, clearing his throat and ignoring the way Galeo tightened his hold on his pen. This was by no means the first time he'd stalled an investigation because something didn't feel right, and although he was usually correct, it didn't mean it annoyed their superiors any less. "There is something about this case that seems strange to us. Particularly the method of suicide and the fact that I told the suspect that it would not face execution for its crimes if it could provide us more information on the organization it was working for. There was just no reason for it to—"

"Maximus." Galeo lifted his head from the report to fix Max with a tight smile, his eyes narrowing in something close to a reprimand. "You and your *family*," he said with such contempt that Maximus was surprised the smile didn't twist into a sneer, "seem to put far too much emphasis on feelings. I don't see where you have any evidence to support that this wasn't suicide. Unless there is something that isn't in this report?"

"No, sir." Max lifted his chin. He felt Quin straighten

his own posture beside him. "It's just a feeling that we have."

"And you got a confession from this demogorgon that it was the one abducting the women?"

"Yes, sir."

"Then there is one less inanimi scum on the streets hurting humans, and you two did an excellent job making sure we arrested the right creature for it. I say we consider this a win, don't you?" Galeo didn't wait for their agreement; he ducked his head again and signed off on the report. Max swallowed down any further arguments. "You're dismissed."

"Thank you, sir." Max took the report for his own files, his shoulders tight. Every step back to their command center was like walking through sand, sinking and weighed down. Likewise, Quin's presence at Max's side was heavy, making Max list a little toward him. Quin didn't have to say anything; Max knew what he was thinking. This thing, whatever it was, it wasn't over.

Nox and Nash were sitting in front of their screens, throwing popcorn back and forth, aiming for each other's mouths, though most of it landed on the floor. Their attention was drawn to Max and Quin when the door swung shut behind them, a piece of popcorn pinging off Nash's eyebrow and down into his shirt, where he shook it out onto the floor.

"What's the word, boss?" Nash asked, shooting his twin a narrow-eyed look.

"Stop calling me that." Max rubbed at his temples. In the back corner of the room, behind the wall of monitors, there was a filing cabinet with drawers that opened on squealing tracks when Max stuffed the file inside with all the others.

The twins must have turned to Quin for an explanation because he grumbled a soft, "Captain said, case closed."

"Even the Timoros thing?" Nox peeked around the monitors to raise a dark brow at Max.

"No." Max shook his head, rubbing his hands on his jeans. "He didn't say anything about the Timoros thing, so as far as I'm concerned, we're still looking for him. I want you two to take that name and run with it. Get me—"

His phone *ding*ed loudly, and Max pulled it from his pocket to frown down at the screen. The contact was a string of numbers he didn't recognize, but the text itself . . .

> Hey handsome, you still owe me a drink,
> and I'm feeling thirsty. ;)

Heat crawled up Max's neck and into his cheeks. He cleared his throat, tucking his phone in closer to himself when he felt one of his siblings trying to peer over his shoulder. A quick glance told him it was Nash, and he quickly smacked him with one of his wings, eliciting a soft grunt.

"As I was saying, get me everything you have on that name. I don't care how old it is, I don't care if it's mythology, I want everything." Slanting a look at Nash, he waited for his little brother to give a salute and slink back to his chair before Max was willing to pull his phone away from his chest and answer.

> I'll pick you up at 7

Then he stuffed it back into his pocket. "While you two are on that, I, uh . . . I have something else to do."

"What else to do?" Nox asked, green eyes narrowed in suspicion.

"Something that's none of your business. Get to work," Max grumbled.

"I don't think it's a what, it's a who." Nash shot a conspiratorial look at his twin.

Max simply grunted and swept from the room. He felt Quin behind him and let out a long breath, grateful that Quin waited 'til they'd at least reached Max's office and had the good grace to shut the door behind him so the twins couldn't eavesdrop as easily.

"That was Ruin." Quin fixed Max with a disapproving frown, and Max almost wanted to shrink under that look. He hated it when people didn't approve of him or something he did, especially when the people not approving were the people he loved most in the world.

"It was. And before you say it, I know what you're thinking: you're worried I'm going to not be myself. But I did think about what you said yesterday, and you're right—don't get smug with me, no one likes a smug Quin." Max shook his finger at Quin, which only made him lift one dark brow. "As I was saying, you were right. I was maybe not trying to be someone I'm not but definitely not being myself. That being said, the game plan for tonight is to take him on a very Max-centric date. If he doesn't have fun or call back, then I guess I have my answer, don't I?" Even as he said the words, something pulled in his chest, a gentle but insistent tug.

"Max-centric?" Quin drawled, his tone almost teasing.

"Yes, Max-centric. Now, you're in charge of the gremlins for the rest of the day. I need to go get some stuff lined up. Do you think you can handle that?"

"I've got it covered, boss." Quin's lips twisted up into a wry smile, and Max grabbed a stress ball the twins had gotten him as a joke when he'd first got an office, then chucked it at his brother. Quin caught it with ease and was already on his way out of the office, laughing to himself softly as he tossed the ball from hand to hand, by the time Max thought to shout any further protests.

He'd known finding the perfect outfit would take forever, but he hadn't been prepared for how much of a mess it would leave his room. Still, Max felt reasonably confident that he looked okay in his mustard-colored jeans, denim button-up, gray cable-knit sweater, and a sturdy pair of boots that wouldn't leave his feet aching by the end of the night.

Maybe he should have texted Ander and told him to wear comfortable shoes. What if he wore something that pinched his feet? Was Max absolutely the worst date for not giving Ander any dress code instructions? He probably was. Maybe he should just call and cancel. This was probably a bad idea. Ander was going to find this date completely and utterly juvenile. And boring. Max should definitely just save them both the—

Ding.

"You've got this, Max," he murmured, running his hands through his hair, no doubt making it stick up worse than it probably already had been, before he stepped off the elevator and made his way to Ander's door. He knocked, his hands tucking into his back pockets to keep from fidgeting more with his clothes and hair. Monnie started yipping, and he heard Ander say something to her but couldn't make it out through the door.

A moment later, the door opened, and the most

beautiful man Max had ever seen came into view. He thought that almost every time he saw Ander, yet the sight of Ander standing there in a pair of artfully ripped black jeans and a sheer maroon shirt that was unbuttoned to his navel—but would have covered nothing besides—knocked Max breathless. He lifted a hand to rub at the gentle tug in his chest again and shook himself.

"I hope you wore comfortable shoes," were the first words out of Max's mouth, and he practically bit his tongue in half trying to call the words back. "I, uh—" Scrubbing at the back of his neck, Max looked down at where he was scuffing his boots against the floor. "I mean, hi, you look . . . you look . . ."

"Why don't you come in?" Ander asked through what sounded like a laugh as he stepped back to let Max inside. "I've just got to feed Monnie and put her show on, then we can head out."

"Her show?"

"She has a thing for *Real Housewives*." Ander shrugged, and Max couldn't help but follow him as they headed into the kitchen to feed Monnie, then to the living room to turn on the TV for her, and make sure her little stairs were set up just so, where she could climb onto the couch when she was ready. "Now . . . why do I need comfortable shoes?"

"It's a surprise?" Why did that sound like a question? Gods of Olympia, he was so bad at this.

Ander eyed him for a moment, seeming to be searching for something, then he shrugged and snapped, a pair of comfortable looking loafers appearing on his previously bare feet. "I don't usually like surprises, but for you, darling," he purred, "I'll make an exception."

"Oh. Oh good." Max brightened, a smile splitting his face. "Then . . . shall we?"

"Hmm. I think we shall."

Max stuffed his hands in his pockets again to keep from reaching out for Ander's, then led him back out to the elevator and down to street level where he'd parked his motorbike.

"I, umm . . . I don't have a helmet that would work with your horns, but I promise I'll keep you safe," Max offered, hesitating as he threw one leg over the seat and waited for Ander to climb on behind him. When Max looked back at Ander, his face was doing something complicated that Max couldn't quite decipher. It might be better if he didn't, honestly.

"No worries, handsome, wouldn't want to ruin my hair." Ander winked, running his fingers back over the hair which he'd spiked into a mohawk between his horns. Max wondered if it was as sharp as it looked, but he didn't get a chance to check as Ander settled in behind him, and all other thoughts fled at the forced closeness. He'd definitely not thought this through. Maybe he should have borrowed his father's Jeep after all. "All set, darling."

"Right." Max cleared his throat, and they were off. It was easier, with the breeze burning his eyes and cooling his skin, to focus on Miami's traffic instead of the warm press of Ander's body behind his own.

They pulled up in front of Max's favorite taco spot a little while later, and Max slid off the motorbike before holding a hand out to help Ander off as well. "Okay, I think I should explain before we get started," Max said, feeling suddenly self-conscious about the choices he'd made for this date. "I know you're probably used to much fancier dates. Expensive restaurants, dancing and whatnot. But I, uh . . . Well, my brother mentioned that I should make sure you get to know me. So . . . we're going to go to a couple of my favorite spots. I hope that's okay?"

Ander tilted his head, seeming to be trying to see past Max's shoulder, which blocked his view of the restaurant. When he couldn't, he wrinkled his nose, and Max couldn't help but notice how absolutely adorable it was. All he wanted to do was lean forward and nip at the very tip of Ander's nose to see if it would wrinkle further. Gods, he was in so much trouble. Quin was right, and he was going to be absolutely insufferable about it.

"Why wouldn't it be?" Ander asked, drawing Max's attention back to the conversation.

Max's wings shifted nervously behind him, out of sight for the humans on the street but very much present. First dates were not a good time to talk about someone's exes—he knew enough about dating to know that—so he just didn't answer. "I just wanted to, like . . . put a disclaimer on this?"

"Here's an idea, Max." Ander smiled, leaning in closer, his hands pressing into Max's chest as he moved onto his tip toes so he could whisper in Max's ear. "Why don't you let me decide for myself?"

Swallowing around a suddenly dry throat, Max nodded eagerly. "I . . . yeah, all right . . . I think I can do that."

"Perfect." Ander pulled back, fixing Max with a dazzling smile that practically knocked him sideways, and held out his hand. Max took it, threading their fingers together, and turned to lead him inside and up to an old airstream trailer that the owners had converted into a taco truck. It was parked in the middle of a high-ceilinged dining room, the tables scattered around full of softly chattering people. "Tacos?"

"They're my favorite food." Max shrugged a little and

offered the woman behind the counter, who clearly recognized him, a wide smile.

"For here or to go?" she asked.

"To go." Max rocked back on his heels to look at the menu, his thumb brushing thoughtlessly across the back of Ander's hand as they ordered their food. They settled into an easy silence while they waited, but it was inevitable that his mind would filter back to the case. The frustration that lingered from Galeo basically dismissing what may have been a murder under the Sanctuary's roof just because the person was an inanimi, just because they'd done something wrong, sat like an ill-fitting sweater across his shoulders.

"Is something bothering you?" Ander asked, giving his hand a little squeeze.

"No. It's nothing. It's just this . . . this case." Max scrubbed at his face, exhaustion suddenly weighing him down. "I can't . . . We shouldn't . . . You don't want to hear about this."

"Au contraire, mon amour. I very much *do* want to hear about whatever has you looking like that." Ander leaned in to poke a finger at the wrinkle in between Max's eyebrows, and Max laughed a little, the weight lifting a fraction.

"It's just . . . Micah killed itself after telling us about this Timoros guy. And it knew more, it was going to give us more. I could feel it. I'd even promised to keep the Princeps from executing it for its crimes. It would have still faced a lot of prison, but it would have lived. But then it just . . ." Max shrugged, then frowned when he looked up to find Ander staring into the middle distance, his brow creased in the middle. This definitely wasn't a first date conversation; the twins were really going to lay into him for it. "Like I said, we shouldn't talk about this."

"Order number 78," the woman called from the pick-up

counter, and Max went to grab their food, then led Ander back outside to the motorbike.

"We're not eating here?" Ander blinked, looking back at the restaurant, confused.

"Nope. Can you hold on to that while we go?"

Ander nodded, and they climbed back onto the little bike before heading out again. Max just hoped the food wouldn't go cold by the time they got to their second stop. Maybe he should have brought a bag to keep things warm or something. Had he spoken to his Papa about this whole thing, or the twins, they'd have had some pointers, but he didn't really want anyone else knowing where he was going or with whom. It'd have been much easier if he were allowed to fly them everywhere, or if he wasn't trying to surprise Ander and Ander could snap them wherever. But . . . he was going to make this work.

They pulled up outside of the Botanical Gardens a bit later, and Ander made a noise of question behind him.

"My dad brought us here a lot as kids." Max dug around in the saddlebags on the side of the bike, pulled out a blanket, then held his hand out to Ander again. "It was one of the few places ignis kids could run around without people bumping into our wings by accident before we learned how to maneuver in crowds."

Ander was silent as they walked down the main path, and Max wondered if he'd royally screwed this whole thing up. Maybe he should have just taken Ander out for drinks and dancing. He had said Max still owed him a drink, and yet here Max was taking him for tacos and a picnic. The twins were never going to let him live this—

"Oh, Max," Ander said on a breath as the path led them to a small patch of grass under a spindly tree. "This is beautiful."

The smile that crawled up his face at those words made Max's cheeks ache. "Oh . . . oh good. Well, you can take a look around. I'll get us set up?"

"No need, darling." Ander shook his head and snapped his fingers. The blanket on Max's arm disappeared and was laid out onto the grass, accompanied by throw cushions of all shapes and sizes and a few candles. "How about that?"

"That's perfect . . . actually." Max laughed a little, tugging him over to the blanket so they could both sit and eat their dinner. "I'd have taken you to the orchid garden, but they don't look like much this time of year."

"Maybe next time," Ander offered, picking at his food, and Max's heart leapt in his chest. *Next time.*

"Yeah, maybe."

The night ended far too soon. Max wasn't sure where the time had gone, but then they were in front of Ander's door, saying goodnight.

"I, uh . . . I had a lot of fun," Max mumbled, cheeks heating as his gaze flicked down to Ander's lips, then back up. "Is it okay . . . is it okay if I give you a goodnight kiss?"

Ander's lips spread into a delighted smile, and he nodded quick enough that he almost knocked his head against the doorframe. Max didn't give him time to say anything before dipping down and pressing their lips together in a soft, chaste kiss that sent his heart into a gallop. He lifted a hand, thumb brushing over Ander's jaw for a moment, then pulled back to offer Ander a shy smile.

"Goodnight, Ander." Gods, why did his voice sound so

rough? He needed to get out of there before he made a complete ass of himself.

"Goodnight, Max."

Max laughed, soft and disbelieving, then stole another quick kiss before spinning on his heel and heading for the elevator. Best to make a quick exit before he tripped over his tongue again.

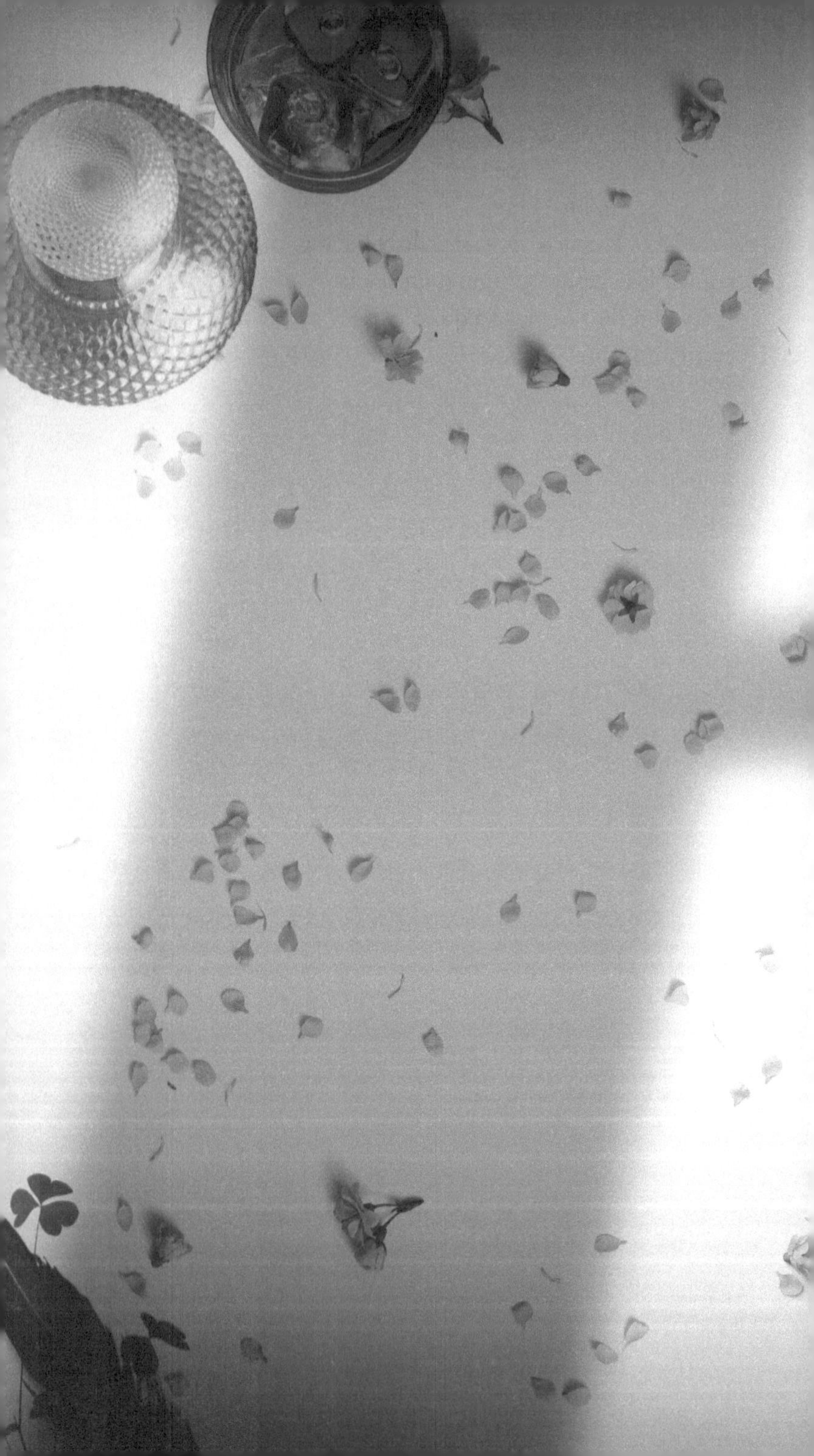

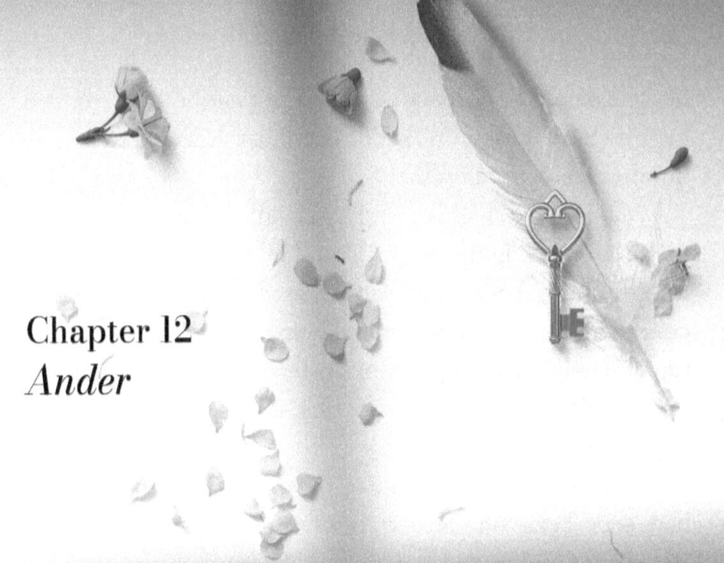

Chapter 12
Ander

Ander stretched beneath his soft down-filled duvet cover, enjoying the feel of his naked body on the silk sheets. A smile tugged at his lips as the memory of his dreams twirled through his mind. Max. Tall, broad-shouldered, beautiful-eyed Max. He'd dreamt of them dancing on a cloud that Maximus had flown them to in the sky. The moon had shimmered down on them in their sparkling attire while they shared a kiss that set the sky ablaze.

His red-painted fingertips lifted to press against his lips that remembered the feel of another pair of soft, plush lips pressing against them in the sweetest, most chaste kiss he'd ever received. Ander didn't think he'd been kissed so innocently since he was a wee one running around the palace at Helicon, chasing Solara through the garden until she offered him his first kiss behind the statue of a naked dancer.

After their date, Ander had gone to Inferno to work late into the night, finishing up paperwork, payroll, and putting in a much-needed order of alcohol to get them through the next few weeks. Max had been frequently on his mind. His nervousness. His respectfulness. The way he never forced too much of himself on Ander yet always seemed to be one hundred percent himself.

Maximus Schields wasn't at all what Ander had pictured most ignis to be like. He was so candid and unassuming. Ander had anticipated consummating the bond with their evening out and being able to finally put the tug of need to rest within him. Instead, a little hand holding and a soft kiss at the end of the night was all that had happened.

And yet, it had been one of the most endearing dates he had ever been on. Seated beneath the glass sky of the Botanical Gardens, with the scent of flowers in the air, Max had asked Ander simple yet personal questions. Seeking to get to know him. But he had never pressed too far, only dusting the surface. Max's sweetness was a danger to him, threatening to pull him into this more deeply than he should. Ignis weren't capable of love. If Ander let himself get swept away by his attention and thoughtfulness, he was only going to end up hurt.

It had been such a good night, it was hard *not* to get swept away.

The one spot of darkness on the whole night had come about when Max was discussing the present case with him. The name Timoros tugged at Ander's memory, invoking feelings of distaste. Ander simply hadn't been able to put his finger on the why and how of recognizing the name.

There had also been the small matter of how Max referred to Micah. *It.* Ander was certain an ignis referring to the dark creatures in such a way was normal, and demogorgons didn't exactly spawn in standard methods. But they weren't *its*. If anything, demogorgons were actually theys. An intersex creature possessing both reproductive organs within themselves.

It felt cold. Distant. *It* was impersonal. *It* was easy to kill.

They were vicious creatures that preferred to feed off mortals above all else, but they were still living, breathing beings.

Ander knew Max hadn't meant anything by his words. The death of the creature was clearly still weighing on his mind. This manner of speech was simply how he'd been raised within the Sanctum. The memory of it still weighed on Ander, though, reminding him of how poorly all inanimi were viewed by the very governing body meant to judge them.

Other than that, Ander had to say the evening had been stellar.

Rolling out of bed, Ander reached for his phone on the nightstand and saw that he had a message from Max.

> Thank you for going out with me last night

The text made his insides feel warm and gooey.

Quickly, Ander's thumbs flew over the keyboard of his phone.

> Any time, darling

With a whistle on his lips and a delighted smirk tugging at his features, Ander disappeared into his bathroom to shower, shave, and put on his face for the day. A little over an hour later, he moved into his closet, his eyes lined in black and hair spiked into a messy mohawk, showing off the undercut on the sides of his head.

Still singing a happy song, Ander moved into his walk-in closet to dress in a pair of black skinny jeans and a loose white T-shirt covered in the outline of gray flowers. The neckline was scooped enough that it hung off one shoulder. White thong sandals finished off his look.

He stopped long enough to feed and soothe Monnie, taking her out for a potty break and turning on her shows, before he snapped his fingers and teleported himself to just inside his friend Rashad's loft apartment.

"Finally!" Rashad cried from where they lounged on the modular sofa seated beneath the window overlooking Miami. "I thought you'd completely forgotten about us spending the day together." Rashad looked at their watch as they stood. "Forget that, the day is pretty much gone."

"Well, excuse me for being a nightclub owner who has to work until almost daybreak. Shame on me for wanting to get some sleep," Ander drawled, crossing his arms over his chest.

"Mmmmhm." Rashad walked toward Ander and pulled him into a hug. Ander curled his arms around their thin waist and hugged back tightly, grinning into Rashad's neck. "It's nice to see you. Now! Let's get going!"

"Wait, what's the hurry?" Ander pulled back. "I thought we were doing pre-drinks here before we headed out to brunch?"

"Ander, it's three in the afternoon. Brunch has long been forgotten by this point. And pre-drinks would have happened had you showed up at ten. Now, I need to go pick up something before it's too late. Then we'll find some cute bar to grab drinks and food at."

"Fine," Ander sighed, acting as if he were being entirely put out. "But where do you need to go in such a hurry?"

"I'm late to pick up a special little treat for the club

tonight." Rashad wiggled their dark brows and ran a hand over their tight cornrows, decorated with a series of gold rings looped through them. Rashad was one of the caucus, a race of fire-breathing giants native to lands just outside of Helicon. Typically, caucus grew to over seven feet tall. Both males and females had bodies of firm, rippling muscles and intense burning-red eyes.

Rashad was none of these things. Though still tall by human standards, they were slender and delicate looking. Much like Ander, Rashad had not been accepted in their homeland, and when the two of them met, a bond of understanding formed.

"Drugs."

"Not so . . . contemptuously, please. Especially from you." Rashad gave him a little push. "And, since you made me late, how about you snap us over there?"

"Fiiiine." Ander looped his arm around their waist, pulling Rashad in. "Where are we off to?"

"Do you know Bourgeois Estates?"

"Your drug dealer lives in those insanely overpriced condos?"

"He's not a drug dealer, he's a specialist. And yes, he lives in the penthouse."

"So pretentious," Ander quipped.

"*You* live in the penthouse of your condo."

"Bitch." Ander grinned at Rashad, and the two of them chuckled together as their arms wound around each other so Ander could easily snap them away.

He didn't take them directly into the penthouse, as he assumed whomever Rashad was dealing with would not approve of the sudden appearance of the two inanimi in his home. Instead, Rashad gave his name to the doorman at the front desk, and after a quick phone call, they were escorted to a private elevator that had only one option—up.

"Pretentious," Ander reaffirmed with a whisper.

His friend only rolled their eyes, leaning back against the elevator wall as they took the box up many floors to the top of the high-rise.

When the elevator doors dinged open, the two of them stepped out into the open foyer of a luxurious condo. A gold and crystal chandelier hung from the eleven-foot ceilings. Black and white marble tiles spread out before them, enclosed by gold papered walls.

"What exactly is your 'friend' selling?" Ander asked, making air quotes around the word "friend".

"Mermaid's Lament."

Ander frowned. "Rashad . . ." There was a warning in his tone.

"No! Not for that!" Rashad had the decency to look aghast. "It's not always used to knock people out. When you use a little dose of it mixed with the normies' ecstasy, it creates this super funky trip. You feel like you're floating, and everything feels like a dream—on top of providing you an incredible sexual experience."

"Not in my club."

"I know, I'll be using it elsewhere. Promise."

"Just be careful with your dosage, yeah?" Rashad nodded. "And please, don't just hand that out to anyone. Some Underworlders would use that for someone other than themselves." The hairs on the back of Ander's neck stood up, and he felt a terrible uneasiness come over him. Mermaid's Lament—mermaid venom—was often used to knock magical creatures unconscious, erasing their memories of what happened to them in the process.

The thought of that drug being here in the city disturbed him.

"You know I never handle these things carelessly."

Nodding, Ander stepped farther into the foyer, beginning to snoop. "Where is this dealer of yours? He knows we were brought up."

"He works on his own time. I'm sure he's making me wait because I was late."

Ander peeked into the living room, which opened onto a large deck with sliding glass doors. A huge fireplace took up almost the entirety of one wall, fur rugs lined the floor, and leather sofas created a welcoming but expensive looking sitting area before it. In one corner, there was a wet bar and a built-in floor-to-ceiling bookcase that displayed more delicate pieces of glass and ceramic than literature.

"Ander, get back here," Rashad hissed.

"I'm just taking a friendly gander." Ander waved their concern off and stepped farther down the hall to peer into an open doorway. It was a dark, wood-walled study. A big, heavy, carved mahogany desk sat in the middle with a leather chair behind it. The room smelled of Cuban cigars and scotch mixed with a hint of vanilla.

Behind the desk, mounted on the wall, was a white pair of wings, gleaming in their purity. Spread to their full length of almost twelve feet, the sight of them made Ander's heart palpitate in a dangerous manner. Suddenly, he was transported to the dungeons of Acheron, staring down at a beaten and battered Ikari, begging for Ander to end his life and set him free.

His heart tripped erratically with adrenaline, his body preparing for flight as the fear of being discovered returned along with the desperation to free the wounded being before him. Having trouble swallowing, Ander grabbed the frame of the doorway to steady himself. He peeled his eyes away from the wings on the wall and looked toward the broad desk. At the corner, an engraved canister sat, fifty, sixty—maybe many more—feathers in a vast array of colors protruding from it.

"Rashad, we have to get ou—"

"So, you decided to come after all. I thought perhaps you had decided to break our appointment. Very unbecoming of you." The familiar voice that called out to them from across the foyer sent ice washing through Ander's veins.

The frantic pounding of his heart only increased, to the extent that he was starting to become lightheaded. He felt trapped, frozen in place. *Was his vision blackening at the edges?*

"I apologize. My friend Ander was late meeting with me, and I was waiting for him to arrive. I hope I can still grab the stuff from you?"

"Ander?" There was surprise in the man's voice. Surprise that hinted at a mixture of delight and fury.

Slowly, Ander turned on his heel to face his living nightmare. Someone he had evaded and avoided for almost one hundred and sixty years, wishing to never lay eyes on them again.

Enrique.

"Oh, do you two know each other?" Rashad sounded intrigued, their face lighting up with interest.

"Yes." Enrique's eyes slowly relaxed into a predatory gleam, his lips curling into a charming smile that Ander knew was deceptive and hid a heart of cruelty. "We're old friends."

Ander couldn't breathe. Faced with the god of punishment, he found the old terror returning. The decades of separation and healing disappeared in the blink of an eye, and he was there in those horror-filled days, thinking that death would be the only release he could possibly hope to find.

"Amazing!" Rashad was grinning, until their eyes landed on Ander and their expression quickly switched to concern. "Ander? Are you all right?"

It was enough to snap Ander out of the emotions and pain coursing through him. Hurriedly, he moved back to Rashad's side. "I wouldn't call us friends," he stated coldly. "But yes, we know each other."

Rashad looked quickly between them, clearly unsure what to think of this moment.

"So . . . can I get—"

"Of course," Enrique murmured, his dark gaze never leaving Ander's face as he extended a hand. Opening his fingers, a small vial of liquid rested in his palm. "Money?"

Rashad dug into their back pocket, pulling out a brown wallet, and fetched a number of bills, which they crossed the foyer to hand to Enrique. The exchange went quickly. "Once again, so sorry that I was late."

"Don't worry about it. You're forgiven now that you've reintroduced me to Ander. It's been so long." His words made Ander's skin feel dirty. He wanted to go home and instantly wash himself in vodka, then light himself on fire just to make the sensation go away. "Too long."

"Personally, I was thinking the exact opposite. Rashad, I think we really should be going, darling. We've got those reservations to make."

There was a question in Rashad's eyes. But instead of asking what reservations, they nodded and returned to his side.

"Until next time, then," Enrique murmured, his gaze

skimming down over Ander's body in one fell swoop, then taking their time to return to his face.

The desire to skin his very flesh off with a carrot peeler anywhere and everywhere Enrique's eyes had landed washed through Ander like a vicious, uncompromising wave. He hated himself for how he couldn't help but wonder if Enrique thought he looked as beautiful as before, or if he saw where Ander had gained some subtle weight in muscle over the years.

Unable to stand being in the penthouse any longer, Ander turned on his heel and punched the button. Luckily, it was a private elevator, so the doors swung open immediately. Stepping inside, Ander spun to face the penthouse, feeling the way Enrique's eyes followed his every move.

Thankfully, Rashad took the hint and soon joined Ander. Crossing his arms in a protective manner over his chest, Ander stared back at Enrique until the elevator doors closed.

"Don't come here again, Rashad," Ander warned softly. "Enrique is actually Orcus, right hand to Hades and Acheron's god of punishment. He is not to be trifled with."

Many names had followed him through the centuries. Enrique was the favorite he'd stuck to for this millennia, the one Ander had called him from the beginning. But if he remembered correctly, in the early 100s, the Grecian people had referred to him as Timoros. Another loving moniker for a punisher.

Ander cursed and shut his eyes. *Max.*

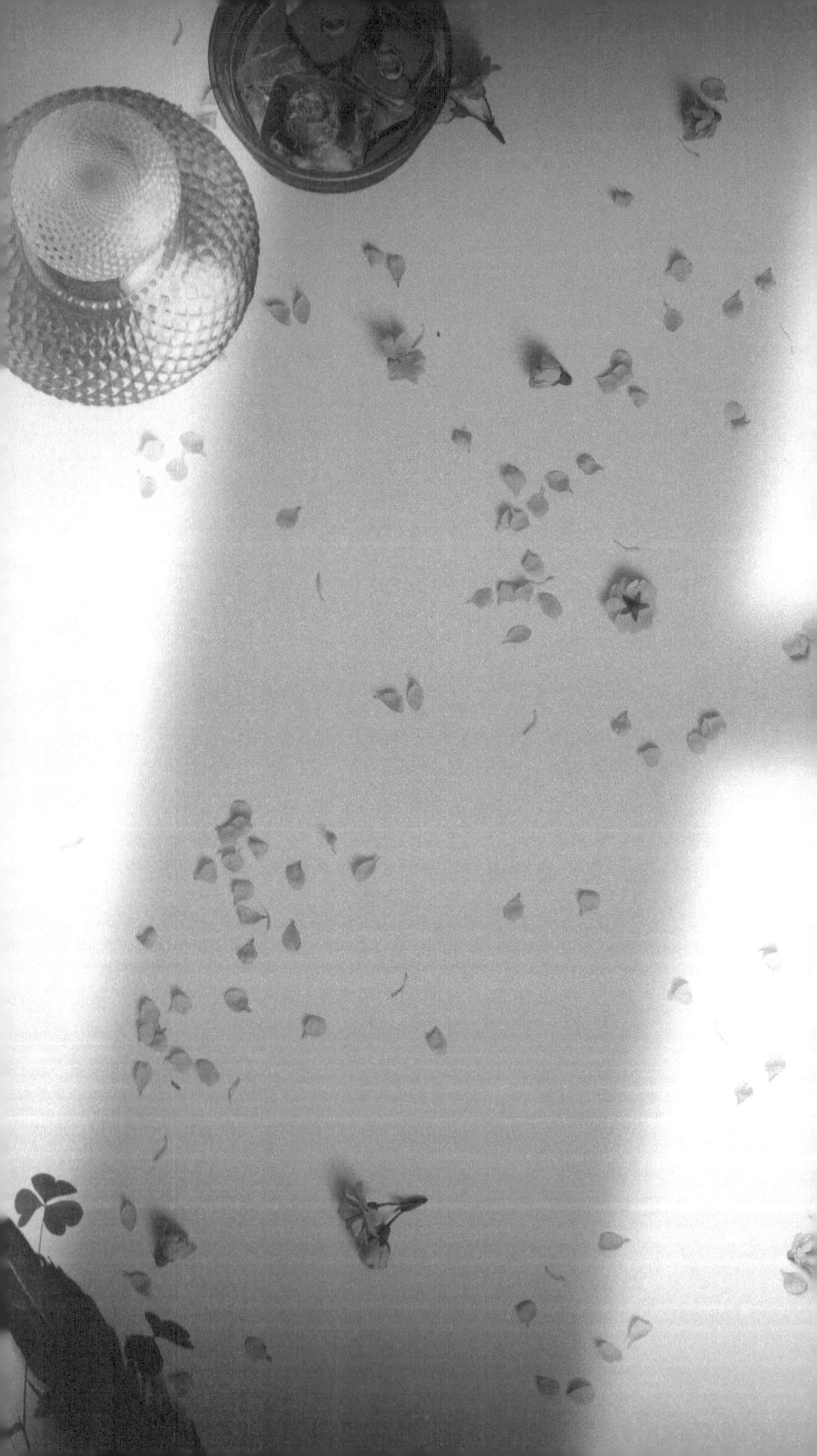

Chapter 13
Max

Max had a smile that just wouldn't quit. Admittedly, he hadn't tried very hard to *make* it quit, but still, his cheeks ached, and his chest was full with the feeling of new . . . *something*. Not love, it was too early for all that, but adoration maybe. Ander was beautiful and smart, and had the most wonderful laugh when he let himself really get going. Max couldn't help but feel enchanted after their evening together. Lighter than air, really—which was saying something considering he could fly.

He could feel Quin watching him, his brother's eyes like a physical weight on the back of his neck, but not even that could drag Max back to earth. Because Ander liked him for *him*. Ander had said, *Any time, darling*, when Max texted him thanking him for the date. And Max was already planning their next one, maybe to the aquarium, or that sculpture garden Quin had found a year back and dragged Max to. There were places sprinkled all over Miami that Max suddenly wanted to share with someone other than his family. Ander might not like all of them, and that would be fine, but Max could give him the chance to at least experience them with someone who did. And Max would get to see the light flicker to life in Ander's eyes when he found delight in something Max had shared with him. It would be wonderful, he was sure of it.

A daydream of them walking hand in hand against a sunset on the beach flitted through Max's mind, making his cheeks ache all the more. The montage was unfairly cut short by the ringing of his cell phone. Grumbling, Max dug the device out of his pocket, and the smile that had fallen immediately grew two sizes at the sight of Ander's name on the Caller ID.

"Hello?" Max asked, unable to keep the giddiness out of his voice.

"Max!" Ander shouted into the phone, loud enough that Max had to drag it away from his ear with a wince.

"Shhh," someone hissed in the background. "Too loud, Andy, too loud."

"Oh. Right. Sorry. *Maaax,*" Ander whispered, dragging out the 'a' sound in a way that made Max's chest tighten, that uncomfortable pulling feeling tugging at him a little. "Can you come get us?"

"Come get you from where?" Max stood, already grabbing his jacket and heading for the door of his office to find Quin. He could probably handle Ander alone, but whoever he was with might be a handful too, and honestly, Max wasn't willing to risk everyone's safety by not coming prepared.

"From where?" Ander repeated, and Max could imagine him wrinkling his brows together in thought. Gods, he was so cute. "Maberella, where are we?"

"Fuck if I know." Mab snorted. "In a tree."

"We're in a tree, Max." Ander sounded proud of

himself, and Max could hear the branches and leaves rustling in the background.

Swallowing down a laugh, Max shook his head. "Where is this tree?" He thought to ask how they'd *gotten* in a tree to begin with but figured that wasn't really information he needed at the moment.

"Ummm . . ." Ander hummed, and there was more rustling on the other side of the phone. Gods, Max hoped they didn't fall out of the tree before he and Quin got there.

"I need you to come with me," he signed to Quin, the motions a little jerky from having to balance his phone on his shoulder, and waited for the inevitable raise of Quin's brows.

"Where?" Quin stood, already heading for the weapon cabinet along the wall.

"To pick up Mab and Ander. They're apparently in a tree."

"I think I see a Pottery Barn!" Mab hissed excitedly.

"Mabbers says she sees a Pottery Barn!" Ander shouted, and Max winced again, holding the phone away from his ear. "Sorry. Sorry."

"Does Mab see a street name?" Max tugged on his jacket, carefully perching his phone on his shoulder so he could slide his arms through the sleeves. Quin was watching him with murder in his eyes, but Max chose to ignore it for the greater good.

"Mabinson, he needs a street name."

There was more rustling and a little squawk from Mab, which was followed by a "For the love of gods Mab, don't fall out of the tree!" Which was then followed by a "I'm not trying to!" before they finally got themselves settled again.

"17th and Michigan Ave," Mab said. It sounded like she'd taken Ander's phone from him, her accent thicker than Max had ever heard it. "It looks like we're in Miami Beach. Ander! How the fuck did we get to Miami Beach?"

"Who knows." Ander giggled. "Who cares. Just tell my Max to come and save me from this vicious tree spirit before we both fall and break our beautiful necks."

"You heard the man, before we both break our beautiful necks." And then Mab devolved into giggles, and the line went dead.

Max choked down another laugh, rubbing at the back of his neck where Quin's irritated gaze sat like a brand. When he turned around to face his brother, Quin's eyebrow was twitching so hard that Max worried it might become a permanent tick. "They're in Miami Beach, on the corner of 17th and Michigan, near the Pottery Barn."

Quin's eyes narrowed, his lips pursed, and he signed, "You owe me. Big."

"Right. Right." Max brushed him off—he could worry about that later; right now, he was stuck on how Ander had called him *his* Max—then led him outside into the humid Miami night.

They found the "vicious tree spirit" less than ten minutes later, with two very drunk inanimi hanging from its branches. It wasn't even a particularly tall tree . . .

Max chewed on the inside of his cheek to keep the squeal that threatened to crawl up his throat down in his chest. Mab and Ander would have been fine getting down and calling a cab on their own, but they'd called Max to come get them. He tried not to think of what that meant.

"All right, you get Mab, I'll grab Ander." Max nodded as they crossed the street to stand beneath the branches.

"My Max!" Ander shouted.

"Wonderboy! And Stink Eye!" Mab yelled at the exact same time, her voice sounding hoarse and raspy, like she'd been screaming all night.

"Big," Quin signed again, then moved forward to help Mab from the branches. Max took note that, in spite of how irritable his brother seemed, he was also careful to untangle Mab's curly hair without pulling it too much.

"Are you ready to tell me how you got into a tree in the first place?" Max asked, his voice only wavering a little with a laugh as he held his arms up to Ander and waited for the other man to slip from the branches down into them.

"No-*pe!*" Ander said, popping the 'p'.

"Didn't think so." Max laughed softly, shaking his head. Once Ander was on his feet again, Max took a step back, ready to let him walk it off on their way home. But Ander swayed dangerously, and Max was quick to grab his waist and keep him from falling to the ground.

"Walking's no good." Ander shook his head, then seemed to think better of that too. "That's no good either."

"I see." Max smiled, his fingers flexing against Ander's waist. "Do you think you can manage to hang on if I put you on my back?"

Ander's head lifted from where he'd been examining his expensive shoes, his eyes suddenly bright in the streetlamps. "Piggy-back's *so* good."

"Of course it is!" Mab griped loudly, but she didn't seem to be holding up any better, leaning heavily onto Quin's shoulder like he was the only thing keeping her on her feet. "That's why you got us stuck in that tree isn't it?!"

She pointed a finger at Ander, shaking it in reprimand and accusation.

"Noooooo. Mabette, noooo. I didn't do it on purpose. Listen to me." Ander stumbled a little like he was going to try to reach over to Mab but belatedly realized Max was the only thing holding him up. He looked pointedly down at where Max was holding his waist, then over at Mab, and Max followed behind him as they stepped closer so Ander could give Mab's shoulder a little shove. "Listen to me. I would never put us in a tree on purpose."

Mab squinted at him, and her nose wrinkled. "You smell like sap!"

Then they were both cackling so loudly that Max was glad they weren't in a residential area, because someone probably would have called the police on them.

"All right, come on, let's get you two home," Max said when Quin shot him another pointed look. He bent down carefully and let Ander amble up onto his back, his hands tight on Ander's thighs to keep him from sliding down. "Good?"

"I don't smell like sap, do I?" Ander asked, his face buried in one of Max's wings to the point that Max could feel his breath against the delicate skin below the feathers. It made a shiver roll up Max's spine that had nothing at all to do with the chill of the night air.

"No. You don't smell like sap. Are you comfortable?"

"Super comfy." Ander brushed his fingers through Max's wings for a moment, humming in thought. "See, Mabunzel? I don't smell like sap." Then he blew a raspberry that had Max choking on another chortle.

"You most certainly do!" Mab poked her head out over Quin's shoulder. It seemed to be a struggle because she had to hook her chin over it just to maintain the position. "Just because your boyfriend doesn't think so doesn't mean it's not true."

Max's heart thudded loudly in his chest at the word "boyfriend", but he bit his tongue to keep from saying anything. It would be better not to get either of them into another argument that might make them louder. Especially since Quin was already giving Max the kind of glare that meant whatever favor he was going to ask for was something Max probably wouldn't want to give.

"So, where are we taking you two?" Max hoped this might get them over the argument as he started their trek back down the street.

"My place is closer," Mab volunteered before disappearing back behind Quin again, likely in search of her phone. There was a soft curse, and it looked like she almost lost her balance before Quin shifted his wings to keep her more tightly in place. "There! Now that bitch Siri can give you directions."

Max heard the application's muffled voice and started in the direction it indicated.

"'That bitch, Siri.'" Ander snickered from behind Max, his face pressed in closer to Max's wings again, eliciting another shiver when his warm breath ruffled a couple feathers. "Remember that bitch . . . what was her name again? The one in Paris?"

"What one in Paris? You're gonna have to be more pacif —specific," Mab mumbled, and when Max looked back, she'd pressed her cheek into Quin's shoulder, her eyes lidded as the gentle movement seemed to lull her. Good. It'd be better if they both went to sleep; then maybe they'd sober up a little.

"Persifal's wife." Ander flapped a hand out at Mab,

snapping his fingers to try to get her attention. "Mabster. Persifal's wife. What was her name?"

"Trifine." Mab yawned. "Her name was Trifine. She was *way* worse than Siri."

"*So* much worse!" Ander crowed, cackling.

"Still can't believe she tried to shoot us."

"What?" Max frowned. He'd seen some reference to an incident in Paris from a few hundred years ago, but nothing about Mab and Ander almost being shot.

"It was all right. We stole a carriage, and Mab drove it into the Seine." Ander patted Max's wing as if trying to comfort him.

"You *what?*" Max turned his head to try to look back at Ander, but all it did was make his eyes hurt, and Ander had taken to stroking his wing in a slow pattern that was making it very difficult to focus on anything else. Quin shot Max another look which was an *I told you so* and judgment all rolled into one.

"We jumped first," Mab mumbled lazily. "And Andy saved the horses."

"Very quick thinking on Mabellina's part. They all thought we were dead!" Ander laughed, rocking his weight back a little, and would have fallen off Max's back if not for the hold Max had on his thighs. "Oh! Mab! Mab! Mab!"

"Whaaaaaat?" Mab groaned, poking her head over Quin's shoulder again.

"What was that song? That one you taught me from Ireland. You know the one. The one mama always hated." Ander flapped his hand at her, seemingly trying to reach out to swat at her. Mab reached back, and Max had to slow his steps so they could link fingers while Max and Quin continued to carry them.

Mab began to hum, her voice off key and scraping

against her throat, then they were both singing at the top of their lungs in a language that Max had never heard before, their words warbly from laughter and drunkenness. Max couldn't help but hum along, his lips twitching upward in a smile. It was nice. It sounded like two cats drowning slowly and painfully, but it was nice.

Putting Ander and Mab to bed had been more difficult than Max would have thought, but the whole experience left him with a strange tingling in his chest, the fuzzy feeling spreading through his veins, leaving a happy hue on the world around him. It wasn't sustainable, he knew that. Still, he didn't think that the event that ruined it would be so . . . *heartbreaking.*

The Feugo City Sanctuary was buzzing. It had been nearly a year since the last time they'd gotten any new ignis, and everyone was excited.

Hazel and Jasper, the guardians of the incoming ignis, were perched on the chairs in the waiting room and had hardly moved an inch since dawn. Not that Max could blame them; ignis younglings were the absolute cutest thing on the planet, and he couldn't wait to meet the newest member of their community. If he were closer to Jasper and Hazel, he might have even brought one of Georgie's old toys in for the child. But he wasn't, so all he could do was sit in his office and watch as Hazel shifted around on the edge of her seat, Jasper's hand on her knee. Every time the door opened, Jasper's head would jerk upward, and he could see Hazel's shoulders still like she was holding her breath.

It was mid-afternoon by the time the retrieval team

finally returned, each of them looking the worse for wear, their faces solemn. Five ignis approached Hazel and Jasper. The leader, a woman named Euphrates, murmured softly to them, and Max watched as Hazel's shoulders drooped and she flopped back into the chair she'd been sitting on all day.

He frowned, slipping from behind his desk and through the Schields' control center to meet Euphrates before she could make her way to Galeo's office.

"What's happened?" Max asked, his own wings unreasonably tight behind him.

"We were attacked," Euphrates said, her voice lowered. She should have waited until she gave Galeo a report first, they both knew this, but there was something sad and beaten about her that seemed to leave her unable to resist, her pale brown wings sagging behind her. "They . . . Hebe didn't make it."

"Attacked by who?" Galeo's commanding voice carried in the quiet that had taken over the main lobby of the sanctuary. His dusty blue wings spread out behind him, making him seem so much larger than Max knew he was.

"We don't . . . we don't know, sir." Euphrates shifted back on her heels. She had blood on her clothes, and one section of her right wing was missing several feathers, Max noticed now that he was looking. "But they were waiting for us, like they knew where the youngling would be. Like they —Like they had access to the oracle. Or they had their own. Or—"

"Go get cleaned up. I want a full report on my desk as soon as you can." Galeo stepped forward to stand beside Max and waited until the group had scurried off to turn to him. "What are you working on right now, Maximus?"

"We're still on the Timoros case, sir. The person the demogorgon abducting humans from Inferno was working for." Max stood up a little straighter under Galeo's assessing gaze.

Galeo squinted up at Max. He had to tilt his chin back a little, as he was a half a head shorter but no less intimidating for it. "I want all hands on this, have I made myself clear?"

"But sir, if we have an inanimi ringleader who is—"

"Have I made myself clear?"

"Yes, sir." Max blew out a breath, trying not to sag under the weight of it all. The missing youngling. Galeo's orders. The nagging feeling that they were making a mistake by dropping the Timoros investigation.

"Good. We have to look after our own, first and foremost." Galeo nodded to himself and turned on his heel. "I'm putting everyone else on this too. So you won't be working alone."

"Yes, sir." Max bit down hard on the inside of his cheek to keep from saying anything else and headed back toward his command center to inform his siblings of the change in plans.

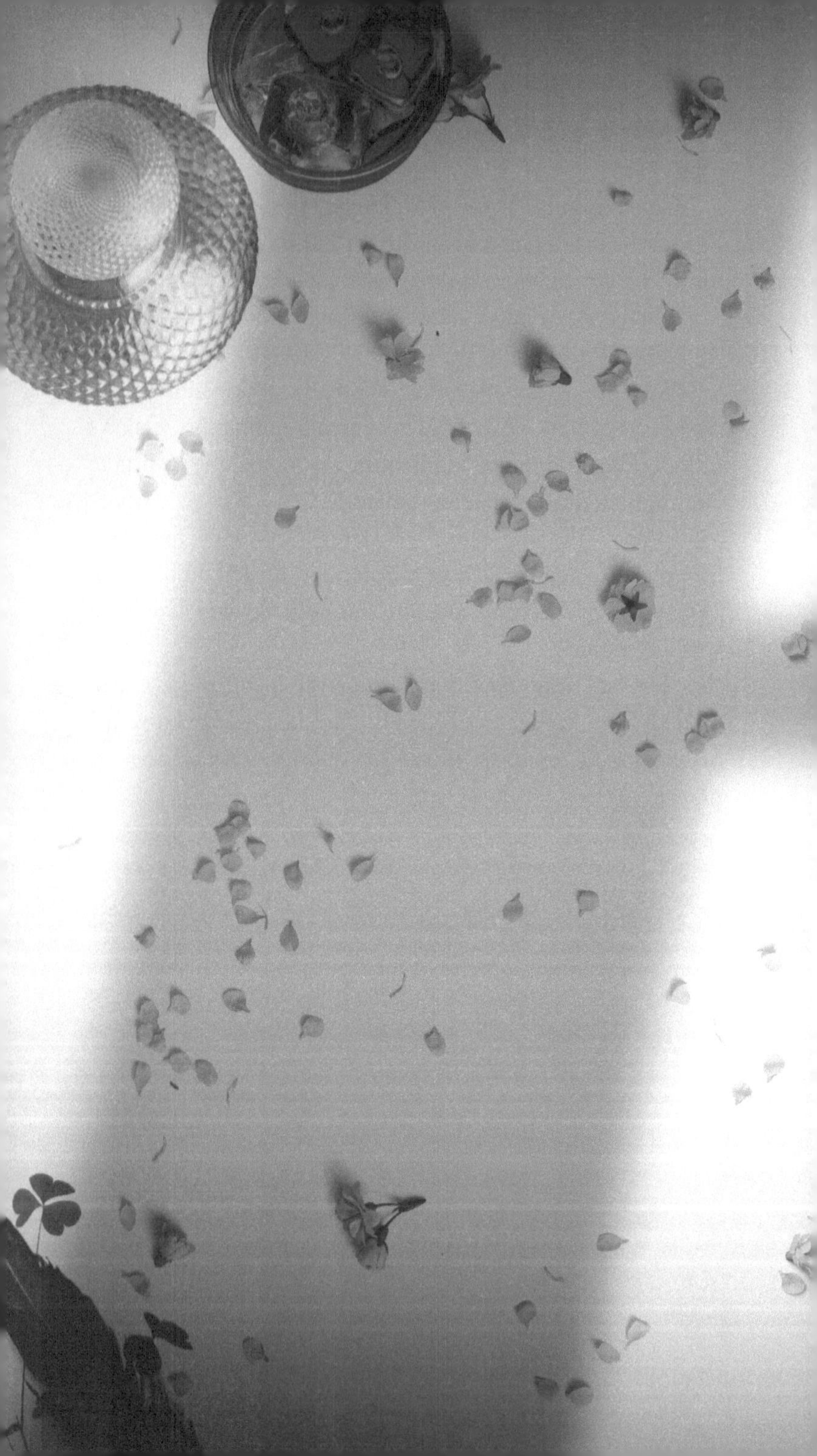

Chapter 14
Ander

He was a boob. That was what Ander settled on. He was a giant boob.

Ander had phoned Max drunk off his ass from a tree branch and begged him to save him from it like a stray cat needing the fire department. This was what drunk snapping got him. The next morning, when he woke up in Mab's bedroom with a splitting headache, he wondered how he was ever supposed to look Max in the eye again.

As it turned out, it had not been a problem.

There had been little to no contact with the ignis since the eventful night of drinking, and Ander couldn't help but think that he had chased him away. However, the ache in his chest that begged to be united with his arrow-bound was driving him to distraction.

Desperate, he purchased a bag of tacos from the truck Max had taken him to and hauled himself over to the sanctuary.

Ander walked through the doors of the highly protected fortress dressed to the nines. White sheer blouse, skin-tight black jeans, alligator-skin ankle boots, and dark, smokey eyes with just a hint of glitter on his horns. The sanctuary was not a place a random inanimi was meant to be able to penetrate, but just as the cells had not been able to contain him, their wards did not sound as he entered.

Stepping up to the reception desk, Ander found a stunned looking ignis staring up at him from her desk. "Excuse me, but could you be a dear and direct me to the station of Maximus Schields?" Ander drummed his fingers lightly on the edge of his jaw as he smiled sweetly down at her.

"H-how . . . how did you—"

"Ander?"

Looking up, Ander found Max himself standing in a doorway leading off the main reception area, appearing shocked to see him. Ander's heart tripped rapidly while his gut lurched. Maybe this had been a terrible idea. What if Max wanted nothing more to do with him? What if his drunken phone call had done irreparable damage?

"Hey!" Ander forced sunshine into his voice, hiding his nerves. "I brought you tacos." He lifted the bag up before him.

Max's face split into a wide grin. "Amazing." The little ball of terror within Ander began to lessen at the smile, and his shoulders relaxed a little. "Come on." Max waved him forward.

Ander blew a kiss at the receptionist and strolled happily after the ignis, following him down the hall and into an office that appeared to belong to him. Max turned to face Ander while leaning on the desk, continuing to grin brightly at him.

Ander felt a little bashful beneath the smile and so ducked his head as he moved to the desk and began to unpack the tacos. "I wasn't sure which kind you would prefer, so I kind of grabbed one of everything."

"You really didn't have to, but tha—"

"Max! Did you go get tacos without us?!"

"We could smell them in the hall!"

The office was suddenly filled with more bodies, as Nox, and someone who Ander could only assume from the looks of him was her twin Nash, came barreling through the door.

"Oh, Ander! Hey!" Nox lifted her hand into the air for a high-five.

Accommodating her, Ander watched the young woman drop down into the lap of her twin, who was now perched in Max's chair, already munching down on a taco.

"Ah, those were for Max . . ." he stated weakly.

The twins glanced up from their tacos at the same time, looking at him with eyes that had gone wide with innocence. "He won't mind," they chimed in unison.

Max rubbed at his neck and shrugged. "It's fine, they can have some."

Ander sighed. Seeing that his lovely was not going to kick his siblings out, he waved his hand over the desk, and the amount of tacos on the desk tripled.

"Holy Acheron, this man is a *god*! Can we keep him, Max?" Nash trumpeted and helped himself to another taco.

Ander decided he liked the boy twin a little more now. As the mongrels feasted, Ander stepped closer to Max.

"Just ignore them . . ." Max murmured. "They'll feed, then they'll leave." Max eyed his siblings as if he weren't entirely sure if they might stick around just to irritate him. "Maybe."

"It's fine." Ander waved it off. "Listen, I came for a reason . . ." Max focused his eyes on him, looking so intently and earnestly that Ander felt his throat go dry. *What were words again?* "I just . . . haven't really heard from you since the night I called you from that tree." *Oh gods, am I blushing?* "And I wanted to make sure I hadn't completely scared you off."

Max blinked, his beautiful hazel eyes looking confused for a moment, then clearing before they widened. "Oh, no! That's not it at all. I actually . . . Well." He coughed. "I really liked that you called me for help." It was now Max who was blushing, and the sight of it finally eased the ball of nerves inside Ander entirely.

Feeling his shoulders relax, Ander stepped closer to him, letting his knee press into the ignis'. "Yeah?" His voice had grown a little husky, and he bit at his lip as he peered up at him. "It was very kind of you to tuck me into bed as well. I deeply appreciated it." He purred his last words, unable to stop himself. The memory of Max laying him down in the bed elicited all sorts of naughty thoughts within him.

"You're welcome," Max whispered back, the flush becoming something more than nerves. His eyes gleamed with a growing desire that tightened Ander's stomach and made his own mount.

They were leaning toward each other when a gagging noise sounded from beyond them. "Ew, please, not in front of my tacos."

They whipped their heads to the side, staring at Nash, who just grinned back, a cocky smirk on his face and a cheek full of taco.

Max shot his brother a glare, then straightened up, clearing his throat. "I'm sorry I haven't had time to text a lot. We've all been on high alert. We lost a member of our retrieval team this week, and an ignis youngling went missing. So everyone has been busy searching for them and—"

His voice faded into the background as Ander focused on the words. An ignis had been killed. An infant kidnapped. Someone had taken a youngling. An ignis youngling. Unbidden images of Ikari floated into Ander's thoughts, the pain and devastation inflicted on his body. His wings taken like a trophy.

The room began to spin as Ander pictured Enrique standing in his penthouse office with a baby ignis in his arms and a set of wings on the wall behind. Panting, he staggered to the side, reaching for the desk to keep himself upright.

"Ander!" It was Max, hands reaching out to steady him. "Ander, what's wrong? Are you all right?"

Ander allowed Max to guide him into a chair, sitting down with his elbows on his knees and his head hanging forward. He gulped in air. "I'm okay," he panted. "I just haven't had much to eat or drink today and have spent too much time out in the sun," he lied. He wasn't ready for Max to know about Enrique. To introduce him to that nightmare. He lifted his head to see Max staring back at him from a kneeling position, concern ripe on his face.

"Are you sure?"

"Here." Nash held out a taco, he and Nox having left their chair to come over. "It's chicken."

Ander took the taco, offering a flamboyant smile he did not feel. "Thank you. But I swear, I'm okay." He met Max's eyes. "I swear."

Max's hand was on the side of his leg, and he squeezed gently before nodding. "Okay, but maybe eat that before you get up again, yeah? Nox, will you go grab Ander some water please?"

"Sure, one bottle of water coming right up!"

In due course, Ander had half the taco eaten and a cold bottle of water creating condensation in his hand. It felt strange to be at the center of their attention, but the three Schieldses all seemed vastly concerned with how he recouped from his moment of weakness.

"I know I'm lovely, but could you all stop staring at me as if I were behind glass at the zoo?"

Laughing, the twins turned away, gathering up a number of tacos—some of which they promised were for Quin—and left the two of them alone. Finally.

"You're sure you're all right?" Max questioned again.

Ander stood, setting aside the rest of his taco and the water, and stepped up to him. "I am truly okay." He lifted his hands to rest on Max's waist, smiling up at him. "And I will be even better if you swear I didn't scare you off."

"Scout's honor," Max murmured. "And I'd really, really like to go out again. If you want." He was quick to tag on the last bit.

"I'd absolutely love to."

Max grinned brightly. "Amazing."

Ander couldn't help but chuckle. "Okay. Good." He leaned in and pressed an ever-so-gentle kiss to Max's lips. "I'll leave you to your work and your tacos. Why don't you give me a call when things lighten up a little for you. We can go out again." His voice had grown soft and throaty.

Max nodded, eyes a little dazed. "Okay," he murmured.

Smiling softly, Ander pulled away. Turning on his heel, he blew Max a kiss before heading out the door. His footsteps picked up speed the closer to the main door that he got, and once he was outside in the sunshine, he released the pent-up breath he had been holding.

Enrique couldn't have anything to do with this, could he?

This was an ignis matter, but Ander couldn't imagine unleashing the god of punishment on any of the beings in that sanctuary, let alone sending Max off in his direction. No. Not if it was for nothing. It was too dangerous if it was all for nothing.

After casting one final glance back at the gate that led to the Feugo City sanctuary, Ander snapped his fingers and teleported himself to Mab's house. She was lying on her couch watching a movie, her bunny, Gizmo, curled up on her lap.

"Um . . . knock much?" she grunted, seeing him appear in the middle of her living room.

"Enrique is back."

"*What the fuck?*" She bolted upright, startling Gizmo and sending him leaping off her lap in a blur of calico fluff. "Where? How? *When,* Andy?!" She looked around the room, grabbing up the TV remote to brandish it like a weapon.

Ander eyed it, his head tipping to the side as he studied her. "Do you plan on bludgeoning him to death with that?" His brow lifted.

"Where did you see him, Andy? And I swear to gods, if you tell me you're mixed back up with him—"

"*No!* Give me more credit than that. I met up with Rashad, who had to go meet with his dealer, and to my fucking surprise, in walks that *asshole.*"

Mab was on her feet, tossing aside the remote and coming around to him quickly. She grabbed onto his upper arms, squeezing tightly. "Are you okay? He didn't do anything to you, did he?"

"I'm fine." Ander adjusted himself so he could wrap his

arms around Mab's body, pulling her in against his chest and resting his chin on her shoulder. "But it's not good, Mab."

"No shit, Sherlock," she grumbled, but wrapped her arms around him in return.

"No, it's *really* not good. I think there were ignis wings on his wall. I think there was a whole jar of their feathers on his desk. I think . . . I think he's kidnapping them. Lots of them."

Mab released a curse under her breath, tightening her hold on him. "You need to tell the Sanctum."

"No."

"What?" Mab pulled back, looking into his face. "What do you mean *no?* This is the sort of thing they need to know about."

"Not yet." Ander shook his head. "I can't involve Max and his family until I'm sure. Enrique is too much of a risk." The concerned faces of the three Schields siblings gathering around him to feed, water, and care for him filtered through his mind. They were too soft. Too kind. They needed to be protected.

"Ander—" There was a warning tone in her voice.

"No, Mab. Not yet. I can't."

"Then what are you going to do?"

"I don't know."

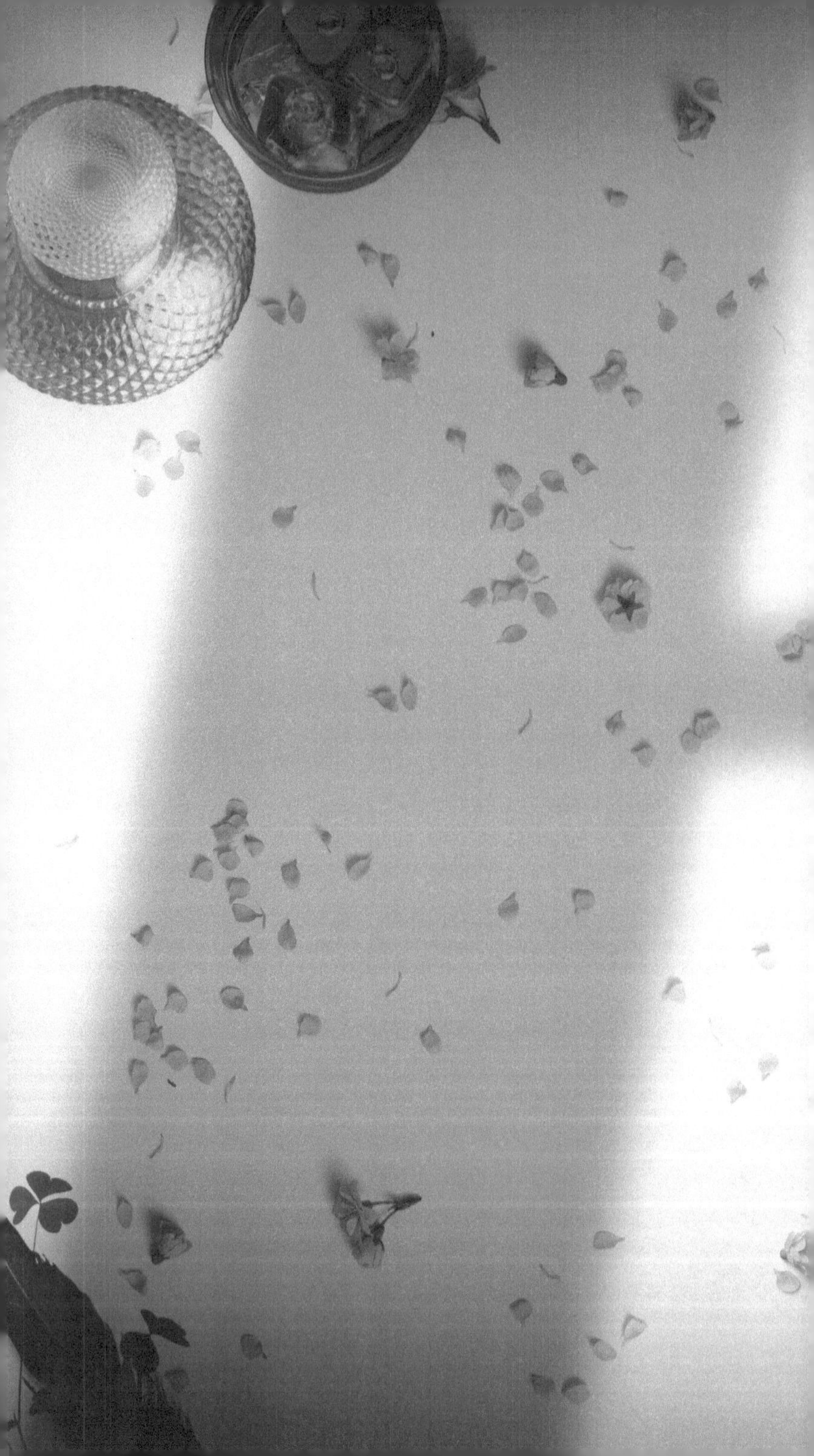

Chapter 15
Max

There were no clues.

There had been another report of a disappearance out on the west coast. An ignis that was already housed with their guardians, had been for a couple of months. Both guardians died, and all that was left of the youngling was a single pale-gray feather. Max had seen the incident photos of the scene and immediately wished that he hadn't told Nox to put them up on the big screen in the conference room.

Whoever took the youngling had left nothing behind, and just like with the incident in Florida, no one had been able to give witness statements on what they saw. From what Max could tell, they were using some kind of cloaking spell, or perhaps even a drug that altered the memories of the people who they interacted with. Max had Nox and Nash pull footage from the area, but that turned up nothing as well.

"So where does that leave us?" Nash asked. His face was drawn—all their faces were—dark circles hanging heavy under his eyes, mouth pinched at the corners. It didn't seem fair to Max that whenever there was an instance of younglings suffering, the Schields family found themselves at the heart of it. He wouldn't have it any other way, though, because he knew out of the entire Feugo Sanctum, they were the best equipped for it.

Max swallowed down a sigh, glad that Quin was in the training room working off some of his nervous energy for the moment. Out of all of them, Quin was the closest to this, having seen what could happen to a youngling who disappeared firsthand. His kidnappers hadn't been so brazen though . . .

"I want you to search the records of any ignis disappearances for the last . . . fifteen years." Shifting his weight onto his heels, Max leaned back to poke his head out the door and check that Quin wasn't on his way back yet. "Maybe further back, but definitely fifteen years. I don't care how unrelated they seem, I want all of them."

"You think there might be a pattern?" Nox chewed on her bottom lip. It had grown chapped, and her long dark hair was tangled into a haphazard bun that likely hadn't been brushed today. He couldn't blame her for it; he'd been pushing all of them harder than he normally would, searching desperately for answers where there didn't seem to be any.

"I don't know yet. But I'd rather be safe than sorry." His toes flexed in his boots, trying to ground himself when it felt like a breeze might knock him over. Gods, he was so tired.

"What about . . . ?" Nash's eyes flicked to the door over Max's shoulder, a question in his gaze.

"Yes. Everything. Whether we found the child or not. I want them all. Just don't put *that* file on his desk, put it on mine." Max knew his brother could handle it—Quin was strong, so much stronger than the rest of them. But he didn't think he should have to. Not when Max was perfectly capable of weeding through that particular file himself. "There might not be a connection to Quin's case, but I want to be positive before we rule it out."

Nash nodded, his fingers already flying over his keyboard. "Has anyone else looked at this angle yet?"

"No. They're all focused on the recent abductions. Captain seems to think this is new." But Max knew better; the whole Schields family did. They were intimately aware of the fact that not every youngling who fell to earth was picked up by their guardians.

"They tend to blot out any past failures," Nox mumbled under her breath.

"Don't let the captain hear you saying that," Quin said from the doorway. When Max turned, he frowned at what he saw. None of them were handling this very well, but Quin had been having nightmares for days now, and Max worried he'd collapse if he didn't get some real sleep soon.

"It's true." Nox huffed petulantly.

"Go get dressed." Max might not be able to order his brother to go home and get some rest, but he could get Quin out of the sanctuary for a couple of hours to hopefully get his mind off of things. It wasn't as good as a solid night's sleep, but it was what he had.

"Why?" Quin's blue eyes narrowed on Max, a frown pinching his brows together.

"The twins have the research covered. You and I are going out to track down some leads." This probably wasn't Max's best plan to get his brother's mind off things for a little while, especially considering all the grumbling he'd done after they'd had to rescue Ander and Mab from that tree, but Max knew the power irritation could wield. It could blot out almost anything else. And, honestly, what better place to get a feel for if anyone in the inanimi community had something to do with this than a nightclub?

Quin's eyes squinted further, but he turned on his heel to head back to the locker room and get cleaned up without another word.

"Do you really think that's a good idea?" Nash's tone was knowing and perhaps a little smug at having figured out Max's angle. Brat.

"I don't have a better one at present. Do you?" Taking him to a gallery would probably be a better idea. Or sitting Quin down with his sketchbook and a set of pencils. But then Quin would feel like he wasn't helping. This was more productive. And if Quin huffed and rolled his eyes and complained that Max was only doing this so he could see Ander again, well . . . that was still better than the haunted expression he was currently sporting.

"Not really."

"Then shut up." Max ran his fingers through his hair, hoping it still looked halfway decent. If he'd had the time, he'd have put some concealer on the bags under his own eyes, but beggars couldn't be choosers.

Inferno was packed—far more than Max would have thought for a Thursday night—wall-to-wall with people. He strategically didn't meet Quin's gaze as they walked up to the front door, not needing to see the judgment to know it was there. Max pushed his way through the crowd to the bar to find Ander lounging on the edge of it, one foot perched on the top while his arm draped artfully over his knee. A big cat ready to pounce. He was chatting with Mab while she shook a drink tumbler. She saw them first, her dark eyes narrowing in distrust. Then she said something, nodding to the pair of ignis making their way across the dance floor. Ander whipped around with a smile so bright across his lips that Max had to squint.

"Max! Darling! What an unexpected and delightful surprise." Ander slid from the bar, shouting over the music as he floated through the crowd toward them, the people parting for him like a field of swaying grasses.

"Ander." Max breathed his name, his cheeks aching with his grin, hands itching at his sides to pull Ander to him and bury his face in his neck. Gods, he had it bad, didn't he? "This isn't . . . uh . . . It's not a social call, I'm afraid." Max shifted under the knowing glare pricking at the back of his neck from his brother.

"No?" Ander pouted prettily, his nose wrinkling, and Max had the unreasonable desire to press his lips to the wrinkle to see if he could smooth it out. Ander's gaze flicked over Max's shoulder to where Quin stood behind him, and the pout twitched a little, threatening to turn into a frown.

"No. Why don't we go up to your office to talk about it?" Max tilted his head so he could see where Quin had pushed forward to stand beside him. "You go to the bar and see if Mab has heard anything about what's going on. The bartender always hears more than they think."

"I thought this was part of the investigation," Quin signed, his fingers moving in sharp, irritable motions.

Right on time.

"It is," Max signed back, his hands moving smoothly over the words the way they did when he was lying. Like he was trying too hard to make the transition between signs too easy. "Just trust me?"

Quin huffed, but he didn't say anything. He just pushed

past Max, banging their shoulders together, and headed for the bar. Max bit back a laugh and turned his attention back to Ander, offering him a knowing grin, like, *siblings, what're you gonna do?*

"Shall we?" Ander asked.

Max nodded and followed him through the crowd to the metal stairs that led up to his office. Once the door was shut behind Max, he spun on his heel to find Ander leaning against the edge of his desk. His long body stretched out lazily while he braced himself on the desktop. Max swallowed thickly against a suddenly dry throat. How was it fair for one person to look so good? It just didn't seem like it should be.

"So . . . you were saying?" A smile lit Ander's face again, like he knew just what Max was thinking, and honestly, he probably did. Max had always been terrible at keeping his expressions in check. Everything that went through his head somehow wound up playing out across his face. Made him a terrible poker player. The twins were always taking him for everything he was worth.

Max had come here to get more information, he really had, but what he'd said to Quin was true: out of the two of them, Mab would know more than Ander. She worked the bar. She listened to people talk when they weren't paying attention. There was likely very little Ander could provide. And besides that, this was the first time they'd been alone in a room together in over a week, and Max was finding it hard to think about anything other than how soft Ander's too-tight leather pants looked. He wondered how they would feel under his hands, his cheek.

"Darling," Ander called, drawing Max out of his thoughts, "my eyes are up here."

"Right. Sorry." Max laughed, his cheeks heating at

being called out. "I mostly came because I needed to get Quin out of the sanctuary for a little bit. He's been . . . Well, we all have, but he especially has been taking this case rather hard."

"The missing ignis?"

"Mhm. There was another disappearance recently. Out on the west coast. And I just . . ." Max faltered, his breath leaving him in a huff. He wasn't going to tell Ander why this was bothering Quin especially—it wasn't his business to tell people, and he knew Quin would be pissed if he did. "I don't know . . ."

"Shh . . . It's all right." Ander was suddenly right in front of him, his hands lifted in question, asking if he was allowed to touch. Max swayed forward into him and melted a little under the warmth of Ander's palms gripping his arms, grounding him. He pressed his face into Ander's neck, inhaling the smell of him: the expensive cologne, the undertone of spring flowers that came from muse magic. Ander's hands slid up his arms, brushing soft fingertips against Max's neck, into his hair.

Then they were kissing. Because that seemed the next reasonable action, and Max was too wound up to think about it. He wasn't even sure who had initiated the kiss, but Ander was suddenly tugging him back toward the desk, his blunt nails fisted in the long sleeves of Max's shirt. Max's hands fell to his hips. The leather was as buttery as he'd imagined.

Ander shifted under his grip, wriggling up onto the desk so he could be closer to Max's height, his fingers drifting back to brush through the soft feathers at the base of Max's wings, eliciting a full-body shudder.

"Sorry. Sorry. Was that not okay?" Ander pressed the question into his lips, not seeming able to move away even enough to speak, and that was okay, because Max didn't want him to.

"More than. They're . . . they're really sensitive." Max broke the kiss enough so he could press his forehead into Ander's, trying to catch his breath. A soft noise of complaint rose in Ander's throat that he soothed away with a chaste kiss to the corner of his mouth. "I want to go out with you again," Max breathed, almost afraid of saying the words too loudly in case he broke whatever spell had settled between them. "Tomorrow. I want to go out with you again tomorrow."

"I can make that work." Ander laughed, sounding giddy. "What about your case?"

"It's going to take the twins a couple of days to compile all the data I asked them to get. And I need . . ." Weak. He was so weak. He hated admitting it, but something inside told him he could trust Ander with this weakness. "I need a break from it. They're just . . . they're just *babies*, Ander."

"Shhh. Shhh. I understand," Ander soothed, his fingers brushing over Max's feathers again, making every other thought blur in a haze of want. Gods, he had never wanted anyone like this. His heart racing in his chest, Max tipped his head to kiss Ander again, deepening it, letting his tongue scrape against Ander's teeth, and the roof of his mouth, drawing out a soft groan. He tasted like alcohol and sugar rims, and Max was drunk on it.

A loud cheer went up from the bar below at a song change, and it drew Max back into himself. Away from the heat of the moment. He pulled back again, hissing as Ander nipped at his lower lip. "Tomorrow?"

"Tomorrow."

"Okay. I should . . . I should go. Quin is gonna be pissed." Max laughed, the sound raspy and throaty.

"That's funny?" Ander pulled his head back so he could cock it at Max. His lips were a little puffy, but they had quirked up on one side in a half-smile.

"It is. That was kind of the point. I figured if I could get him irritated, it would provide a bit of a distraction." Max huffed another chuckle and rolled his eyes. "I'll let him beat my ass a little bit in the training room, and he'll sleep better tonight."

"You're a good brother."

"Yeah." Max ran his tongue over the stinging spot on his bottom lip where Ander had bitten down a little too hard. He wondered if it was red. Would Quin be able to tell what he'd been doing up here? "Guess so."

"We shouldn't leave him with Mab too long, though, she might undo all your hard work," Ander teased, his hands seemingly unable to make up their mind about whether they should push Max away or pull him in closer.

"Probably." Max nodded, ducking his head to let it rest against Ander's shoulder for a moment so he could inhale deeply the smell of him. Sweat and expensive cologne and something fizzy and bubbly that made Max feel like he'd drunk that glittering champagne his Papa loved so much. "Thanks for this."

"Any time, sugar." Ander's fingers brushed through his hair, ruffing it gently. "Seriously, you need to go. Or I'm going to be tempted to lay you out on this desk." His voice rumbled up through his sternum, vibrating against Max's skin.

"Not yet," Max murmured and drew back finally. He pressed another soft kiss to Ander's lips and stood. "I'll see myself out."

"Yeah . . . you do that." Ander leaned back against his

hands on the desk, his chest rising and falling in heavy breaths.

"See you."

"Tomorrow."

Max nodded. "Tomorrow."

Then he spun and strode from the room and back down the steps. Not even the judgmental once-over Quin gave him could bring Max down.

Tomorrow.

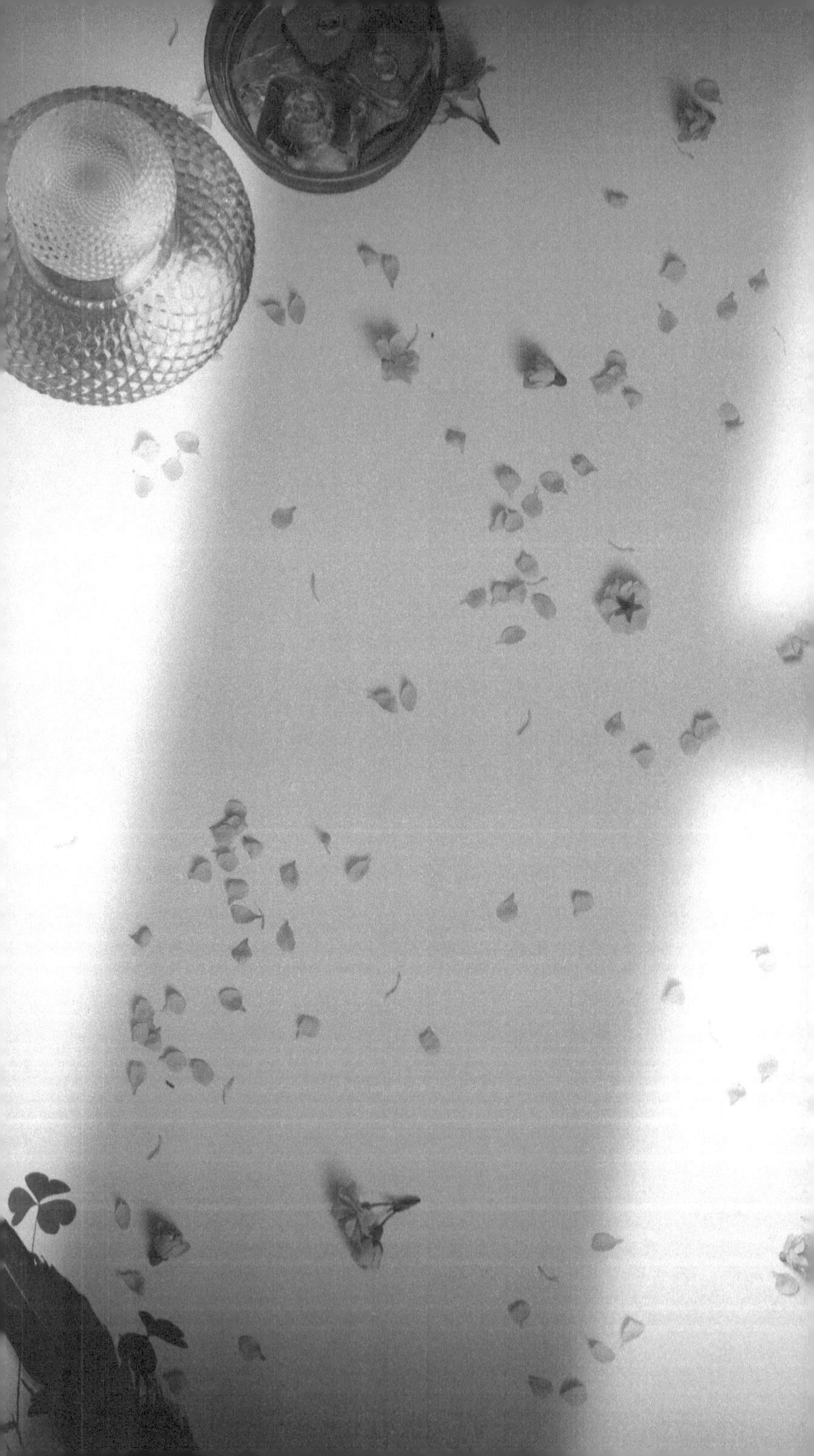

Chapter 16
Ander

Max's impromptu visit and make-out session left Ander in a complete fog. So much so that he forgot to submit the payroll. This realization only struck him as he was finishing his preparations for their date.

Which was why Ander was currently sat at his desk logging into his payroll program while dressed for a romantic night out. He'd chosen a black sheer dress shirt with hand-embroidered roses all over it and satin cuffs and collar. The dress shirt was tucked into a pair of slim-fit black slacks that ended at his ankles, showing off that he wore no socks with his Italian leather shoes. His dark hair was styled messily into his signature wavy mohawk, and he'd used magic to turn the tips red.

Tonight, he'd decided to go all out, so his lids were painted with an ombre of white, fading into pink, fading into red and ending in black at the corners, all lined with a thick black cat-eye.

His long, tanned fingers that clicked rapidly over the keyboard of his laptop were adorned in many gold rings, and one earlobe bore a sparkling cuff at the top corner. He felt good. Which helped the ball of nerves that had nestled in his belly. It had been a very long time since he had so much hinging on a date.

"I thought you weren't coming in tonight?" Mab's voice drew Ander's eyes up to the door.

"Forgot to submit payroll. Figured there may be a mutiny if no one gets their checks."

Mab snorted and nodded. Crossing her arms beneath her breasts, she leaned against the doorframe. "Did you tell Wonderboy about Enrique while he was here last night sucking your face?"

Ander froze, frowning down at the computer screen. "No."

"And why not?" Her voice was soft, but with an underlying chord of steel. She was trying very hard not to snap at him and send him into a dramatic fit; he could tell.

"Because I am not going to throw that monster into Max's path until I am sure there is something to be concerned about."

Although he wasn't looking at her, Ander could tell Mab had rolled her eyes. He was positive she'd rolled them hard enough, everyone downstairs was also aware she'd done it.

"Ander—"

"You won't change my mind on this." He pressed submit and sent off the payroll. Shutting his laptop, Ander stood.

"But—"

"No." There was firmness in his tone as he met her gaze. "I can't let that innocent young ignis face such a nightmare unless absolutely necessary."

"Then what do you plan to do?" Her eyes narrowed on him.

"I'm going to get back into Enrique's condo and get ahold of one of those feathers so I can make sure they're ignis."

"Abso-*fucking*-lutely not!"

This time it was Ander who rolled his eyes. "I'm the only one he's going to let in there, Mab!"

"And you're the only one he's held hostage!"

"Listen, I don't have time for this. I know the risks better than anyone. I'll get in, get the proof I need, and get out. When I know he's messing with ignis, I'll let the Sanctum know. Until then, Max doesn't need to know."

"Ander, listen. I don't think—Don't you dare sna—"

Before she had a chance to finish, he had snapped himself away and reappeared outside the Schields family residence.

Ander felt a momentary twang of guilt. Mab was only concerned, and rightfully so. She'd helped him pull the pieces back together after Enrique destroyed him. But it also meant she should realize why he couldn't just send Max and his siblings after him. Enrique was a god. The ignis were not. They would not be strong enough to end him if it were needed. The one intentional flaw in their design. Only a god could harm a god.

Ander pulled out his phone and sent off a quick text to Max:

I'm here.

The white stucco house sat back off the main road, a high white plaster wall up around it, with just the peak of the terracotta tiled roof peeking over the top. Ander could only assume that it was secluded so that the children would have been able to fly when they were young and learning how without worry of being spotted.

Max must have been anxiously waiting for him inside because he'd barely finished sending the text, and Max was there, opening the gate and panting like he'd run the whole way across the yard. At the sight of Ander, Max's eyes widened, and his breath seemed to hitch. It made Ander's entire body tingle.

"Wow," Max breathed out. "You look stunning."

Ander feigned bashfulness, then winked at him. "Thank you, sugar. As do you." And he meant it. Max was dressed in a white V-neck T-shirt with a beige and tan plaid blazer over top. His thick, muscular thighs were lovingly wrapped in dark blue denim, with dark brown loafers on his feet. He'd attempted to style his hair, but the mess of dark brown locks seemed intent on doing as it pleased, giving him a bit of a windswept look. Ander, however, approved.

As always, the bond within his chest panged fiercely at the sight of Max, leaving Ander breathless. He wanted—no *needed* to be near him. To consummate this thing between them so he could finally rest and move on.

Max blushed at his words. "Thanks. So, um, where are we going?" His eyes drifted around them, looking for a means of transportation.

Smirking, Ander closed the distance between them, slipped his arm around Max's waist, and pressed his hand to the small of his back, pulling his hips in flush against his own. It made Max gasp, and Ander nearly cooed in delight.

"It's a surprise," he purred. Lifting his free hand in the air, he snapped his fingers and teleported them to the rooftop of his favorite inanimi-owned restaurant.

The rooftop was heavily decorated with potted trees dripping with hanging votives, each with their own flickering candle inside. All around the base of the trees were potted flowers and ferns, and in one corner sat a bubbling fountain. The rooftop had the appearance of a lush garden, blocked off from the rest of the world. Just one table set for two, and the open sky above.

"Welcome to Te Quiero. I know the owner. We have the whole rooftop all evening." Ander held out his hand to Max, pleased when he accepted it, and drew him over to the table.

"This is beautiful." Max sounded shocked, and it sent another little thrill through Ander.

He pulled Max's chair out for him, waiting until he sat down, brushing fingertips lightly down his shoulder, then moved to take his own seat across from him.

"I hope you like Cuban food?"

Max nodded. "I do."

"I'm happy to hear it. I also hope you don't mind, but I told Chef Ramon to create a menu especially for us tonight. So it'll be a surprise for both of us." Ander waited, wondering if he'd overstepped and would be faced with a hidden alpha male side of Max who wasn't pleased with his choices being made for him. He was a warrior. There had to be one there, surely?

Instead, Max smiled brilliantly at him. "That actually sounds really fun."

Ander released a relieved breath, sliding his hand across the table to place it over Max's and was pleased when Max rolled his hand over so that they could clasp fingers. That pang in his chest flared almost violently at the contact, eliciting a gasp from Ander that caused Max to look at him questioningly. To hide it, Ander smiled brightly.

"Did I tell you yet how wonderful you look?"

Max smiled bashfully and nodded. "Yes, you did."

"Well, I think it bears repeating."

Max's fingers tightened a little around Ander's hand. "Thank you. I really wasn't sure what to wear tonight. You always dress so beautifully, I was sure I was going to look dull in comparison."

"What? Never. You are far too beautiful to *ever* appear dull. Not with that magnificent height, that jawline to die for. Gorgeous eyes and the most sinfully delicious looking lips I've ever seen."

If Max was blushing before, it only increased tenfold as Ander spoke. The ignis opened those very lips to say something, but he seemed unable to form a thought because they closed back up shortly afterward. Ander pulled their hands across the table, twisting them slightly so that he could press a kiss to the inside of Max's wrist.

Before either of them could say anything, Chef Ramon came out to say hello, carrying mojitos for both of them. Once the chef left, promising that their first course would be out shortly, Ander lifted his drink to make a toast.

"To a wonderful night." As their glasses clinked together, Ander smiled over at Max and took a sip of his drink. "Speaking of wonderful nights . . . how are you? I know the last few days have been rough on you."

"We don't need to talk about that tonight."

"No, we do," Ander insisted. "So?" He quirked a brow.

Max offered him a sweet smile. "It hasn't been great. There are still no real leads, and it's hard knowing that we're failing younglings."

"Hey." He frowned. "You're not failing them. You're actively searching for them. Doing everything you can to find them."

"How do you know?"

"Because you come across as the sort of being who puts

their all into everything that they set their mind to." Or at least, Ander hoped he was. Another wave of longing went through him. So much keen focus that could be aimed solely on him and bringing his body pleasure. He wanted to be the center of all of it.

"I try."

Chef Ramon was not wrong, and soon their first course had arrived. As the two of them began to eat, their conversation turned to lighter things. Max asked what brought Ander to Miami, and after he explained his desire to open the world's best nightclub, Max went on to talk about his siblings.

"You care a lot about them, don't you?" Ander took a bit of the shared flan between them, then sat back, content.

"I do. They're my family. I know they always have my back, and so I'll always have theirs. It's my duty to protect them."

Ander wanted to argue, but he couldn't. Not when he thought of Mab and everything he would do for her. "I can understand that. I would walk through fire if it meant protecting my Mabbers."

He watched Max finish off a good portion of the flan once he was sure Ander wanted no more of it, and when the ignis finally settled back against his seat, Ander grinned. "Did you enjoy that?"

"I did. Thank you. This was a wonderful meal."

"I'm glad you thought so." Ander sipped his fresh mojito, pondering over something else he had wanted to speak to Max about. "Max . . . can I ask you something?"

"Of course, anything."

"Why did you refer to Micah as *it*?" He sipped his drink once more, peering over the rim of the glass at Max.

Max, sitting back in his chair, seemed a little confused

by the question. "I . . . I don't know. I guess that's what everyone calls them." He paused and studied Ander for a moment. "Is that not right?" His brow furrowed in the sweetest sort of way. Ander could see the troubled thoughts running through his mind.

The male had no idea how to hide his emotions.

"No," Ander said, shaking his head gently. "I presume the Sanctum started referring to demogorgons as its because they are wildly known for being an intersex race. They carry both reproductive organs, thus making it easier to reproduce. When two mate, both are able to conceive, and their race actually spawns faster. Which helps as they have a two-year gestational period." Max was nodding, clearly already aware of this information. "Some beings are neither, or they are both, Max, but they are always a living, breathing, sentient being. They are never *it*."

Max's mouth opened, a little air whooshing out of him, but then his lips closed once more. Ander didn't want him to feel bad, he simply wanted him to know. "I—" he started, then stopped, and Ander held his hand up.

"I know you didn't think anything of it. I also know that demogorgons are a vicious race and making them seem more like mindless beasts helps when taking them down. But all life deserves respect, even if it is monstrous by nature."

Max nodded. "I'm sorry."

Ander shook his head. "I didn't say something hoping to receive an apology. Only for educational purposes. I know what it's like to be the thing no one knows how to name." He smiled in a self-deprecating manner.

Max looked a little saddened by this, and not looking for anyone's pity, Ander downed the remainder of his drink.

"Would you like to head down to the beach for a walk?" he asked, changing the topic.

Max seemed hesitant for a moment, like he wanted to say something else. Instead, he smiled and nodded. "Yeah, that would be nice."

Ander stood, extending his hand to Max and pulling him in against his chest once more. The scent of him and the nearness made Ander's heart trip faster. He had to snap them away to the beach before he gave in and claimed his lips for his own.

Once on the beach, both shed their shoes to walk barefoot in the sand, and it only seemed natural and right to clasp hands as they walked. As the sun set over the horizon, casting bright reds and oranges over the water, Ander considered pinching himself. When was the last time he felt this at peace while on a date? He often felt relaxed or in his element, but never at peace. Never so near swooning over the presence of another.

Was this what it was like for everyone who was arrow-bound to another?

"Ander?"

"Mm?"

"Can I just say once again how truly sorry I am for putting that cuff on you. And for . . . and for speaking of Micah incorrectly."

Ander sighed. "You don't need to apologize, it's fine."

"No, it's not. I just . . . I feel like there's so much I don't know sometimes. About inanimi. About you. Mab told me how bad it was for you, and I know it's none of my business . . . but if you wouldn't mind telling me about it, I'd like to know why." Max glanced over at him, a gently prodding look on his face.

Ander blew a few stray pieces of hair off his forehead,

that peace inside him melting away to be replaced by a tight hand of dread that gripped at the back of his neck. This was not exactly romantic date talk.

"About one hundred and sixty years ago, I met a god. Orcus, the right hand of Hades and punisher of oath-breakers and other terrible things." He took a deep breath, steadying himself for the rest. "At the time, Enrique, as he was known by then, was the most beautiful thing I'd ever seen, and I believed myself in love with him, and he with me. Or at least, what I thought was love." He cast a quick glance at Max. He was listening intently. Ander didn't want to expose himself this way. To let Max see all of the truly ugly parts of himself so soon. But perhaps it was best to get it over with quickly if it was going to be the end of them. "But he used that love to make me doubt, hate, and lose myself until I was dependent on him. I made excuses, looked past the terrible things he would say and do. Let him tear me away from Mab and my mother.

"When they tried to pull me out of that toxic, abusive relationship, he convinced me to accept an aeternus ring from him. Then there was no escape." Max gasped at this, and Ander shot him a quick look. "I saw a violent, angry side of him after that, and it was truly terrifying. There was no saying no—to anything—despite how badly I wanted to. Despite how many times I said it out loud." The pain made a resurgence, clenching tight within his chest and making his voice tremble. Max squeezed his hand, and Ander felt a sense of calm in the contact. In the gentle yet firm strength Max was offering. "What Enrique wanted, he took, whether it required force or not." Ander paused, throat tightening with the years of unshed tears he'd refused to let fall after those first weeks. "I was essentially a hostage in Acheron for the worst year of my life, until death seemed a preferable choice to staying and being used by him for the rest of eternity. The cuffs just brought back that feeling of being trapped and unable to flee no matter how badly I wished to."

Ander's eyes had drifted out over the water at some point, focused directly on the last spot of sunshine. Letting it blind him to the world and to the memory of pain that washed through him. That was until Max spun him to face him, his strong, battle-roughened hands lifting to cup his face.

His hazel eyes were so earnest as he peered down at Ander. "I promise I will never make you feel like that again. I vow it on my life."

Max was so sincere that Ander couldn't resist rising up and pressing his lips to Max's. His own hands wound around the back of Max's neck, sliding up into his unruly hair, and a murmur slid out of him as Max's hands gripped his hips and drew him nearer.

The taste of him, so warm and earthy, washed all the darkness out of him, like the first rays of dawn chasing away the night. Perhaps he could stay kissing Maximus Schields until all the shadows within him were burned away.

When they broke apart, both of them were breathless. Chuckling a little, they fell back into step alongside each other, hands once more clasped together. Their walk was silent after that, just the soft pad of their bare feet on wet sand and the gentle fall of waves along the shore.

"You don't think less of me, then? After hearing that?" He hadn't told any of that to anyone. Only Mab and his mother were aware of what had happened to him in that hellhole. Ander hated the thought of appearing weak.

"Of course not," Max insisted. "None of that was your fault. It was the fault of the one who treated you badly. This

Enrique." He spat the name like it was poison. Foul and tainted. "No one should ever use your feelings against you." Ander glanced over at Max and found that he was looking at him. "It doesn't make you less, Ander. It makes you more. Because you're stronger for having survived something like that."

Ander's fingers tightened around Max's, and not for the first time, he wondered if he were dreaming all of this.

Feeling that everything was getting a little too deep and a little too serious, Ander pulled away from Max to stoop down near the water, wet his hand, and fling some of it in Max's face. The other male squawked in surprise, then launched himself in his direction.

With laughter bubbling up out of him, Ander darted down the beach, his bare toes digging into the sand.

The sound of something large beating against the air followed behind him. Ander looked over his shoulder and found that Max had launched himself into the air, long, glorious wings stretched out in flight. Before he could register what was happening, strong arms were wrapping around him, lifting him from the sand before they both tumbled to the ground. A firm hold and white wings surrounded him, protecting him from the fall as they rolled over the beach.

When at last they came to a halt, Ander was on his back, and Max lay on top of him. Laughing breathlessly, they gazed at each other, then their mouths were together once more, hands tugging at hair, hips rocking lightly together, breath mingling in the most excellent of ways.

Max was sweeping him away, Ander could tell, and he was starting to think Max would welcome the tidal wave, allow it to crash over him and carry him out to sea.

"Back to my place?" he rasped against his lips, nipping

at the corner of them then down over his jaw toward Max's neck. The feel of the firm body above him and against him was driving his senses wild. He needed to feel Max completely. To connect with him fully.

But there was a sudden hesitation in Max that made Ander stop and pull back so he could rest his head on the sand beneath him. Max, though panting from their efforts, was also suddenly looking shy.

"I, um . . . actually want to take it slow."

"Oh." The air whooshed out of Ander.

Seeing his reaction, Max rushed on. "I just—I don't want this to only be about sex. You're too special for that, and I'm not looking for that anymore. I want what my parents have. I know it's out there for me, and I just . . ."

Ander stared up at Max, feeling a little stunned and a little confused. "Maximus . . ." he whispered. "Are you saying you're looking for love?"

Max nodded his head.

"I didn't—I didn't think you could."

Max looked a little affronted. "Of course I can! All living things can love."

"I'm sorry . . . it's just—"

"I know what everyone believes." Max frowned. "I know Quin has never shown interest in sex, let alone dating, and I don't know what the other ignis feel, but mostly it's the Princeps. They don't want us to." He jammed his fingers through his hair, mussing up the already disorderly strands. "There is this belief that love makes us weak and will distract us from our purpose. From a very young age, it's preached to us how our lives are meant to be the battle. Our duty. That our fellow ignis are our brothers and sisters. The only family we need. And if we were meant to be distracted with our own families, we would have been born with the ability to reproduce. But my parents—"

"They wanted more for you," Ander supplied.

"Yeah . . . they did—they *do*."

Ander studied Max, his heart tripping away in his chest. *Up yours, Erotes. Maximus Schields can love.*

What did this mean?

He lifted his hands to cup Max's face, staring up into those lovely hazel eyes that held such a mixture of innocence, determination, sincerity, and lust that Ander knew for certain he was a goner. Whether it was the amare bond or something altogether more, he wasn't sure. But Ander could feel himself already willing to sacrifice too much if it meant the smile would stay on Max's lips.

"We'll take it at your pace, sweetheart. I would never pressure you into something you weren't ready for."

Their lips met in a gentle, soul-searing kiss that made Ander melt into the sand, and the darkness, for the moment, burst into oblivion.

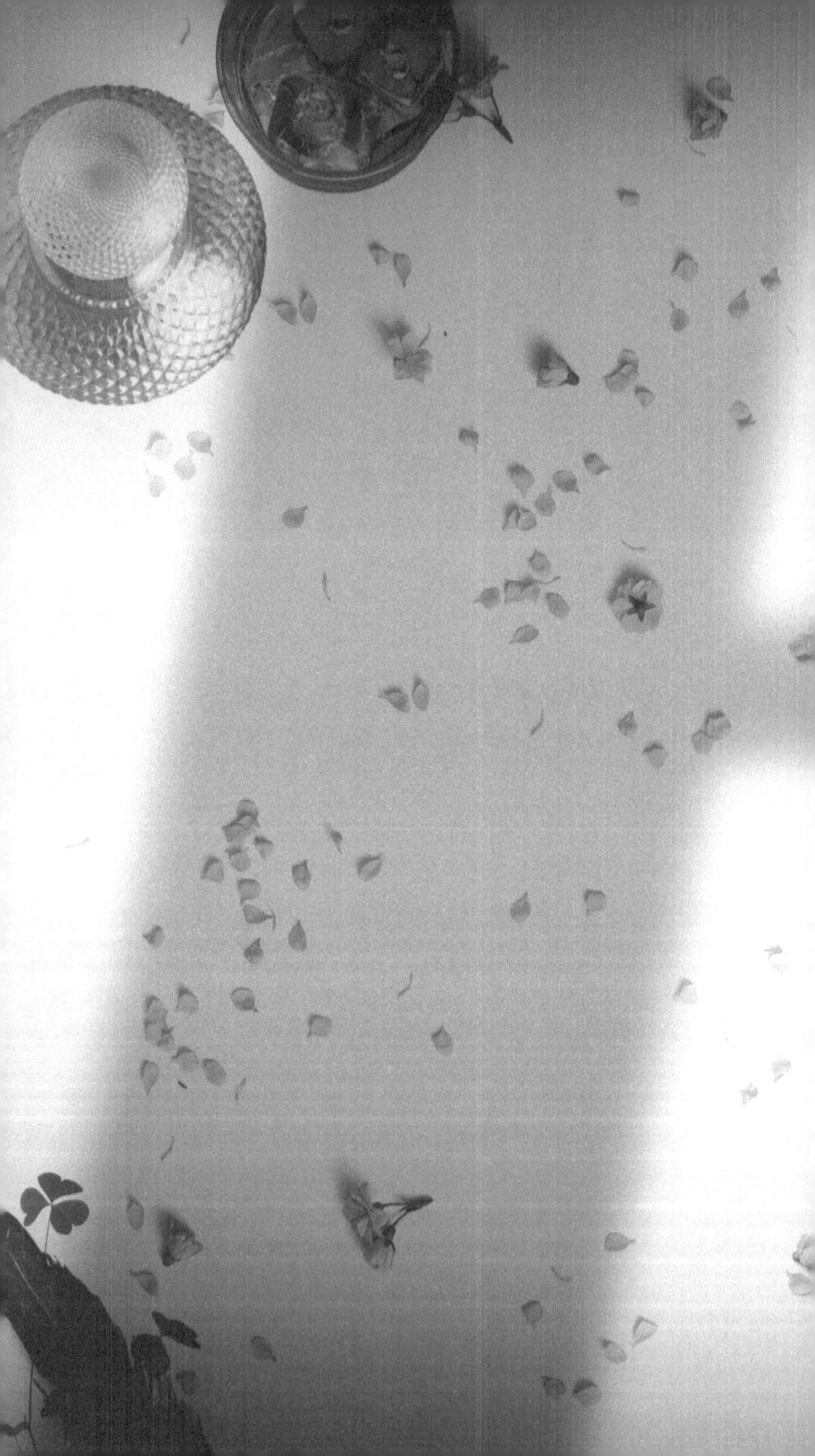

Chapter 17
Quin

Quin slid out of the shower, wrapping a towel around his waist and walking to the sink to wipe the condensation off its surface. There was a bruise just under his right eye that was puffy and sore; he'd taken a scaled hand to the face while he and Max were battling a gorgon that had been terrorizing a local shopping area. The creature had not come quietly, and they'd had to dispatch it rather than lock it up.

He pressed his fingers to the underside of the bruise and grunted as he dropped his hand. It would be gone by the following morning, despite how terrible it looked. Not that it mattered; there had been far worse injuries inflicted on him over the course of his twenty-three years, some of which had been bad enough that they left scars despite the innate ability to heal that each ignis possessed.

Some wounds just could not be hidden. Just as some scars could not be seen.

Quin stared at his reflection in the mirror, and instead of the grown ignis he was, he saw the small child of five, finding his own image for the first time in the surface of a dirty puddle. The image rippled into blurred nothingness as drops of his own blood fell to distort it.

He shut his eyes against his reflection, pressing his hands into the surface of the counter and willing away the memories. So much fighting. So many screams of agony and death. Taunting jeers of the crowd and their harrowing cries of victory when one gladiator fell to another.

A shudder coursed through Quin, and he turned to the toilet instead, leaning over it to retch up what was left of his breakfast. It had been thirteen years, but the stench of death still clung to his nostrils, the hunger still gnawed at his belly, and his muscles still tensed in preparation for any unsuspecting blow. The night terrors didn't happen as often these days, nor did the terrible setbacks where he lost all sense of where he was and found himself trapped inside the horrors of his own mind. Most days, it was easy to put one foot in front of the other and leave behind the trauma of his childhood.

Today was not most days.

Dad promised the fighting rings had all been shut down by the Sanctum. All orchestrators hanged to prove a point. Monsters weren't meant to have ignis in their clutches, and if they were found to, death was the only outcome.

But someone wanted ignis younglings again. Someone who was willing to kill to have them, and it couldn't mean anything good—it never did.

Quin flushed the toilet and moved back to the sink. Grabbing up his toothbrush and toothpaste, he quickly brushed the sick out of his mouth.

He had just finished rinsing his mouth when knuckles rapped on the doorframe, and Max walked into the bathroom without so much as a "can I come in". Quin said nothing as he straightened up, just gave his brother a questioning look. They didn't always need words.

When their dad first brought Quin home, Max hadn't understood why Quin didn't speak, or why he shied away from all touch and most interactions. Yet he'd been so patient with him, sitting for hours doing their own thing, only talking to him when it was necessary. In the end, Max had become a steadying, calming presence for Quin—he still was.

Even when he annoyed the hell out of him.

"I need you to come to Inferno with me."

Eyeing him dryly, Quin signed, "Why?"

"I want to surprise Ander, and I need you to come be my wingman." Max shuffled his feet a little as he gave Quin an imploring look.

"No," he signed in response, quick, short, decisive.

Max sighed and stepped farther into the steamy bathroom. Linking his hands together, he lifted them before himself in a pleading look. "Please?"

"You've gone on two dates with him already, you don't need a wingman," he said out loud so that Max could hear the irritation in his voice.

Max's eyes took on that sad, puppy dog look that tended to get most of their family to give in, whether he realized he did it or not. "But I don't want to just show up by myself. I'm braver when you come with me. Pleeeease, Quin? I need moral support!"

Quin growled. He knew what Max was doing. Knew what all of his family were doing. Every day, they tried to keep him busy with mindless, stupid things so he didn't have time to sit alone and think and remember. He appreciated their love and concern, but he hated being treated like he was broken. Or as if they needed to walk on eggshells and avoid the elephant in the room.

"Fine. But can I get dressed before you throw something else at me?"

"Sure!" Max grinned brightly at him before heading back out the door.

Shaking his head at his sibling, Quin looked back at the mirror, seeing himself as he was once again. Tall, broad-shouldered, muscled torso covered in an array of scars and dents that would never go away. Unfurling his wings, he stretched them out and gave them a rustle, shaking out the last of the water. His wings were black, but much in the way a raven's were, with hints of blue and green along the tips. He was the damaged demon to Max's angel.

Inferno, as usual, was loud and chaotic. Quin didn't like it. The pounding of the bass made it feel like his body was constantly being buffeted by an attack, and his eardrums rang from the noise masquerading as music. He didn't understand why people enjoyed this.

"Thanks for coming with me," Max said as they slipped farther into Inferno.

Quin grunted, but he doubted Max was able to hear him. "I'll be over here." He pointed in the general direction of the bar, then headed for it.

"Hey!" Max shouted over the music, causing Quin to turn back and look at him.

"Where are you going? You're supposed to come with me," Max signed.

"You don't want me up there with you. Signal if you actually need me," he signed back.

At the very end of the bar, there was a free spot. Relieved to be able to sit down away from the dancefloor where the music was the loudest, Quin claimed the stool and pulled the small charcoal pencil out of his pocket that he always had on him. If he was going to have to sit here for a while, he was going to at least sketch a little; maybe take his mind off of how much he hated being where he was.

"Stink Eye," a voice said from above him. "What are you doing here?"

Quin looked up to find Mab Duchan before him. She always looked at him as if he had seven heads and all of them wanted to spew fire and burn her world down around her. "Max," was all he said in return.

Mab quirked a brow at him. "Max?"

"He wants to see Ruin." Quin didn't bother to hide his eye roll, spinning the pencil in his fingers where his hand sat on his lap beneath the bar.

Mab just nodded. "What can I get you?"

"Just water is fine."

"Water?" The banshee scoffed. "If you've got to trail along for another make-out session, you may as well have a drink for your troubles."

"I don't drink." He didn't like being out of control of his body.

"How about a mocktail?"

It didn't seem like she was going to let up and just leave him in peace. "Sure."

Duchan nodded, then stepped away to begin mixing something that seemed to have a lot of juices and sparkling water in it. When she turned back to him, it was with a martini glass full of a bright peach liquid fading into red. A small skewer of fruit sat nestled against the rim. "On the house."

"Thanks."

"Enjoy." She stepped away to start working on other orders.

Quin picked up the glass and took a sip. It was very sweet, though it wasn't bad. Not really his choice of drink, but it was palatable.

He reached over the bar and picked up a few napkins. Laying them on the bar in front of him, he began sketching a couple down the bar, capturing the light of desire in the male's eyes every time he peered down at his companion. When he was finished with that portrait, he began quickly doodling the back bar, shading where he could to capture the bright sparkle of lights off the vast array of bottles on the shelves.

The napkin was a terrible medium to work on, but it suited his purposes for the moment, especially since he'd forgotten the small notepad he usually had on him. If Max hadn't dragged him out here, he may have gone to his studio to work on his current piece. Yet Max seemed to think that if he left him alone, he'd end up off his rocker with trauma responses.

Quin pushed the still life drawing aside, looking up from the bar to find the next most interesting thing. Mab Duchan stood at the counter, mixing a large number of drinks for one of her waitresses. Without much thought, he began to sketch the outline of her form, the large puff of white hair on top of her head, the slender, capable hands mixing and shaking drinks without pause.

She seemed entirely at home in this atmosphere. He was fully aware of her and Ruin's history, but Duchan didn't put off the air of a partier. Not the way her business partner did. So it surprised him to see her so in her element like this.

As he began to sketch in the shape of her face, the slope of her button nose and the full lips, his eyes fell on the scars that marred her cheek. Or at least, they could have. But there was something powerful in the way Duchan wore them without attempting to hide them. The scars Quin had were all tucked beneath layers of clothing. Out of sight and out of mind. But hers were there for all the world to see and question.

There had been nothing in her files about how she'd obtained them, but from Quin's own knowledge of injuries and scars, they looked like deep scratches.

"What did he say Timoros wanted us doing?"

Quin froze as he heard the name uttered behind him.

"Mermaid duty, *again*."

Quin spun on the stool, seeking out the bodies belonging to the voices he'd overheard. At first, it was just a sea of partygoers, but then he saw them. Two males dressed in black, muttering to themselves and not paying any heed to the nightclub around them.

He pushed off the stool and followed them outside, where they slid into a car parked across the street in front of Element 79. Quin hurried after them, pulling his phone out of his pocket to snap a photo of the license plate for the twins. Hurrying back inside, Quin pushed his way past dancers, despite their protests, and mounted the metal stairs to Ruin's office two steps at a time.

He didn't knock but wished he had. As he stepped into the office, he found Ander perched on top of his desk with Max between his thighs, their arms wrapped around each other and the two of them attached at the mouth.

Quin grunted, and the pair pulled apart. Max looked

over his shoulder as he panted, and he looked both irritated and concerned at the disturbance.

"Wh-what?" his brother squawked.

"I found a connection to Timoros."

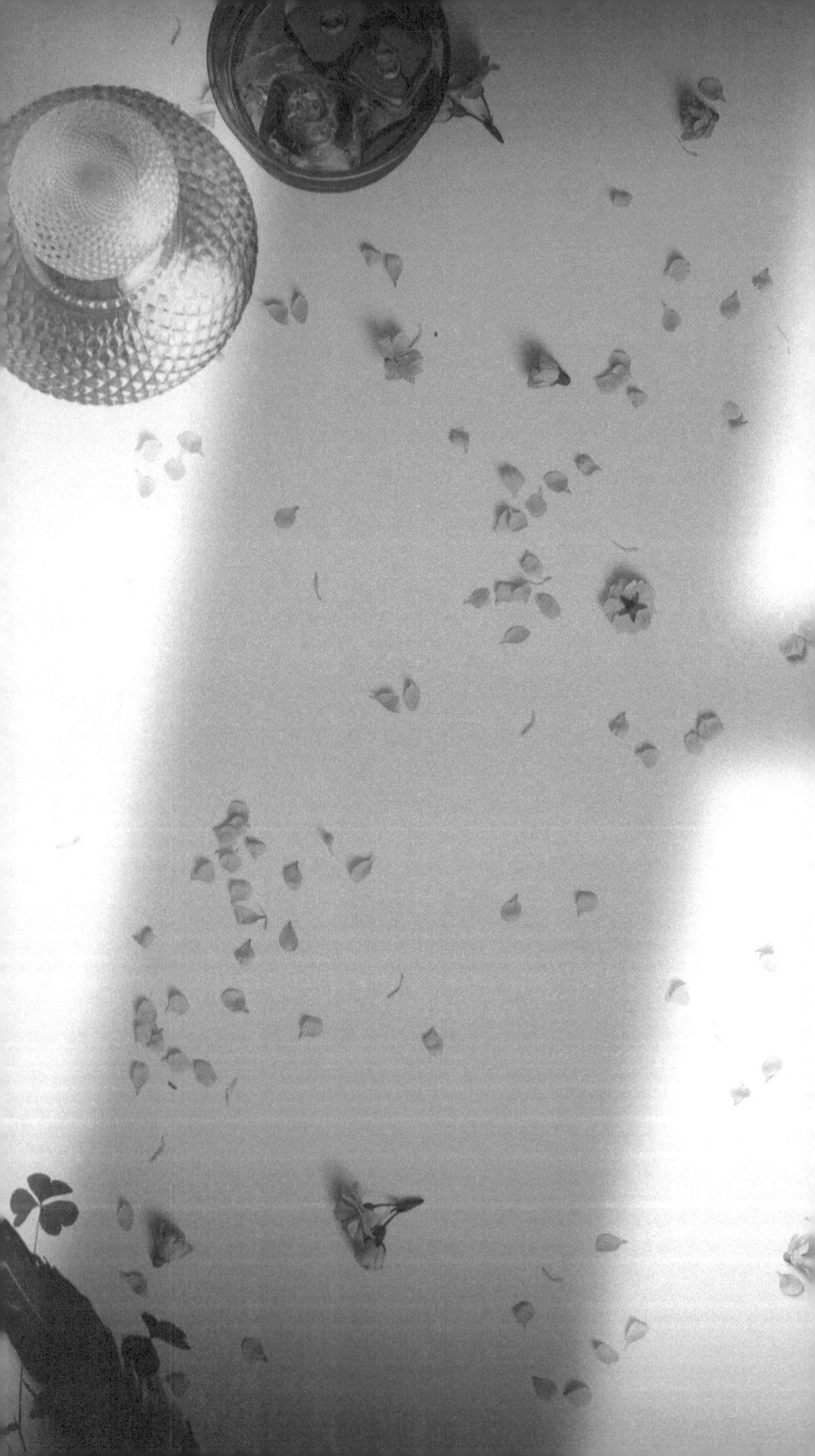

Chapter 18
Max

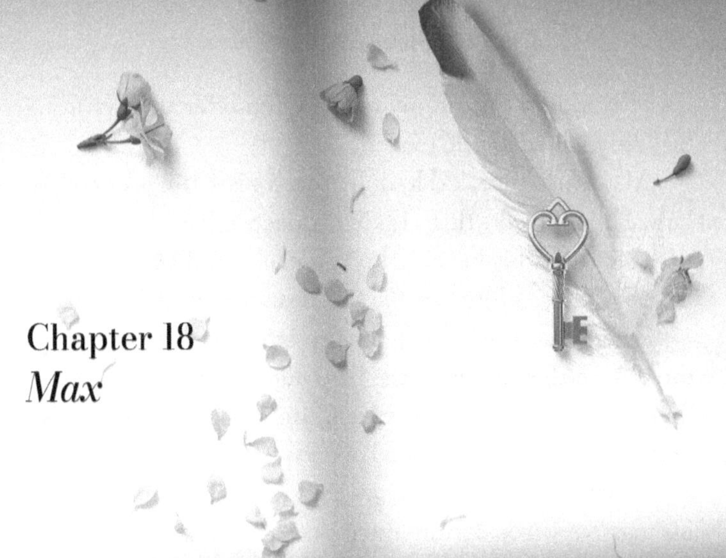

Open water made Max twitchy. He was aware of the irony of this, given that he lived in Miami and was thus surrounded by water, but that didn't change facts. So he wasn't exactly pleased when he found that the license plate was attached to an Uber with credit card transactions linked to a name that led them to a fucking *houseboat* of all things. Not pleased at all.

Add that to the way Quin's eyes kept shifting from the end of the floating dock they were standing on, out to the open water, then back to his brother. Max couldn't see the twitch of his gaze, but the pressure of it sat like a weight against his skin, threatening to push him into the water. It probably didn't help that when he was a child, one of the elder ignis had told him that if an ignis went into salt water, their spark would go out and they'd die instantly. Gods, that guy had been a tool. Max had never been so happy to see an ignis transferred in his life. But he was an adult now. A fully trained warrior. He should be over this nonsense. He knew that. Still, his toes curled in his boots, muscles twitching with the desire to step away from the edge of the dock.

"I could do this on my own," Quin offered when Max had dillydallied a little too long.

Max wasn't weak. He didn't need his siblings to coddle him. He could do this. Taking a deep inhale through his nose, he shook his head. "No. You can't. And you shouldn't have to." *Especially given the circumstances* went unsaid.

There likely wouldn't be any ignis younglings out on the boat in the middle of the bay. But in the off chance that there were, Max couldn't leave Quin to face that alone. No matter how much he disliked open water.

"Fuck. Okay. Let's just get this over with." Max flapped his massive wings, letting them pull him off his feet and up into the air above the water. A second later, he heard Quin join him. With a glance back at the dock, Max swallowed down his fear and pushed forward, heading for the coordinates the twins had sent to his phone before they'd arrived.

It took less than a minute for the gentle silence of the bay to be broken by the growl of a cigar boat speeding past them. The loud whoop of someone on a parasail being dragged behind made Max's shoulders tense further. It would be so easy to be ripped from the sky and dragged under the waves. For the engines of every passing boat to tear through the thin membrane of his wings and—

"Over there," Quin called, cutting Max's spiraling thoughts short.

"It looks like the mortals are giving them a wide berth." Likely for the best. If this crew was truly working for Timoros, then they were a danger to more than just the ignis; they were a danger to every other creature they came into contact with, mortal and immortal alike. "It doesn't look like anyone's home," Max said when they got close enough to see the deck of the boat devoid of people.

Quin shrugged, his fingers working smoothly over words as he signed, "Only one way to find out."

They shared a brief glance, quick and fleeting. Then, with a nod, they both dove toward the boat. Max felt the wards pop like a bubble just before the shrill sound of an alarm blared in his ears, making him wince. A second later, just as he was touching down onto the deck, someone dove out of the door on the side of the cabin and into a fan boat that he hadn't seen floating there before—likely hidden to keep their exit strategy a surprise.

The engine on the fan boat whirred to life, then a second person dove from the door, almost missing the deck of the fan boat, and it was off like a shot. Max only had enough time to register that their suspects were making a quick and clean exit—one that would no doubt help them to slip into the crowd of mortals using the bay as their own personal playground, making them impossible to track or apprehend—before he leaped into the air again.

"Make sure no one else is inside, then follow me," he called over his shoulder, his wings beating hard as he took off through the air after the escaping suspects. As he regulated his breathing, the air around him shifted with an ignis' innate magic, and he hid himself from not only the mortals on the water but also the people he was chasing, hoping to give himself the element of surprise. If he could just circle around and get ahead of them, cut them off before they reached the nearest cluster of normies, that would be ideal. But he wasn't about to let up even if he didn't manage it. He wasn't walking away from this. He couldn't.

A dinghy cut across the path of the fan boat, making the driver take a sharp left, slowing their progress, and Max knew he had them. His wings burned, the muscles unused to such heavy exertion in such a short span of time, especially with the winds of the bay buffeting him, but he pushed harder, faster. It paid off, because a moment later, the engine stalled out, either from lack of gas or divine intervention, making the motor sputter and whine. They kicked at the controls, trying to force the boat to continue, but the engine had well and truly locked up. Max dropped down onto the deck, fingers flexing at his sides.

"All right, guys, we can do this the easy way or the hard way." Someone snorted in the comm in his ear—probably Nash, but Max ignored him in favor of giving the two satyrs on the fan boat his most serious expression.

The male who'd been driving the boat picked up a pole that looked like it was for grabbing lines from below his feet, his knuckles turning pale as he gripped it tight, thrusting one end at Max in warning.

Max rolled his eyes and grabbed the sword from his back to hold in front of himself. A little push from the fire at his center, and it lit like a torch, blazing hot enough to rival even Miami's scorching sun. Was he using intimidation techniques to dissuade these two goons from fighting him in a confined space in open water? Yes. Did he think it would work? Well . . . maybe.

They looked at Max, looked at each other, looked at his sword, looked at him again.

"It's not worth it, man," the shorter male muttered, then knocked the pole out of the other male's hands.

"I'm not telling birdbrain shit," the taller one snarled, spitting at Max's feet.

"Now that's just uncalled for." Max sighed, pulling a pair of cuffs from one of the many pockets on his black pants and yanking the taller male's wrists forward to cuff them together. There was some struggling, but Max almost wondered if it was just to make it look like he'd tried, lest the ringleader get it into his head to off another one of his underlings. "What about you? Are you going to talk?"

"Not planning on it. But I'll come quietly," the shorter one said, holding his wrists out and letting Max cuff him.

"Coward!" the taller snapped, lurching in Max's hold to try to get at the shorter. What he intended to do once he did, Max had no way of knowing, but he kept them firmly apart. "If you tell them anything, I'll make sure that—"

"Why don't you just keep your fucking mouth shut, you moron?" The shorter one tilted his head and lifted one dark brow, an air of confidence and security about him that Max didn't think he much cared for. It sent unease crawling up his spine. This male wasn't worried. About what Timoros would do to him for being caught. About what the ignis would do to him for his indiscretions. About anything. He seemed wholly relaxed with the situation, and that left Max's feathers standing on end.

"Need a lift?" Quin asked as the houseboat puttered up to them. A smile had crept up one corner of his mouth, the expression invisible to anyone else, but Max could see it—he always would be able to see it. Max let out a huff of a laugh and shook his head.

"Help me get these two on board. We'll want to haul the boat back to the Sanctuary's docks for processing."

Quin nodded and pulled the fan boat in so he could tie it off on the houseboat. "We've got an underwater tank on this boat, accessible by a floor panel. Three mermaids inside. I've let them know they're safe now and will be released once we've had a chance to question them."

"Good."

With the two of them working together, getting their prisoners secure and the boat turned back to shore took less than a few minutes. But even then, something didn't sit right with Max. The way the shorter male had acted . . . they weren't the actions of a caged man. They were the actions of someone who knew they wouldn't face repercussions for their deeds. And the mission? It had been too easy.

Max's hands were shaking, had been shaking since they'd stepped off the boat onto the Sanctuary-run docks. Quin hadn't said anything, and Max should really have thanked his brother for that. He should also probably have stayed to help search the boat, but that's why they had the twins. That and maybe even to check in with Quin to make sure that he was all right. But Max needed to get away from the water and the perceived danger that it posed him.

His siblings would understand.

The walk back to Max's office had never felt so long as sweat cooled all along his spine, pimpling his skin. Every step, an exercise in self-control over his own anxiety. By the time his office was finally in sight, Max felt like he was running to keep from being stopped by anyone wanting an update on the mission, and his heart didn't start to slow down until he'd shut the door behind himself and leaned against it.

The sound of a deep exhale filled the room, drowning out the sound of his heart beating in his ears. *One. Two. Three. Four. Five. Better. So much better.* Nodding to himself, Max shuffled across the room to slump behind his desk to at least pretend to start the arduous task of paperwork.

It took him about a half an hour to realize that he'd read the same line at least a dozen times, zoned out, and the paperwork wasn't getting done. An afterimage of the sun-bleached water flashed in his mind, and Max found himself reaching for his cell phone on the side of his desk before he'd even fully thought about what he was doing and calling Ander on FaceTime.

Ander picked up on the second ring with a delighted, "Darling! What an unexpected, and delightful, surprise. To what do I—" Ander stopped, his expression falling a little when he got a good look at Max's no doubt still slightly pale and sweaty face. "Max, honey, what's wrong?"

"Nothing. It's nothing. It's—" Max sucked down another breath that threatened to catch in his throat, squeezing his eyes shut. "We got a lead last night while we were at Inferno."

"Yes. I recall your brother coming in and rudely interrupting our intimate moment," Ander said, his voice a soft, lilting tease. Like he wanted to make light of the situation but wasn't sure if it was appropriate. "Max. What happened?"

"It's really nothing." It really *was*. Just his overactive imagination running away with itself and taking the rest of his anxiety along with it. Nothing to get so worked up about.

"Did someone get hurt?"

"No. No, everyone's fine." Max shook his head and fixed his gaze back on Ander, smiling a little. Ander's right eye had a perfect cat-eye along the lid, but the left was lacking its twin yet. Ander must have been getting ready when he'd called. He'd stopped what he was doing to talk to Max. Max's heart thrilled at the thought. "We had to chase down a boat, out on the bay. And I kind of hate open water." Rubbing at his neck sheepishly, Max let out an uncomfortable laugh. "Actually, not just hate. Have a phobia about? I guess? I don't know. It's stupid."

"You were scared, and you called me?" Ander's tone had lost its teasing edge, going tentative and hopeful.

"Yeah. I guess I did."

"Okay." A long exhale ruffled Ander's unstyled bangs—he looked wonderful this way, all soft and cozy, domestic—and he looked at whatever was beyond the phone, the mirror probably, then nodded. "Okay. What can I do to help? Do you need me to come and see you? I can pick up dinner? I'm supposed to be at the club in about an hour but—"

"No. No. There's really no need for all that. I just . . ." Heat crawled up Max's neck, warding off the chill from earlier. "Can I sit and talk to you while you get ready?"

"Of course, darling!" Ander's smile brightened again. There was some shuffling, the camera jerking wildly as Ander propped his phone up on something so his hands would be free to finish up. "I'm all yours."

"That's . . . That's really great. You're really great." Max relaxed back into his chair, feeling the muscles in his back loosen one by one as he settled in. "Tell me about your day?"

And Ander did. The conversation came easily after that. So easy that Max hardly noticed that Ander's preparations had gone from purposeful to fiddling, as if he were looking for something to do just so he'd have an excuse to keep talking. It wasn't until someone knocked softly on the door to his office, and Nox let herself in without first waiting for his invitation, that he realized they'd spent the last forty-five minutes talking about seemingly nothing.

"What is it?" Max asked, forcefully dragging his gaze away from Ander to raise a brow at his sister.

"We found something. We're all in the conference room." She tilted her head in question, loose bun bobbing with the motion. "And, uh . . ." She stepped into the room, a thumb drive in her hand. "I got the list of the missing younglings you asked for. It's—Max, it's a lot more than we thought."

"How many more?"

She shook her head and set the thumb drive on his desk with a soft click.

"All right, I'll be out in a minute."

"Okay. Tell Ander I said hi." Nox waggled her fingers and disappeared back out into the hallway without another word.

Shaking his head, Max turned his attention back to Ander. "I'll talk to you later?"

"Until then, darling." Ander blew him a kiss before reaching forward and ending the call.

Max locked his phone, scrubbed over his face to try to massage the smile out of his cheeks—no luck—and followed Nox to the conference room. "All right. What is it?"

Nox clicked a button on the remote, and an enlarged photo of a table popped up on the screen. "This is everything someone would need to extract mermaid venom for Mermaid's Lament."

"The magical knockout drug?" Max asked, settling into the seat at the head of the table and ignoring the way Quin was watching him. There was no judgment in that bright blue gaze, but Max didn't think he liked the curiosity either.

"Exactly." Nash perked up from where he'd been drooping like a wilted sunflower in his chair. This last week had been hard on all of them, but especially on Nash, who partied perhaps more than their Papa and now was finding himself almost exclusively bound to the office. Poor kid. Max would have to take them out when all of this cleared up.

"The three mermaids found in the bottom of the boat mentioned that they had only extracted enough from all of them to know that they had a viable venom source. Which means this was only a hunting party, and they are likely holding mermaids hostage somewhere else for the full extraction process." Quin fidgeted with the pen in his hand, tapping it against the surface of the table. He did that sometimes when he really wanted to be drawing but worried it might seem unprofessional to doodle during a meeting. Max didn't know why he bothered; no one else was looking, just them. But then, he supposed Galeo did make a nasty habit of dropping in.

"A full production line means plenty of space. So this is what they were using to abduct their victims from Inferno." Max pinched the bridge of his nose, a headache settling between his eyes. He didn't like how all of the puzzle pieces were fitting together. All of them except, of course, the ones that his captain would find the most pertinent. What did any of this have to do with the missing ignis? "Did the two down in lockup say anything?"

"They gave us a name." Nox smashed another button on the remote, and the image on the screen changed to that of a satyr in a cheap suit. "Hector Hugman is a luxury yacht salesman, and from the surface level at least, he looks clean. But we did a deeper dive on him, and honestly . . ." She sucked her teeth in disapproval. "The man is rolling in it, and we can't quite figure out how."

"He sells yachts," Quin reasoned.

"Not enough of them. Not according to his tax records. So either he's evading taxes somehow, or he's got another stream of income."

"Only one way to find out." Max perked up, the corner of his lips twitching a little. A lead. They had a lead. They had a direction to go in. Maybe soon they'd have answers. "Get me a list of his properties, and we'll raid the places."

"Already one step ahead of you, boss." Nash winked and slid a file folder over to him. "We've even narrowed them down for you."

"Do you want a sticker?" Quin asked, and Nash stuck his tongue out at him.

"If he's hiding his cargo anywhere, it's one of these." Nox hit a button, and the image on the screen changed again to show a list of addresses along the docks.

"That's too many for us to raid." Max shook his head, ignoring Quin and Nash as they devolved into bickering via ASL. "I want you to check any security footage you can get on these places and narrow it down further for me."

"How many are you thinking?"

"We should have enough ignis to raid three addresses. But, Nox . . ." He waited until she was looking at him over Nash's quickly moving hands before adding, "You have to be sure. Once we do this, we're going to tip him off."

"Got it." Her head bobbed, dark hair falling into her eyes, but already he could see her mind working on the best way to get them what they needed.

"Good." Max turned to his brother and swallowed a chuckle at the furious gestures Quin was making in Nash's direction. Most of them were names Max was pretty sure his brother would never call anyone out loud but . . . "Quin."

"Yes?" Quin stopped, his bright gaze still narrowed on Nash.

"Let's go start deciding who we want with us on this raid."

Quin jerked a nod, threw one last aggravated sign at Nash, and rose.

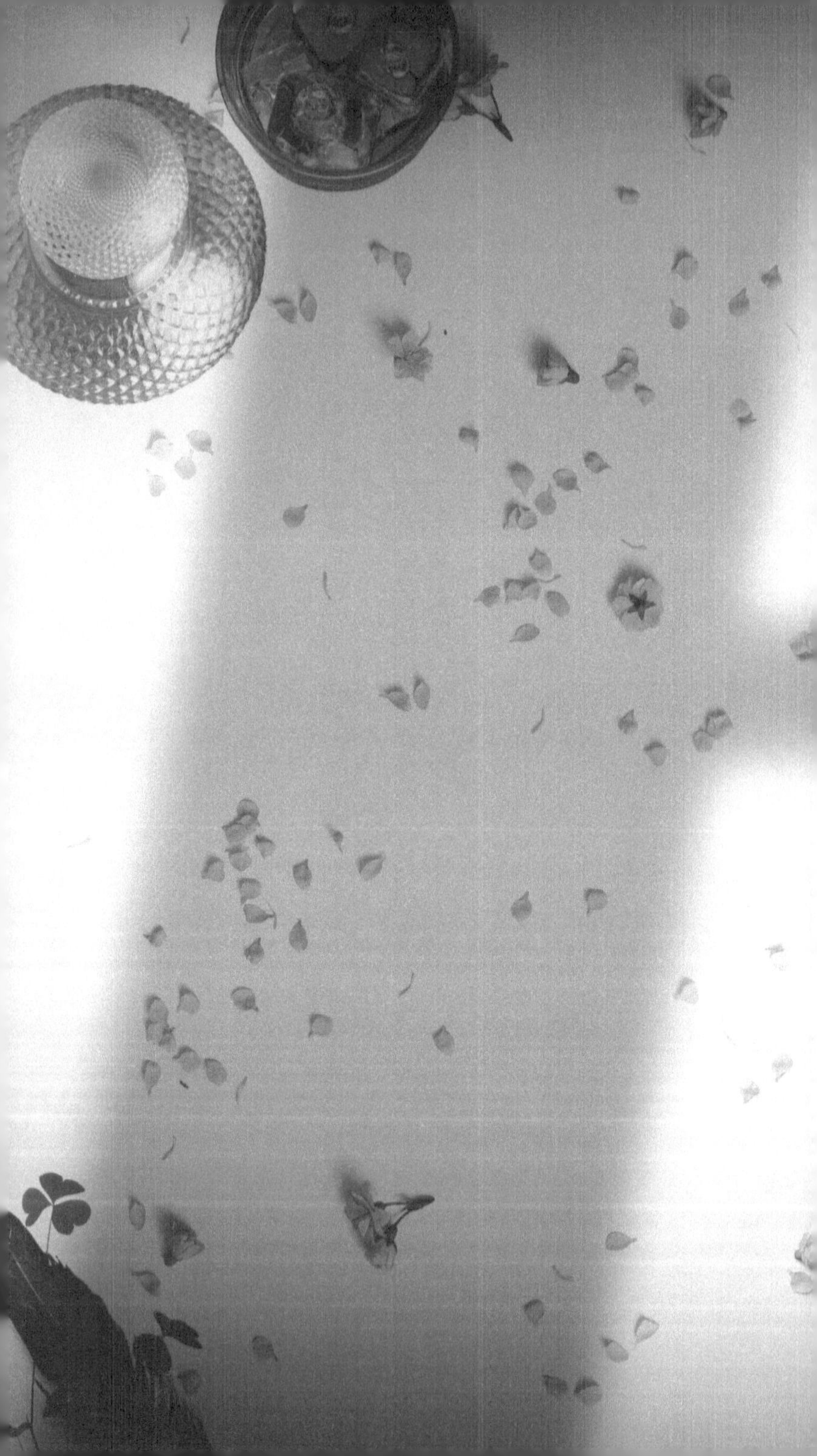

Chapter 19
Mab

"No. Absolutely *not*." Gizmo shifted in Mab's lap, uncomfortable with the sudden tightness of her grip. Forcing her hands to relax, Mab gave the ball of fur a gentle scritch between his long ears, and he settled again.

"What do you mean 'absolutely not'? We talked about this. I can't send the ignis after him." Ander wasn't looking at her; his narrowed gaze was fixed on something in the middle distance. Maybe Enrique's too-pretty, too-perfect teeth. She should have taken the chance to at least chip one of them when she'd had it all those years ago. "They're not built for that. In fact, I know you know this, but I feel like you might need reminding: the ignis were built specifically to *not* be able to fight—"

"Gods. Yes, I remember. Lest they overthrow Indra himself." She deepened her voice to mimic Indra's drawling tones. If he'd been there, he may have smited—Smote? Smoted? Smitten? She didn't know—her on the spot or laughed himself silly. There was never any way to tell which way he'd go with these sorts of things. "But you aren't equipped to handle him either, Andy."

"I'm better equipped to—"

"*No.* You're not." The words were an uncomfortable grate in her suddenly tight throat as she remembered Ander, gaunt and haunted. Remembered how he stared at the wall for hours sometimes after he'd come back, looking like he wanted to die more than he wanted to live. Maybe he had forgotten, but Mab could never, *would* never. And she'd *never* let that happen again. Not so long as she was still breathing. Her hands had started sweating at some point during their argument, but she wasn't sure when. All she knew was that it was starting to mat down Gizmo's soft calico fur. Not that he seemed to mind; the rabbit was perfectly content to perch on her lap when it was available to him or he wasn't causing trouble elsewhere.

"Mabbers," Ander said, tone suddenly quiet as he reached between them and took one of her hands from where it was clutching Gizmo to thread their fingers together. With a gentle squeeze, he pulled her out of that place. "I'll be careful."

"It's not enough." She lifted her free hand to scrub at her burning eyes. She couldn't cry. It would negate the point of this argument. "You aren't going in there without protection. I won't let you."

"And how would you propose I protect myself?" Ander threw himself back on the arm of the couch, giving the hand he refused to release a sharp tug that nearly sent her sprawling into his lap. Dramatic little shit. "Nothing can hurt a god!"

"I don't know!" Sharp and aggravated, Mab snatched her hand away, balling both hands into fists in her lap when Gizmo vacated it due to their raised voices. "But that's the end of the discussion as far as I'm concerned."

"Mab, be—"

"If you say 'be reasonable', I will come across this couch and drown you in that martini." Ander's gaze flicked to the half-drunken martini on the coffee table before he slanted a questioning look at her, likely trying to decide if she'd really do it or not. Which would've been funny in any other situation because they both knew she would; she'd done worse in the past. "If we can't find some means of protection for you, then you aren't going in there alone. I'll be going with you."

This made Ander pause. He began to worry at his lower lip, eyes shifting back and forth but never landing on her face. Mab didn't budge, didn't pull away. This was her final say on the matter. There would be nothing else. Finally, after what felt like a small eternity, he let out a low exhale, his shoulders sagging with the release. He looked back at her, a pinched expression settling around his eyes that almost made him look like he had crow's feet—not that she'd tell him that because it'd send him into a tantrum. "There might be another way."

Mab raised a brow, her head tilting to one side in interest. "Oh?"

"I don't know how true it is, but I've heard tell about this potion called *dues somnum* that can render a god unconscious." His hands moved so he could pick at the letters on his tank top. It read "boss bitch" in sparkling red sequins. It was an atrocity, but as they weren't going out, neither of them really cared.

"And?" It felt like a trick. Like he was lying just to get her off his back. And maybe he was. Ander wasn't above that sort of thing, the self-sacrificing idiot. But Mab would play along for now, if just to see how true it was. She was consistently amazed that he still thought he could lie to her after literally spending centuries at one another's side. "Where do we get this mysterious potion?"

"That's the thing. I don't . . . I don't know. It's just a rumor I heard." Ander slumped in on himself, defeat lining his face. Mab should've felt bad for pushing him like this when she knew all he was trying to do was protect his soulmate. She should've felt guilty that she was forcing him to stop and think when his first gut instinct was to do the right thing. It was selfish of her, but she couldn't lose him again. He was the only family she *had*.

"Well, that's just spectacular news." Mab threw her hands up in frustration. "Because here I was thinking you'd found a solution to our problem. But noooooo. It's just gossip!"

"Hey! It's not my fault you're pushing this! I would be more than happy to just go in—"

"Why are we yelling?!" A third voice joined the shouts, and both Mab and Ander stopped dead, their heads whipping toward the kitchen to see Indra sauntering out of it, a carton of ice cream with a spoon sticking out of it in one hand and a bar napkin flapping in the other. "Who drew this?"

Mab's heart ricocheted in her chest, and she launched herself over the back of the couch, nearly tripping on the rug to snatch the napkin away from him. A careful once-over showed that the pencil lines hadn't been smudged, and Indra hadn't gotten any chocolate smears on it. She let out a slow exhale.

She didn't know why she'd even kept it. It was just some silly drawing someone had done when they'd been sitting at the bar that she'd found during one of her rounds of cleanup. But the way the person had captured her made her heart squeeze and her eyes burn a little. It was similar to how Edward used to draw her, but different. Edward had always put her on a pedestal, seen her as something godlike and unattainable because of their difference in status and her being his patroness. This wasn't like that. This person had captured a softer beauty that Mab didn't think she'd ever actually seen in herself before. And she was ashamed to admit she'd spent an embarrassing amount of time rehashing her evening trying to figure out the artist just so she could look them up on their bar tab. Because she was *not* asking Ander to look at the security tapes.

"So, who drew it?" Indra asked again, leaning down so he could press his face in close to hers, a curious leer etched into his features. "It is a rather good likeness. Although . . . perhaps they made you a little *too* pretty. I don't think your eyes look nearly that sparkly."

"If I've told you once, I've told you a hundred times: Don't. Go. Through. My. *Purse.*" She punctuated the last word by shoving his face away from her with a hand smooshed against his nose. Indra grunted a protest but backed up nonetheless. Holding the napkin closer, she turned her back on him and headed back to the couch, choosing to walk around it this time instead of over it. Indra joined them a second later, perching on the arm next to Ander, where he rested the hand holding his ice cream so close to Ander's neck that it raised goosebumps. Ander swatted him away, but it didn't do much.

"So, what were we yelling about again?" Indra took an obnoxious spoonful of ice cream into his mouth to talk around it.

"Ander says there's a potion that can knock out a god, and I was asking him where we could find it," Mab said, jumping at the chance to change the subject as she set the napkin on the arm of the couch behind her where neither of the males could see it. "You don't happen to know anything about it, do you?"

Sticking the spoon back into the carton with half-melted ice cream still on it, Indra wiped his mouth on the shoulder of his T-shirt and frowned. "*Deus somnum*? I know where to get it. It doesn't really knock us out, it just makes us weak, drunk almost. Consider it a god-like roofie. But I can't exactly be giving that stuff out like candy on mortal Halloween. We've got rules around it, you know?"

Ander turned so he could crane his neck to look up at Indra, his brows drawn together. "What sort of rules?"

"Well, I need to know who it's for first," Indra said, holding up one finger like he was ticking off a grocery list. "And why." He held up another. "If you're planning to prank Hades, then sure, I'm always game for messing with my big bro. But if you're using it to get revenge on Erotes, then I'd have to say hard pass because I really don't need his cantankerous ass pissed at me *again*."

Mab kind of wanted to know what Indra had done to get Erotes mad at him before and what kind of vengeance Erotes had enacted. After what the god of love had done to her and Ander . . . well, Indra had good reason to be concerned about his retribution. But instead of asking, she said, "We need it for Orcus" before Ander could fully explain the situation. The less Indra knew, the better. Probably.

"Oh! Well, that's fine, then. I can totally get you some for that S-O-B. Let me just go make some calls." Shoving the spoon back into his mouth, he stood and slunk to the glass doors toward the beach behind the house.

It wasn't until he'd reached the surf that Ander turned back toward Mab, his eyes dancing with curiosity. Mab had just enough time to register that he was lifting his hand before Ander snapped, and the napkin was suddenly between his fingers. He inspected it for one heart-thudding moment before he smiled. "He's wrong. Your eyes *are* that sparkly."

"Give it back." Mab huffed, heat crawling up her cheeks as she leaned forward to take it.

"Who drew it?" Ander had scooted closer to her, pressing his shin into hers where they'd both bent their legs to face each other on the couch. He had the drawing spread out across his thigh, his fingers brushing over the edges softly.

"I don't know. I just found it sitting on the bar the other night at cleanup." She took it when he handed it back. "It's stupid, I know. But I couldn't throw it away."

"It's not stupid." Leaning forward, Ander pressed his forehead to hers, making her meet his gaze. There was a smile on his face, small and tentative but oh so soft. Gods, Mab loved him so much, sometimes it ached. "You have a secret admirer," he whispered, tone lilting with a tease.

"Shut up," Mab barked an embarrassed laugh and shoved him off. "I do not."

"You dooooo. Look how pretty they think you are! Oh, Mabbers, you did always have a soft spot for artists, didn't you? I'm going to figure out who this is, mark my words. And then I'll set you up, and you'll live happily ever after. That's what friends are for, after all."

Mab threw her head back and laughed again, letting the lightened mood wash over her as Ander babbled on about who her secret admirer could be.

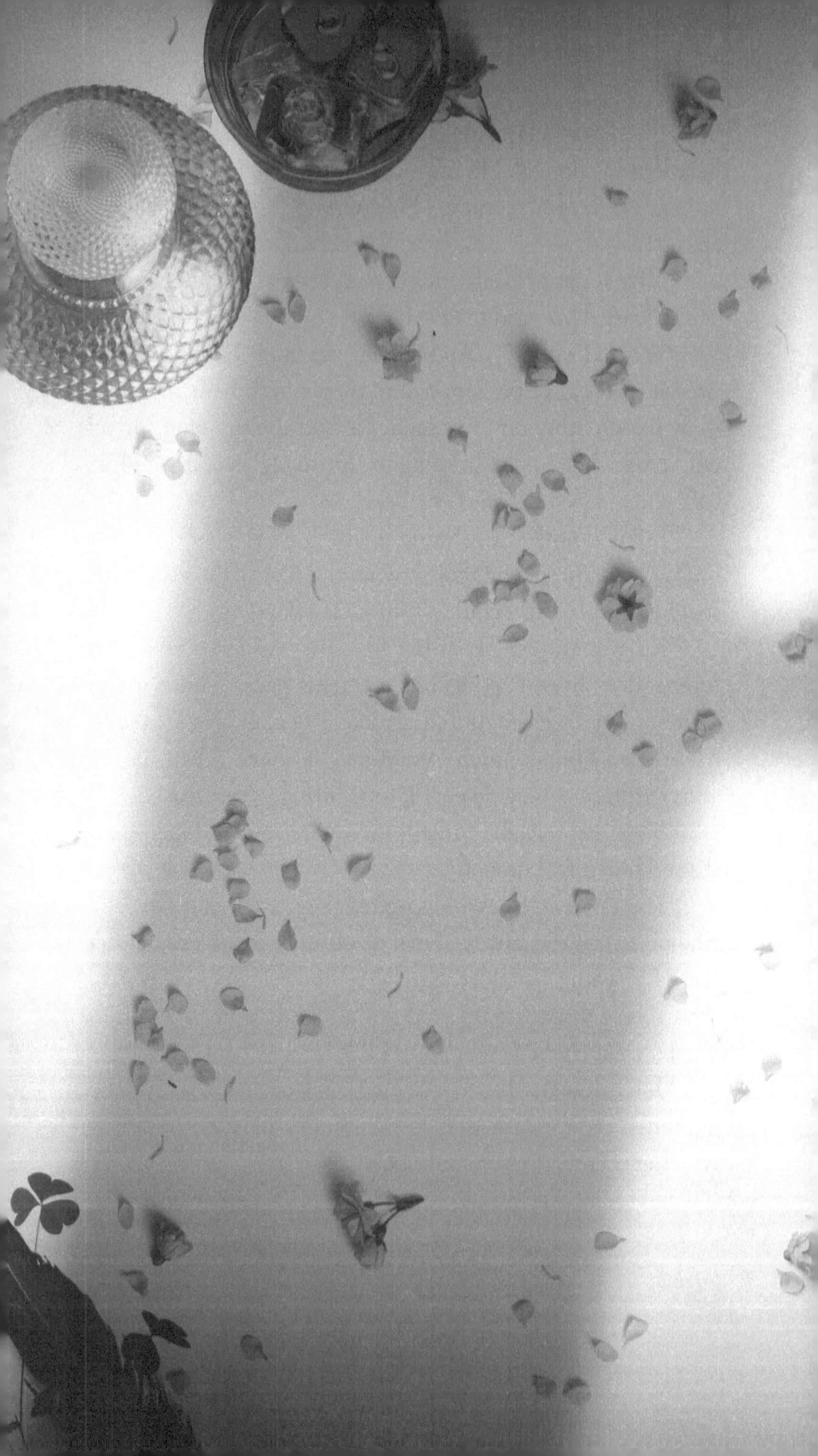

Chapter 20
Ander

The music was loud and overbearing. The bar top was sticky from spilled drinks and the heat from the pressed bodies oppressive. Ander hated Memento Mori. One of the in-betweens, it was a common Underworlder location—if one was interested in activities best hidden from the knowledge of the Sanctum. A doorway on the side of an old warehouse took you not into the warehouse but through a portal into the bar that sat in a disreputable part of Underworld.

It was, of course, the nightclub Enrique would frequent.

After asking around, it hadn't taken long for Ander to figure out from the other Underworlders where the scumbag would be.

As he stood at the bar, a chilled martini in his hand, Ander stared across the nightclub at the tall god, lounging with his knees spread wide in a VIP booth. A young female leaned into him on one side, and a young male on the other. It made Ander sick to think of either of them falling under that bastard's spell—but what was a muse to do?

Ander stared at Enrique as he lifted his glass to his lips and downed his drink in one gulp, then pulled the olives off the stick with his teeth, chewing quickly. He promised Mab that he'd only entice Enrique tonight. No going to any place where they would be alone, not until Indra came back with the brew to drug him.

He hadn't wanted to admit how much the sight of Enrique twisted him up inside, making his skin crawl and his innards feel sick. It was hard to breathe just thinking of being near him again.

But protecting Max was worth whatever nightmares would be dredged up tonight. Slamming the glass down on the sticky countertop, Ander straightened himself up and pushed through the crowd on the dance floor.

He'd dressed intentionally to impress and seduce. Skin-tight leather pants that left nothing to the imagination and a black leather vest that showed off his sculpted arms and upper chest and hinted at the abs beneath. There was certainly more flesh on his body than the last time Enrique had seen him naked, but he also took much better care of himself than he had when they'd first met.

Ander swayed his hips and donned a sassy look as he sauntered into the VIP booth where Enrique lounged, pulled the young gorgon off the bench, and quickly took his place. "You don't really expect these children to keep up with you, do you?" He purred the words and fought down bile.

His skin crawled as Enrique glanced at him in surprise, then took the opportunity to rake his gaze over every inch of his body. If Ander could've plucked those very eyes from his head, he would have. Instead, he forced himself to relax against the pleather seat and tossed his head back.

Enrique's eyes tightened with both suspicion and

unveiled lust. Even after all this time and a hundred years of punishment, he still wanted Ander. It wasn't purely about desire, Ander realized that—it was Enrique's need to possess and control. Ander was a prize that had gotten away. The god of punishment's hopes of one day ruling his own kingdom out from under the thumb of Hades.

"Princeling," Enrique cooed. He lifted his arm to sling it over the back of the bench behind Ander and leaned in a little more. "Why do I feel as if this is not an accident?"

"I feel so called out," Ander purred back. Gods, he couldn't feel any dirtier if he'd rolled in literal shit.

Enrique's eyes lit up. "So, this wasn't a coincidence. You sought me out."

Ander shrugged, playing coy. "I may have asked around . . . I may have not." He reached out, letting his fingers slide over Enqriue's thigh.

Enrique leaned in more. "Would you like to dance?"

Goosebumps of dread rose over Ander's skin where Enrique's breath washed over it. "I'd love nothing more," he purred.

Soon, his hand was in Enrique's, and he was being pulled abruptly to his feet and crashing into Enrique's chest. His scent washed over him, and Ander was instantly transported back to those nights in Acheron, trapped beneath Enrique's weight, pinned to the mattress of their bed, unable to escape the god's cruel, punishing desire.

Ander's hands lifted to Enrique's chest, and he pushed them apart, swaying his hips and making a show of turning slowly so that Enrique could see the way he moved. He took deep, steadying breaths as he did so, searching for his center of calm.

Mab had been right. He wasn't ready to do this. It was more than he could handle.

He squeezed his eyes shut as Enrique grabbed ahold of his hips and pulled his ass tight in against his groin, rocking into him hard enough that Ander could tell the god was definitely enjoying the feel of Ander against him. It took every ounce of self-control Ander had in him not to elbow him in the gut and set his clothes on fire. Instead, he pictured Max's adorable look of happiness when he'd surprised him with tacos.

Tipping his head back onto Enrique's shoulder, he gazed up at him through his lashes. "What are you doing Saturday night?"

"What did you have in mind?" Enrique's brow lifted.

"I'd love to show up at your place with food, liquor, and a sexy movie. Clothing optional."

"That sounds appetizing." Enrique then acted before Ander could react, dipping his head down to bite at his throat.

Ander winced as teeth pinched at his flesh, lips sucking at the skin and leaving a heavy mark there. It made him shudder, which Enrique took as a sign of pleasure, a groan leaving his throat as his hands glided down over Ander's thighs and his hips rocked into him.

He was going to be sick.

Ander spun around to face him, running his hands up over Enrique's chest. "Then it's a date." He leaned in close enough that their lips were almost brushing. "I'll see you at eight."

Ander moved like a zombie through Memento Mori, pushing the door open to transport him back to Miami. Once on the mortal streets, he snapped himself away to the middle of his own bathroom. With shaking hands, Ander tore off his clothes, kicking his shoes across the room hard enough that he knocked a set of bathroom oils over, sending them shattering to the floor.

Finally naked, Ander staggered into his shower stall, darkness threatening to cloud his vision as his chest heaved and he fought to take each breath, struggling against a vice grip around his lungs and a clawing, tearing feeling crawling up his back and around his shoulders.

When the first spray of hot water hit his skin, Ander barely felt it. Instead, he pressed his hands to the shower wall before him and bowed his head, letting the water course over him.

It was the first sob shaking his torso and scraping at the inside of his throat that let him know he was crying. Not even a hundred and fifty-six years was enough time to forget what had happened in his own personal hell. Being touched by Enrique again had been enough to bring it all back. Every agony. Every violation. Every wound inflicted on his body, mind, and heart.

Ander grabbed his loofa. Pouring body wash onto it, he began to scrub at his body, trying to scour away every last trace of Enrique. It wasn't enough, not even after he'd washed until his skin was red and the water in his shower had run cold.

Unable to find the energy to do it himself, he snapped his fingers and deposited himself on his bed, towel around his head and a silk robe around his body.

He needed . . . someone. Something. *Anything* to take his mind off the trauma path it wanted him to go back down.

Using magic to locate his cell phone, Ander opened his favorites and stared at the names on his list. He couldn't call Mab. She'd only tell him she'd told him so. He didn't want her to see just how badly this had affected him. Mab wouldn't let him finish this if she knew.

His thumb hit Max's name, opening up his contact information. Not letting himself second-guess his decision, he pressed the Call button.

"Ander! Hey!" Max sounded happy on the other end.

"Hey . . ."

"What are you up to?"

"Can you . . . come over?" he asked softly, voice rough as tears threatened at the back of his throat.

Max must have heard it in his tone because his own became gentler. "Ander, are you okay?"

"I just need some company."

"I'll be right there." He didn't say goodbye, he just hung up, and Ander could only assume it was because Max was already on his way out the door and headed over.

Ander found the will to pull himself from bed. He hauled the towel off his head, plucked Monnie up from her position on the pillow, and padded into his living room. Ander set the tiny dog down on the couch and moved to the wet bar on the side of the room to mix himself a stiff martini, extra dirty. After guzzling it down, he mixed another one.

He didn't want to be drunk when Max arrived, but he definitely needed to be buzzed. There had to be a way to wash the feel of Enrique's filth off him before his sweet ignis got here.

He had expected to hear his buzzer sound, so was surprised when a knock sounded on his patio door instead. Spinning to look out onto his balcony, Ander found Max standing there, wings still slightly unfurled and his hair mussed by the wind, waiting to be let in.

He had flown.

"Hey," Ander rasped as he slid the patio door open.

Max didn't miss a beat. Ander was soon swept up into his arms and carried down the hall to his bedroom.

"Wh-what are you doing?" he squawked.

"By the look on your face, I can tell you just need to be cuddled and loved on. There's no better place for that than curled up in your bed." Ever so gently, he laid Ander back down on his tussled bedding. "Is there anything you need before I climb in there with you?"

Ander shook his head, staring up at the broad-shouldered ignis. Who was this glorious creature that had come into his life so suddenly?

Max kicked off his loafers and climbed in alongside him. Moving to lay on his back, he then slipped an arm under Ander and pulled him in to his side. Ander went willingly. Resting his head on Max's chest, he let himself relax finally, the heat coming off his body starting to sooth him.

The feel of fingers playing through his damp hair had Ander's eyes closing, and he settled into the comfort that was being offered to him.

"Did you want to talk about what happened tonight?'

Ander shrugged, feeling the tightness in his throat once more.

"Does it have anything to do with the hickey on your throat?" Max's voice was soft but strained.

Ander swallowed roughly, biting at his lip. *Damn you, Enrique, you capital prick.*

"You don't . . . You don't have to tell me. But . . ." He paused, and Ander felt his chest rise with a deep breath beneath his cheek. "You should know, I'm not seeing anyone else but you, and I don't want to. I was kind of hoping that—"

Ander propped himself up quickly on his elbow to cut Max off before he could continue. "It's not like that!" He huffed, hating that the rat bastard had put him in this situation. "I had a run-in with my ex unexpectedly, and he got handsy, and before I could stop him, he tried to lay claim on me like the old days and bit me."

Max frowned. "Your abusive ex, Enrique?"

Ander nodded a little.

"Are you still in love with him?" There was a little pinched frown line forming between Max's brows.

"*Gods, no!* I hate every cell in his body. I wanted to light him on fire tonight. It's why I'm such a mess right now. Every part of me is rejecting his very presence near me. I can't wipe it away. Nothing I do will—"

Max silenced him with a tender kiss to his forehead, and then one to his nose, both of his cheeks, and then his chin.

Seeing that Ander had stopped speaking, Max seemed to take this as a cue to continue. He lifted one of Ander's hands up and began to kiss his fingertips one by one by one. Then his palm, the inside of his wrist, and up his arm to his elbow. Shivers and tingles of pleasure followed in his wake.

"Is this helping?" he asked softly.

Ander could only nod.

Max released his hand, but only so that he could gently grip Ander's jaw and tilt his head to the side. The ignis then pressed his lips tenderly to the bruise on his throat and left a new touch there.

Ander's eyes slid shut as he relished the feel of Max's lips washing him clean. Feeling more content now, he gazed down at the male so sweetly looking back up at him. "Thank you." He pressed a quick kiss to Max's lips and laid his head back down on his chest, snuggling in. "I'm not seeing anyone else . . . Just so that we're clear. And I don't intend to either. Just you."

Ander wasn't sure when he had settled on that, if it was just now or if he had been feeling that way all along. But despite his tendency of bed-hopping, Ander had no desire to be in anyone else's arms but Max's.

He didn't have to look up at Max to know that he was beaming at this. "I'm very happy to hear that." His strong arms tightened around Ander, then his fingers began to brush slowly up and down his back.

"And thank you for coming to my rescue again." How many times could he call him before Max decided Ander was too much work? *I am too much work.*

"It's my pleasure." Max kissed his forehead. "I want you to call me whenever you need me. Or . . . just whenever you feel like it."

Ander tipped his head back a little to look up at the younger male and saw that he was blushing. "You're adorable."

Max blushed even more. "No, you are."

Ander rolled his eyes. "No one could be as cute as you."

"Take that back."

"Why?"

"Because, have you seen yourself?!"

"Excuse me." Ander scoffed. "I'll have you know, I'm sexy."

"Oh, you absolutely are." Max's blush turned into a flush as he peered down at him, the hand on his back traveling downward and stopping just before his bottom. "But you're also adorable."

"Am not."

"Are too."

"Am—" Max silenced his argument with a kiss, forcing his lips open to explore the ready welcomeness of his mouth. Ander groaned as their tongues tangled, and Max's fingers pressed more firmly into the flesh of his lower back.

When Max pulled away, Ander was panting and desperately didn't want him to stop.

"Should we watch a movie?"

Ander just blinked up at him. How could his thoughts move so quickly to a movie when they'd just shared a kiss that had rocked Ander's world? Did it not affect Max as much as it did him? Was he sure that he could feel emotions the same way everyone else did? What if this amare bond *was* all one-sided? Max hadn't ever mentioned feeling the tug of it, and yet Ander's chest felt ablaze with the bond, desperate to connect.

He blinked as Max reached out to tap his nose. "I can see that you're thinking, and whatever you're thinking is taking you down a bad road. So I'm going to say yes to a movie." He reached over to the nightstand and grabbed the remote for the TV on the opposite side of the room. Without asking, he opened up Ander's streaming app and searched for *Lilo & Stitch*.

Ander stared at the screen, then back at Max. "This is my favorite . . . How did you know?"

"You made a Lilo reference about Nox when we first met."

"I am quite positive I did not mention Lilo when you and Quin showed up at the bar."

"No, not then. I mean when we *first* met, outside of Element 79."

Ander blinked, shock ricocheting through him. "What? How do you remember that?"

"How can you think I would ever forget a moment of meeting someone like you? You were amazing." The blush was back. "And the most unbelievably beautiful man I had ever seen."

It was Ander's turn to blush as he brimmed with something akin to sheer joy. He needed to watch himself; it would be far too easy to tumble head over heels and lose himself entirely to Maximus Schields. "I think I'm a little bit obsessed with you."

Max chuckled and pulled Ander back down to his chest. "Shh, watch the movie." But he was smiling a big, endearing smile as he stared at the flat-screen.

With something that felt a lot like contentment, Ander settled in against Max's chest and let himself just absorb the gentle comfort that was coming from his heat, his fingers running up and down his back, and the sheer presence of the other male beside him.

Around the halfway point of the movie, it seemed entirely natural to close his eyes and let himself drift off to sleep. He felt safe with Max beside him. Nothing was going to touch him.

When he woke the next morning, it was far too early. The sun wasn't even up, and Ander couldn't quite figure out why he was awake. Then he heard the gentle rustle of someone walking around the room. Rolling over, he found Max coming back to the bed from the washroom.

"You stayed all night?" he asked, surprise washing through him.

"Of course I did, you needed me."

Ander's throat felt tight with an emotion he didn't really wish to acknowledge. "You're amazing."

"So are you." Max rested a knee on the bed so that he could lean over on his hands and press a kiss to Ander's forehead.

"Oh gods, no I'm not. My hair must be a disaster, and I

don't have any makeup on. I don't know how you're even looking at me right now."

Frowning, Max reached up to grasp his chin and tilt Ander's head up so that he was forced to meet his gaze. "Ander Ruin, you are gorgeous. In any form that you come in. Never let me hear you put yourself down again."

Ander gazed up at him, surprised. "Yes, sir," he whispered.

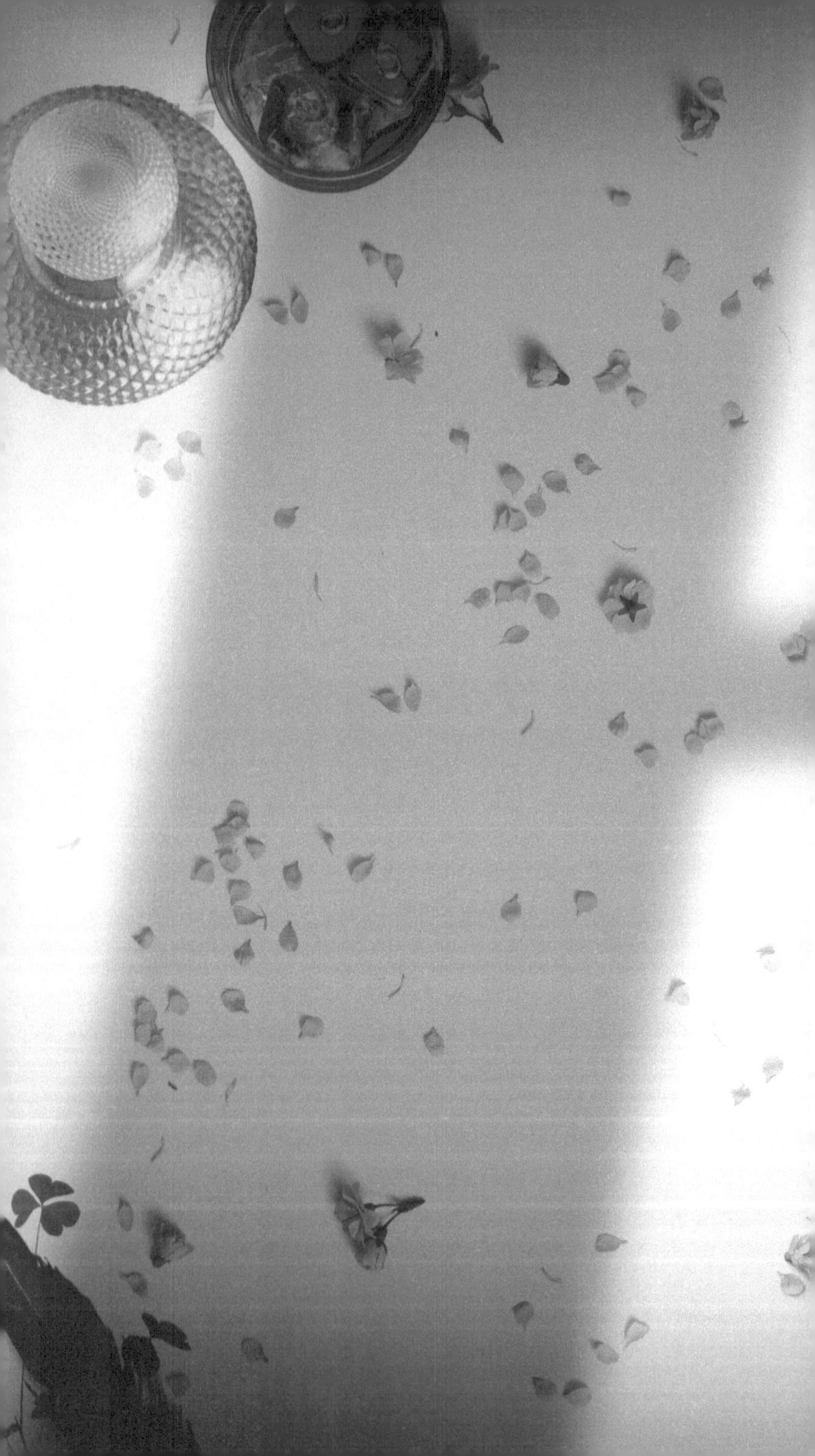

Chapter 21
Max

"Aren't those the same clothes you were wearing last night?" Nash asked. He had paused in the doorway to Max's office, his hand halfway to stuffing the last half of a strawberry Pop-Tart into his mouth.

"And what if they are?" Max didn't look up from the file he was scrolling through to see the wide-eyed look his brother was giving him. He didn't need to; he could imagine it perfectly. It was the same expression Nash had given him when he found out Max wasn't a virgin. He'd taken a particularly vindictive pleasure in keeping the knowledge of his first sexual encounter to himself—and Quin—for a while after it happened. Up until Nash made some joke about Max dying a virgin. Good times.

"Oooh, did you sneak out last night?" Nash lowered his hand, the Pop-Tart forgotten as he skipped into Max's office.

Studiously ignoring Nash, Max flipped to the next page in the report on the buildings Nox had shown them the previous day. He had yet to look at the report on the missing ignis. He didn't think he was ready for it yet, not mentally.

Maybe if he just stayed quiet long enough, Nash would get bored and go away.

"Noxie-kins! You have to see this! Our big bro is blushing!" Nash crowed, leaning back in his chair to put his feet up on Max's desk.

There was a muscle in Max's eyebrow that he hadn't even known existed until Nash learned to talk all those years ago, and it had taken to twitching periodically when his brother was being particularly annoying. Like right now. "I'm not blushing!"

"You are! Is this because of your boyfriend? Noxie-kins! I think Max got some last night!"

"He did?" Nox stuck her head in, her face painted in delight, brows drawn up and mouth twisted into a smile. "How big is he? We've been taking bets."

Max choked on his own spit, coughing hard into a closed fist before he let out a strangled, "Excuse *you*?!"

"Nox thinks he's big. She says it's all in the swagger." Nash shrugged, finally stuffing the last half of his Pop-Tart into his mouth so he could talk around it obnoxiously. "I've seen his toy stash, I think he's compensating."

"We didn't . . . we didn't *do* that." Grabbing the bottle of water from the corner of his desk, Max tried to wash down the tickle in his throat, but all it did was make him feel like he was drowning and set him to coughing again.

"Uh-huh. Sure. That's why you're freaking out, right?" Nash rubbed the crumbs from his breakfast onto his pants.

"Don't you two have *work* to do?" Max coughed into the elbow of his sweater.

"Oh. Yeah, about that," Nox said, dropping into the chair next to Nash and blessedly changing the subject. "We narrowed the list down a bit."

Nash leaned forward to grab the tablet from in front of

Max and tapped on it for a couple of seconds before passing it back. "Based on the activity of these docks and the manifests of the ships coming in and out, I'm down to two locations. If you give me another couple of hours, I can maybe pick one."

"Are you sure about these?" Max asked, looking down at the list of locations. They weren't close together, so they would need two separate teams. He'd have to put Quin in charge of one while he took the other. And if they were wrong about this, they'd be burned for every other location Hugman had his name on.

"I'm positive. He meets with normies at the other locales, likely doing his used car salesman shtick. But these places are only active at night, and it doesn't look like Hugman ever visits them personally. Probably to distance himself from what's going on, or to keep from leaving any trace evidence. He's not stupid. Scummy, but not stupid." Nash drummed his fingers on the wood of Max's desk. "I've got a couple other things I want to look at to help narrow it down further, but we should have it down to one by the time it's dark enough to raid."

"What's your recommendation?" Max set the tablet on the desk again, his fingers steepling to tap at his lower lip.

"Nox?" Nash tilted his head to his twin, a smile curling up his lips.

"We think you should have two teams but focus the majority of your forces on one warehouse and send a smaller force to the other, just in case." Nox brushed a bit of hair back behind her ear. "We looked at the roster for who you planned to take. You should have more than plenty ignis for that."

"All right." Max sat back in his chair to give the twins a wide smile. "Good work, you two. Now get back to it."

The twins nodded and rose from their chairs, but just before they left, Nash turned back to ask, "You really didn't get any last night?"

Grabbing the stress ball from his desk, Max chucked it at Nash, who squawked and disappeared through the door just as the ball smacked against the wall beside the doorframe.

The twins had really done good work with this one, Max had to give them that. Not that they didn't always, but this was of particular note. They'd managed to determine when there would be a shift change and what types of inanimi Hugman was using to guard the facility. All of that meant the ignis were prepared with the right dosage of tranquilizers for their size, and that the guards were distracted, making taking them down and getting inside fairly straightforward.

It was once they had broken the door down that things went off the rails.

The door swung heavily on its hinges, banging against the wall to one side so loudly that there wasn't a snowball's chance in hell that everyone in the warehouse didn't know they were there. And what followed was pure, headache-inducing chaos.

While the twins may have prepared them for the minotaurs on the outside of the warehouse, there was no way for them to know about the demogorgons stationed on the inside. Well-trained demogorgons, who reacted to the intrusion immediately, making the element of surprise practically null.

They could only fit two ignis through the door at a time, and Max and Quin went first. The demogorgons on either side slashed out at them with large fangs and dripping claws. Max stumbled back, nearly losing his footing on the step down into the warehouse and only just righting himself with his wings acting as a counter-balance. Metal sliced through the air as he advanced on the demogorgon, pushing the inanimi away from the entrance to allow others of his team through the door.

Another swipe of claws that dripped, like they'd been dipped in something, tore through his shirt, cutting into the skin of his abdomen and making him hiss. Max spun, feet taking them farther into the open space of the warehouse. Moving onto his toes, Max leaped into the air, away from the tables and cages kept at the center of everything, hoping to keep the innocents safe from the battle.

The demogorgon screeched and flung themself at Max, grabbing onto his ankles and taking him tumbling to the ground in a roll that knocked over everything in their wake. Max just prayed that there wasn't anyone in the way as he grabbed ahold of the demogorgon's shoulders and pinned the thrashing creature to the ground. He'd lost his daggers along the way but managed to pull one of the tranquilizer darts from the pouch on his waist and jab the demogorgon in the neck with it. The creature screeched, teeth sinking into Max's forearm before they finally lost consciousness, and Max could take a breath. He rolled the inanimi over onto their stomach and cuffed them.

The battle was far from finished, however, and Max was quickly on his feet again, spinning to find his team dispatching the remainder of the guards and some of the staff, while one of the workers—or maybe they were considered scientists? They *were* in white lab coats—

shoved a number of things into a duffle bag and started running for the door. Jumping back into the fray, Max made his way through the flurry of battle to catch the person in the lab coat just as they reached one of the back doors. He grabbed them by the wrist, spinning them around to get a good look at the woman's face just before she lifted a spray bottle of some kind and misted something into his face.

Max had enough time to register that it was probably not the best idea to inhale whatever it was but not nearly enough to hold his breath and prevent the inevitable disaster. He wobbled on his feet but didn't let go of her wrist, even as she sprayed more at him. Reaching for the cuffs, he got them on her, knocking the bottle from her hand and slamming her back against the wall, preventing her from escaping. She went down with a hard thud and a hiss, and Max pulled back, his chest heaving as the world began to lose focus, the sounds of the battle muffled.

There was a warm weight on his shoulder suddenly, and Quin was at his side, saying something that he couldn't quite make out before leading Max to the wall to sit down. When he looked out over the open space, he saw that the battle was done. The perpetrators had all been cuffed and set against the wall, where armed ignis guarded them while others from his team worked to free the trapped mermaids.

"I need to get him back to the sanctuary," Quin said, his voice still muffled, like it was coming through cotton, but making more sense now than it had a few minutes ago. He tapped on something in his ear, mouth pinching in frustration. Oh! It was his comm. He must have been talking to the twins. "No. You cannot play with him while he's drugged."

The twins must have said something else in reply

because Quin snorted—actually snorted!—and rolled his eyes.

"I'm taking him home. I'll get him into the sauna, and he should be fine." Quin tapped his ear again, effectively shutting down any further protests before he came to squat in front of Max, his tone soft as he asked, "How are you feeling?"

Max blinked up at him a moment, trying to get his hazy mind to really focus on the question. How *was* he feeling? "Floaty," he decided after what must have been an embarrassingly long time, because Quin had settled onto his bottom across from Max to wait him out.

"I see." Quin frowned, and Max leaned forward to press the tip of his finger into the wrinkle in between his eyebrows, trying to smooth it out. "What are you doing?"

"You're gonna get wrinkles that way." Max snickered, then thought about what he'd said again and started laughing harder. A full-belly laugh that made his sides ache. He didn't know how long he sat there laughing at himself, but when he opened his eyes again, rubbing the burn of tears from them, Quin was gone. Panic gripped Max's chest for a moment, but then his brother was back, and he relaxed. "Where'd you go?"

"Just to see what she sprayed you with. Looks like it was some altered form of Mermaid's Lament. The twins should be able to tell us more once they get this stuff back to the lab, but until then, I'm going to take you home. Papa is there, he'll look after you. Is that okay?"

Quin was so good. How was he so good? He'd had it so hard for so long, but still he'd come out the gentlest person Max knew. Kind in a way Max didn't think he'd have been able to be under the same circumstances. A tiny miracle in the scope of all the awful that surrounded them.

"Max. Did you hear me? I asked if that was okay?"

"Huh?" Max sniffled, scrubbing at his nose. When had he started crying? Gods, he was a mess. Quin shouldn't have to deal with this. He had more important things to handle.

"I'm going to take you home to Papa, and he's going to get you into the sauna, then into bed. Is that okay?"

"But what about the raid?" He pushed himself to his feet, feeling like he was standing on a foam mattress or a trampoline, the ground giving beneath him. Quin reached for him, looping one of Max's arms over his shoulders.

"You're in no shape to finish up here. I've got it." Quin helped him outside, where a van waited by the curb. The fresh air cleared away some of the misery that clung to the insides of Max's skull, and he relaxed against his brother. "Easy, don't go boneless on me yet. We still have to get you into the sauna to try to sweat this stuff out of you."

Max nodded sagely, but a giggle was crawling up his throat, a wild, rabid thing threatening to make him into a childish mess. Thank the gods Quin got him into the van and on the road before it finally reached the back of his throat. Then he was laughing at anything and everything before pulling his phone from his pocket to text Ander.

"Do you really think that's a good idea?" Quin asked from the driver's seat, which was just a bench stretched across the front of the van to make room for his wings, his eyes flicking from the road to give Max a wary look.

"Yu-*p*!" Max popped the p, and that set him to giggling again, just long enough for his eyes to blur with tears and for them to pull up outside of the Schields' family home. He sent a quick text off to Ander as Quin struggled out of his seat belt.

I mess u. clome see me. I lbehaomb he;chdelj

He frowned down at the text, his nose wrinkled. What did that even mean?

"Q, can you text Ander for me? Tell him I love him and I want to see him later." Max pouted up at Quin as he worked to get his seatbelt undone and pull Max from the car.

"I'm not doing that."

"But why noooooot?" Max pouted more, poking his lower lip out in a way that was uncomfortable as well as ridiculous.

"Because you're high," Quin huffed, all but carrying Max toward the door where Papa was already waiting, his face pinched in worry.

Max thought about his words for a moment, letting Quin and Papa push and pull him down the hall to the in-home sauna that Papa had added when they first adopted an ignis. He had been lucky and hadn't *had* to use it since he'd been sick as a baby, but Quin had spent a fair amount of time in there when he'd come home from Syria, sweating out all of the toxins. "So?"

"So, what?" Quin asked, seeming to have lost the thread of the conversation as he pulled Max's ripped shirt from his torso. "Make sure he treats this after he showers. Hopefully the heat will burn everything out of him, but if it doesn't—"

"I know how to take care of a sick ignis, Quin. Don't worry. You get back to the raid and let me handle your brother." Zeke sighed, his hands gentle as he untied Max's boots and helped him step out of them.

"So what if I'm high? Why can't you tell him I love him

and he should come see me?" Max grumbled, wobbling a little when Zeke went for his socks next.

Quin stopped where he'd been reaching for a towel to eye Max wearily, his lips pursed. After considering his brother for a moment, Quin turned to their Papa and said, "And don't let him have his phone until he's sobered up."

"What?!" Max squawked but was ignored as Quin passed the device off to Zeke, although Max wasn't sure how he'd gotten it in the first place.

"Aye, aye, captain." Zeke gave a little salute and tucked Max's phone into his back pocket before Quin considered the matter settled and left Zeke to wrangle a grumpy Max into the sauna.

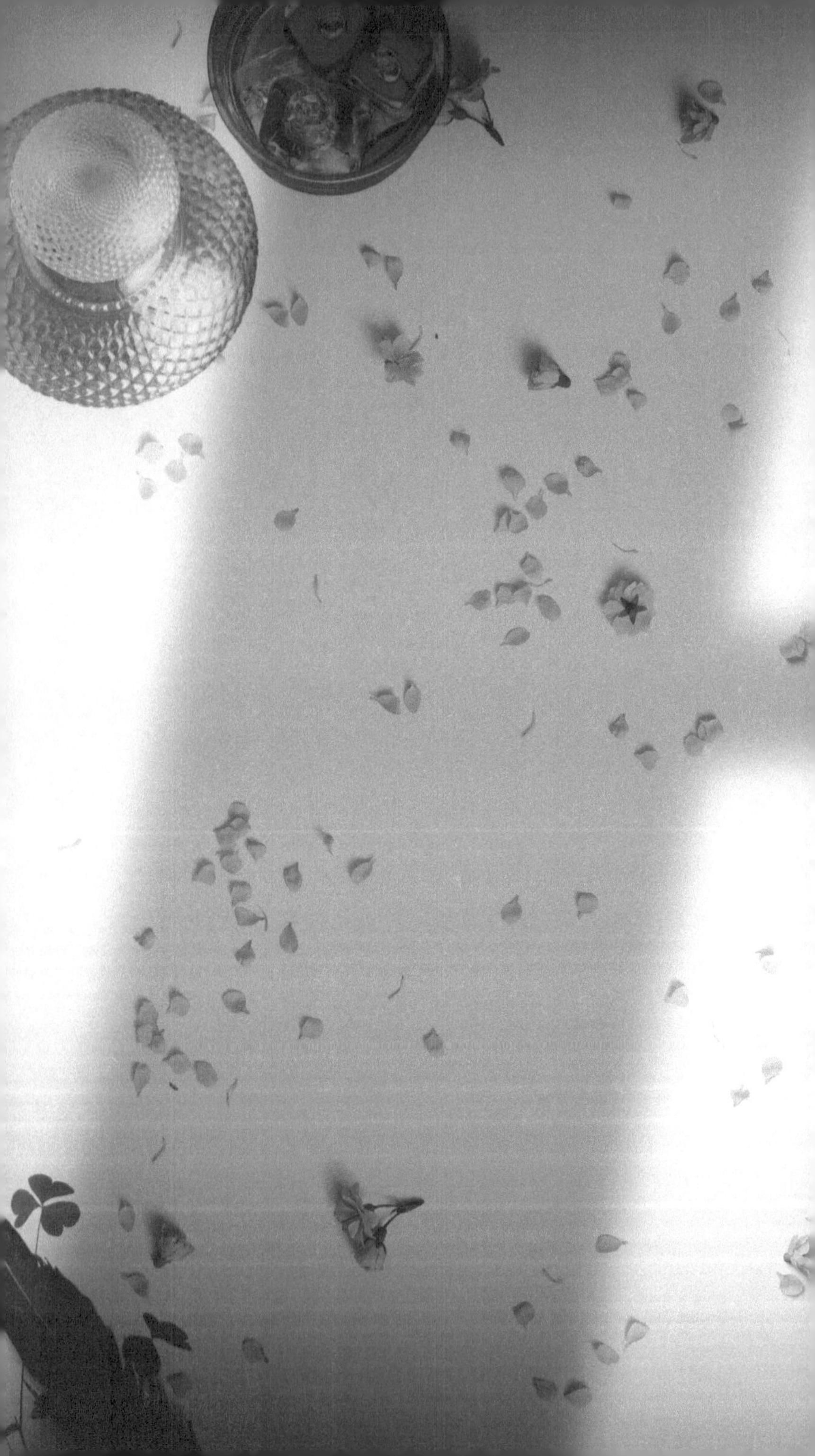

Chapter 22
Ander

Ander stared up at the Burgeois Estate condos, his heart hammering loudly in his ears and his legs feeling weak.

He should have just snapped himself into the penthouse apartment without giving himself the time to think or to back out. Yet he hadn't, and here he stood, dreading the entire evening to come and hating how vulnerable he felt.

Everything with Enrique had been over two lifetimes ago, but the other night in the bar, as his hands had gripped onto his hips and the god had pulled Ander back into him, it felt like all that time and healing had melted away. Ander hated how weak that made him feel.

Filled with nervous energy and dread, he looked down at himself checking his outfit for the hundredth time. He wore a red tank top with thin spaghetti straps and such a low scooped neck that it did nothing to hide his nipples and upper chest. It flowed loose around his torso, and was longer in the back and higher in the front, showing off a hint of abs. As well as the sparkling diamond hanging in his belly button.

Snug black jeans hung low on his hips, with a snakeskin leather belt through its loops. The shiny belt buckle attached read "sex kitten". Army-style leather boots covered his feet, helping him to feel more secure in his ability to flee. The finishing touch to the outfit, besides some cat-eye makeup and a series of bangles on his wrists, was a gold chain around his neck that a small gold vial dangled from. It looked like the kind of thing you might place a hidden note in, or someone's ashes. Ander had poured the potion from Indra into it.

And when he had the chance, he was going to drug the fuck out of Enrique, steal the feathers off his desk, and get the hell out of there.

Squaring his shoulders, the half-muse made his way into the lobby, gave his name to the bellman, and was let into the elevator. Steadying his breathing as he rode the lift up, Ander masked his features, hiding any fear behind a cool exterior of seduction.

When he first met Enrique, Ander had let himself be swept away by his charm and magnetism. Let Enrique run the relationship. He never had to use any of his tactics on the god. Now, it was time to show him what it was truly like to be the center of Ander's attention and seduce the hell out of him.

When the elevator doors dinged open, Ander slipped into the foyer of Enrique's condo, a bottle of ambrosia dangling from his fingertips.

"Hoooney, I'm hooome," he called out.

"In my office," Enrique called back.

Convenient. Ander strolled across the foyer and into the office, forcing his eyes not to dart up to the pair of wings mounted on the wall. Instead, he kept his air entirely casual and uncaring. He was aloof. He was careless. He was here to get fucked in more ways than one.

"I didn't think drug dealers needed to do paperwork until eight o'clock at night . . ." Ander teased, sashaying across the room to lean one hip on the edge of the desk, his arm resting on his thigh.

Enrique's eyes raked him over thoroughly, just as they had in the club. Heat and longing filled his gaze, and he bit down on his lip before he smirked and leaned back in his chair. "While it's quaint you think I would be so low-tier as to classify myself as a drug dealer, I am almost always working."

"Well then, how lucky for you I am here and ready to force you to take a break." Ander lifted his hand, rolling it over in the air. When his palm came up, there were two tumblers clutched in it. "Shall I pour us one?" He lifted up the bottle of ambrosia.

"Yes, pour away." Enrique closed his laptop and pushed his chair away from the desk a little. He was dressed in a pair of dark gray dress slacks and a black dress shirt. The sleeves were rolled up to his elbows and the top two buttons undone at his throat. It was a dom look if Ander'd ever seen one, but where once it would have turned his knees to jelly, it now only made his stomach knot with disgust.

Ander knew all too well just what sort of dom Enrique was, and it was not the loving after-care type.

Setting the tumblers down on the desktop, Ander uncorked the bottle of ambrosia he'd bought in Olympia and poured both of them a healthy share. The dark amber liquid swirled in the glasses, glittering with speckles of gold dust. Offering Enrique one of the glasses, Ander then picked up his own. "To us, and rekindling old sparks."

He would *not* vomit all over the Persian rug beneath his feet.

Their tumblers clinked together in celebration, and both took a healthy swallow of the strong alcohol that tasted as sweet as honey but could knock an elephant on its ass. It was also one of the few things that could properly get a god drunk.

"So, what *was* keeping you working so late?"

"Does it matter?" Enrique took another drink, finishing off his glass and reaching for the bottle to top himself up. He then stood and moved in so that he towered over Ander. "I'm not working now, and my attention is fully on you. That's what you wanted, wasn't it?"

"Absolutely." Ander took another drink of his own to wash down the acidic bile burning at the back of his throat.

He kept himself pliant as Enrique grasped an elbow and pulled him off the edge of the desk. "I believe you said something about clothing being optional tonight?" He cooed the words, desire brimming in his eyes.

Ander licked his lips that had gone dry and swallowed. He could do this.

"I don't just get naked at the drop of a hat—not anymore, at least. Why don't you head out there into the middle of the room and show me what I've been missing out on this last century or so?" He quirked a brow up at him.

"Like a strip show?" Enrique looked like he'd fallen somewhere between intrigued and insulted.

"Unless you don't think you have anything to show me? Maybe I should go find someone else who—" Enrique shut him up by hauling him in by the hip and smashing his lips against Ander's.

Every muscle within Ander tightened in refusal. His heart lurched wildly against his sternum, and his hands raised to shove him away. Instead, he pressed his hands to Enrique's chest and let them sit there, feeling the planes of muscles that had once been so familiar.

The kiss was hard and punishing. Ander wanted to bite Enrique's tongue out of his mouth and spit it at his feet.

Pulling back, Enrique murmured, "That's just a small reminder." He then pulled away and walked around the desk.

Shuddering in revulsion, Ander took the moment to unscrew the vial from his necklace and pour the potion into Enrique's tumbler. He then topped his glass up with more ambrosia and spun around to drop down into Enrique's chair and watch him.

"Please do make it worth my while." He snapped his fingers, and the sound system on the far wall began to play a deep, sexual tune.

Ander sat there, sipping his drink while Enrique began to strip for him, slowly taking off his shirt and tossing it aside. His torso was still as sculpted as it had been before. His biceps thick and strong. The sharp lines over his hips traced down to disappear beneath the waistband of his pants.

He was as beautiful and sexual as he'd ever been. Still a truly fine specimen of male.

And he left Ander absolutely cold.

"You know what . . . This side of the desk is awfully lonely." Ander stood up, grabbing Enrique's drink and carrying it over to him. "I'd rather help you get naked than just watch."

Enrique took the glass. "Why don't you even the score?" He reached out to lift up Ander's tank top a little, then slid his hand around Ander's side to his back, his fingers a hot brand on his skin.

Pulling Ander in against him, Enrique sipped from his drink, then met Ander's gaze

His heart hammered in his throat. Could Enrique tell that there was something else in the glass besides just ambrosia? Would he get enough of the potion into him for it to have an effect?

"I can do that," he purred, then pulled away. Setting down his own glass, Ander began to dance to the music, moving slowly and sensually. If there was one thing he'd learned to do well, it was how to move his body in the most sexual of ways. Turning to face Enrique once more, he began to lift the tank top over himself as he danced but didn't take it off. Not yet. He would taunt and tease and hopefully make Enrique's mouth go dry so that he needed all of that drink to even speak.

It seemed to work because as Enrique watched, his eyes following every sway of Ander's hips and every brush of his hand to expose flesh, he sipped absently at his drink.

How long would it take to have an effect on him? Ander hadn't thought to ask Indra just how long he'd have to wait until Enrique would pass out.

"Enough teasing." Enrique downed his drink, tossing the glass across the room and closing the distance between them. His hands were on Ander's hips before he could think, then he was being lifted off his feet and dropped ungraciously down onto the desk.

Enrique's lips were on his once more, and his hands tore the tank top down the middle, pulling it roughly from his body.

Everything inside Ander froze. Memories and horrors washed over him, transplanting him back to a time when he was helpless to fight back. Trapped and too afraid to do anything to stand up for himself. Believing that he deserved every vile thing that was done to him.

Enrique had shoved him down to lay back on the desk and was working on his pants before Ander remembered that he wasn't helpless. That he wasn't trapped in this situation, and he didn't have to take any more of Enrique's abuse. Never. Ever. Again.

"No!" Placing his hands on Enrique's shoulders, he shoved him back, away from him.

"Excuse me?" Enrique snarled as he stumbled back, his eyes blinking as the potion clearly began to work on him. "This is what you came here for, bitch. You're not going to push me away this time."

Enrique was on him once again, tearing at his clothes and trying to take hold of his wrists.

Ander roared, rage building inside of him for the trusting man he had once been, who'd allowed himself to be broken and torn asunder by this god. Kicking out at him, Ander blasted him with a wave of magic. As Enrique staggered back again, Ander swung his fist without thinking and punched the other male squarely in the face. Gold blood spurted everywhere, coating Enrique's face and glistening on Ander's knuckles.

They both stared at each other in shock for a moment, neither quite certain of what had just happened.

Then Enrique made a feral noise of fury and bunched his shoulders in preparation for attack, and in the same breath, Ander lifted his hand to snap his fingers, teleporting him out of Enrique's condo and safely onto the streets of Miami, miles away.

Panting harshly, he leaned over to rest his hands on his knees and vomited what little was in his stomach onto the pavement below him.

That had gone sublimely wrong.

Enrique hadn't become drunk enough to be contained.

Ander had been mauled.

And there had been no retrieval of feathers.

The only good that had come out of all of this was the knowledge that the potion Indra gave him made it possible for Ander to injure Enrique.

Body trembling and panic still coursing through him, Ander studied his bloody knuckles in the fading sunlight, focusing his mind on this impossibility rather than the ghost of Enrique's mouth and hands traveling over his body. Contemplated the likelihood of the potion working the same way should he try again rather than the darkness threatening to blacken his vision or the chill seeping into his spirit, pulling him down into a fresh pit of self-loathing.

Unworthy. Tainted. Needy. Damaged.

Ander took a deep breath, shutting his eyes and wishing he hadn't. Enrique's angry face swam before him, threatening to consume him once more.

Failure.

He'd failed Max. Failed the younglings. *Failed Ikari.*

Hot tears pricked at his eyelids, threatening to spill out. Not protecting himself was one thing, but why couldn't he protect those he cared about? Would he ever be of any use in this life?

Worthless.

His phone dinged, pulling him out of the spiral. Digging into his pants, Ander cursed when he saw the screen had been crushed by Enrique dropping him onto the desk's surface. Opening the message, a soft sob slipped out of him. Max. Drunk or somehow equally inebriated.

I mess u. clome see me. I lbehaomb
he;chdelj

Max wanted him to come see him. Sweet, adorable Max. Erotes had truly screwed him. Not because Maximus could not love, but because no matter how hard he tried, no matter what he did with his life, Ander could never in a million years deserve the ignis he'd been arrow-bound to. And it was a truth that would haunt him for all his days.

Swirling his hand before him, Ander snagged himself a bottle of vodka. Twisting the cap off and pinging it away, he tipped the bottle back and drank from it deeply. Perhaps he would walk and drink and do this until he was ready to take himself home.

He couldn't possibly take himself to visit Max in this state. Not with the grime of Enrique on his body and his favorite red tank top torn off, leaving him shirtless. He likely looked like a hot mess.

Ander walked and drank until the vodka bottle was three quarters empty. Eying the sloshing liquid as he swirled it around in front of his face, Ander decided he was ready to go home. The world at large felt topsy turvy, and if he didn't snap home soon, he'd wind up in a tree again.

"Time to go back where I belong," he rasped to the empty street around him. Snapping his fingers, Ander found himself suddenly in a bedroom he did not recognize.

The bed was large and incredibly comfortable looking, with more blankets than anyone living in Miami needed. All around him were a series of Disney souvenirs and a full wall of Mickey ears. Had he snapped into a child's room like some creep?

It was a shocked gasp that alerted him to the fact that he was not alone, and spinning on his heel, Ander found himself face to face with a shirtless Max, dressed only in a towel low on his hips.

"A-Ander?"

Uncontrollable giggles slipped out of Ander, and he lifted the hand holding the vodka bottle to his lips, trying to contain them.

Max stuttered something unintelligible, grabbed some clothing from his dresser, and quickly darted into the bathroom attached to his room.

"I wouldn't have peeked!" Ander shouted after him, giggling more until he was forced to drop down onto the edge of the bed lest he fall over.

Max returned shortly dressed in a pair of gray sweats and a white sleeveless shirt, looking sheepish as he toweled his hair dry. His wings were so white behind his back, they almost glowed. He truly was an angel. "What are you doing . . . *here*?" His eyes shifted toward the door anxiously.

"You told me to *clome* see you." Another giggle slid out of Ander, and then he sobered up a little, looking at Max. "You don't want me here. You didn't actually mean you wanted to see me tonight." Dread began to sweep over him, making his scalp tingle and goosebumps pop up on his arms. Wobbling to his feet, he held out the hand with the vodka bottle still clutched in it. "I'll go."

"Ander . . ."

"No, I'm sorry. I shouldn't be here," he said, slurring a little.

Max was before him, curling his fingers around his hand to stop him from snapping himself away. "That's not what I meant," he said softly.

Ander gazed up at him. "It seems like it is."

Instead of saying anything else, Max slid his arms around Ander and pulled him tenderly in against his chest, one of his strong hands angling Ander's head into just the right position so his cheek could nestle against him and his antlers wouldn't poke out an eye.

Ander's bottom lip trembled, and he shut his eyes against the room, which had become a little blurry. Being held by Max was so comforting and perfect. It was more than a failure such as he deserved.

"Just relax," Max murmured. His hand rubbed gently over Ander's bare back, soothing him.

Releasing a pent-up breath of anxiety, Ander melted into his frame, letting everything he'd been holding out. "I failed tonight," he rasped painfully.

"Failed what?"

"To keep my word." He'd promised Mab he would get in and get the feathers, and that he was the best one to do it. That he would be okay. But he wasn't okay.

Max was silent for a moment, then he pressed a kiss to Ander's temple. "Well . . . tomorrow is another day." His voice sounded a little strained, but his touch, his hold, remained gentle and tender. "Why don't you sit down again? We'll get your boots off, I'll give you a pair of pjs, and we'll cuddle up in bed?"

Ander lifted his head so he could look up at Max. "You don't want me to leave?"

"No." Max shook his head. "I don't want you to leave."

"Even though I'm such a mess and far too much drama?"

"Even though you're such a mess. But no one could be more drama than I'm used to." Max kissed his forehead.

Ander sighed once more and buried his face in Max's chest, arms clinging to him, just accepting this grace that he had not earned in any part of his lifetime. "You're the sweetest, most wonderful being alive," he breathed out.

Max laughed a little awkwardly "Okay, let's just get you sat down" then helped him to make his way safely down to the edge of the bed.

Once Ander was seated, Max kneeled and began unlacing his boots. Ander watched him with wide, amazed eyes, lifting the bottle of vodka to his lips once more. Max quickly grabbed that from him as well and set it aside.

"How about no more of that for tonight?"

Ander sighed and pouted. "You're as bad as Mab with your liquor limits." He thought about sticking his tongue out, but by the time he remembered how to do it, Max had pulled both of his boots off.

"Okay, I'm going to get you some pj bottoms. Do you think you can get into them on your own?" He crossed the room and pulled a pair of pants out of the dresser.

"Of course I can! I'm not a child, no matter what Mab says . . ." He stood up, and the world spun on its axis, making the floor tilt, and Ander had to compensate by leaning the other way, which only made everything spin and tip even more.

Max was at his side to catch him before he faceplanted. "So, that's a no . . ." He held the pants out to him. "Here, put these on, I'll hold you up." His eyes shifted up to the ceiling.

Taking the pants and beginning to undo his jeans, Ander giggled. "You're allowed to take a peek if *you* want."

Max blushed deeply. "Now doesn't seem the right time."

Ander sighed. "Fiiiine." Relying on Max's hands to keep him upright, he managed to kick his way out of his jeans then pull the cotton-polyester-spandex-blend pajama pants up over his hips. "You should invest in some silk bottoms," he announced.

Max's eyes shifted down carefully, and relief showed in his face when he saw that Ander was, indeed, dressed once more. "These are comfier and warmer." He spun Ander around and gave his bottom a soft little tap. "Into the bed."

Ander snickered, crawling over the bed to drop down into the fluffy covers and pillows. "Was that tap a promise of what's to come later?'

Max slid beneath the covers and began pulling them out from under Ander so that he could pull them over him instead. "Someday later."

Ander turned his head on the pillow to gaze over at him. "Promise?"

"Promise." Max leaned in and kissed his nose. "Want to watch my favorite movie this time?"

Ander nodded, scooting over so that he could tuck himself into Max's side as Max reached for the remotes on his nightstand and turned on the TV and DVD player. The menu for *Legally Blonde* came up.

"Was this just in your DVD player?"

"Yeah . . ."

Ander giggled. "How often do you watch it?"

"Shhh . . . the movie is starting," he said, avoiding the question.

A smile on his lips, Ander snuggled into the warm ignis even more. "I apologize if my antlers poke you in the face," he murmured sleepily.

"You're fine. Don't worry."

"Mmm, 'kay."

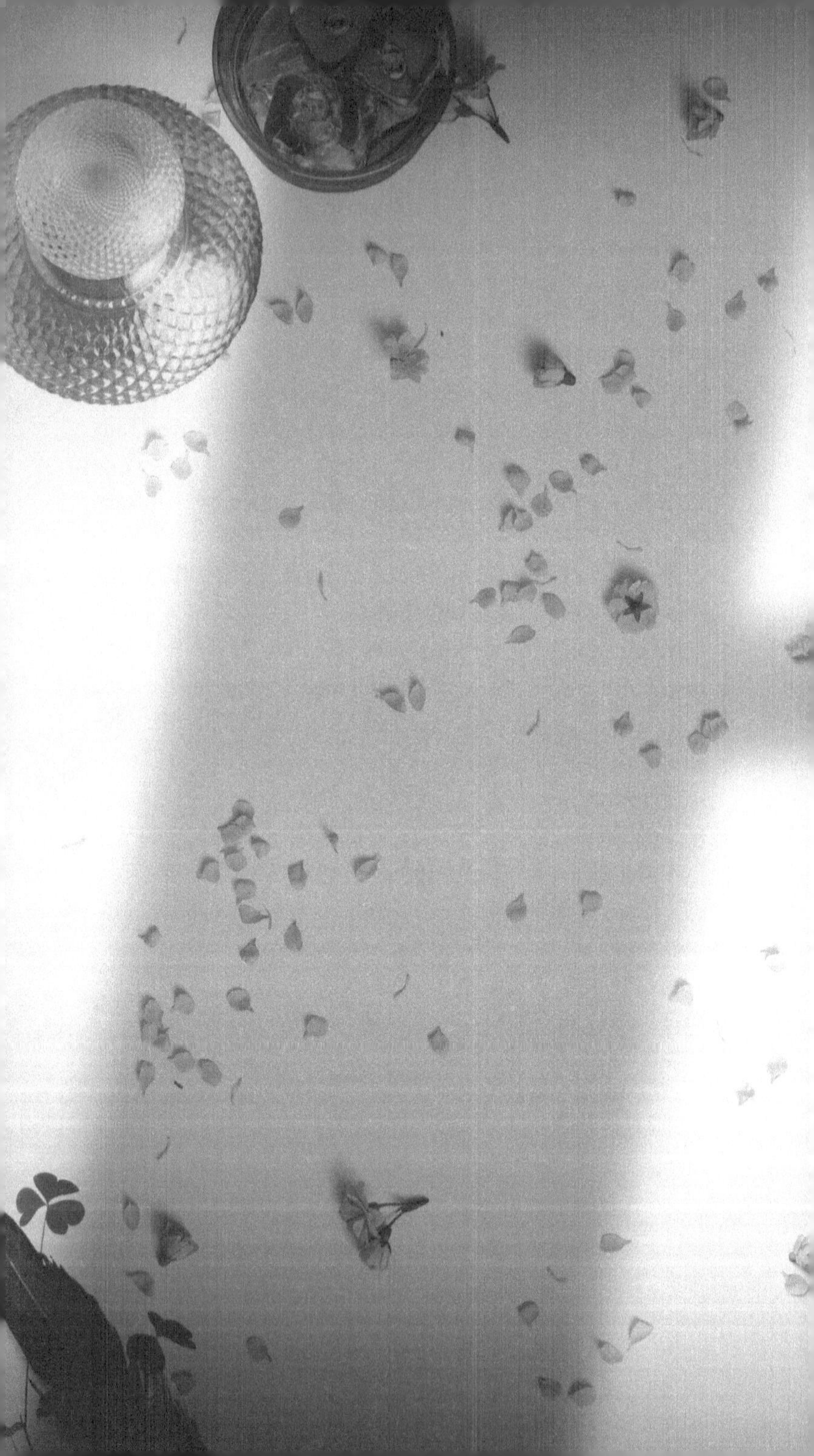

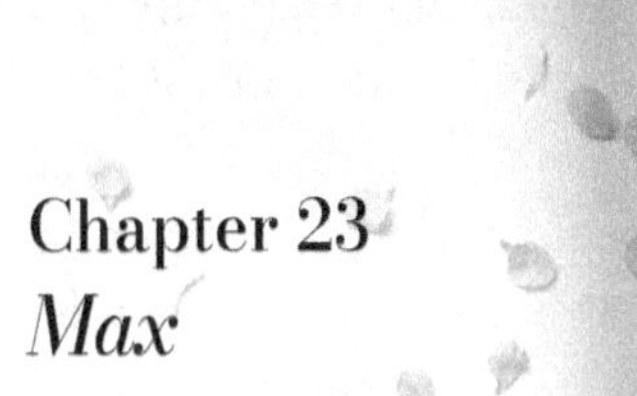

Chapter 23
Max

It had been easy—*right*—to fall asleep with Ander in his arms. Max couldn't explain it, he just knew that the subtle tug that had developed into something more insistent over the last few weeks had settled and now buzzed warmly in his chest. A contented cat, purring loudly at having the inanimi close.

It didn't make a whole lot of sense, Max knew that. Ignis weren't supposed to feel like this, especially not about inanimi. But something about Ander had drawn him in since day one, and Max was beginning to realize that, even if he did get burned by this—Quin made himself very clear that he disapproved for that very reason—he didn't think he'd mind. Let all of this end in a blaze; it'd be worth it. Just to have known what it felt like to have someone like this in his life. Just to know what it felt like to maybe, *almost*, love. Max wouldn't regret it, whatever his brother might think. It would be worth it. *Ander* was worth it.

That being the case, curling up around the inanimi was like coming home, and Max drifted off without even a second thought as to where they were and the fact that his entire family was on the other side of one very thin door.

A grave miscalculation.

The next thing he knew, he was being woken up by a garbled scream of something unintelligible that might have been his name.

Max bolted upright in the bed, knocking Ander off of his chest, his hand flying out to grab at the dagger he kept on his nightstand. But before he could fully raise it to defend himself, his vision focused, and he saw his Papa standing in the doorframe, his mouth hanging open, light brown face flushed furiously.

"What *is* this?!" Zeke all but roared, his face turning a deeper red, verging on purple.

Max opened his mouth to remind his Papa about his blood pressure and what the doctors said about getting himself worked up like this, but then Georgie's strawberry-blond head popped into the doorway, phone in one hand, kitchen knife in the other.

"Oh. It's just your boyfriend." Georgie deflated, her grip on the knife loosening a little in disappointment.

"*What* is going on here?!" Zeke shouted again, his voice echoing off the bare marble floors and the high ceilings of Max's room.

Georgie's expression shifted from forlorn to bloodthirsty again in the span of less than a second as she tapped something on her phone, holding it up higher to get a better angle. "Oooooh," she cooed, a delightedly vicious smile curling up her freckled face. "You're in soooo much trouble." Then more quietly, "The twins are gonna be so mad they missed this."

"Get out, Georgette!" Max hissed, grabbing the pillow he'd been laying on and reeling back to chuck it at her and the infernal device in her hand. Georgie stuck out her tongue but didn't move.

"*Maximus Schields*, answer me," Zeke hissed, taking a step into the room.

Max winced at the use of his full name and opened his mouth for a second time to answer his Papa, only to stop when his Dad came barreling down the hallway. He hardly noticed the snickering Ander beside him as Colt took one look at the situation and grabbed his husband's arm to bodily remove him from the doorframe.

"Come on, Zeke. Remember what the doctor said about your blood pressure? Deep breaths. That's it," Colt said, voice a deep, smooth drawl as he pulled Zeke away. "You too, Georgie."

"But Daaaaad," Georgie grumbled, never once taking her eyes off of Max and Ander, the phone still aloft, little demon child that she was. Max had forgotten how much he hated teenagers now that the twins were technically "adults", but he really *hated* teenagers.

"Georgette," Colt called back, an order.

"Awww, fine." Georgie huffed, tapping something on her phone as she spun on her heel. Likely sending what little footage she'd acquired over to Nox and Nash. "Don't do anything exciting where I can't see you."

"Go *away*, Georgie!" Max growled, throwing another pillow at the door and slamming it shut with the force.

He heard her say something back, but he couldn't make out the words, just her high, taunting tone. That left him muttering "brat" under his breath.

The room was silent for a moment, quiet enough that Max could hear the sounds of his parents in the kitchen again, bickering over breakfast. Then Ander let loose the loudest, most undignified snort Max thought he'd ever heard before he collapsed entirely into uproarious laughter so violent, it shook the bed.

Max's phone dinged beside him on the nightstand, and he didn't have to look at it to know that it was his Dad telling them to come to the kitchen when they were presentable for a family meeting. Great. Scrubbing at his face, Max turned to watch the still-laughing Ander. It was nice to see Ander looking so free, so open, when just the night before, he'd come to Max with his shoulders sunken, trying to make himself as small as he could. It hadn't escaped Max's notice that Ander's knuckles were scraped up and his lower lip bruised, like someone had tried to force themselves on him. They'd have to talk about that eventually. But he'd decided to let it go, at least for the time being, in favor of providing comfort and getting Ander to settle down.

Now wasn't the time to bring it up either. Not with his family waiting just down the hall, likely gossiping like old hens.

"Keep it up, chuckles," Max scoffed, rolling from the bed to head to the bathroom to at least wash his face. Maybe that would make him feel less foggy, the previous day's dose of Mermaid's Lament still clinging to him like a bad hangover. "Dad's called a family meeting."

"A what?" Ander stopped, his eyes suddenly wide and owlish as he pulled the blanket tighter to his neck.

"Family meeting," Max called from the bathroom over the water. "He wants us to sit down and talk about this. To keep the peace."

"Should I—Should I go? I should go." There were sounds of scrambling as Ander rolled from the bed, looking for his discarded boots from the night before. He'd just thrown the extra blanket that they'd kicked off at some point back onto the foot of the bed when Max caught up to him, catching his wrist in a soft grip.

"You shouldn't go." Rubbing the pad of his thumb over Ander's pulse, Max pulled him in close, pressing a kiss to his forehead. "You should come have breakfast with us. Dad makes the best spread when he's home to cook." Ander's gaze flicked nervously around Max's face, a cornered animal looking for a way out. "You don't have to if you don't want to."

Ander made a sound like a deflating balloon and leaned forward to press his head into Max's chest, his horns poking lightly into Max's collarbones. He was going to say no. He was going to leave Max to face this alone. Max was sure of it. Could feel it in the way Ander's weight pressed against him. This was a goodbye, likely in more ways than one. Ander had gotten a glimpse into the absolute insanity of the Schields family and decided it was all a bit much for him. Max couldn't blame him. He wouldn't be the first boyfriend who had decided the Schields were just too much, and Max doubted he'd be the—

"Okay," Ander said so quietly that Max almost missed it. But then, he was pulling back so he could offer Max a smile, although it was strained at the edges, forced bravery in the face of a lion. "Let's go have a family meeting."

"Okay." Max let the word out on a breath. Then he took hold of Ander's chin, gentle as ever, tilted his head just so, and dipped down to kiss him, long and slow. Ander pressed in closer, his arms curling around Max's neck, a soft, pleased sound on the back of his tongue, and Max nearly turned into a puddle right then and there. Likely would have if it weren't for the sound of someone banging a pan loudly in the kitchen, his Papa no doubt, impatient to get some answers. "We've gotta go."

Ander sighed, shaking his head, likely to clear the dazed expression that lingered after the kiss—and honestly, Max could relate; he was feeling quite floaty himself—then straightened his shoulders. "Let's go."

Max grabbed Ander a shirt, and with their fingers threaded together so tightly that Max could feel their bones grinding against each other, they made their way down the hall to the kitchen, where Zeke was pouting. Georgie was flitting about, grabbing plates and setting the table, and Colt was at the stove.

"Good of you to join us finally." Zeke scowled then let out a grumpy huff when Colt cleared his throat in a quiet reprimand. Max pulled Ander over to sit next to him at the table, and silence descended upon the kitchen as Colt finished plating breakfast.

When all of the food was finally in front of them, Max looked over at Georgie to find she'd perched her phone on the island, the camera no doubt already recording. "Motion to have Georgette Schields removed from these proceedings as she is not here to add anything of intrinsic value to the discussion. Her goal in attendance is solely amusement."

"Motion denied," Georgie said, stuffing a big bite of pancake into her mouth so she could talk obnoxiously around a cheekful. "I act as a representative for the Schields siblings who could not be in attendance due to prior obligations."

"You don't have the authority to deny a motion!" Max snatched the syrup bottle as she reached for it and held it just out of reach because if she was going to be a brat, so was he.

"I do so! Tell him, Papa!"

"Your sister has just as much right to be here as anyone else," Zeke hissed, pulling Georgie into a hug so tight, it looked like it hurt, and she stuck her tongue out at Max like the petulant child that she was.

"Dad, Georgie is just going to make a spectacle of—"

"Enough." Colt's voice was quiet but firm, and it worked like it had every other time. Colton Schields, head of the Schields family, did not need to raise his voice to command the attention of a room. He never had, probably because he wasn't the type to shout. Max envied that about him, had tried to emulate it in how he commanded their team, but more often than not, it felt like the act that it was. Like he was just a child trying to fill his daddy's shoes. Quin was the one who had mastered the skill of silence, even for all the Schields siblings made it seem that he hadn't sometimes. When he spoke in that quiet, deep way, people listened. Just like their dad.

Max slanted a look at Ander and found him biting back some expression. A smile, maybe. A laugh, perhaps. Or maybe he was trying not to scowl at the sheer ridiculousness that was Max's family. How embarrassing.

When everyone around them gave their murmured acknowledgement, yielding the floor to Colt, Colton Schields leaned forward, plucked an orange from the bowl at the center of the table, and held it up for everyone to see. "This," he said, tone serious, "is the feelings orange. Whoever holds this orange is allowed to speak. No one else."

Zeke leaned forward to grab a second orange from the bowl and opened his mouth to talk, but Colt smacked it away quickly.

"No. One at a time, Zeke. You know how this is done. You'll just have to wait your turn." Zeke huffed again, pouting as he crossed his arms over his chest, and Colt handed the orange over to Max, then winked. "You're up, Max."

"Ah . . . right." Max laughed, his grip too tight on the orange, as his other hand lifted to scrub at the back of his neck. "Ander and I are dating. And before you say anything, Papa, I know you're upset about it because of the whole *'he's my nemesis'*"—Max did what he thought was a reasonably good impression of his Papa's irritated voice—"thing. But you two have been fighting for years, and both your clubs are doing really well. So isn't it time you just put this behind you and called a truce? I mean . . ." He shifted, Ander's stare on the side of his face like a brand, hot and curious. "I really like Ander. And he makes me happy. And I don't—I don't think it's fair of you to tell me who I can and cannot date. I'm an adult. And this whole thing is over something silly that happened years ago." The last part was a little rushed, mumbled, almost inaudible as Max stuffed the orange into Ander's hand.

"I—I make you happy?" Ander whispered. His grip had gone so lax and disbelieving around the orange that Max was surprised he hadn't dropped it. His hair was mussed around his horns, his skin pale and eyes drawn from an obvious hangover. Max's shirt was overly large on his more slender frame, and he looked every part a hot mess. He had never looked more adorable in Max's mind.

"Ecstatic." Max grinned down at him, the world melting away as he dipped to press his forehead against Ander's, forming their own little bubble, their own little universe. Max wanted to live in that universe for as long as he was allowed. Bask in the light, and warmth that was Ander Ruin for as long as Ander would permit. Forever, if he could. He would settle for today.

"You make me happy too." The words came so softly

that Max was sure no one else at the table had heard them, but it didn't matter. Because Ander had pressed them into Max's mouth, a secret and a promise all in one, and Max's heart was hammering loudly against his chest. A war drum.

"Fine," Zeke said, ripping them both from their little world. "A truce. I can do a *tentative* truce."

"Good." Colt clapped his hands. "Now, let's finish breakfast." He held his hand out for the orange, and Ander passed it over with a soft smile.

But even as the atmosphere around the breakfast table settled, Max wasn't so sure his Papa would let this lie. He liked to think he knew Ezeqiel Schields a little better than that.

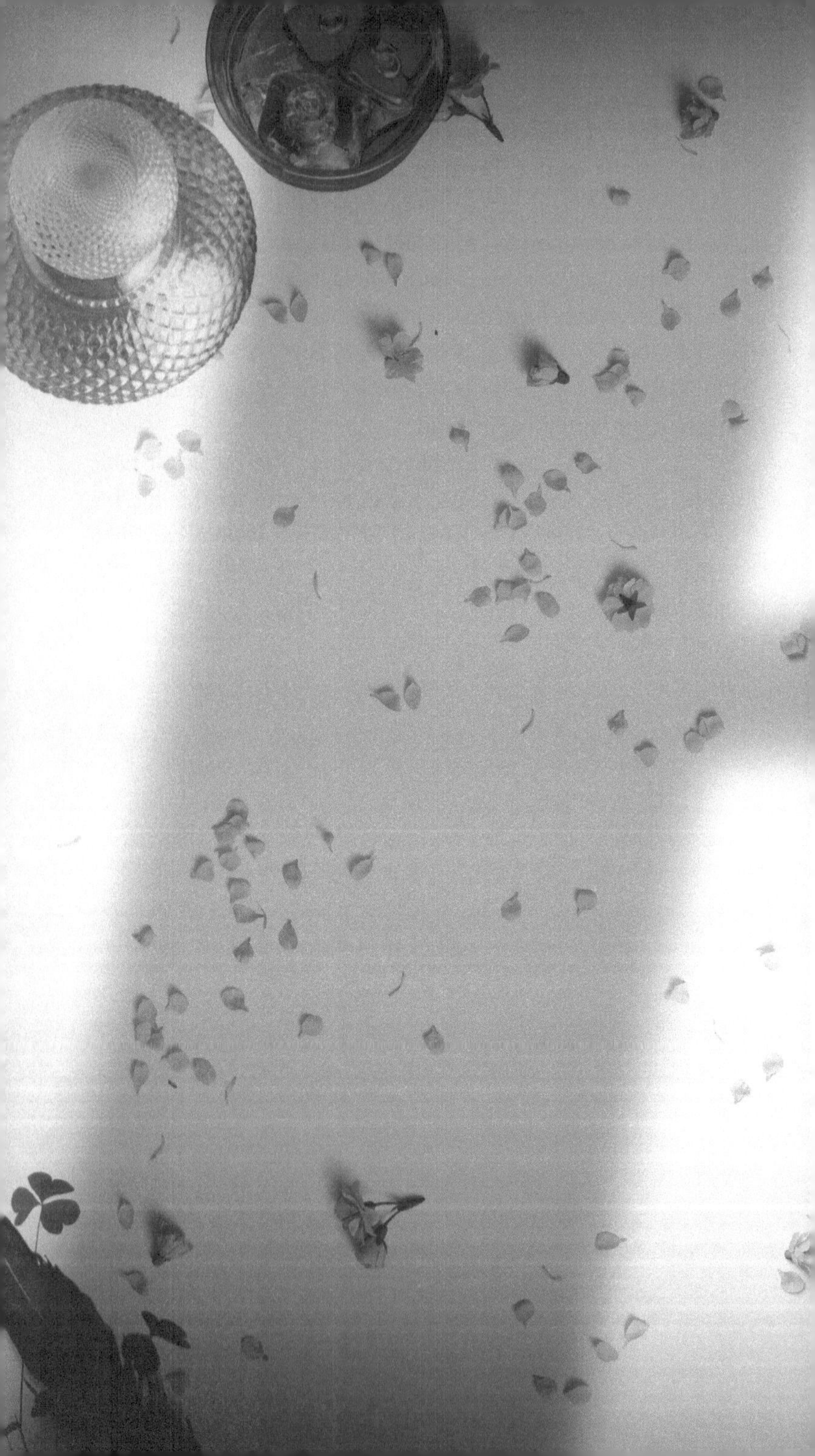

Chapter 24
Ander

Well, *that* had been a whole world of awkward.

Ander stared at himself in the mirror. Dressed in a pair of Max's pajama pants and a T-shirt, he hadn't exactly presented himself in the kind of made-up fashion he would have preferred for that particular showdown with Zeke Schields. But maybe being found in his son's bed then appearing at the breakfast table in said son's clothing was even better?

Either way, he and Max were officially out in the open.

Sighing, Ander leaned down to splash water on his face, then dried it with the hand towel. His head still pounded, and he felt like a truck had run him over, but a clean face helped. Feeling a little more refreshed, he stepped back into Max's room—and found Zeke standing there waiting for him.

"Ezeqiel."

"Ruin."

Ander cocked a brow at him.

"I know my husband made it appear as if this is all okay,

and for my son's sake, I played along, but don't think for one second that it is. I *will* be watching you."

Ander snickered, which made Zeke's brows bunch in annoyance. "You'll be watching me, will you? Watching me, what . . . Work? Play? Fuck?"

Zeke reddened a little, exactly what Ander had wanted. Because he knew just what the other man was picturing. Ander Ruin bedding his precious baby boy. There was something dark and twisted inside Ander that delighted in the knowledge that, just by happily falling into bed with his arrow-bound, he would also stab his enemy right in the heart. Metaphorically speaking.

Zeke took a step closer to him, shoulders squared in an imposing manner. "You listen here, if you hurt him in any way at all—"

"You'll what?" It rankled Ander's nerves that Zeke thought *he* would be the one to hurt Max. Did he not have any idea that Max possessed more power in his little pinky to utterly destroy Ander than Ander thought he possessed in his whole body? "What could you possibly do to me, mortal?"

Zeke puffed up like a peacock about to squawk its lungs out. "I will find a way to wipe your immortal ass off the face of the Earth and clear off the ends of Underworld while I'm at it. I will make you feel so much pain, you will—"

"Babe . . . you wouldn't be going back on everything you promised me at the kitchen table, now, would you?" Colt Schields stood in the doorway of the bedroom. Arms crossed over his broad chest and a stern look on his face.

Ander and Zeke froze like two small children caught by their mom in the process of doing something they'd both been forbidden to do.

Zeke's shoulders dropped, and his body took on a more lax appearance. He slowly turned back to face his husband. "What? Of course not."

Colt's eyes narrowed. He wasn't buying it.

"I was just making sure Ru—Ander didn't need anything."

"Babe . . ."

"Yes?"

"Out of Max's bedroom. *Now.*"

Huffing, Zeke cast Ander one last death glare before he sulked out of the room. When he was gone, Colt gazed over at Ander.

"I apologize for his behavior. While a great deal of it does come from your past issues with each other, know that he is also concerned about Max. We all are. We love our son, and we will protect him, no matter who it is against." His words were gentle, conversational, yet ten times more effectively threatening than Zeke's had been.

Ander nodded. "And believe me when I say I would burn this whole world down if someone hurt him."

Colt nodded respectfully, then left the room.

A shaky breath left Ander, and he realized his hands were trembling.

Was it too soon to feel this strongly about someone? Was this due to the amare bond? Or was this just a failing of Ander's?

He'd become absolutely besotted with Estelle, shown his true self to her, and that had ended in devastation.

He'd fallen too quickly for Enrique, and look where that had gotten him.

He knew he shouldn't be so quick to trust. So willing to just hand himself over, body and soul, to another individual who had the ability to utterly destroy him. Would he never learn?

Ruin. It was in the name.

Only, lately, it seemed to be Ander that was getting the ruining.

"Hey, are you all right?" Max. Beautiful, sweet, endearing Max. The ignis stepped into his bedroom and quickly crossed the floor. There was a concerned furrow to his dark brows.

"I'm fine. Just a little hungover."

"Is that why you didn't eat much of your breakfast? I thought maybe you were a little too nervous about the whole thing."

"Nah . . . I'm just not a morning person." Plus, food. Ander had a lot of deep, personal thoughts surrounding food. Most of them not so great. Another parting gift from Enrique. "Thank you, though, for breakfast. And letting me crash here last night."

"Of course. You can come here anytime you need to." Max stepped closer, a hand lifting, then falling back to his side, like he was afraid to touch Ander in case it would cause him to flee.

Ander solved the dilemma for him and stepped into his arms, circling his own around the younger male's waist beneath his white wings. Ander sighed as Max's arms came around him.

"Are you okay?" Max whispered.

"I'm fine."

"Are you sure?" Max paused, clearly puzzling over how to word his next statement. "Last night you seemed . . . distressed. You also, well . . . Ander . . . were you—did someone attack you?"

Ander squeezed his eyes shut and held his breath for a

moment, remembering Enrique on top of him, tearing the red tank top from his torso. A look of lust and dominance in his eyes that made Ander shudder again.

"Ander?" Max's fingers pressed gently beneath his chin, tipping his head up so he could read his face. There was deep concern within his hazel eyes, and it made Ander wish that he was better. That he deserved this kind of tenderness.

"I'm okay." His voice was soft, hiding the strain. "I just had a bit of an altercation last night. No big deal." Max was looking at him like he didn't believe him. "And I meant to go home . . . But somehow, I ended up here when I snapped." Their eyes locked. "Wait . . . You sent me a drunk text. But you weren't drunk when I got here, were you? What happened?"

"You're deflecting," Max quipped.

"No, I think *you* are. What happened?"

Max sighed. "I was drugged during a raid at a warehouse—"

"You were *what*?! Are you okay? Why didn't you say anything?" Ander stepped back so he could grab Max's face and pull him down a little closer to inspect his eyes more carefully.

Max squawked at the sudden movement. "Ander, I'm fine. I promise. I came home, and Papa put me in the sauna for an hour so I could sweat out all the toxins. You know we're built to be resistant to these kinds of things."

Ander chewed on his bottom lip, studying him a little more before he released his face. "You should have told me. You were the one who needed taking care of last night, not me."

This time it was Max who took ahold of Ander's face, making him look up. "Who hurt you last night?"

"No one."

"Ander . . ."

Ander huffed and looked to the side. "It was just a handsy guy. I punched him, and he backed off." When his eyes shifted back to Max's face, he was looking at him dubiously.

"You know you can tell me, right? About anything that happens, no judgment." He looked so sweet and earnest.

"I work in a bar, it happens."

Max looked disgruntled, so Ander rose up on his tiptoes to press his lips firmly to Max's, and to his delight, it worked to distract the other male. Max's hands slid around his waist, resting just over his hips, and he pulled him in against his firm chest.

In return, Ander's hands slid up Max's body to rest on his shoulders. Although Ander had started the kiss, it was Max who took control, parting Ander's lips with his own and exploring his mouth hungrily. The glide of Max's tongue against his own made Ander's knees feel weak, and his fingers dug into the muscular shoulders beneath them. A moan slid from him as one of Max's hands slid from his waist down around the curve of his ass, pulling his hips in tight against Max's.

Ander couldn't hold himself back and rocked against him in response, feeling the press of Max's hardness against his own. A shudder coursed through his body, and the throb in his chest both increased and blossomed until it was a humming force, sweeping through his body, making the hair of his scalp tingle and his nerve endings quiver.

"Gods, Max," he gasped, pulling his lips away. "You make it very difficult to behave and wait."

"Sorry." Max blushed. "I can't help myself around you."

Ander slid his fingers up into Max's hair, tugging gently

on it. "You never have to, sweetheart. I am all yours for the taking, whenever you so choose." He purred the words, his lids lowering in a languid, promising manner.

Max's cheekbones burned brightly, but there was a responding heat in his eyes that told Ander his words had resonated.

"I should go home."

"What?" Max blinked, like he'd forgotten Ander didn't belong in the house with him.

"I need to feed Monnie. And take her out. She's likely bursting at the seams, the poor little fluffers."

Max grinned in a dopey manner. "Fluffers?"

"Yes."

"You're adorable." He dipped his head to kiss Ander once more, and Ander willingly went back into his arms.

He wasn't adorable, and he wasn't sure how Max saw him in that light. But he would continue to accept the words. Because he wanted to be adored by Max. He wanted him to hang on every word and action of Ander's. Maybe then he'd feel like the scales were tipping a little more evenly.

"I really do have to go," he rasped, breaking away from Max's lips finally.

"I'll take you home." Max nuzzled his throat, sending shivers through his body.

"That's not necessary. I can just snap—" Max pressed a finger to his lips, silencing him.

"I'm going to take you home. I want to." Ander nodded. "You can borrow the T-shirt to wear back."

"Sure thing, love." Ander pulled away then, smiling a little. Stripping out of the bottoms, he pulled his own jeans back on and shoved his feet into his boots.

When he was dressed, Max swooped him up in his arms.

"What are you doing?" Ander squawked, then laughed, his legs kicking a little.

"I said I was taking you home."

"So you're *carrying* me?"

"How else am I supposed to fly you back to your condo?"

"Maximus . . ."

"Crown Prince Ander . . ."

"Okay, okay. Break the rules for me." Ander giggled a little and slipped an arm around Max's shoulders, planting a kiss firmly on his lips before they left the Schields home by way of a back door.

Outside, the Miami sun was bright and hot, already promising another scorcher of a day. Ander paid it little mind. Instead, he focused on the firm arms holding him securely as the stark white wings spread behind the ignis and began to flap. As Max launched them into the air, Ander strangled a noise of surprise deep in his throat, not wanting to sound too afraid of what was happening. But for someone who didn't even have to bother with airplanes, hurtling through the air freely was a little terrifying.

"For the love of gods, please don't drop me!" he finally shouted when he found himself able to.

Max laughed. "Are you afraid?"

"No!" Ander argued. "Just highly aware of how far down the ground is!"

Max chuckled again and kissed his cheek. "I promise I won't drop you."

Ander nodded and appreciated the way Max's arms curled around him a little more tightly.

Gratefully, the flight was rather quick. Ander wasn't sure he could have stomached a prolonged period of time in the air. When Max's feet touched down on his balcony, Ander sighed in relief.

"See? Safe and sound."

"While I appreciate the speedy nature of our trip, I'm thinking next time we should just snap."

Max pouted a little, like a giant, sad golden retriever puppy—with wings. "But then I don't get to cuddle you."

Ander's lips tipped up at this, and he grabbed Max by the front of his shirt to pull the tall ignis in closer. "Well, if you'd said that was the reason . . ." Their lips met once more, a happy hum releasing from Ander.

The moment was broken by the sound of angry yips coming from the other side of the sliding glass doors. Breaking away from Max, Ander spun around to spot his tiny white dog pawing frantically at the glass.

"My poor little darling!" Ander hurried to the door to open it up, letting Monnie out onto the patio so that she could race to the patch of grass he'd had installed there just for such emergency purposes.

Once the tiny dog had gone, she pranced back over to them. Sniffing disdainfully at Max, she climbed onto Ander's foot and nipped his ankle in retribution.

"Ow! Okay, I'm sorry!" Bending down, he plucked her up and carried her into the kitchen to get her food and fresh water. He pressed several kisses and nuzzles to her fluffy white fur, cooing sweet nothings of devotion to her.

Setting her on the floor, he prepared her breakfast.

As he milled around the kitchen, he noticed Max watching him. Peeking at him from the corner of his eye, Ander looked at him questioningly. "What?"

"Nothing."

"You're staring."

"I'm not staring . . . I just like watching you at home and comfy in your own space."

"I'm pretty sure that's staring." Grinning, Ander gave Monnie one last pet as she dug into her food, then stepped up to Max, his arms slipping around the other male's waist easily, like they had been made to wrap around him.

"You like it, you know you do," Max murmured, his own arms wrapping around Ander in return, curling him into his chest happily.

Ander could have purred, he felt so content where he was. "I do. I won't even bother pretending that I don't."

In their current position, it seemed only natural for Max to dip his head down once more, and for Ander to stretch up a little so that their lips could connect. This. This right here. This must've been what it felt like to be in heaven.

There was a peace and safety in Max's arms that was almost terrifying. Ander couldn't help but wonder when the shoe of complete and utter disaster was going to fall. Nothing could be this good and real, and last. Not for him.

"I should go," Max whispered against his lips.

"Mmm, you should." Ander's fingers slid around the back of his neck, and he pulled him back in for another kiss, their lips meshing eagerly.

Max's hands slid down his back, pressing into the dip just above his bottom, pulling him in tight. Ander went willingly, leaning against him.

"You've got to work, don't you?"

"Yeah, I can't be late." It was Max this time who initiated the kiss. After being locked together for another moment of bliss, Max pulled away at last. "Okay, I really have to go."

"Of course . . . of course. But just . . . one more—" Ander pulled him in again, nipping playfully at his lips so that Max laughed, wrapping his arms around his waist and lifting him off his feet, spinning him around a little.

Monnie yipped excitedly at the display of happiness.

Laughing, Ander felt a little breathless when Max set him back down on his feet.

"Okay, go." Ander gave him a little shove, but Max grabbed onto his wrist and tugged him in once more, pressing a quick peck to his lips.

"Thank you for staying for breakfast this morning. It meant a lot. I'll see you again soon, okay?"

Ander nodded. "Okay. Go to work. And be safe, my *ignis*."

Max grinned, his hazel eyes bright. "I will be." He kissed Ander one last time, then ducked out the patio doors and was off.

Ander watched him go with a sigh, then fell back against the kitchen island. He had so much to share with Mab.

Mab!

Gods! He hadn't called or messaged her last night once he finished at Enrique's.

Snapping his phone into his hand, he saw that Mab had indeed blown up his phone with phone calls and text messages, which grew progressively more frantic as the time had gone on. In his drunk, distraught stupor the night before he hadn't noticed.

Realizing that a simple phone call was not going to be enough to earn his way back into his bestie's good graces, he quickly snapped himself to Mab's house.

She was there, pacing in her living room, hair a mess, bags under her eyes, and face pinched with stress. At the sight of him, she visibly sighed with relief, then raced over to him to give him a fierce, rib-cracking hug.

"You're alive!" Squeezing him again, she pulled back and began to beat at him. "*Damn you!* Why didn't you answer your phone?! I thought you were dead!"

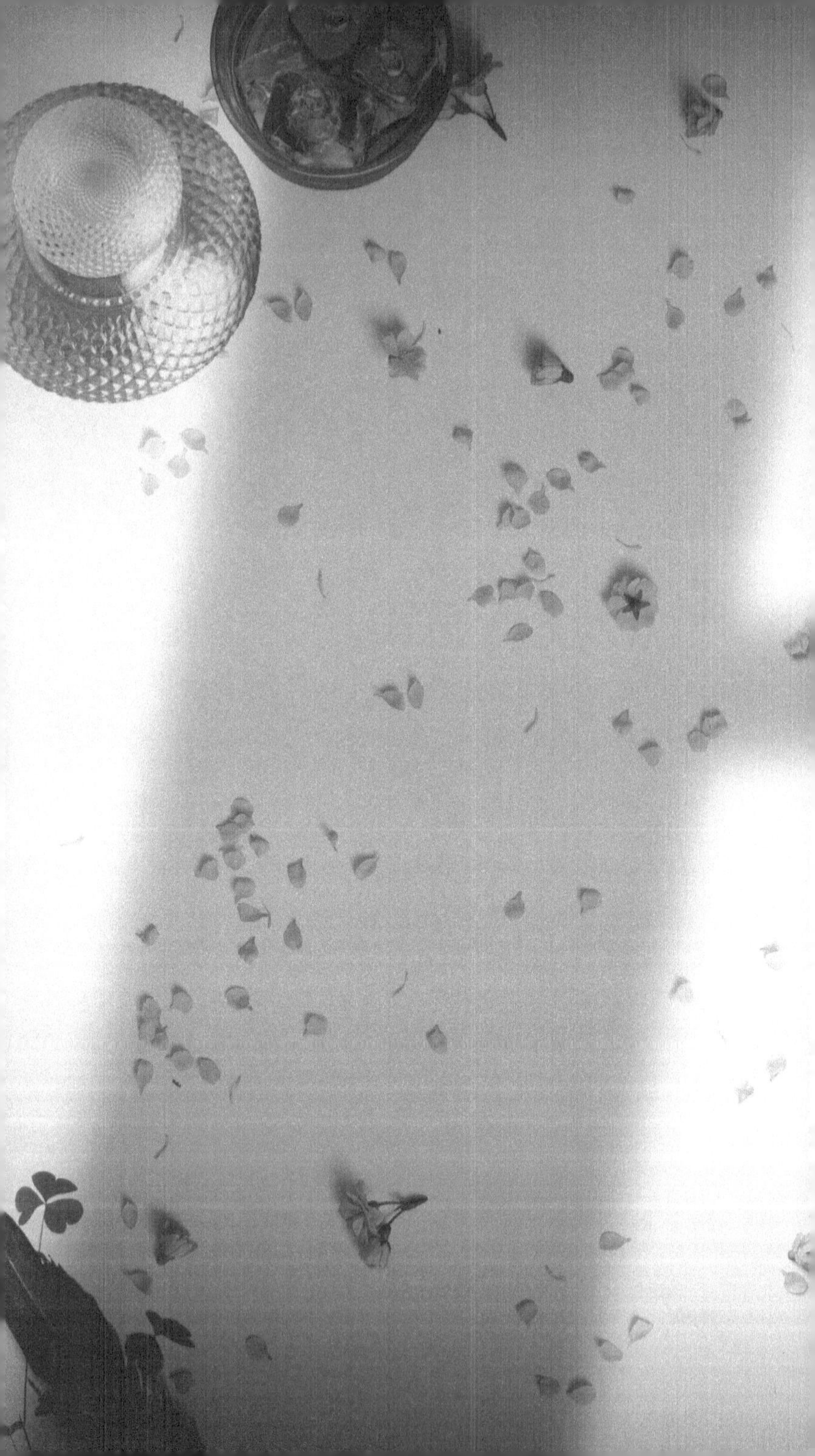

Chapter 25
Mab

Panic.

It lodged in Mab's throat, a thick wad of feelings she couldn't swallow around or cough up even though she had tried. She spent an hour curled up on her knees in her bathroom trying to retch it into her toilet so she could breathe properly again. But despite spilling the contents of her stomach into the bowl, nothing else had come up, and the terror sat like a lump of cold, hard dread in her throat, threatening to suffocate her.

Anxiety added itself to the mix a while later. Making her skin feel too tight and itchy. She'd scratched at it in spots so hard that she was sure she'd have sores come morning, maybe even scars like the ones on her cheek. Gizmo had come from his hutch to try to calm her, hopping around her feet and rubbing himself against her shins like a cat might, but that didn't help either.

Nothing did. Nothing would.

Seeing Ander was the only solution. Holding him in her arms, pressing her face into his chest, and screaming at him until her throat was sore, that was all that would cure this.

But he wasn't answering his phone *at all*, which was unlike him. No calls. No texts.

And when the sun rose too hot in the blue-pink sky over the water, Mab resolved to call Aemiliana, even as dread pooled in her stomach, threatening to make her sick again. Because how was she going to tell the queen of Helicon that Mab had lost her son? *Again.* That she'd failed. *Again.* There was absolutely no excuse for it, and all Mab would be able to do was hope that whatever punishment Aemiliana chose to dole out on her was swift and efficient.

She was just gathering the ingredients to contact Aemiliana when the air pressure in her house shifted, her ears popped, and Ander appeared in front of her. Words crawled up her throat, scraping it raw, though she didn't hear them over the pounding of her heart in her ears as she thumped a fist against his chest as hard as her exhausted body would let her.

Ander let out a soft chuckle, which sounded distinctly wet, and pulled her in against him, burying Mab's face in his shirt. She took a moment there, letting her heart and breathing settle before she pulled back to narrow the most cutting glare she could manage at him.

"Where in the name of the gods *were* you?" Mab hissed, her voice still raw from the crying and the panic.

Taking a step back, Ander scrubbed at the back of his neck, and Mab got a good look at him finally. At the scrapes on his knuckles. At the shirt that hung a little too baggie off of him, clearly not his.

"Whose shirt is that?" The shoulder stitching showed it was too wide for him, made for someone with a broader chest, and not in the way that Ander's too-big shirts usually hung. This was . . . Horror had her by the throat again. "Don't tell me you slept with—"

"No! Gods no! Mab. I'd never. Come on." Ander frowned, but then he grabbed her by the hands and tugged her over to the couch, said, "Come on, I'll tell you all about it," and she went willingly.

A half an hour later found Mab nursing what was left of the coffee and scones Ander had snapped for her, crumbs littering her lap and her exhaustion really starting to sink in now that she was no longer jittery with anxiety. She had slumped into Ander's side, her shoulder pressing into his.

"I think I want to try it again. He just needs a higher dose," Ander said, his tone soft and careful. Like he knew what reaction this would garner from Mab. Honestly, if he didn't know, then he was stupider than she thought.

"What?" Mab sat up to blink at him blurrily, then frowned. "No. Absolutely fucking *not*."

"Oh, come on, Mabbers, it's not like—"

She squinted, her lips pursing, and Ander deflated.

"What would you suggest instead?"

"We're going to go to Underworld, and we're going to get more information on this stuff." Mab suddenly felt wide awake, a plan already forming in her mind. "We need to know what dosage to use. How it might react with other substances." She rose from the couch, heading into the kitchen to grab a pad from the counter and start making a list. "What's in it. If we can make it ourselves."

"Mab, I really don't think—"

She threw the little pad at him, only just missing him as he ducked to avoid the sharp corners.

"All right. All right. We'll go to Underworld. Jeesh! No need to throw shit at me!"

There was a back door tucked away behind a crate of the most expensive vodka Inferno boasted, at the back of the stockroom. The bottles had dust on them because most of their customers couldn't afford it, and that worked just fine for Mab and Ander's purposes because one step through that back door dumped a person out into Helicon. It traded the musty air of the stockroom for the fresh, green scent of the valley where the muses roamed.

Mab pulled the door shut behind them, turning the deadbolt and hoping that Parker and Hazel would be able to handle the bar while they were gone because they would, sadly, be out of cellphone range for the next couple of days. Hopefully not longer, but time moved differently in Underworld, and Mab wasn't going home until they had figured this out.

Aemiliana was waiting for them with hugs, fresh clothes, and a letter that would let them in to see Juno in Olympia, and Mab had never been more grateful for Ander's mother. She never asked, she always just provided. She was a saint among beings. Pressing kisses to their cheeks, Aemiliana stepped back from them and waved goodbye as Ander snapped them away.

The streets of Olympia shone gold in the sunshine, making Mab squint. She wished she'd opted to keep her sunglasses when Aemiliana had forced her into a traditional toga to better fit in with the people of Underworld. Who cared if they looked out of place? *She* was out of place here. Underworld had never been her home, even Aemiliana's land, and never would be. She belonged to the land of the mortals.

"I'm not keen on this plan," Ander mumbled out of the corner of his mouth as they walked up to the main gate of the palace.

"Stop complaining." Scrubbing at her face, Mab rolled her eyes and pressed her fingers into the tight braids Ander had done for her on the sides of her head. They created a fauxhawk out of the top length of her hair, making her and Ander a matching set of sorts and also making Mab feel more akin to a warrior than she ever had. "Indra isn't even here. We're just going to talk to Juno, get some straight answers, and go home. We'll be back in Miami sipping mai tais before you can say—"

"Prince Ander of Helicon, and escort," the footman announced, his tone bored. In any other circumstance, Mab might have been annoyed by the lack of introduction, by being relegated to a footnote beside Ander. But there were more important things right now, and she wasn't looking to ruffle Juno by throwing a fit in her royal chambers over something so meaningless.

"Ander. Mab." Juno's wide smile crinkled the skin around her eyes but wasn't as comforting as she probably meant it to be for someone whose condo had once been set on fire by a raging Juno after she'd found out about Indra's latest lover. Honestly, if Mab could stay out of Juno and Indra's constant squabbles long enough to see her five hundredth birthday, she'd be surprised. Any immortal who was friends with them was unlikely to live past a few centuries.

"Nice to see you, peaches," Ander purred, leaning in to brush a kiss to one of Juno's cheeks and then the other. Mab followed the greeting, even though she felt strange doing it. It never paid to be rude to the queen of the gods.

"To what do I owe the pleasure?" Juno pulled back, her smile slipping a little as her eyes flicked over them, assessing.

They waited to answer until she had led them to a small sitting room off the side of her personal receiving hall and had wine before them. Mab's fingers drummed against her goblet, trying not to shift too much in her seat.

Ander sat forward a little more, his hips shifting to the edge of the lounge cushion. "Indra gave me this potion that he said could knock out a god, *dues somnum*. I used a little of it on Orcus, but it . . . Well, it didn't work quite as well as we'd hoped."

"And?" One dark brow lifted, and Juno's eyes sparkled dangerously. She knew what they wanted, what they'd come for, but she wanted to hear them say it, wanted them to beg for it. Gods, Mab had forgotten how much she hated the gods sometimes. Indra was easy enough to deal with for the most part—all she had to do was ply him with a little bit of liquor and some ice cream, and she could talk him into things. Like warding her property just in case they ever needed to hide out there. Granted, that was partly for his benefit as well, as he semi-regularly showed up when he was in trouble with Juno and needing a place to lay low.

"And we'd like some more information on it." Mab set down her goblet and pulled her list from the pocket of her toga before sliding it across the low table to Juno. "If you wouldn't mind."

Juno took the list, her dark gaze flicking over it for a moment while her face remained perfectly impassive. When she was done, she asked, "Are you planning to use this on my husband?"

"No." Ander shook his head, but he'd relaxed a little beside her, and Mab took that to be a good sign.

Looking back up at them, Juno's lips quirked into a little bit of a smirk before she said, "Pity."

"So, will you help us?" Mab pressed her leg into Ander's, needing the warmth of his presence at her side to soothe the anxiety crawling under her skin.

"I don't see why not." Juno shrugged, and the list disappeared in a tiny purple flame. "Unfortunately, much of this you'll need to see my brother-in-law for more information on. But I'll have word sent to Hades that he should give you everything you need. You can get there on your own, can't you? Or do I need to give you a ride?"

"I think we'll manage." Mab's shoulders drooped in relief. Returning to Hades' realm was at the top of her list of things she did *not* want to do, but if it meant they could get rid of Enrique once and for all, she'd do it. Ander, however, had gone rigid beside her. She reached over to take his hand, squeezing it tightly, and heard him let out a long, slow breath.

"Very well. I have sent your request along to Hades." Juno rose, straightening her toga as she did, and led them back the way they had come. "But do think about what I said. Using this against Indra would be . . ." A vicious grin crawled across her face, knife-sharp and deadly. Mab was suddenly very glad her name had not been in that sentence.

"We'll think about it," Mab said, ushering an unresponsive Ander out. Once they were out of earshot, Mab tugged them into an abandoned corridor off the main hall and spun Ander so she could face him. Much of the color had drained from his face, and his eyes had a distinctly hunted look to them. "Are you all right?"

"I'm fine, Mabbers. Fit as a fiddle. Why wouldn't I be?" But his words sounded hollow.

Mab swallowed around something snarky and mean about him being an absolute idiot before saying, "We don't have to go there if you don't want to. Or I could go alone. You don't have to do this."

Ander grabbed her wrists where she was squeezing his shoulders perhaps a little too tightly. "I do. I have to do to this."

"Andy. No. You don't. I could—"

With a shake of his head, Ander sighed. "No. I'm going with you. Come on, let's just get this over with."

It wasn't a good idea. It was a *terrible* idea. She should really have insisted on going alone. But then the image of Ander cowering on the porous black stone of Hades' palace flashed through her mind, and she knew even if she wanted to, she wouldn't be able to. So instead, she nodded and reached down to thread her fingers through his, squeezing tight enough to cut off circulation.

Hades' realm was so similar to how it had been on that day all those years ago that Mab struggled to keep the image of Ander rail-thin and cowering from her mind. Every hall they turned down, every door they walked through, seemed to bring it back to her. The smell of blood and sulfur. The racing of her heart as she almost lost the most important person in her entire world. But none of it, absolutely none of it, could be worse than what Ander was going through.

She didn't think he'd noticed, but his hands had begun to tremble. His thin fingers were so tight around her own hand that she could feel his rings digging into her skin. But she didn't say anything. She didn't complain. Because she didn't want him to let go. Not ever.

"Juno told me what you want," Hades said, his voice echoing in the empty hall, deep and threatening. Mab thought she might've heard the whispers of the dead lingering in it, but she couldn't be sure, and she knew it was better not to think about it too much. She'd only freak herself out. "And while I'm always happy to help a fellow noble"—his dark eyes did look truly dismayed by what he was about to say—"I'm afraid I cannot do this for you."

"Why not?" Ander asked, but the words sounded almost choked, his hand tightening around hers so much that she felt the bones of her knuckles rubbing together.

"I think you know why not." Sighing, Hades ran a hand down the dark brown skin of his face. He looked tired all of a sudden, his broad shoulders hunching in a little on themselves. Mab was reminded keenly of the fact that Hades very rarely got visits from the other gods, his brothers included. Of how welcoming and kind he had been the first time she had visited Acheron. He was a kind god, for all he was also terrifying. And he seemed so very lonely. Meanwhile, all Ander and Mab had done was come to ask him for a favor. She would have felt bad for that if it weren't for the danger of Enrique looming over them.

"We need it." The trembling had grown worse, making Ander's voice shake. His upright posture was slowly slouching, shrinking. Mab wanted to loop her arm around him to hold him up, but she wouldn't, not in front of a fellow noble.

"I'm sorry, I can't jus—"

"Orcus is abducting Ignis," Mab blurted, cutting Hades off.

The god's eyes widened, his jaw falling slack as he stared at her. "Do you have proof of that?"

Mab nudged Ander gently. "Tell him what you've found."

Ander sucked in a breath, straightening his posture. "I was at his place a few days ago, and he has a pair of wings mounted on the wall."

"That doesn't mean they're ignis wings," Hades reasoned, but even he seemed to hear it for the hollow thought that it was. They all knew what he'd found when he'd searched Enrique's chambers the last time Mab had been to Acheron. "And even if they were, that is a matter for the ignis or Indra, not me, to handle."

Mab gave Ander's hand a firm squeeze. She had known this might be an issue. The other gods hadn't wanted to interfere with Enrique's experiments the first time. He hadn't even been punished for them. But surely they couldn't be stupid enough to not see what was going on here, what he must be doing.

"He also had a jar of feathers of all different sizes. If those were all ignis feathers, then that means he might be raising an army. Wouldn't that make it your problem? Where do you think he'd start?" Ander pressed, his pulse ratcheting up another notch where it was pressed against Mab's own wrist.

Hades' frown deepened. "Very well. But you will report your findings to me. If one of my underlings is raising an army, I need to know."

"Yes, Your Highness." Mab tugged Ander down into a shallow bow, and when they stood again, Hades was holding out a tightly wound scroll with a piece of black twine holding it closed.

"No one else is to see this. Have I made myself clear?" He raised one dark brow, eyes narrowing in a threat.

"Of course. Once I've learned all I need to know, I'll burn it." Ander snatched the paper away, then he returned to Mab's side, ready to escape back to Helicon.

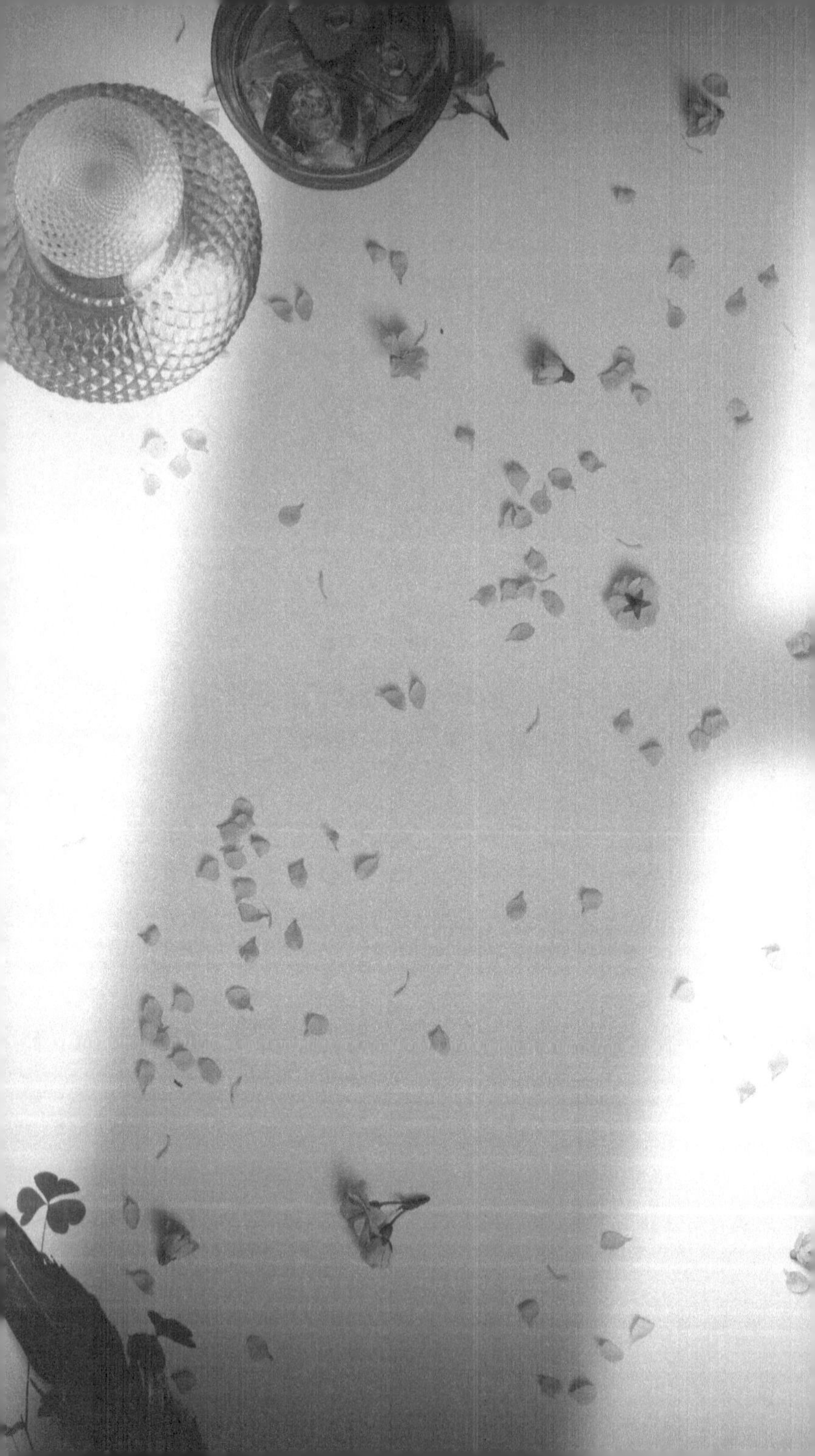

Chapter 26
Ander

With the scroll from Hades in his hand, Ander made a final bow and quickly left the throne room, forcing his steps to remain as evenly paced as possible and counting out a slow rhythm in his head to keep himself from sprinting away.

He'd forgotten just how clouded even a bright day could be in Acheron due to the billowing fires in the pits of Tartarus filling the sky with smoke. It had been that faint scent of sulfur in the air that triggered the most memories upon their arrival. Transporting him instantly back to those claustrophobic days of knowing he was confined in a tight, controlled space with Enrique ever looming. Watching. Demanding. Taking.

Ander had known it was going to be terrible, but he hadn't judged correctly just *how* terrible it would be. Each step he took toward Hades' fortress drove him deeper and deeper into the feelings of despair that had coated each one of his days here. The helplessness. The pain. The absolute desire to end it all at any cost.

Now, standing outside once more on the steps of the fortress, Ander was sick to his stomach. His recent encounter with Enrique didn't help matters either. His touch lingered on his skin too recent. The memories of his weight bearing down on Ander too real.

He hadn't realized he was literally gasping for each breath until Mab was before him, her hands on his upper arms and her concerned face peering back into his. "Just breathe, Andy. One deep breath in, one deep breath out. Come on, do it with me."

And he listened, because focusing on Mab and her breathing as she walked him through it was much better than focusing on the landscape around him. Better than remembering the day he had been forced to harm Ikari and was sick on these very steps as he realized just what sort of monster his "beloved" was and how absolutely trapped he had let himself become.

With each deep inhale and long exhale, Ander felt a little bit of calm returning.

"How about we go spend a couple of days with your mom?" Mab suggested.

"But—" he began, holding up the scroll.

"No." Mab was quick, and she was final. "We do personal healing first, then we worry about others."

It was selfish. He knew that. But he nodded. Sometimes it was just better to listen to Mab the first time rather than realize later that he should have. "Fine." He wrapped his arms around her, pulling her into a tight hug, and snapped them away from the obsidian hells of Acheron to the sunny, crystal, fresh breezes of Helicon.

He had transported them into his favorite space within the castle: a small courtyard situated in the middle of the music conservatory. Here, marble pathways twined through lush grass, artfully crafted waterfalls trickled into ponds of gold and white fish, and scrolling benches sat, hand-whittled into the side of large trees or natural stone. Within this courtyard, the sweet tunes of perfectly honed instruments floated down to an expectant ear. Looking up at the many stories of arched windows could also provide a glimpse of a gracefully extended hand or arched foot, or the masterfully controlled spin of a ballet dancer.

This courtyard had been Ander's escape from society.

A muse's true magic came from their affinity for crafting things of beauty. It was in the lilt of their voice, the perfect pitch of their ear, their ability to sculpt lifelike replicas out of any material. Their magic also lay in healing with their craft: music, art, and finery. Spells woven into each cord plucked or every fine stroke of a brush.

But with this ability came a taste for fine things, and in turn, a need for perfection around them.

Ander, with his long, elegant horns, had not been the definition of perfect written into the scrolls of the muses long ago. His magic worked differently, not requiring an act of art to be called upon. He was tainted. A mix of something *other* that was not acceptable

With a deep breath of relief, Ander dropped down near the pond. His hands fell behind him, resting in the grass to prop him up. The coolness of the earth beneath him and the gentle tickle of the sun on his upturned face brought a sense of ease that had not been present in Acheron.

"Are you okay?" Mab asked, dropping down to the ground beside him.

"Yeah . . ." He opened his eyes and peered over at her. "Thanks."

"Always."

They smiled at each other across the grass. The soft lilting sound of a voice came from one of the floors above.

"Ander? How did it go, sweetheart?"

Ander glanced up and smiled a little at the sight of his mother. He'd always meant to ask her if she had some kind of sensor spell in place, because whenever he appeared unannounced, his mother always managed to find him shortly afterward.

Without saying anything, he climbed to his feet and was at her side quickly, wrapping his arms around her slender form. Ander drew his mother in against his chest and just held her tightly. She seemed surprised at first but quickly melted into him, her own arms curling around his waist. Ander buried his nose into her hair, smelling the honeysuckle of her soap. A fragrance that had brought comfort to him all his days.

"Are you going to tell me what's actually going on?" Aemiliana's voice was muffled against his chest.

"Later," he whispered back. Pressing a kiss to the top of her head, Ander released her enough that she was able to look up at him. "First, I want to drink, and eat, and dance . . . and just enjoy being home." Home. Was it, though?

Wasn't home actually his condo in Miami? Inferno? Princess Monaco? Mab . . . and Max?

"Very well." Queen Aemiliana stepped back and held out her hand in welcome to Mab. "Let's get you both some light nibbles to hold you over. Then tonight, we'll throw a feast in honor of your visit." Mab smiled a little and took the offered hand, and Aemiliana drew them both out of the courtyard. "I'm also going to assume this means you're staying for an extended time?"

"Yeah . . . a couple of days, at least."

"Good." She was smiling brightly. "It's been too long since my children were last home."

The table before Ander was spread with every delicacy known to Underworld. The kitchen had certainly rolled out the red carpet for him and Mab, clearly listening when their queen said this was a celebration.

"Here, sweetheart, have some of this. Chef made it especially for you."

Ander looked at the steaming dish of moussaka and felt his stomach clench at the notion of so many carbs going into his body. "I'm good for the moment, Mother." He pushed around one stuffed grape leaf, debating whether to bother with it or just stick with the olives and small selection of roast lamb he'd taken.

Mab was frowning at him from across the table, but he chose to ignore her.

"Are you sure? You always loved moussaka."

"I'm not that hungry right now. Maybe I'll raid the pantry for some tonight. Might help stave off tomorrow's hangover." Ander grinned at her, his insides feeling greasy. If any of this stayed down at all, it would be a miracle.

"You should really have some of these veggies, Andy." Mab held out a medley of roasted tomatoes, eggplants, peppers, and onions.

He knew what she was trying to do.

"Actually, I've got plenty of veggies already."

"Olives don't count."

"Vodka is made from potatoes. Potatoes are a veggie. Let me introduce you to my vegetables." He saluted her with his martini glass. While there was a plethora of wine and mead on the table, Ander still preferred his mortal realm cocktails.

Mab eyed him like he was a wayward child, the glint in her eyes warning him that she was debating how best to shove some of the medley down his throat. Swallowing roughly, Ander gulped his martini and looked instead to the entertainment before them.

Lovely, slender muses dressed in nothing but gold skin paint and sheer slips of fabric arched and twirled to music being played by an ethereal looking lyre player. The song was joyful with a twinge of sadness just beneath the surface that tugged at Ander's heart. It was a skill the muses were known for. Creating works of art that could lift you to the highest heights and at the same time leave a taste of heartbreak in your mouth.

When the piece concluded, everyone around the table clapped, and Ander was surprised when one of the dancers, a youthful male, stepped up to him. He was tall and lean, lovely in the way that all muses were.

"Your Highness, we performers had hoped that you would show us a dance from the mortal realm." He bowed gracefully, then slowly lifted his head so that piercing dark eyes could connect with Ander's. A bold move for someone not born to a noble house.

Ander didn't feel like dancing. But dancing would pull him away from the dining table and both Mab and his mother's scrutiny of everything he wasn't eating. "It would be my pleasure, darling." Ander picked up his martini and downed the rest of it, watching the young male lower his eyes and blush becomingly at the casual endearment. "Mother, Mab, I'll be back. My fans beckon." He winked at both of them as he stood from the table.

Ander walked to the open floor of the dining hall—always left barren for entertainment and performances—and turned to the lyrist.

"We will need something with a dirty rhythm. Is there a percussionist here?" Another male stepped up from a nearby alcove, clearly waiting for his turn to come before the royal family. "Perfect." Once the male had set himself up with his toubeleki between his knees, Ander stepped up to him and quickly tapped out a fitting rhythm. "Got it?" The male nodded. Ander then looked at the lyrist. "Now, I need you to match his beat with something dirty and seductive." He listened while the lyrist strummed away at his instrument, trying different melodies until something caught Ander's ear. "Yes, that's it."

Pleased with the music, Ander returned to the dancer who had beckoned him out onto the floor. Extending his hand to him, he waited until the young male accepted it, then drew him in with a twirl to face away from him and tugged him in against his chest. The dancer was just a little shorter than Ander. Perfect for the dance he had in mind for this exhibition.

"Watch closely," he informed all the performers now circling around to watch. With his hands on the dancer's hips, he pulled him tight enough against himself that he would be able to follow his movements. "Move with me," he instructed.

Slowly their hips began to glide to the music, rocking lightly and dipping lower to sway back up. After they'd all had a chance to watch, he spun the male around and pulled him against him once more, his arm around his waist, and began to dance and grind more naturally to the music, his body fluid and graceful. The male's face was flushed, and he glanced at Ander through his lashes.

He was interested. It was written plainly on his face for Ander to read. And while he was beautiful in the elegant, perfect way muses were, he wasn't *right*. He was missing the height. The broad shoulders taut with muscles. The pair of hazel eyes that connected with something deep inside Ander he couldn't even explain.

The heat in the young male's eyes did nothing for him. Ander pulled away from him, putting space between them. "And if I wanted to dance on my own, I would move like this." He swayed his hips, dipping low and slowly rising back up. Spinning on his foot, he continued to sway and grind to the music, dancing like he would if he were in the club. Seductiveness had always come naturally to Ander. It was far easier to communicate with someone else through his body than it was to do so verbally.

He quirked a finger at another dancer, encouraging her out before him. With an eager smile on her face, she began to mimic his movements. Soon they were all surrounding Ander, dancing along with him, and it felt almost like he was on the floor at Inferno. Except this was Helicon, no matter how much he tried to change it, and it would never truly be his home.

Ander broke free of the dancers, who all gave him a happy clap of appreciation, and returned to the table, a little flushed and glistening with a hint of sweat along his hairline.

"Well, that was . . . something," his mother murmured. "Is that how all mortals dance now?"

"At least at our club, it is." Ander waved his hand over his glass and refilled it, snapping his fingers so that a toothpick full of olives dropped into it with a little splash.

"Fascinating. Humans are terribly obvious with their mating habits."

Ander chuckled. "They can be. Though not always so brazenly." He bit at the corner of his lips as his mind drifted to Maximus. *Max.* So sweet and earnest. So totally without that brazen heat he was used to. All tenderness and fumbling uncertainty.

Silence had fallen over the table, and it took Ander a moment to realize that both Mab and his mother were gazing over at him, his mother's gaze one of deep study.

"Are either of you going to tell me what brought you to Helicon today? Or better yet, what took you into that hellish landscape of Hades'?"

Ander swallowed roughly, lifting his glass to his lips and looking across the table at Mab, trying to tell her with his eyes not to say a word.

"Only Ander thinking he needs to be the one to handle Enrique rather than let the Sanctum do their job." Her face was stone cold, exasperation shining in her eyes with a hint of worry pinching at the corners.

He narrowed his eyes on his best friend. *Bitch*, he mouthed at her.

Queen Aemiliana frowned. "Ander." His name on her lips was enough to draw his gaze to her. "Why in the name of the gods would you think you ever need to deal with that ingrate again?"

Ander scowled. "Because I am perhaps one of the few who truly understands what a terrible monster he is."

"So? The Sanctus Ignis were created by Prometheus to combat monsters. Allow the Sanctum to do their job if Orcus is up to his old ways once more."

"Exactly what I said," Mab championed from across the table.

"It's not that simple."

"Oh?" His mother's brow shot up. "Please do explain why."

"Because! The ignis weren't made to deal with gods. If I send them in after Enrique, they're just going to die." Panic caught at his throat, squeezed his chest, and caused his diaphragm to spasm. He couldn't put Max in that kind of danger.

Aemiliana's eyes narrowed on him suspiciously, and Ander felt exactly like a virus under the microscope.

"You've never concerned yourself with the welfare of the Sanctum or its soldiers before. Typically, you're the one causing them the headache." She wasn't wrong about that. "Why the change now?"

"I've always cared!"

Mab snorted and placed her elbows on the table to lean forward, staring him down.

Ander did his best not to squirm beneath their pointed looks.

"Sweetheart." His mother's voice was soft but insistent.

He sighed heavily, feeling pinned in place. "I've found my soulmate." His mother inhaled sharply but did not interrupt him. "It's been twenty-three years since Erotes shot my arrow at a descending ignis youngling, and I've found him."

This time, when his mother gasped, she was not able to stay silent. "Erotes arrow-bound you to an ignis?!"

"Mab too."

"When did this happen? Why did you not tell me?" Her dark eyes traveled between the two of them quickly.

"It was in Germany, happened sort of out of the blue. Didn't seem like an important thing to mention at the time," Ander muttered.

Mab rolled her eyes at him. "More like he didn't want to mention how he got himself into this mess due to a one-hundred-and-thirty-year grudge Erotes held against him, and then proceeded to get *me* involved because he couldn't keep his mouth shut."

Ander hissed. "Traitor. Tattletail. Mama's little snitch."

Where's the lie? Mab's eyes asked him. It didn't keep him from glaring at her.

"Oh, Ander, how do you always manage to—" His mother cut herself off, fingers rubbing at her forehead. "Let me get this straight . . . Enrique is up to something terrible enough that you felt you had to go speak to Hades about it. And you refuse to enlist the Sanctum because you don't want this ingis you're arrow-bound to mixed up in whatever it is."

Ander shrugged his shoulders. "More or less."

"Sweetheart—"

"No. Mother, listen . . . If you had the chance to meet Maximus, you would understand. He's not like any ignis you or I have ever met before. He's sweet, and kind, and far better of a person than I could ever hope to be. I don't know exactly what Enrique is up to, but if my suspicions are correct . . . it's something absolutely awful. But I can't send Max in until I know for sure there's something worth risking his life over. So, I'm trying to figure out if what I think is happening is actually happening."

He felt like he'd just talked himself around in a circle. His heart and his mind were all twisted up inside him, wound tightly by the tangled mess that was his binding to Max.

His mother studied him intently until her eyes softened. "You love him."

"What?" Ander laughed, shaking his head. "No. It's simply that I'm bound to him through the arrow . . . I just need him to stay alive long enough for us to consummate this bond so the ache in my chest will go away. That's . . . all . . . ." His mother was already walking around the table toward him.

Before he could finish his half-assed refusal, her arms had slipped around him, and she'd pulled him from his seat and into a hug.

"I can't wait to meet this ignis who has filled your eyes with such light." Aemiliana smiled softly and pressed a kiss to his cheek.

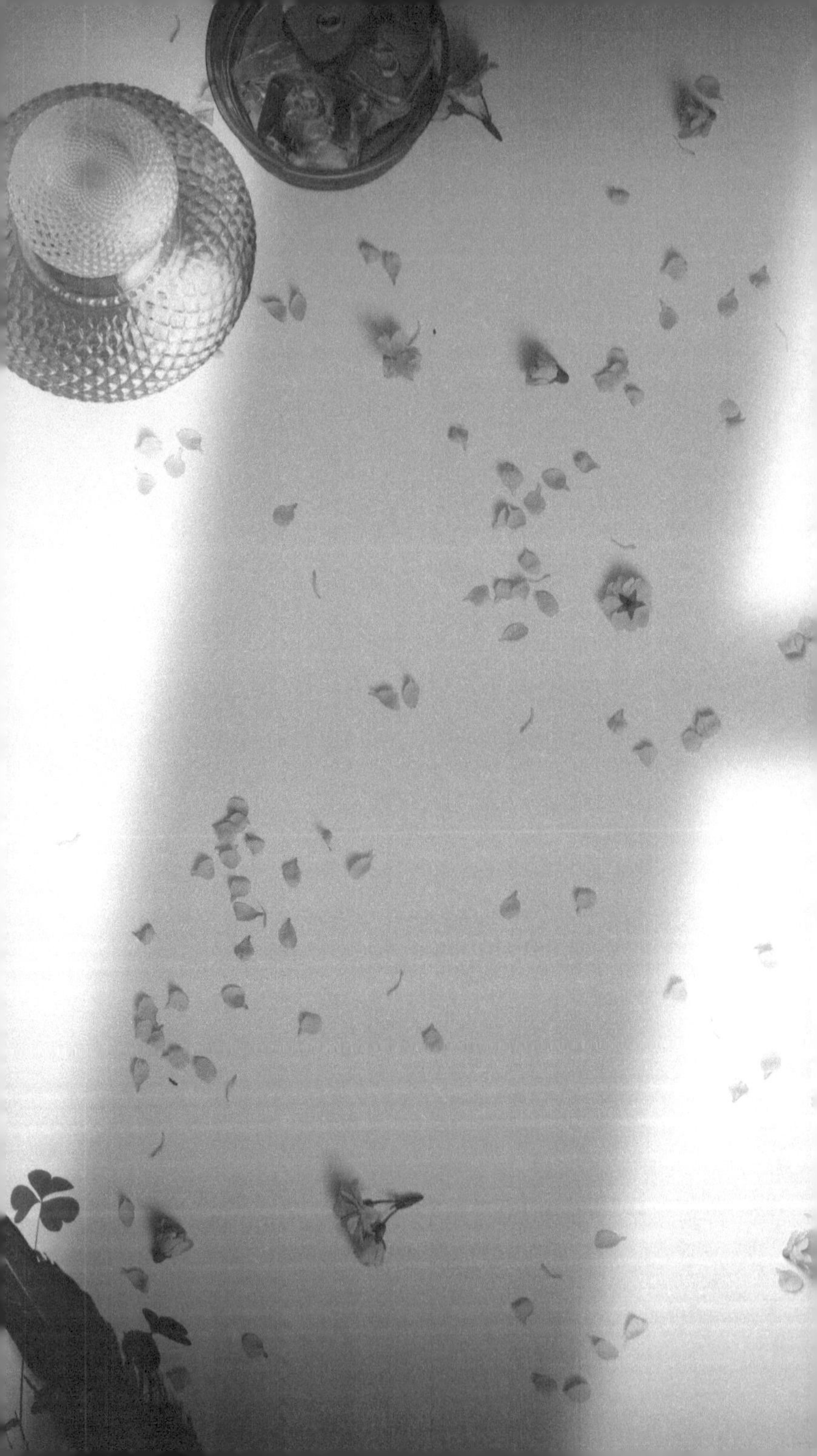

Chapter 27
Quin

Hector Hugman had done nothing but stare straight ahead since they'd captured him at his home and brought him in, no matter who attempted to taunt him into speaking. The satyr was locked up tight, face and body giving nothing away. It frustrated Quin, who had done his best to break the suspect. In the end, they needed something to force him to talk. Something that would make his position weak and make him crack.

Returning to the warehouse to search it alongside the forensic team had been the only viable solution either he or Max had seen.

It stank of filth: blood, piss, and fear. A number of truly terrible things had happened in this building, and there was a good chance they would never know all of it. The world was filled with so many dark and twisted creatures. Too often it felt as if they were fighting a losing battle, that there would never be a way to overcome all the darkness. But when Quin could feel the despair sweeping over him, putting out all his hope, he looked to his brother.

Max had always been a light to him in the dark. The

one bright spot that kept him going. Especially when their dad had first brought him home from Syria and Quin had been too afraid to even speak. He hadn't really even known what it was like to have a voice he could use. Max had learned ASL with him, so happy and pleased to take on this entirely new language so that he could communicate with his new brother. That alone was a struggle, Quin's vocabulary consisting of fragments of English and Syrian. Snippets that he managed to pick up as his captors moved him from cell to fighting ring.

Max reminded Quin that there were still wonderful beings in this world worth fighting for. That no matter how dark things got, it was worth going on because of creatures like him.

"I've got the west side, if you'll take the east," Max said as they entered from the southern end of the building.

The forensic team, headed up by Nox and Nash, were beginning at the south end and working their way down, one thorough inch at a time. They'd already been there for hours, and processing all of the grit and grime inside the warehouse was far more of a headache than Quin wanted to contemplate.

While the twins were chaotic and a nuisance half of the time, he had to give it to them for setting their minds to the specialized task of combing a crime scene from top to bottom. Their focus and drive in these situations was admirable.

In the center of the room sat several tanks filled with murky water that they'd rescued fifteen mermaids from last night during the raid. Two forensic officers dressed in scuba gear were inside collecting samples.

Quin nodded at Max's words. "Sure." Clicking on his flashlight, he swept it over the floor, illuminating the areas the forensic lamps didn't quite reach. Yellow caution tape trailed from around one beam and dipped into a puddle of water that had formed from a hole in the roof. It still dripped from a small shower they'd had overnight.

The pool of light highlighted a dark corner and exposed the outline of a door. Quin stepped up to it, twisted the knob, and threw the door open. Inside was a small office that had been trashed. Old papers lay all over the floor, dirtied from boots treading on them. A broken chair lay on its side, and the desk was covered mostly in dust and old fast-food wrappers.

Seeing nothing of importance, he left the small office and continued walking the eastern side of the building.

The windows were covered in dark paper, keeping any potential sunlight out. The occasional burst shone through where the paper had torn or crumpled. The cement floor, thick with dirt and papers, also seemed free of any trace amounts of evidence.

Quin grunted with irritation and moved farther down the warehouse, trailing the flashlight beam up the walls to check out the ceiling and upper mezzanine, then back down to the floor level. As he did so, a flash of silver caught his attention on the other side of the warehouse.

He moved quickly, following that twinge of instinct that guided him on occasion. Never as good as Max's, but it served him well enough.

A wall was framed out with metal studs but only partially covered by drywall. Half of it was missing. Like someone had simply given up on finishing their job, or perhaps run out of material.

Quin lifted the flashlight and shined it into the small partitioned-off room. Several cages sat abandoned beyond the metal studs. He walked around the partial wall, ducking through the door that was framed out so his wings did not catch, and stepped up to the cages.

There were scratch marks on the floor, and partially bent bars where something incredibly strong had tried to free itself. Quin kneeled down, shining the flashlight into the back corner of the first cage.

A shiver of apprehension wove its way from the top of his head to his neck and straight down his spine.

Several pieces of white down lay long forgotten in the corner of the cage, along with a dried puddle of shimmering blood. Heart hammering, he pulled his knife out of the sheath on his thigh and stretched his arm into the cage to scrape some of the blood up. But he already knew what he was going to find.

Quin brought the blade of the knife close to his face. He shined his flashlight onto it, moving it back and forth. The blood not only shimmered but, even dried, the darkest red shifted with living flame.

Quin shuddered. Ignis blood.

He fell back onto his bottom, inhaling a sharp breath. The cages were too small for adults. Hugman had been holding younglings here. What was he doing with them? Did this mean Timoros was also involved in an illegal youngling trade on top of the Mermaid's Lament and the human trafficking?

Quin's head spun, leaving him dizzy and nauseous.

The large spear clanged against the rungs of his cage. In fear, he scrunched back against the opposite side, trying to seem small and uninteresting.

"What about this one?" a dark voice growled.

"It's a child. The battle will be over too quickly."

"No, this one is a spitfire," the one with the spear insisted.

He tried to curl up on himself more. He was insignificant. He was weak.

He was trembling in fear. He couldn't go back out to the arena. Not again. The wounds on his back and legs were only just healing. His left wing ached from where the sphynx had latched on with her claws and nearly torn it from his flesh.

The screaming of the crowds was too loud. So many bloodthirsty faces bearing down on him. Wanting to see him hurt. Wanting to see him die.

He didn't want to die. He didn't want to be like the others who grew cold and still. Whose eyes turned cloudy and stared into nothingness, seeing no more.

"Doesn't look like much."

"Just watch," the satyr holding the spear stated. The door to the cage swung open, and the satyr reached in to grab one of his arms.

He knew he shouldn't react, but his instincts said to fight. To do everything he could not to end up in their hold once more. Not to end up back in that bad place, where pain and death happened.

Screaming, he lashed out at the hand, kicking and hitting with as much force as he could. The satyr cursed, while the demogorgon laughed.

From behind, the hard end of another spear jabbed into his back, forcing him into the middle of the cage. He clawed at the floor, doing his best to hold himself in place while kicking out, but the satyr grabbed his ankle and yanked him out of the cage. His nails bent back as he dug into the dirt floor beneath him.

Once out of the cage, his black wings started flapping frantically. They flapped strongly enough, he managed to right himself and began to lift the satyr off the floor. However, a spear swung through the air, connecting with his *temple. A cry of agony left his lips as he fell to the ground, hands clutching at the fresh wound in his hairline.*

"You were right, it does have a lot of spunk. How old is it?"

"About six."

"Can it win?" the demogorgon asked.

"It has before."

"Quin."

He pushed up onto his knees and growled, blood dripping into his eyes. He refused to blink, but glared up at the two.

"Quin, you're safe."

He growled again, swatting out at the satyr with the spear.

"Q!"

Quin blinked, staring over at Max, who was kneeling down in front of him, his hands on his shoulders.

"You're not there anymore. It's over. You're safe."

Quin nodded, but his heart pounded loudly in his ears, and his breath came in short, sharp gasps. He could still smell the dank must of the basement confines they kept them in. Could feel the dampness of his clothes from the excess moisture. Still ached in his bones from sleeping on the floor and fighting through the exhaustion of malnutrition and dehydration.

"Just breathe with me," Max murmured softly, then took a slow, deep breath.

Quin stared at him, fighting to regain control. He took a slow breath but ended up panting quickly once more.

"That was good, that was a start. Take another one with me, then breathe out slow."

Max's fingers were firm but steady on his shoulders. Quin let that ground him in the present. He focused on his brother's kind hazel eyes and took a slow breath, then forced his lungs to hold it in for a moment before slowly letting it out.

"That's good." Max somehow managed to give him a smile that was kind and encouraging without being condescending. But then, that was Max. Tender without ever being judgmental.

When Quin once again had control over himself, he shrugged off Max's hands. "Thanks," he signed, not feeling quite up to speech yet.

"What happened?"

Quin pointed his flashlight into the cage. "Ignis down," he signed slowly.

Max turned to look. "Gods . . . they're not only trafficking humans as food, they're trafficking younglings."

"That means another fight ring has popped up," Quin rasped. It was the worst possible scenario for where the missing younglings had gone.

Max turned to look at him, hand grasping his shoulder once more. "We'll find it, Quin, no matter what it takes."

Quin stood, needing to put some distance between himself and Max's concern. His skin felt raw, like every nerve inside him was on high alert, sending electrical impulses at the mere suggestion of touch or movement.

"I'll go get the twins, let them know forensics needs to start in here right away."

Max nodded, standing but keeping his distance. Max understood him, perhaps better than anyone.

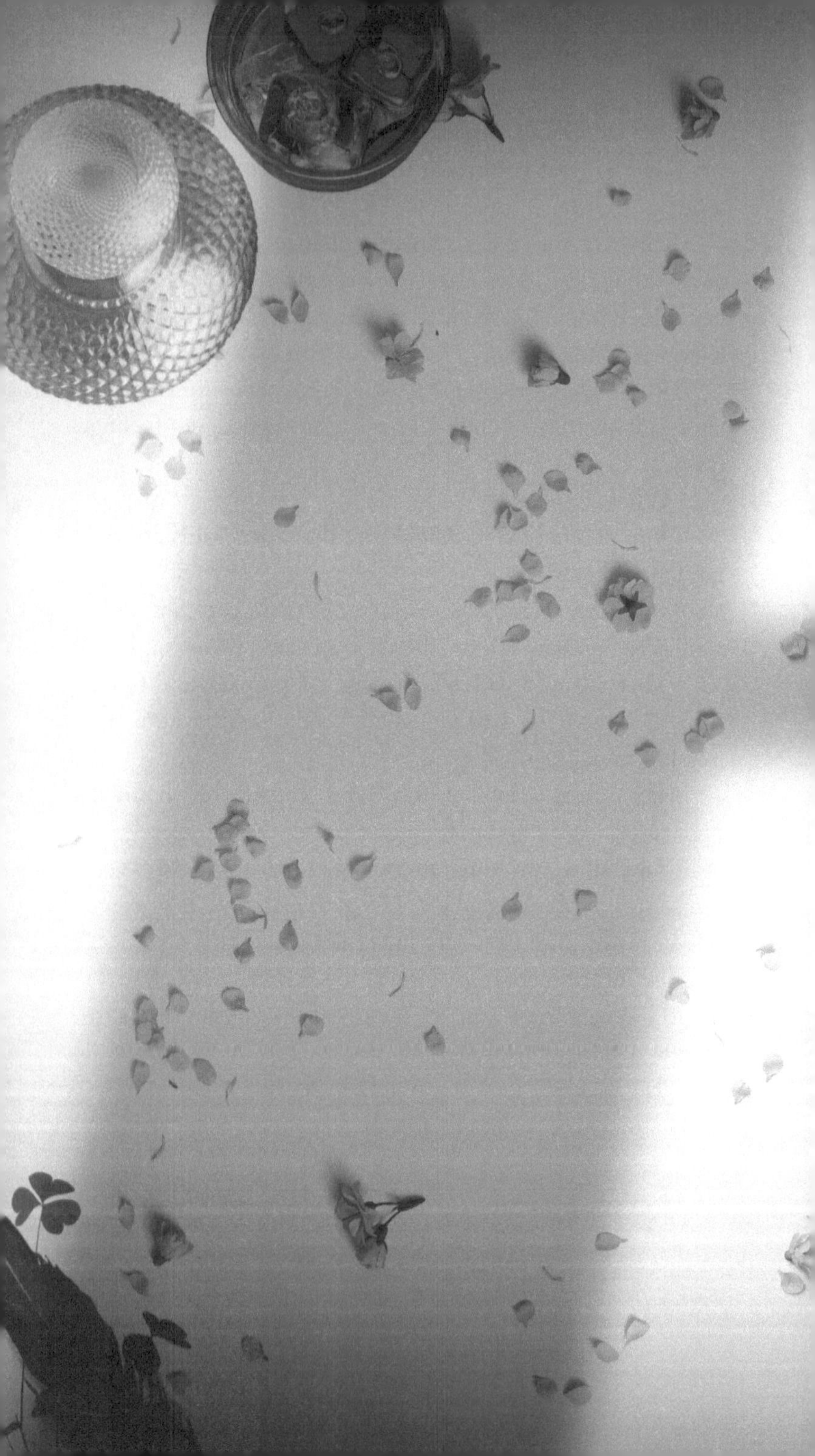

Chapter 28
Max

No news is good news. It was something Max had grown up hearing from his papa. Ezekiel Schields would say those exact words whenever they hadn't heard from Colt for a stretch of time, and Max would find comfort in them, even when he didn't really know what they meant. Because if his Papa wasn't worrying, then neither should he.

But the older he got, the more he realized those words were an empty platitude. An infuriatingly contrary phrase that didn't really *mean* anything and never really did anything to make anyone feel better.

Funny how growing up could shine a different light on things, exposing all the ugly edges. And there was nothing uglier than what he and Quin found in that warehouse just a few short hours ago. *Nothing.*

So, when the twins at last returned from the warehouse he asked them what they'd found while digging deeper into the records for Hugman and they just shook their heads . . .

No news is good news.

Max tore himself away forcibly from the control center,

needing now more than ever to distance himself from that world and the horrors therein.

He needed air.

He needed space.

He needed to beat Hugman into a bloody pulp until he told them everything he knew about what was being done to the poor innocent creatures that those monsters had stuffed into filthy tanks and cages.

Tanks and cages.

Like they were no more than shelter animals. No. *Worse.* Shelter animals at least had blankets and affection. The creatures Max and his team had rescued from Hugman's warehouse had neither. Just torture and cold.

And the younglings were still out there, more than any of them could have imagined, if the report he'd finally read from Nox was anything to go by. Over a hundred younglings missing in the last twenty to thirty years. The bottom had dropped out of the world at the sheer breadth of those numbers. It was like fighting the tide. A swirling undertow, dragging him to the depths to steal the fire from his heart, the breath from his lungs.

Max's feet, with no permission from his mind—or any other part of his anatomy, really—led him through the sanctuary and to the door that kept the medical wing separate from the rest of Miami's Sanctum operations. There was a narrow window in the door, reinforced with chicken wire between two plates of glass, eerily similar to hospital doors Max had seen so many times on normie television. And through it, Max could see the mermaids his team had rescued as they were treated with a kind of care many of them may have never seen before.

Each face, no matter how young or old, held the same

guarded lostness that Max had seen so regularly on Quin's in those first few years, that he *still* saw sometimes, even now. A hollow pang went through his chest, making him lift a hand to rub at it, trying to force away the ache.

"Where's Q?" Colt asked from where he had joined his son looking into the medical bay—just to check, just to see, just to know that they were all right.

Thankfully, no one seemed to be fighting back against the medical professionals tasked with helping them. Not the way that Quin had when he'd first moved into the Schields home. But that didn't mean they wouldn't. There was a long road to recovery in front of each and every one of them, and most of it wouldn't be physical.

"Sent him home." Max shrugged, not turning to face his father. He just needed a minute, just one, to remind himself that they'd done well the last couple of days. They hadn't gotten to the very heart of things, but they had saved beings. So many living, breathing beings. He should have felt good about that, right? He should've felt accomplished? He didn't. "Papa came to get him after we got back."

"That was probably the right call," Colt said with a hum of approval, moving to stand beside his eldest child, his shoulder brushing against Max's in a way that was meant to be a subtle comfort in a way only Colton Schields could provide.

On a normal day, that approval would have made Max puff up with pride. He'd spent his entire life wanting to make his family proud, striving to prove his father had been right in going against guardian norms by raising his ignis alongside human children. By treating them as people first and warriors second. But now? Now his father's words were hollow praise. Just like *Max* was hollow.

"I need to report in," Max said, falling back on the good little soldier he'd always been. It was easier to be that than to be this. Whatever *this* was. "Galeo is waiting."

"Why don't you call Ander first?"

"Tried. He's not picking up." With a long sigh, Max scrubbed at his face and turned to lean against the wall beside the door. "Besides, I don't have time for that right now. I'm a man down."

"Max." Colt's tone was soft but chiding. "You're allowed to take a minute to process. No one will fault you for needing time. Especially not with what you found this afternoon." He clasped his son's shoulder, giving Max a gentle squeeze that did nothing to warm the chill that had settled in, bone-deep. "Go and see Ander. Let yourself find comfort in someone you love for a few minutes before diving back in to all this."

"I'm not gonna put this on him." Max shook his head, brushing the hair that fell into his face away with a rough hand. "It's not his job to make this okay for me. He didn't sign on for that."

Colt huffed, shaking his head. "I didn't say go and unload on him. I said find comfort in him, in something good in the world." He gave Max's shoulder another hard squeeze before pulling back and putting some distance between them. Both men lifted their heads to glance down the hall at the approaching footsteps of Georgie.

She looked so small now when compared to what Max found in that warehouse. Her bright pink wings curled behind her neatly, doing nothing to make her look any less the little girl that she was, not even fourteen yet for gods' sake. And Max could imagine her there, brilliantly pink wings washed into dullness from the trauma and the dirt, stuffed into a cage right alongside a much younger Quin.

Max shook himself, but he knew the image would haunt him in his nightmares for the foreseeable future. "What is it?"

"Nox says she found something," Georgie murmured softly, keeping her tone low so as not to disturb the stillness of this side of the sanctuary.

"Good." Max pushed himself off from the wall and stood up straight, his spine stiff. He turned to give his father a nod, but Colt stopped him with a hand on his shoulder again.

"Think about what I said," Colt murmured gently, as if afraid to scare Max off. "You might find that you're wrong about some things."

Max wasn't sure what that meant, and Colt didn't expand upon it. He turned and headed through the swinging doors into the medical wing, leaving Georgie and Max alone in the hall. When Max turned back to his sister, she was watching him with her brows pinched together, the same expression he'd seen on her face so many times when she tried to solve a math problem.

"Are you okay?" she asked after a moment of silent inspection.

And although the lie sat heavy in his mouth, Max said, "Yeah, I'm good. Come on, let's go get this son of a bitch."

Then he headed back down toward the command center to see what it was the twins had dug up.

"There was a co-signer, sir," Max said after he'd finished his report on everything they found in the warehouse. His hands were clasped behind his back to hinder the fidgety, jittery feeling that had started up in the muscles and would only make him appear incompetent in the face of his superior. They couldn't have that.

"A co-signer?" Galeo asked, his head tilted to one side where he sat behind his heavy desk.

"Yes, sir." Max licked his lips, shifting his weight a little on his feet, a subtle fidget that did nothing to ease the tension racing through him. Maybe his father was right. Maybe he did need to go see Ander, give himself a little happiness in the darkness that surrounded him. "We didn't find it at first because the property was lease-to-own. But there was a second name on the original leasing agreement. A name we've been able to track to property in other areas that have experienced ignis disappearances. There seems to be a connection."

"I see." Fingers tapping on the dark surface of his desk, Galeo hummed softly in thought. His blue wings shifted behind him, spreading out a little in something that was likely involuntary but also intimidating.

Max waited through the silence as Galeo considered everything, taking his time to parse it all out, and tried his best not to fidget more under the weight of the quiet. It lasted far too long for Max's comfort, and he was almost to the point of asking Galeo if he could dismiss himself before Galeo's eyes cut to him again, pinning him in place.

"I'm going to put more hands on this. I'll get a set of teams together; you'll meet with them tomorrow."

An order, not something Max could even argue with. But it left him feeling raw. Galeo didn't trust him to do this alone. Max had proven himself incapable. This was too big for him. Maybe the Princeps were right about him after all. His fingers twitched.

"Yes, sir." Max didn't wait to be dismissed. He spun on his heel and left, headed back to the command center where the twins were still behind their screens. Both of them had a distinctly glassy look to their eyes, like they hadn't slept nearly enough over the last couple of weeks, but they turned to look at him when he entered, mirrored expressions of concern pinching their features.

"Well?" Nash asked, not even waiting for Max to say anything.

"We're being given more men for this." Max slumped down into the extra wheely chair they left shoved into a corner, usually piled with paperwork. "Galeo is putting together a task force this evening, and I'll meet with them tomorrow."

"That's . . . good . . . right?" Nox frowned at him, her bright green eyes taking in much too much of what was likely playing across his face. Max sat up again, making the conscious effort to school his features. Whatever doubts lingered. Whatever insecurities buzzed under his skin. Max couldn't let them show, not in front of his team. They needed him to be strong, confident, in control. "It means he's finally taking this seriously."

"Yes." *Not really. It means you failed them, all of them. It means you weren't good enough. It means—*"You two should head home and get some rest. It's been a long few days, and it's not looking like it's going to get less hectic anytime soon."

They both looked like they wanted to ask him something, likely the same thing Georgie had asked, but Max wasn't going to give them the chance. He couldn't. So, he pushed to his feet and headed for his office to grab his sweater.

He threw a simple "I'll see you guys in the morning" on his way out the door and didn't wait for any further probing.

His father's advice still ringing in his ears, Max found himself in front of Ander's building before he had even made the conscious decision to head there. He stood for a moment, his feet rooted to the sidewalk, staring up at the reflection of the setting sun on the windows, not really seeing it.

Should he drop in like this? Were there rules about this kind of thing? His exes wouldn't have liked this. They wouldn't have appreciated him just showing up at their place looking for a bit of comfort. But . . .

But he couldn't go home. Not like this. His papa would see through him. Quin would see through him. He couldn't let them see this sad, aching piece of him. Not right now. Not until he'd soothed it a little, made it less ugly. He needed to be strong for them.

And besides, he was already there wasn't he? Why not just go up and see if Ander was home?

With a deep inhale, Max forced himself in through the lobby entrance, not even feeling the chill from the AC unit over the door because he was still cold from the warehouse, and strode right to the elevator. He tried not to look at himself in the chrome panels on the inside of the little box but still somehow managed to catch the wild tangle of hair, the bags under his eyes, oh yeah, and the smudge of something that could have been dirt, could have been blood, on his jeans. Gross. He was gross. He should just leave. Ander shouldn't see him like this.

Beautiful, wonderful, vibrant Ander should never have to see Max like this. Fresh from hell and looking for a place to curl up and just sleep for a week.

But the elevator dinged, and his feet carried him to Ander's front door regardless of what he thought. Then his hand pushed the doorbell, and the door was flung open seconds before Max could change his mind and flee.

The first sight of Ander was like breathing again after being too long under water. Max inhaled, his shoulders relaxing for the first time in what felt like centuries.

"Come in," Ander said without any prompting and ushered Max inside, heedless of the dirt and grime still caked on his boots and clothes as he deposited Max on his sofa. A blanket was thrown over his shoulders, and Ander disappeared for a long minute before he returned with a glass of water.

"I—I—I'm sorry," Max mumbled, his fingers trembling as Ander pressed the glass into his hand. "I couldn't—I didn't want—I shouldn't be here."

Ander shushed him gently and nudged his wrists until he lifted the glass to his lips and took a long, slow sip. It helped, but only until the moment when it hit his empty stomach and began to slosh around.

He took another sip anyway, because Ander had been nice enough to get it for him and because his tongue felt like sandpaper, making it unwieldy and hard to speak with. When the glass was drained, his mind was a little clearer. "I'm sorry to just show up like this. It was a hard day."

"Max." Ander's tone was firm, no-nonsense, so unlike how he usually spoke, and when Max finally met his eyes, he saw that Ander had fixed him with a penetrating stare, kind brown eyes pinning him in place. "You're always welcome here. Do you want to talk about it?"

Max curled his fingers into the blanket around his shoulders, tugging it so close to his face, he could smell the scent of Ander's home on it. Soothing. He opened his mouth to respond, to tell Ander everything, to lay himself bare, then his eyes caught on a pair of Ander's shoes abandoned beneath the coffee table. Black dust coated the toes.

"What's that?" Max asked, reaching down to brush his fingers over them, and pulling his hand closer to his face to examine the dirt. It was black, and glittering, like—"Why were you in Acheron?"

"Just visiting with Hades," Ander said, flapping his wrist flippantly as if to say *as one does*. Which, no. One did not.

"Why were you visiting Hades?"

Ander shook his head and leaned in closer, his hand reaching to brush lightly against Max's, effectively brushing away the proof while he pushed the shoes farther under the coffee table with his foot. Then he teased, "You're deflecting."

No. You are. Max heard the refrain in his head, a mirror of the last time those words had been said between them. When he'd asked Ander if someone had attacked him, a gnawing feeling in his belly that it had been his ex. Max couldn't pinpoint why he thought that, how he just *knew*, but he did. And . . . suddenly, he didn't feel like he wanted to be so vulnerable with Ander anymore. Not if . . . not if he was keeping secrets about his ex.

"I don't want to talk about it."

"All right." Ander nodded once, the decision made, and slipped to his feet, taking Max's hands in his to tug him off the couch. "Then let's go get cleaned up, and we can get into bed. You look like you could use the rest."

And Max didn't fight him on it. Didn't make him explain.

Why bother?

Ander would just lie again.

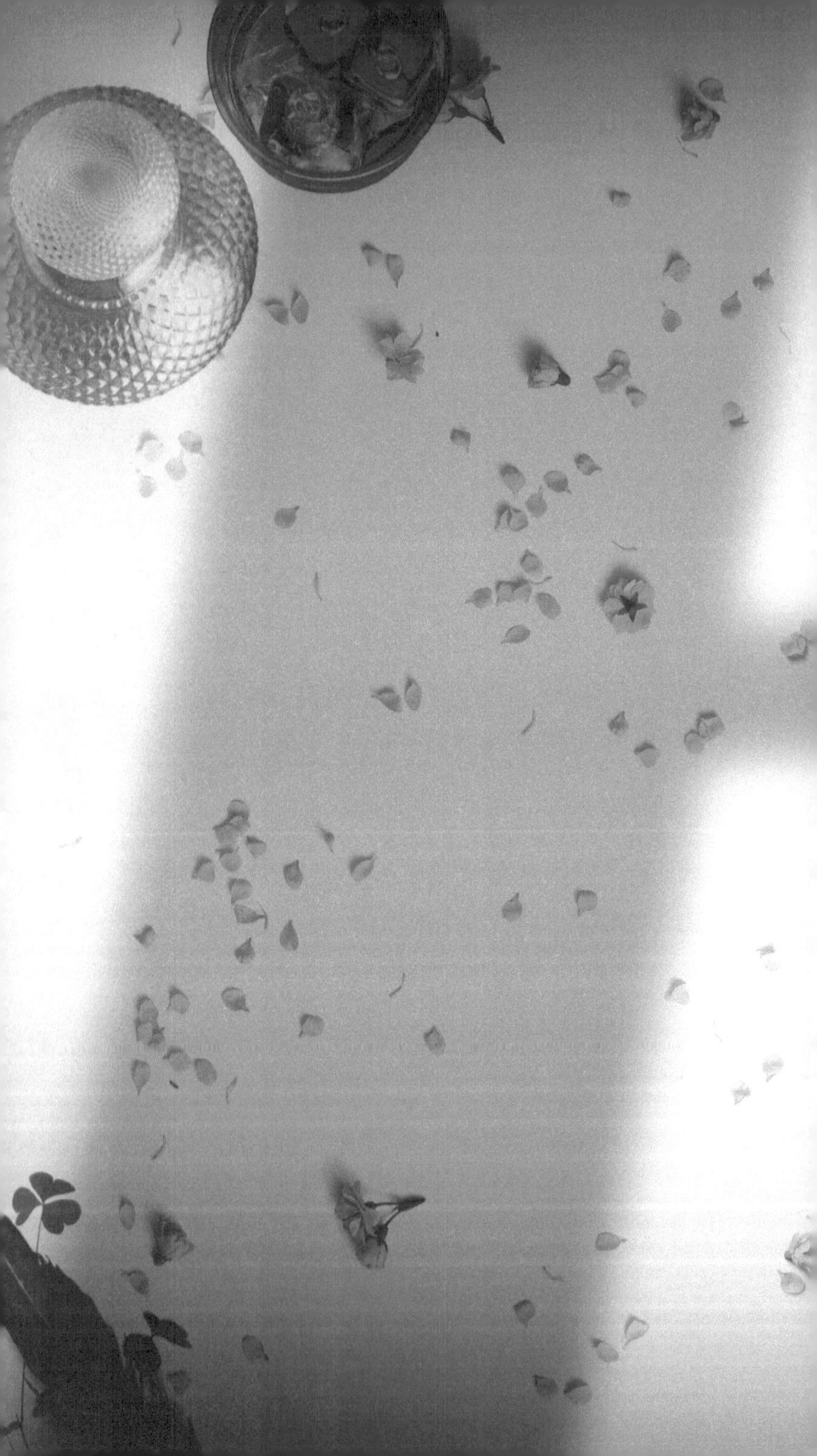

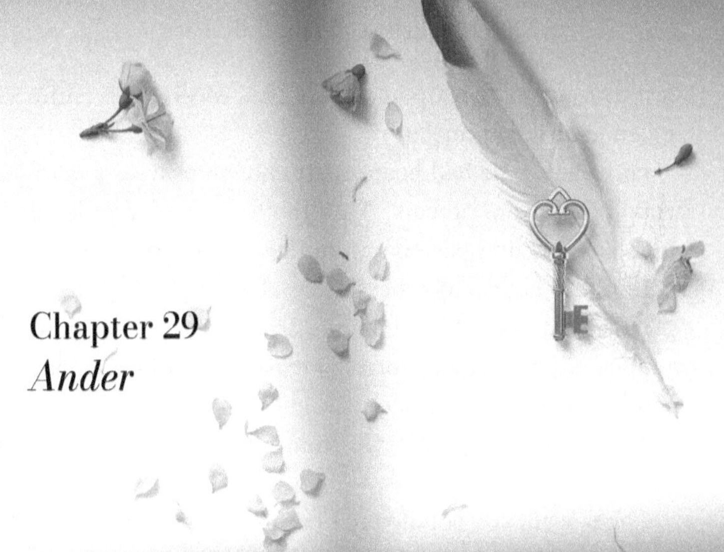

Chapter 29
Ander

Max was gone, and Ander felt empty.

He'd shown up out of nowhere looking like his world was crumbling down around him. Ander had wanted to do everything that he could to help, but instead, Max shut him out.

It hurt.

Ander was so used to dealing with Mab, who didn't always wish to discuss her feelings but after a pointed look from Ander would eventually come clean. Max was the complete opposite. Typically, his face was an open book to his emotions, everything he felt worn on his sleeve. Ander was sure that once he had him sat down and comfortable, he would open up. Especially since he had shown up unannounced, clearly needing Ander's company.

Instead, Max had been a closed door. He'd snuggled in and accepted the physical comfort Ander could give him but not the emotional.

It was always the physical with Ander. That was what he was good for. Even to his arrow-bound.

"Damn you to Acheron and back!" Ander cursed as his

latest concoction blew up in front of him, covering his entire kitchen in dust and smoke.

Fortunately, he had been smart enough to wear a mask through this entire process. After the first attempt, at least, which had left him passed out on the floor for three hours. Mab laughed her ass off when he'd told her.

He snapped his fingers irritatedly; the mess disappeared, and Ander tore his mask off his face, giving himself a moment to breathe.

Monnie let out a little yip from her daybed across the kitchen.

"That is enough out of you. I'm pretty sure I know what I did wrong, and this next batch will be perfect."

The dog sniffed derisively.

Ander snapped his mask back into place and began working on the different ingredients required to create *dues somnum*. He hummed, distracting himself from his internal thoughts of doubt that concerned him and Max and instead focusing on mixing the magical concoction.

He broke up the petals of angel's trumpets, using only two instead of the full bloom like he had last time. If he mixed it just right, the potion wouldn't only make Enrique feel drugged and sluggish, it would possibly even knock him out. He dropped the petals into his mortar and picked up his pestle to begin the slow process of grinding up the dried flower. Known in the mortal world as devil's breath, the scent emitted from the flower acted as a powerful hallucinogen. On a god, it wouldn't have the same effect. However, it would work perfectly for transporting *dues somnum* in powder form.

Rather than trying to get Enrique to drink it, this time he would simply blow as much of the powder into his face as he needed. Enrique's body would absorb it much faster through the airways than it would when digested. From what he could tell, however, the potion had never been turned into a powder before. Thus the catastrophic status of his kitchen currently.

The mixture had to be perfect though, and he wasn't going to stop trying until it was. Ander had only one more try for this before Enrique became suspicious of what he was up to.

Once the angel trumpet was ground into a fine powder, Ander began adding the other ingredients, each rarer and more expensive than the last. He had called in a number of favors to get his hands on everything he needed. But if this worked, it would all be worth it.

As he added in the final drops of mermaid venom, Ander held his breath and stepped back. He counted to ten and then relaxed. "I think this is the one!" he declared happily.

Across the room, Monnie yipped once more.

"Don't doubt me! I just need someone to test it out on."

Ander gazed around his condo. That was the next question . . . Where was he going to come up with a god to test this on before he called Enrique up for their next and *final* date?

As if he had beckoned him out of thin air, a lean, blond figure emerged from the back of Ander's condo by way of his bedroom.

"Have you never heard of a front door?" Ander grumbled, staring at the king of Underworld and his wife as they stepped into his kitchen.

Indra flashed a bright and happy smile. "When have friends ever needed to announce themselves?"

Ander huffed at the way Indra felt so completely fine with entering his home without permission. He scooped up a handful of the powder and rounded his island, lifting it palm-up. He brought it to his lips and blew out a deep breath.

The white powder filled the air, going straight into Indra's face.

The King of Underworld took a moment to blink at him, coughing as he inhaled the dust. Then he swayed on his feet and fell to the floor, only stopped from smashing face-first into it by the pillow Ander snapped into place at the last minute.

Ander was elated. It worked! Then crushing realization filled him as his eyes lifted from Indra's prone figure to that of his wife standing across from him.

"Juno!" Ander sputtered out. Juno had said he should use it on Indra, but what if that had been a joke?

"Oh, how convenient," she smirked. "I was trying to figure out how I was going to ditch him to go meet up with my date." Without concern, she took a step over her husband's body and patted Ander on the shoulder. "See you later."

Ander turned to stare at Juno over his shoulder, his mouth falling open a little. It was still open when Mab passed Juno on her way out.

"Ander, when did Ju—*What did you do?*" she shouted, spotting Indra on the floor.

"I needed to test the powder on someone . . ."

"And you chose Indra? In front of his *wife?*"

Ander shrugged. "She thanked me."

Ander was anxious about his second attempt at drugging Enrique. After what happened during his first attempt, just getting into Enrique's good graces would be hard enough. There would be no third try if he didn't succeed. And he *had* to get his hands on the feathers. *Had* to find out if Enrique was collecting an army of ignis younglings to do horrible, vile testing on.

The memory of Ikari haunted his dreams now, reminding him each night of what happened in the dungeons of Acheron and the debt he owed the Sanctus Ignis for his participation. Forced or not.

The anxiousness was turning into a feeling that something was going to go terribly wrong, and he just couldn't have his last time seeing Max be what it had been the night before. Which was why he found himself outside of the Schields' family home, a bouquet of flowers in his hand and his finger on the doorbell.

He was dressed in a pair of red, drop-crotch pants, a black tank with slitted sides, black suede sneakers, and a number of gold rings on his fingers. The long strands of his hair on top were styled into a wave over his forehead, flicked up at the ends, and his undercut had been redone. Ander had even splurged on some heavy eye makeup in reds and blacks, with just a hint of gold dust at the inner corners.

When the door swung open, it was not Max, but Zeke. He took one look at Ander and slammed the door.

Or he would have, had Ander not stuck his foot in the way. "I'm here to see Max!" he shouted quickly, foot throbbing.

"He's not here!" Zeke shoved at the door.

Ander pushed back. "I know he is."

"No. He's. No—"

"Papa!" Max's shout came from beyond Zeke, deeper in the house. "Open the door for Ander."

There was a growl from Zeke, and the door swung open once more. "Fine," Zeke deadpanned, eyeing Ander unhappily. "I guess he is home." He stepped out of the way but continued to glare at Ander as he walked down the hall.

Ander watched him for a moment, then turned his attention to Max. "Hey!" He grinned and held up the bouquet. "I am here to take you on a date."

Max's dark brows shot up at the sight of the flowers, and he took them, a blush coming to his cheeks. "A date? Where?"

"It's a surprise." Ander grinned.

Max eyed him over the bouquet as he buried his nose in it, shoulders a little tight. "Can I have a hint?"

Ander pursed his lips as if thinking. "Wear comfy shoes."

Max laughed, the tension in his shoulders easing a little, and nodded. "Okay, just give me a second."

"Of course."

Ander watched him hurry down the hall, to grab footwear, he could only assume.

"Shut the door, you're letting all the heat in!" Zeke shouted from somewhere in the house.

Ander rolled his eyes as he stepped into the house and closed the door behind him. Zeke Schields may have agreed to let Max date Ander, but he certainly wasn't going to make it easy on him.

Fortunately, Max wasn't gone long, and came back dressed in dark blue jeans, a light pink boatneck T-shirt, and a cream cable-knit sweater.

"Gods . . . you're adorable," Ander murmured, grabbing ahold of the sweater and pulling Max in against him, then lifting his chin up to claim his lips in a kiss that started out chaste but quickly became heated.

The taste of him was overwhelming, the scent of him inciting every dark, dirty thought swirling around in Ander's mind. But he pulled away and hauled in a deep, needy breath. "Ready?"

Max looked a little dazed and only nodded his head.

Ander looped his arm around his waist, tugged his hips in close so that they pressed against his, and snapped them away from the Schields family home.

When they reappeared, they were in the middle of Disney World's Magic Kingdom.

Max gasped and spun around. When he turned back to Ander, his eyes were wide. *"How did you know this was my favorite place?!"*

Ander laughed. "I've been in your room."

Max blushed once more. "Oh, right." For a moment, he looked embarrassed by this admission.

Ander broke the tension by taking Max's hand in his, threading their fingers together. "Come, I'm assuming first things first: we must buy ears."

Max grinned brightly and nodded. "Absolutely."

Ander allowed himself to be dragged off to the nearest shop, where they waded through squealing children, complaining teens, and a group of thirty-somethings singing "Hakuna Matata" to get to the large wall covered in ears.

Max zeroed in on a set quickly and pulled them off the wall to plop onto his own head. It was a yellow and gold pair with a red rose in the middle. He then plucked another blue and gold version off and turned to Ander. "Will you wear these?"

"Really? *Beauty and the Beast?*"

Max nodded, holding the ears up close to his lips,

looking shy and adorable. "It's my favorite . . . I always—" He got embarrassed and looked away.

"You always what?" Ander pressed.

"Dreamed of finding my Beast," he admitted quietly.

"Well, I *am* a horned prince." Ander flashed a cocky grin and swiped the ears from him, setting them in place on his head in front of his horns.

Max audibly gasped. "You're my very own Disney prince!"

Laughing, Ander pulled Max in by the sweater once more and kissed him quickly. "I think I'm more horny toad than Prince Charming, but I can work with that."

Max slipped his arms around Ander, holding him tightly. "You're definitely a Prince Charming, you don't even realize how much."

Ander shook his head but decided not to argue. "Come on, ma belle, let's go pay for these." He swirled his hand before him, and when he turned his hand over, the tags from both were in his palm.

A quick swipe of his credit card later, and they were headed out of the shop and back onto the street. Knowing he would need alcohol to survive this adventure at magic sunshine land, Ander tugged them over to the nearest kiosk selling fruity drinks in large cups and bought both of them one.

Once the large slushies were in their hands, Ander snapped himself a small bottle of rum. Winking, he added it to his own, then offered it to Max, who shook his head.

"Suit yourself, darling." He tucked the bottle into his back pocket for later. "Okay, what do you want to do first?" Ander looked up at Max and sucked fruity alcohol through a long bendy straw.

"I want to take our picture in front of the castle." His

eyes glowed with excitement, and Ander wondered if he would ever be able to say no to anything when Max looked at him with that kind of happiness.

"Absolutely." Hand in hand, sipping their drinks, they made their way farther into the park, heading straight to the castle.

Ander frowned at all the people milling about, hating that there would be so many in the shot. So, while Max found someone who was willing to snap their photo, Ander wove his hand in front of him, using his magic to encourage everyone to step away from the castle, clearing the background of any stragglers.

When Max stepped up to him, he was ready, all smiles, and curled into his side for a series of pictures. After the first two, Ander set their drinks aside, then turned to face him, wrapped his arms around Max's neck, and kissed him, one foot lifting off the ground.

Max laughed happily against his lips, his hands tight on his waist.

"Wanna dip me?" Ander murmured to him.

Without warning, Max's hands shifted to his upper and lower back, and he dipped him backward. Ander squealed in delight, then broke out in laughter, leaning back into the dip. Together, they looked at the camera. Then Max was kissing him, and Ander lost himself to the moment.

Breathless, they straightened, and Max retrieved his phone, thanking their impromptu photographer.

Retrieving their drinks, they walked farther into the park. Ander allowed Max to lead him to several rides but only suffered through the wait for the first one. After that, he snapped them to the head of the line for the rest. Max tried to protest, but Ander said there were many things he would do, but waiting in line just wasn't one of them. He'd never been a line person for anything.

It was after their second ride on It's a Small World that a stuffed Stitch on a shelf near the doorway of a souvenir shop caught Ander's eye. Drawn to it, he squeezed the soft, plushy foot.

"Do you like that?" Max asked.

"*Family means no one gets left behind*," Ander murmured, more to himself than anything. There had always been something about that movie that got to him. Perhaps because family, whatever that truly meant for an individual, had always meant more to Ander than anything else he had in this life.

Mab. His mother. A smattering of friends here and there. They were all that truly mattered when he totaled up what he had. Family was not always who you thought it would be, but your darkest times told you who would be there to lean on.

He blinked as the Stitch was snatched from the shelf in front of him. Frowning, he looked at Max. "What are you doing?"

"Buying you a stuffy."

"I don't need a stuffy."

"Yes, you do."

"No. And *I'm* taking *you* on this date!" Ander protested.

Max ignored him and took the stuffed creature to the cash register and did not return until he was able to hold it out to Ander, fully paid for.

Sighing, Ander took the item from Max, wrapping his arms around it and resting his chin on its fuzzy, plush head. "Thank you."

"You're welcome." Max leaned down to press a kiss to

the tip of his nose. "Teacups?"

"Huh?" Ander blinked.

"Should we do the teacups next?"

"Oh. Sure." Ander was glad he was only tipsy and not drunk. The last time he'd been here and ridden the teacups, he'd been so trashed, he'd barely made it off before hurling.

Max grinned and slipped his arm around Ander's waist so that he could lead him in the direction of the spinning teacups. This time, Ander didn't protest as Max pulled them into the line to wait. Instead, he used the time to lean against Max, inhaling his deep amber scent and absorbing the feel of his muscular body wrapped around him.

"You're adorable, you know that?" Max murmured, looking down at him with an adoring light in his hazel eyes.

Ander shook his head. "You're mistaken. You are clearly the adorable one here."

"No-*pe*." Max popped his p, and Ander rolled his eyes. "Don't fight me."

"Why? You gonna pin me down if I do?" Ander wiggled a little, eagerness taking over his face.

Max blushed. "Stop that."

"Stop what?"

"Flirting." Max squeezed his waist.

"It's my love language."

Max laughed and pressed a kiss to his forehead. It made Ander feel gooey inside. There was a warmth and ease that came with being with Max that he had never felt before. Something new and fresh. Good. Terrifying.

They moved farther up in line, and Ander watched the families spinning furiously around in circles as the colorful teacups twirled. He felt a little like that on the inside. Gleeful and riotous. Like at any moment, he may go spinning off into the cosmos, laughing uncontrollably all the while.

"Where'd you go?" Max murmured into his ear.

Ander leaned into him more, hugging his stuffy close. "Just getting dizzy."

"Don't worry, I'll hold you close."

Ander tipped his head back, gazing into Max's beautiful eyes, filled with tenderness and something absolute. "Never let go?"

Max shook his head. "Never." He smiled, then his head lifted, and his eyes lit up. "Come on, it's our turn!" He pulled away, but only so that he could claim one of Ander's hands, tugging him to a lavender-colored teacup.

Together they climbed in, and Max pulled Ander down beside him, tucking him into his side. Holding onto him with one arm, he lifted the other to rest it on the side of the wheel in the middle.

Ander clutched onto his stuffy with one hand and used his free hand to mirror him. Grinning at each other, they began to turn the wheel, and slowly, their teacup started to spin. As the ride went into motion, turning all of the cups together, Max and Ander spun themselves faster and faster, until it was all Ander could do to stay sitting up. And just like the others he had watched, he began laughing uncontrollably. Max's own laughter followed.

When it ended, they fell into each other, their snickers turning into tired giggles as their vision slowly stopped swirling about them.

"Gods . . . if I fall over and chip a tooth, it's all your fault." Ander snickered again and climbed out of the teacup.

"You're fine," Max encouraged, climbing out after him and wobbling a little on his feet.

Ander snickered more and wrapped his arm around Max's waist. "C'mon, I don't need you falling over either."

Their laughter rang out as they made their way off the ride and back onto solid ground. When they were a safe distance away from squealing children, Ander pulled Max in against his front and gazed up at him. "So, this was a good surprise?"

"It was the best surprise."

"Good." Ander wanted nothing more than to gift Max all the most wonderful things in the world. To see him happy and smiling as he was now.

His thoughts were cut short as Max dipped his head and pressed his lips to Ander's. Ander murmured in welcome, wrapping his arms easily around the ignis' neck. As he did, his fingers brushed the edges of Max's wings, and Ander could feel the shudder that went through him. The responding moan echoed in Ander's mouth and made his knees weak.

He wanted to hear more, and so he brushed his hand up along one wing, delighting in the silken softness of the feathers. Max groaned, the fingers at his hips biting pleasantly into his flesh.

"Back," Max rasped, sounding winded.

"Home?"

Max nodded and then captured his lips once more.

Ander didn't need to be asked again. Clutching his Stitch and holding onto Max, he snapped his fingers, teleporting them quickly away from the park and directly into Max's bedroom. The door wasn't closed, but Max took care of that with his foot, kicking it shut, then dropping them both down to the bed.

Ander gasped as he hit the mattress, Max's weight half landing on him and half on the bed. Wanting control, he rolled them so that Max was fully on his back, his gorgeous wings spread out beneath him, making him look like a fallen angel splayed out for Ander's pleasure. He wanted to leave him disheveled and panting. To wreck him in the most glorious of ways. And yet, he also wanted to protect him. To make sure nothing ever sullied the purity and wonder that resided within his heart.

Straddling his hips, Ander settled on top of him easily. Resting the palms of his hands on his stomach, he slowly pushed Max's T-shirt up, exposing the rock-hard abs for his viewing pleasure. Ander groaned and bit at his lips.

"Gods, you are a wonder to behold," he breathed out.

Max blushed and reached up to loop his hand around the back of Ander's neck to pull him down into a deep kiss.

A moan slipped from Ander as his fingers slid up under the shirt, tracing over hard ridges and soft skin. Exploring everything within reach as his lips parted to Max's exploring tongue. He rocked his hips down over Max's hardening member, and a shudder coursed through his own body. He wanted him so badly. With every fiber of his being. He wanted to feel their bodies connecting, to share intimate breath and forget there was ever an existence where he was not one with Maximus.

Max's hand left his neck and slid down his back, moving to dip into the back of his pants. His touch was warm, the heat of his ignis body almost scalding him but in the best of ways. It made Ander's form melt beneath it, and he moaned once more, nipping at Max's lips.

Unable to figure out how he was meant to take the shirt off over the wings, Ander just snapped it and the sweater away. Though he had seen Max shirtless before, he still couldn't help gasping at the sight of his bare flesh. He pulled away, but only so that he could lean down and begin nipping and kissing his way down Max's throat, over his collarbones, and across the slope of one peck.

Teasingly, he tongued a small nipple until it was a sharp peak and was delighted when Max's hips lifted slightly off the bed in response. "Good boy," he purred, and Max blushed oh so becomingly.

His fingers brushed down Max's sides as he scooted farther down the bed, nipping each ab adoringly and trailing his tongue between them. His own heart hammered quickly in his ears, and his need made it hard for him to think. But as he reached Max's belt buckle, his fingers ready to undo it, he remembered Max's words. How he said he wanted to take things slow, to make this special.

Ander shut his eyes, pressing his forehead against Max's abdomen, his horns gently scraping his skin. He took a deep breath to steady himself, reining in his desires. He wouldn't push Max. As much as he wanted this to go further, he wanted to respect Max's wishes even more.

When he lifted his head, Max was looking at him questioningly. "What's wrong?"

"Nothing, sweetheart." Ander smiled tenderly, his heart squeezing tightly at the sight of him. Slowly, Ander crawled back up to him and pressed a deep but tender kiss to his lips. "I had a wonderful time with you today."

"I did too." Still panting lightly, Max's fingers skimmed over his back, and he tried to pull Ander back down to him, pressing another hungry kiss to his lips.

Ander returned the kiss for a moment but lifted his head when his desires flared too strongly once more. "But I should go now."

"Wh-what?" Max blinked, looking up through hazy eyes.

Ander smiled gently and brushed his fingers lightly

down the side of his face. "I'm going to head home before I stop being able to control myself. You have the best night, my darling. I'll send you kisses from bed."

He stole one more kiss, imprinting the feel and taste of him, before he finally hauled himself from the bed to snap home.

His body screamed at him in dissatisfaction, but his heart was happy and full.

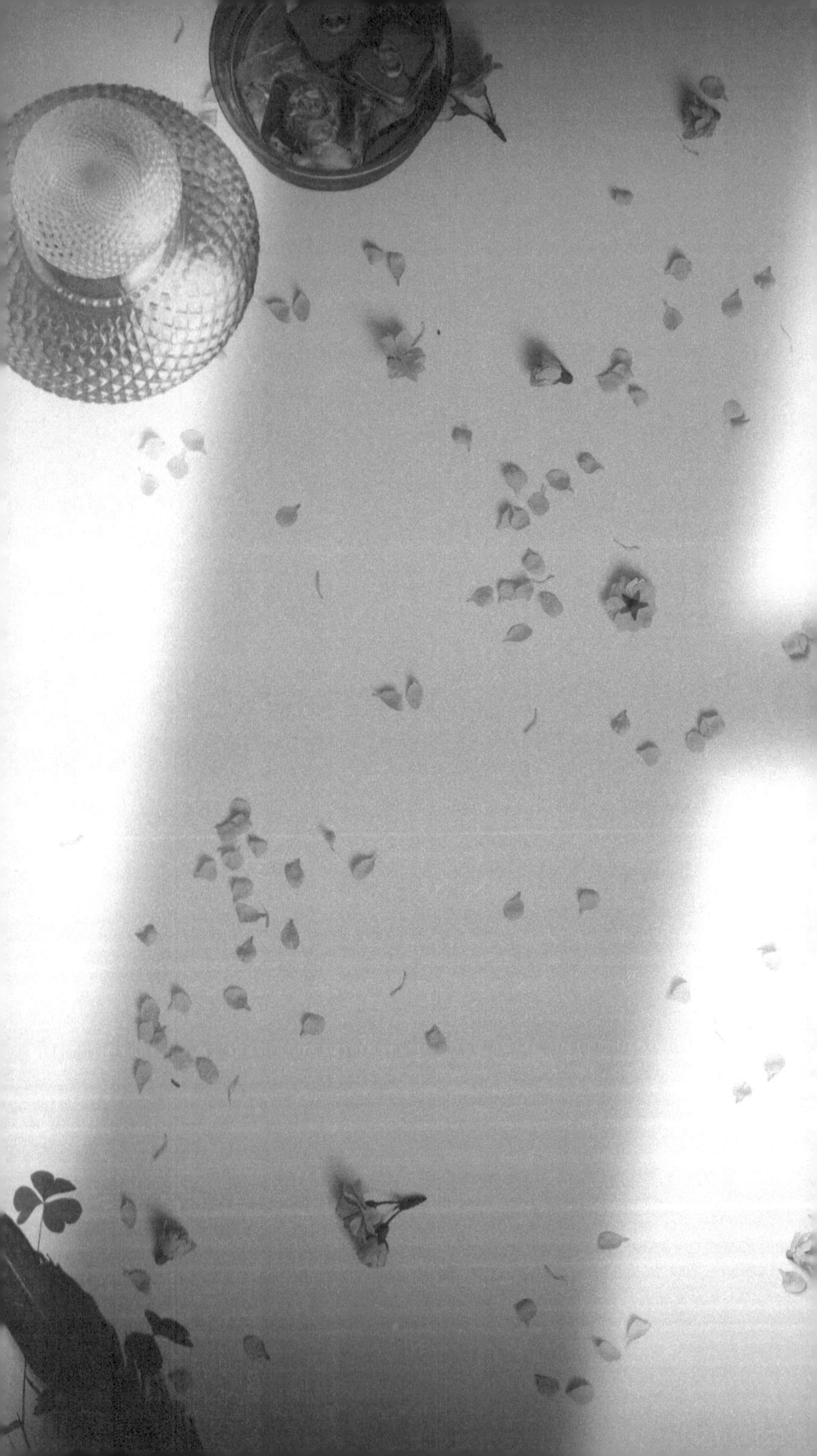

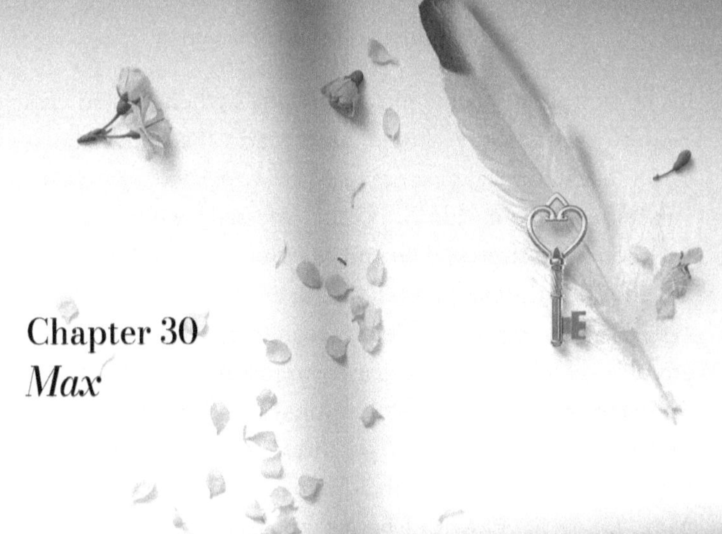

Chapter 30
Max

Quin landed a heavy blow to Max's stomach with his staff, no doubt leaving behind a healthy red mark that would bruise, and narrowed his eyes on Max. "You're distracted."

"I'm fine." But the words were hollow, even to his own ears, ringing false in the training room they'd booked for their weekly sparring session. It was meant to keep them in top form. To allow them to hone their teamwork. And for years, it had worked as such, making them one of the best ignis partnerships the Feugo City Sanctum had ever seen. But today . . .

Well, Quin was right. Today, Max was distracted.

With a scoff and a movement that was all brutal efficiency and brotherly admonishment, Quin knocked the staff from Max's hand. It clattered sharply to the floor, the sound ringing through the empty space and making Max wince when it hit his ears.

Quin didn't say anything; he just raised a brow as if to ask, *really?*

Leaving Max only one choice, which was to blush, scuff his boots against the floor, and duck his head as he retrieved his bo staff. Not looking into Quin's eyes when he said "It's Ander" theoretically should have made the conversation easier, but it didn't.

"What about him?" Quin pressed when silence between them stretched on and Max refused to meet his eye as he twirled the staff in his hand for a little too long.

Max shrugged, suddenly regretting that he'd said anything at all. It would be easier to just not talk about this. To ignore it until the problem went away. Only the problem probably wasn't *going* to go away. It would end in a breakup, or a fight, or something equally unpleasant for Max. Damn it. How did he get himself into this position again? Tied to someone who was going to break him. Was lying to him.

"Max." The tone was soft, chiding. Quin wasn't going to let Max retreat back into his shell now that he'd said something. There was no escape. He had to face this. Maybe it was better this way. Maybe talking it out with Quin would put everything in perspective. Maybe voicing the thoughts inside his head would make them sound silly.

"I'm . . . confused? Conflicted?" Max shook himself. None of those seemed the right word for the spiral he found himself tumbling down after Ander left him the previous evening. Well. Not right after. Because right after, he had a serious problem he needed to take care of that involved imagining how things might have progressed had Ander not pulled away. Ander's hot mouth wrapping around him, his lacquered nails scraping red marks into Max's thighs, his—

"Which is it?" Quin asked, ripping Max from the daydream and forcing him back into the real world where Ander might be . . . he might be . . .

"I think Ander might be seeing his abusive ex."

"What?" The stillness that took over Quin made Max's

heart stop. It was the posture of a man waiting, watching, listening. Max had seen Quin fall into this stillness before, and it always, *always* preceded something terrible. Something bloody.

A sigh left Max, his shoulders drooping as he hunched forward, using the staff to bear his weight. "There was dust on his shoes the other day when I showed up unannounced."

"Okay?"

"Acheron dust. Ander's ex works for Hades. Spends part of his time in Acheron."

"Max, that doesn't mean—"

"There were bruises." Max licked at his lips, hating himself even as he said the words. Ander was all-in when they were together. He was attentive and affectionate. He was wonderful, everything Max wanted from a partner, everything he'd always dreamed of. But . . .

"A hickey, a little while ago, on his neck. He admitted that he had a run-in with his ex, and the guy got handsy." He swallowed around a throat gone tight and sharp. The thing was . . . he didn't blame Ander for this, not really. Couldn't blame him if he was still in an abusive relationship or if he'd been pulled back into one. But he needed Ander to be straight with him, to tell him what was going on, so he could help him, protect him if need be. He couldn't do any of that if Ander refused to be honest with him.

"And you think . . . what?" Quin's staff tapped against Max's leg, an attempt to draw him out of his own head that Max appreciated far more than he ever thought Quin would know. "That he's cheating?"

"I don't think cheating is the word. Not really." A squeak echoed through the room when he scuffed his boot on the floor again, leaving behind a little black mark.

With pursed lips, Quin looked like he was trying to suck back something sour. He did that sometimes when there were words on his tongue he knew he shouldn't say. Things that would hurt people's feelings. Because Quin thought over his words carefully. When he had finished sorting it out, he asked, "Then, what?"

"I think maybe he needs help." Which was a better alternative to cheating and more likely. Right? It had to be the case. There was no way sweet, wonderful, charming Ander was cheating on him. No way this was all one sided. It just didn't fit.

Quin squinted at him for a moment, searching Max's face for the answer to a question he hadn't asked, and Max shifted under the attention, feeling naked and exposed. He hated it sometimes that his brother could see down to the heart of him. Hated how there were never any secrets between them, at least on Max's end of things. Quin could keep secrets. Quin could disappear into his own head and hide things. But Max was always an open book, and it left their relationship feeling terribly one-sided sometimes.

Then he said in the most reasonable tone possible—because that's what Quin was, reasonable—"I think you should go and talk to Ander about this." Quin rubbed cooling sweat from his brow, frowning a little. "Sooner rather than later. You don't want this to fester."

Max slumped further in relief. If they both weren't sweaty and gross, he might have wrapped Quin up in a bear hug and kissed him on the cheek for his patience and understanding. "Yeah. I should."

With a nod, Quin snatched Max's staff away from him and swatted him on the butt with it. "Now."

A yelp, then a startled laugh left Max, and he spun to

head for the showers and do just that. Sometimes, he realized, siblings gave the best advice.

Bodies and sound pressed in on Max from all sides, making it hard to think, to focus on the faces that surrounded him. But he was a man on a mission, and he had some idea of where Ander would be. And if he was wrong, he could always ask after him with Mab.

But the closer he got to the bar, the more he wished he had brought Quin with him. Not that Quin would have done anything—he'd likely have just stood behind Max like a wall of slightly disapproving muscle—but it was nice sometimes to have his brother there. Nice to know that he wasn't alone.

The little bag of tacos crinkled as someone bumped into him, nearly sending his and Ander's dinner to the floor where it would be trod upon and ruined by too-expensive shoes, joining the sticky mess of splattered alcohol. He wasn't sure how Inferno could be so packed when it had literally just opened. Maybe there was some magic woven into the walls, whether intentionally or not, that drew these hordes of people in even on a weeknight. A siren call all its own.

It was almost easy to spot Ander through the crowd, his long antlers towering over everyone else and shimmering in the dancing lights, making Max's gut give a kick. A soft tug at his chest drew him closer, and the crowd parted to reveal Ander—

Ander and a tall, dark-haired man whose groin Ander was grinding against. The man's hands were splayed over

Ander's hips, possessive. Max's stomach dropped out through his feet.

Still, his body seemed to be moving of its own accord, dragging him forward, forcing him to bear witness to his own destruction. Like when people rubber-necked past a wreck, unable to take their eyes off the carnage that their own hubris and a multi-ton vehicle could have wrought.

Ander didn't see him at first, his eyes closed as he focused on something. Perhaps the movement of his hips. Or maybe it was the lust that simmered in his veins. Lust that Max clearly didn't inspire in him as Ander had pulled away, *always* pulled away. Even when Max was ready and willing. Even when Max wanted nothing more than to see where things took them.

He wasn't enough, and the realization hit him like a sledgehammer. Likely would never be enough. Not for anyone.

"Max!" Ander's tone was too high, surprise or guilt or something else that Max couldn't make out above the music coating it. He pulled away from the man behind him, even as the man tried to maintain his hold, patting the man's hand lightly and murmuring a soft "I'll just be a moment, Enri" before making his way over to Max. "What are you— What are you doing here?"

"I brought you dinner." The words left him with no consent from the rest of him, no conscious thought, and Max held up the bag now stained in grease to show Ander, his motions strangely distant from the rest of his body. Like that would make this all go away. Like it would make what he'd just seen any less real. Then he added insult to injury and said, "I missed you."

An expression flashed across Ander's face, one that Max couldn't read through the fog in his own mind.

Because it was clear, it was all so *very* clear now: Ander didn't want him here. His invitation to come to Inferno hadn't been open-ended. Ander didn't want Max here, anywhere, or at all, outside of the times of his own choosing.

What did . . . what did that make them?

Nothing.

"Who's this?" Enri said, his voice husky and deep, as he reached for Ander again, reeling him back in. And Ander went, soft and willing. No fight. No hint of distress. Like this is what he wanted. Max's stomach churned, the sugary smell of alcohol and the musk of sweating people nearly causing him to vomit on the dance floor.

Ander tilted his head back to fix Enri with an adoring look. "Just a friend, darling. Weren't you just saying we should get out of here?" He gave his hips another pointed roll, and the nausea in Max's gut threatened to lurch up his throat. "Back to your place."

Enri's keen eyes were still on Max, assessing him, making Max feel pinned down, but Max couldn't look away from Ander. Ander, who hadn't looked at him since Enri reappeared at his side. Ander, who wouldn't even face Max. What did that mean? Were they . . . were they over? Had they even been anything to begin with? Gods. He was so stupid. So fucking *stupid*.

"Ander. We need—we need to talk." Max fisted his hand more tightly around the paper sack holding their likely now cold tacos.

"You should go home, Maximus," Ander said, and though the words were soft, the tone gentle, they landed like a blow. Freezing Max to the spot as Ander and Enri wrapped themselves more tightly together, and Ander snapped them away without even bothering to so much as look at Max.

Something shattered in his chest. Sharp. Ripping. Cutting into the fleshy bits of him. And all Max could do, all that was left for him, was to abandon the bag of tacos on a table and leave the way he'd come.

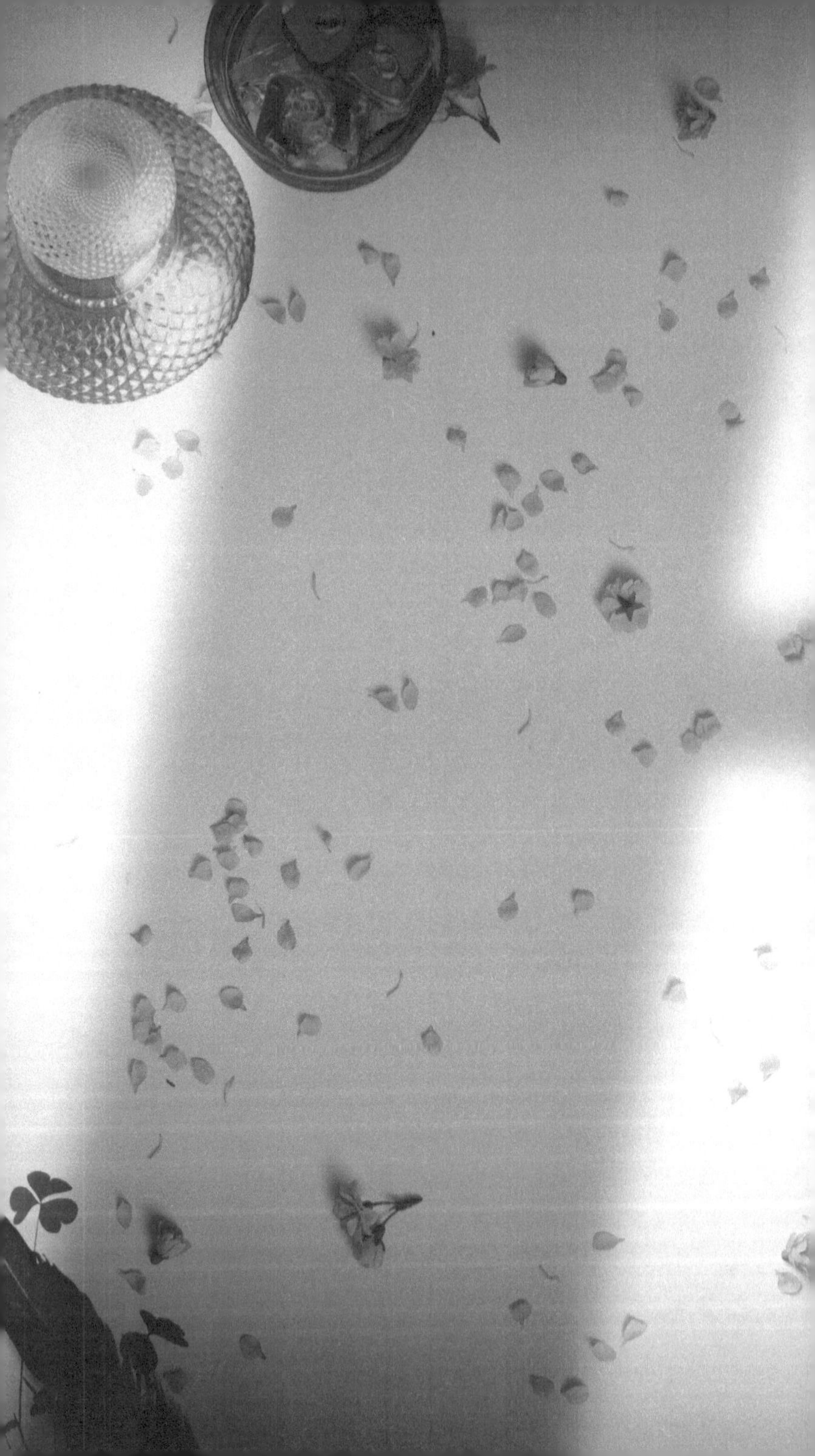

Chapter 31
Ander

He was a monster. Or, at least, that's how he felt the minute the words came out of his mouth and he saw the devastation in Max's eyes.

Why had he come? And unannounced. If only he'd stayed away just one more night, Ander would have had this whole Enrique mess taken care of, and things would've been fine. Instead, Ander had possibly just done irreparable damage to his relationship with Max, and the thought of it made him sick to his stomach. The pain from the amare bond flared so fierce in his chest, he fought against a gasp. Every inch of him wanted to go back and explain. To fix what had been done. The only thing keeping him from doing so was the knowledge that he was doing all of this *for* Max.

As they appeared in Enrique's penthouse, the god growled darkly, his hands slipping around Ander's waist to grab onto his ass tightly. He pulled Ander in against his body and smirked down at him in delight.

"Seeing you crush that ignis boy to come with me was

delightful, princeling. We should play that game again some time."

The name "princeling" brought bile up the back of his throat, and Ander had to swallow it back down, lest he be sick all over Enrique's pristine white shirt. "Who would pick an ignis over you?" he cooed, fighting with the urge to push Enrique away from him.

Everything about the male disgusted him, and if he could've physically harmed the god, he would have.

Not even a part of Ander had doubted that Enrique would see him again despite how their last interaction had gone. The need within Enrique to claim Ander, to show that he was the one in control was so strong he couldn't resist another chance to stake his claim. Now he'd been able to do it in front of someone else who wanted Ander too. His victory had been made even sweeter.

"Mmm, I do enjoy hearing you say it. But it's also fun to make them think they have a chance." His dark brown eyes gleaming, Enrique dipped his head to bite at Ander's throat, purposefully bruising the flesh there.

Ander's eyes slid shut, and he clenched his jaw. His hands tightened on Enrique's shoulders, and he could not contain the shudder of revulsion tearing through him at the feel of the other male's lips and teeth on his flesh. Fortunately, the reaction made Enrique excited as he mistook it for Ander's pleasure.

It should have been impossible for Ander to find himself in this position once more considering how things had ended between the two of them last time. Fortunately the drugs had worked enough to leave Enrique with only vague memories of their night. Enough for him to know there had been some nudity, but no sex. And Ander was waving the possibility of sex before him tonight; bating him like a fish on the line.

The god's excitement was undeniable as it pressed into Ander's abdomen.

Every instinct within him screamed to smash a vase over Enrique's head, stake him through the heart, and spit on his corpse as he walked away. Ander instead threaded his fingers through the hair at the back of Enrique's head, holding his mouth to his throat. It only encouraged him, and the male covered his throat in nips and open kisses, growling against him as his hands tightened more on the curve of Ander's ass.

Looking over Enrique's shoulder, Ander saw that he had indeed snapped them into the living room of the penthouse. Carefully, and much like leading a partner through a dance, Ander began pushing Enrique backward, steering him in the direction of the sofa.

When his calves hit the front of it, Ander pulled back enough that he was able to plant his hands on Enrique's chest and shove him down onto the cushions. Then, within seconds, he was straddling Enrique's lap, pressing against him. Enrique growled, a pleased look in his eyes. He grabbed Ander's hips and pulled him firmly against him, rocking up into him suggestively.

The sick feeling in Ander's stomach lurched, and he swallowed once more, forcing himself to continue.

When Enrique pulled his face in for a deep kiss, Ander went with it. *Don't bite his tongue off and spit it in his face,* he told himself. He needed this distraction so he could snap the powder into his hand.

However, the instant he felt the powder nestled in his palm, he pulled back. Enrique went to speak, but Ander acted before he could. He lifted his hand and took a deep breath to blow all of it directly into Enrique's face. The god inhaled sharply in surprise, then sneezed. He blinked, his brow furrowing as his lips fell open to speak.

Instead, his eyes blinked, and his body swayed. "What . . ." he began, tongue making his voice sound thick.

For good measure, Ander lifted another handful of powder and blew it into the god's face. This time, the deep inhale of *dues somnum* had Enrique's eyes sliding shut, and his entire body fell back against the sofa.

Ander swung out and slapped him sharply across the face. His head lulled to the side, but there was no other reaction from the god.

Without hesitation, Ander climbed off his lap, shuddering at the remembrance of the other male's hands on him. "Never again," he spat at him. "Gods, I hope I've killed you."

There was no time to lose, and Ander hurried down the hall into Enrique's office. He threw on the light and stepped in, eyes going to the desk where the canister of feathers had sat.

It wasn't there.

"Well shit on a stick!" Why had he moved his little collection of trophies?

Several more curses slid from between his lips as Ander crossed over to the desk and began to rummage through the drawers. Files, canisters of suspicious powders, and a bottle of scotch were the only things he found. He plucked the scotch from the bottom drawer, opened it, and took a large swig. After swishing it around in his mouth, he spit the liquid on the floor, effectively washing away all of Enrique's germs. The next swig he swallowed.

Wiping the back of his hand over his lips, Ander spun

to the shelves. With quick motions, he knocked everything onto the floor, searching for the jar. With each crash, he thought for sure Enrique would come rampaging into the room to stop him. Slam him up against the wall, beat him, try to take his life. And he would be successful; while Ander's magic could help him fight, he could not kill a god. That ability belonged to the gods themselves.

As each second passed, his heart beat all the more fiercely. He refused to fail this time. This chance would not come again.

At last, he knocked a painting onto the floor and found the jar of feathers nestled behind it. Ander let out a woosh of breath, deep relief filling him. He snatched the jar up, clutched it tightly to his chest and snapped his fingers, getting himself the hell out of that condo and away from Enrique for good.

He didn't go home. Enrique would look for him there. Instead, Ander snapped himself outside of Mab's little bungalow. It was a contemporary home of white cement with a flat roof and beautifully manicured lawn. From the front, all one could see were the tall black doors at the end of a paved walkway leading from the driveway. The true beauty of the home was when one walked around the right side, leading to the back, where the entire south wall of the living room was made of glass looking out over a gorgeous view of the beach.

Because his dear, sweet Mabbers was also paranoid beyond everything else, she'd once convinced Indra to put several magical wards up around her home. Those wards could keep even a god out unless they knew the specific phrase to let them pass.

Mab was able to change that phrase at any time, so even

Indra could be locked out by his own wards, making it the perfect place for Ander to hide away.

Ander, fortunately, always knew the phrase.

He placed his hand on the front door and felt the thrum of magic blocking his entry. "Ander is a giant dildo." He huffed at the words. The wards rippled, and his hand passed through to the knob.

Mab had changed the phrase one drunken night when she was annoyed with him and still refused to switch it. She found it highly amusing to hear him say it.

Once inside, Ander fell against the door, letting out a massive sigh. Relief caused his shoulders to sag, and he rested his head back against the solid oak behind him. It was done. Finally. Monnie came running from the kitchen, yipping excitedly. Ander stooped down to pick her up, cuddling the fluff ball to his chest. He'd brought her here before heading to Enrique's, wanting to make sure she was safe while this all went down.

His phone was out of his pocket in a moment, and he hit Mab's name at the top of his Favorites list.

She picked up on the first ring. "Are you okay?"

"Yeah."

"What's wrong? You sound like something's wrong."

Of course she knows from just one word. "Max saw me with Enrique." Ander swallowed and buried his face into Monnie's fur against the fresh wave of regret and a suspicious prick of tears. "I had to blow him off so Enrique wouldn't suspect anything."

"Oh." The noise of the night club could be heard behind her. So much happiness when the weight of the world seemed to be resting directly on his chest.

"He hates me now."

"Wonderboy doesn't hate you. He just doesn't know the

truth. Once you tell him, it'll be water under the bridge," Mab assured.

"I dunno, Mab . . ." Ander scrubbed at his face. "You didn't see the look on his face."

"Don't think about it right now, Ander. Test the feathers, and then you can go to him with the truth."

Ander sighed and nodded even though she couldn't see him. "You're right. I have more work to do."

"I love you, Andy. It's going to be all right."

"Thanks, Mabbers. I love you too." He hung up, slipping his phone into his pocket. He lifted the jar of feathers up before him, his heart clenching once more.

All he could see was Ikari, wounded and broken. Trapped in Enrique's dungeons and begging for death now that his wings were gone. There had been so many signs that Enrique was a monster leading up to that moment, but seeing the ignis he'd kept solely to torture in those dungeons had been a sign even a delusional Ander in denial couldn't ignore.

"I won't let him keep doing it, Ikari. Not to anyone else," he vowed softly to the jar. Ikari's own feather sat safely tucked away in Ander's jewelry box at home. A reminder, always, of what had happened in the hellish dungeons of Acheron.

Ander moved into Mab's kitchen. Carefully, and with great reverence, he took each feather out of the jar and laid them on the counter before him. There were so many. Dozens. More than he cared to count. Though he felt like he owed it to each one of them to do so.

Fifty-seven.

All different: size, color, and type of feather. Everything from pin to down. Some so small, they could only have come from a youngling, while others were long and majestic. Adult.

Ander extended his hand out over the feathers and began to slowly murmur, calling to the feathers. Asking each one of them to reveal themselves to him. He hummed softly, his magic rising and calling for each to tell their story.

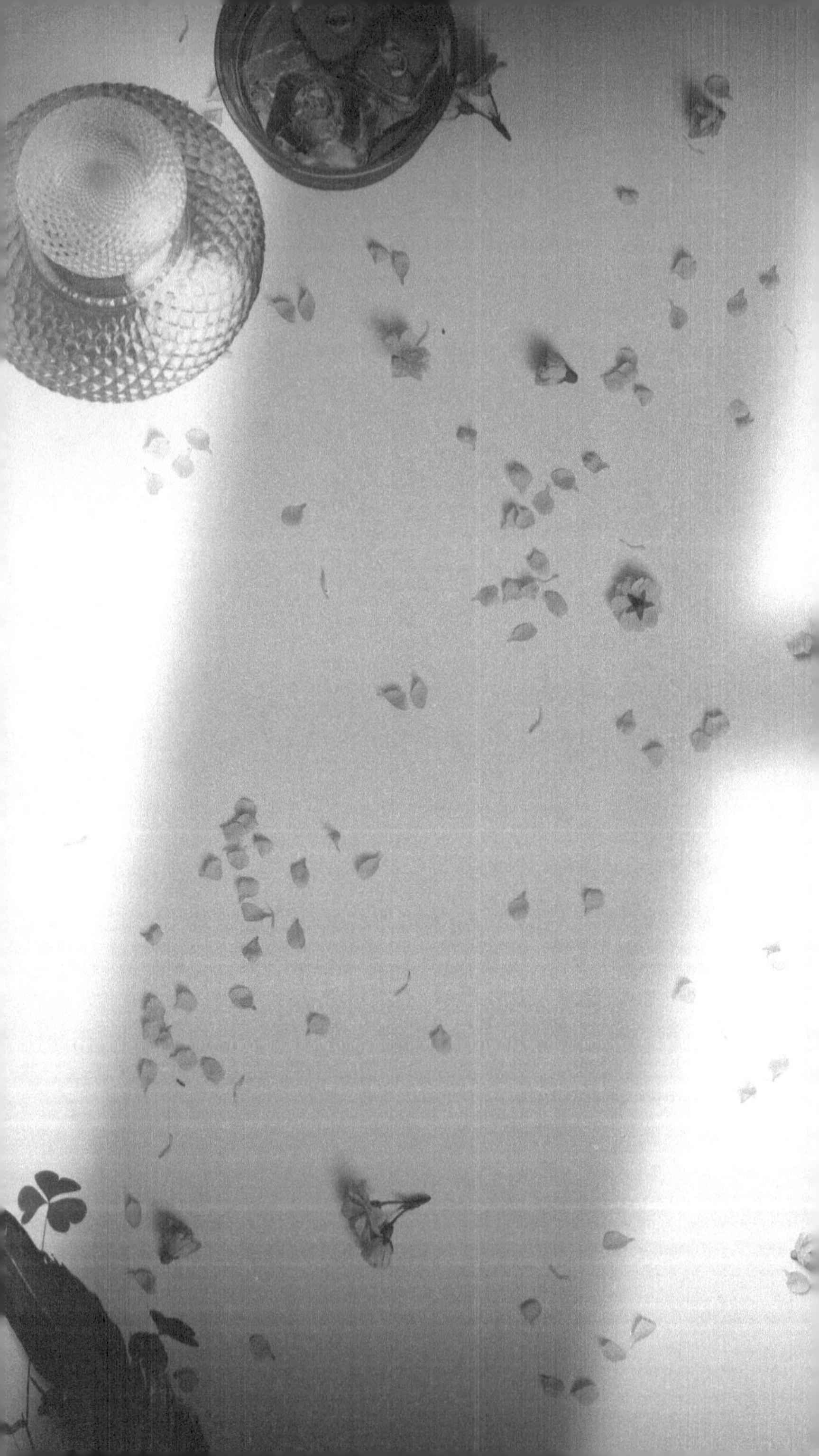

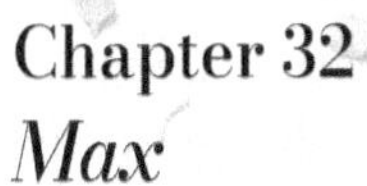

Chapter 32
Max

Time passed in a fuzzy, distant sort of way. As if it were separate from Max himself. And, really, it was, wasn't it? Years could pass. Decades. Centuries. And Maximus Schields would remain exactly the same.

Dark hair without a hint of gray.

Skin unwrinkled.

Heart in pieces.

Being immortal was funny that way. It forced itself on people, making them realize how much things stayed the same, even when everything around them seemed to change.

And *he* was the same. He thought he had changed. He thought he had grown. He thought he had maybe found something . . . someone to pass the years with. To stay still with him while the world shifted around them. But he wasn't wanted. Wasn't needed. He was just . . . what? A distraction? A fun little game?

It had all seemed so *real* at the time. He remembered looking at Ander and feeling like he was basking in the first of the summer sunshine. The warmth heating his skin and chasing away a long, cold winter that had left him aching on the inside. It was more than he'd ever experienced, and so much more than Max thought he would ever get to have, would ever deserve.

Because ignis didn't fall in love. They weren't built for it —or that's what people said, anyway. They didn't feel things the same way everyone else did. They were incapable of it. Their only love—their only purpose—was the unending battle to keep rogue inanimi in line. Just soldiers. Just tools for the gods to move around like pieces on a chess board. Just—

"Max?" a little voice asked, dragging Max away from the nihilistic spiral. He looked down and found Flo staring up at him, her eyes too wide, too big in her round face. Her little fists tugged at his shirt, leaving it wrinkled and stretched out from a strength she still didn't quite understand. "Max, are you okay?"

"I'm fine, sweetheart," he lied through his teeth as he bent to scoop her up into his arms. It was good she was the only one left behind after their lessons. Good that all the others had been picked up by their Guardians already. He shouldn't be seen doing this. Hugs and comfort and cuddling weren't a part of the way an ignis was supposed to be raised.

Oh sure, he'd had those things, and so had his siblings. It was one of the ways the Schields family were raised differently than the rest of their brethren. The other way was that they'd been brought up with human siblings, not just other ignis. They went on vacations. They were allowed to have things like favorite Disney movies, unbalanced breakfasts, ice cream at midnight when they'd had a rough breakup. They were allowed to have breakups, while most ignis didn't date. It was always about the physical needs being met. Never about the emotional, the mental. And Max had thought—Max had thought—

"You look sad," Flo said, her chubby fingers pressing cold into his cheeks, not letting him disappear back into his head for long. "Why do you look sad?"

"It's just been a long couple of days, Flo. I'm okay, I promise." He wasn't, though. He didn't know that he would ever be okay again. The shards of his heart caught rough against his insides, like every broken bone he'd ever experienced. Only, unlike those bones, this one wouldn't knit itself back together in a couple of hours. No. It remained stubbornly shattered, making every breath ache. Maybe this is what dying actually felt like. Maybe it was a slow, painful slip into oblivion. "You did very well today in training. Your sword skills are very much improved."

"I know." Flo tilted her chin back in smug satisfaction at the praise from her teacher, and Max ached all the more.

He'd been so close, hadn't he? So close to everything he'd always wanted. A family of his own. A love of his own. A home of his own. Except. No. He hadn't been. It had only seemed that way. Ander was playing him, like some twisted game, and those things had never really been within reach. Never would be, very likely, because who would want that with him?

"Make sure to tell your Guardian. They should know you've done well." They should also give her a special treat for her vast improvement, but they likely wouldn't. Max knew her guardian. They were a stern battle-ax of a person who didn't seem to understand that Flo was a child first. But then, that was most Guardians. Even the ones who thought there might be some merit in Colton Schields' methodology. They just couldn't get past the fact that the ignis weren't human, weren't *people*. The Sanctum, under the guidance of the Princeps, had drilled that into their heads.

"Yes, sir." She gave a little salute that was unbelievably adorable, and Max heard the clearing of a throat from the door to the training room. Quin was standing there, Flo's Guardian at his side. They didn't look pleased by the obvious affection Max was giving Flo, and he could only hope they wouldn't take it out on the youngling. Flo didn't know she wasn't supposed to be allowed things like this.

"Time to go, Floriane," her guardian said, holding a hand out to the child, their eyes still fixed pointedly on Max. He wondered if Flo would be allowed back in his classes after this. Probably not. No matter how knowledgeable a teacher he was, that wouldn't excuse the weakness the Guardians would see in him. He wondered if he'd even be allowed to teach another class. Maybe not once Flo's Guardian told everyone what they'd seen.

Max set Flo on her feet, his hands itching, even as she toddled across the mat, to draw her back to him, to hold her close. Which was stupid, and he knew that. Flo wasn't his ignis to look after—none of them were. And ignis didn't raise other ignis. They didn't have families. They weren't *fathers*.

"She's right, you know," Quin said once Flo and her Guardian were gone, "you look like hell."

"I feel like I'm in Hell," Max mumbled, only half hoping Quin would hear as he made his way over to the wall of practice weapons. Maybe if he wore himself out, he'd be able to sleep. Or at the very least stop remembering what Ander had looked like while saying "just a friend". Why was it that the good memories were already starting to fade? Becoming worn with age as he went back to them over and over again. But the bad ones were still just as sharp and crisp and cutting as they'd been the moment they happened.

"Talk to me." Quin frowned at him, batting the practice sword away when Max held it out to him.

Max tapped him on the shoulder with the point of his sword, hoping Quin would give in. He didn't want to talk. He didn't think he'd ever want to talk about Ander Ruin again. Maybe if he stopped talking about Ander, then the memories and the heartbreak would fade. It wasn't like the relationship had been long. There was no reason for Max to not be able to get past this.

"Talk. To. Me." The words were said with more bite than Quin had ever spoken to Max before, his teeth gritted so hard, Max could see his jaw tick beneath the skin.

Max's answer came in the form of a swipe toward Quin's open midsection that Quin parried easily. His brother was furious at the lack of communication, Max could see that. It probably wasn't fair of him to hold this all in like he was. To silence himself and cut himself off from the people who did love him. But he couldn't seem to help it. He didn't want to be their burden. And hurting alone always seemed so much easier than sharing it with others.

Quin's reactions were all brutal efficiency, a warrior not hindered or weighed down by the sadness that made his brother too slow and too distracted to see the swipe of his leg in enough time to react. Max went down hard, the mat knocking the breath from his lungs, and he wondered, staring up at the ceiling, how many times Quin had knocked him on his ass in the last couple of months. It was probably more than five. Which was just . . . Wasn't that just *perfect?*

"Talk to me," Quin said again, flopping down next to Max's head, knocking on it with his knuckles lightly. "What's going on up there?"

"I think . . . I think we broke up," Max told the ceiling, because he couldn't look at Quin when he said this. Couldn't let his brother see how absolutely pathetic he was.

Quin released a long, slow breath, a sign that he was gearing himself up for something or that he was exceedingly frustrated with the situation, Max knew from experience. "So, all this moping," he said slowly, as if sounding the words out would make them less infuriating, "is over some *guy*?!"

"Ander isn't just—He's not just *some guy!*" Max turned his head to glare at his brother. Although he wasn't sure why. Shouldn't he be allowing himself this? Allowing the room to bitch and moan and shit talk Ander after what he did? It didn't feel right though. Didn't feel like all the other times a guy had broken up with Max, and Quin had curled up with him on the couch with a tub of ice cream and a bunch of movies, and they'd talked about how Max's now-ex wasn't really that great anyways.

"Yes. He is," Quin bit out, his hands flexing into fists beside him, angry on his brother's behalf. "You went on a grand total of, like, three dates. You've only known him a few weeks, Max. He's just—"

"I'm in love with him," Max blurted suddenly, his mouth moving faster than his mind, spilling the words out into the air like they were the truest thing in the universe, even for all he hadn't known it until a second ago. Because it *was* the truth. Max was in love with Ander Ruin. Gods. How long had he been in love with him? Since the first moment? Or was it more recent than that? The moment Ander placed those gaudy Beast ears on his head and declared himself Max's very own Disney Prince Charming, his dream come true. Or had it always been there? Had he opened his eyes all those years ago to the sun burning his retinas and the ground hard beneath him while he waited for Colton Schields to find him, and been in love with Ander Ruin even then? He didn't know. He didn't know, and it didn't matter.

"Fucking *finally*!" someone shouted from behind them, and Max sat up, whirling around to glare at where the twins had taken up residence in the door of the training room. They were each leaning on one side of the doorframe, like gargoyles, smiles stretched so wide, it was likely hard to see through their thick lashes.

"Finally?"

"Yes. Finally! We knew it all along," Nash bragged, his tone smug.

"You owe me a twenty, Quin," Nox called. There was a wad of cash in her hand that she appeared to be counting.

"I hate all of you." Max groaned and pushed to his feet. He didn't stop to put the practice weapons away, didn't even stop to cut the twins a disapproving look for taking bets on his love life. He needed to get away. He needed space to deal with all of this. To fully process how he'd realized too late, too late—*far* too late—that he was in love with Ander. In love with him, and now he was gone. Lost.

He turned the corner, heading for the locker rooms, and came face to face with his worst fucking nightmare at that particular moment.

"Ander," Max squeaked, taking a step back to keep distance between them. Because if he didn't, he'd reach out. He'd try to pull Ander in close. He'd try to fix this. There was no fixing this. "What are you doing here?"

"I need to talk to you. I need to tell you something about Enri—"

"I don't want to hear it." Max pushed past him,

knocking his shoulder hard into Ander's, sending him stumbling.

"Max, you need to—"

"Oh? It's *Max* now, is it? Not Maximus?" Max growled, baring his teeth as his heart stuttered in his chest, his breath starting to come in hard pants. He needed distance. He needed space. Whatever Ander had to tell him could wait until the wound had calloused or he'd cauterized it. One way or the other, he couldn't talk to him now about this. Not with the realization of his feelings so very fresh.

"Please," Ander all but begged, grabbing for Max's arm. Max ripped it away, speeding up to put more distance between them. But between one breath and the next, Ander had snapped to be in front of him, his hands outstretched as if to stop Max from running away, like he was a spooked animal. "You have to talk to me."

"I don't have to do anything. You made yourself pretty clear the other night when you left with Enri. I don't have to listen to you at—"

"We're amare-bound."

"What?" Max stopped dead, his heart lurching in his chest. *Amare-bound.* That didn't—That didn't make—But it did. It *did* make sense. It made perfect sense. Because ignis didn't love, they weren't capable of it. So of course Max's first brush with love, the reason it had all happened so fast, was because it was fated. Because the gods were fucking with him *again*. Moving him around like a piece on a chess board. And what did that mean? What was their plan? And of course—of course—of *course*, that meant Ander didn't feel for him in turn the way Max did. Because it was all magic. All some fucked up twist of fate. All—

"I—" Ander started. He looked half-wild, his fingers shaking where they were still held out in front of him to stop Max from leaving. "I cast a spell. Many years ago. And Erotes, he—"

"I can't deal with this right now." Max pushed past him again and all but ran toward the locker room, slamming and locking the door behind him, because he needed space, distance. The walls were closing in. There was something sitting on his chest. Darkness closed around his vision. He was going to pass out. He was going to vomit. He was going to—

Amare-bound.

Why wouldn't the gods take one more choice away from him? Why wouldn't they turn him into a puppet on a string entirely?

The floor was blessedly cool beneath him, but when the frenzied heat of running away wore off, it left him shivering, sobbing, freezing, barely holding himself together as his entire world shattered.

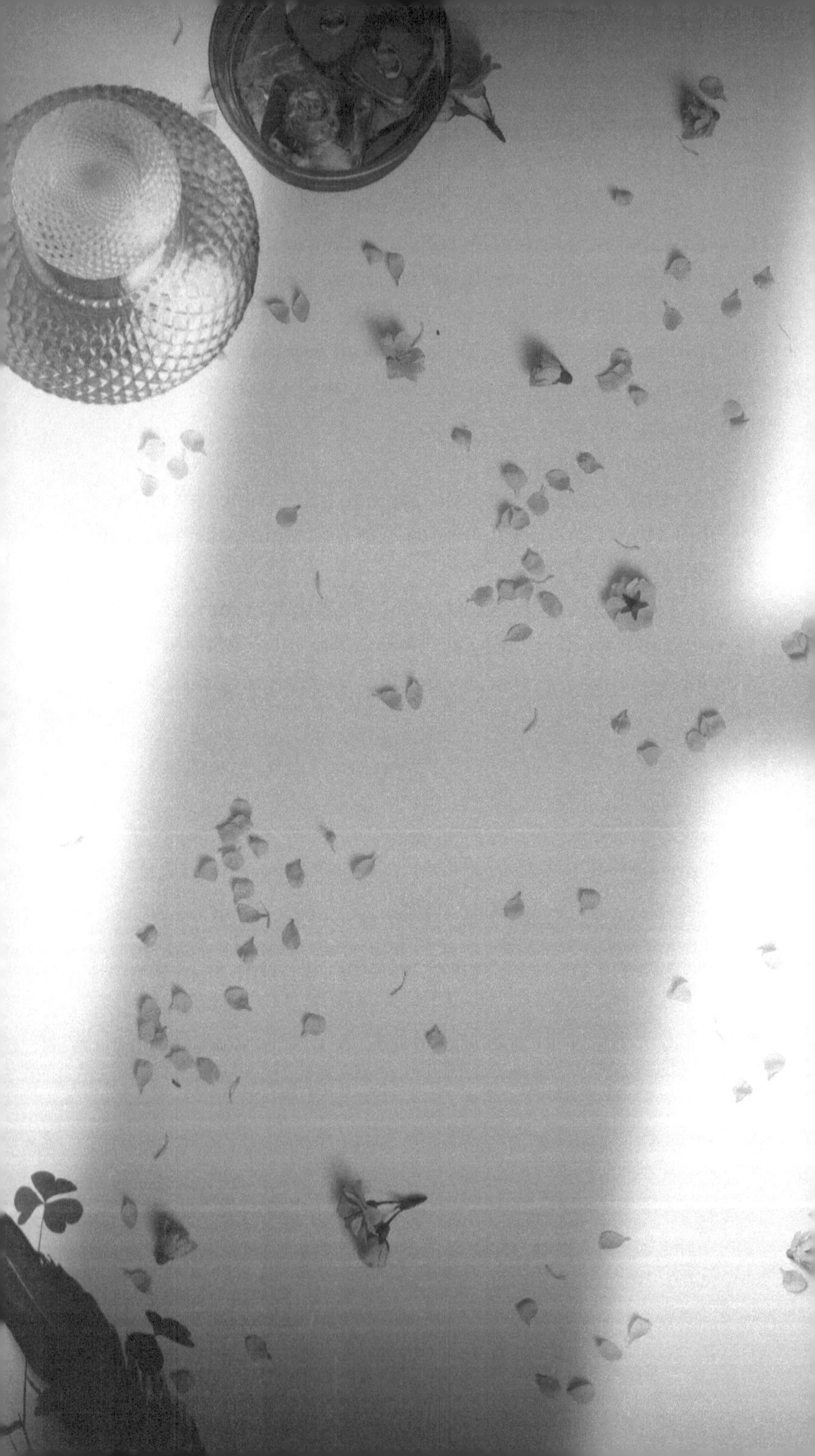

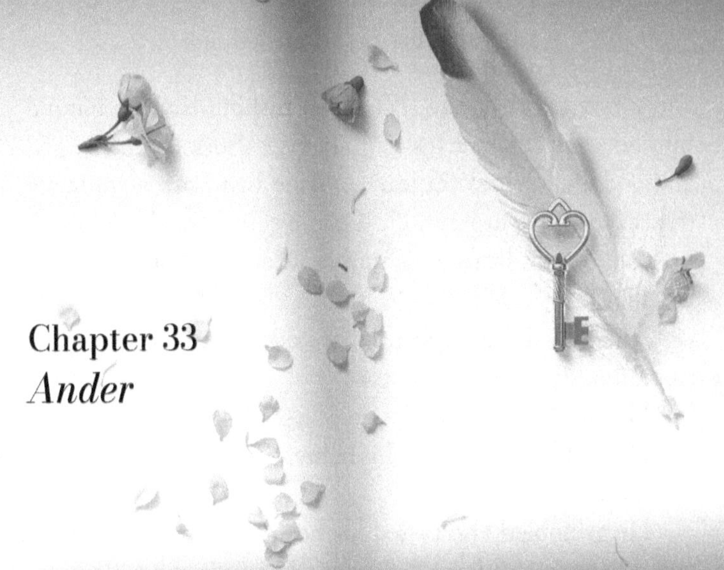

Chapter 33
Ander

Ander stared up at the ceiling fan that swirled around oh so slowly. He hadn't looked at anything else in at least an hour. Not since he'd stumbled drunkenly across Mab's living room and tripped over her damn rabbit.

Mab had taken the bottle from him then, declaring he'd had enough. And sprawled out on his back on the floor, Ander hadn't had it in him to stop her. Instead, he lay there, accepting his fate. Max hated him. Wanted nothing to do with him. He'd had something wonderful within his grasp and, as usual, had managed to ruin it all. He was never going to have a happily-ever-after. Eventually, Monnie climbed on top of him, settling down to sleep on his chest. Not even the weight of her fluffy little body brought him any peace of mind.

"Andy, you need to eat something."

Ander simply grunted at Mab's prodding. There was a hole inside of him that seemed to be eating away at everything there was. Food wouldn't fill the gaping wound. Nothing would.

Every time he thought he had happiness wrapped up

and pinned with a bow, life came rushing back to remind him he wasn't meant for happily-ever-afters. Even the god and goddess of love couldn't provide him with a soulmate that would stick around. He'd made certain of that himself, breaking Max's heart and ruining whatever shot they'd had together.

Ander had managed to chase even the destined away from himself.

He didn't deserve love.

He was the epitome of his name. Ruin.

"Andy . . ."

He grumbled and tossed his head to the side so that he could stare over at her, dead-panned and annoyed. "What?" he snapped.

"Don't give me that tone," she scolded. "I'm just trying to help."

He sighed and brushed the side of his arm over his eyes. "I know you are . . . but in my attempt to protect Max, I've gone and destroyed our relationship. Now he won't even talk to me!"

"I told you that you shouldn't keep this from him. This is his job, he should have been a part of it from the beginning."

Ander glared at her more furiously, his heart panging so viciously with regret, he winced. "You're not helping!"

Telling him what he already knew wasn't going to change things. Telling him that things would get better wasn't going to help either.

There was a severed bond inside of him, one that had been created by Erotes' arrow, and it was tearing him in two. The only thing that would fix this would be Max's arms slipping around him once more, and his gentle words and kisses slowly putting him back together.

If he'd thought the constant pain in his chest from the unresolved bond was bad, it was nothing compared to the shattered nature of it now.

Ander bit his tongue against the sob threatening to slip between his lips. Wailing was highly undignified. He needed to save that for when he was home alone and could sob away in his bathtub.

"Well, you're going to have to find a way to talk to him. You need to tell him about Enrique."

Ander sat up, glaring at her from the floor of her living room. The motion knocked Monnie off his chest and into his lap. After a growl of displeasure, the small dog pranced away indignantly. "Did you not just hear me? He won't *talk* to me."

"Well . . ." She paused for just a moment. "Text him, then."

"Mab!" Ander was aghast and angrily swiped the tears out of his eyes. "This is not a conversation meant for *texting*."

It was Mab's turn to huff with annoyance. "One way or another, you have to tell him."

Ander just stared at her, holding his hand up as if to say, *I'm waiting on your idea.*

"Well, he's got about eighty siblings. Why don't you contact one of them?" She offered him a proud look.

He opened his mouth to tell her she was crazy only for his lips to snap shut. While Max did not have eighty siblings, he *did* have four. At least one of which Ander had the phone number of.

"That . . . might actually not be the worst idea ever."

Mab rolled her eyes. "Gee, thanks."

Ander waved her off and looked around the room, wondering where his phone might be. He couldn't actually remember when he had last had it. Everything was fuzzy beyond Gizmo tripping him up and landing him here on the floor.

Swirling his hand around, the phone appeared on his palm. He pressed the Home button and quickly typed in his password. Or tried. His thumb didn't seem to want to work.

Then he dropped the phone.

He let out a frustrated hiss and clumsily picked the phone back up, finally succeeding in typing in the password. When he found Nox's name, he typed out a message consisting of a lot of typos but that still seemed to get the point across. He needed to speak with Max. It was imperative. How did he achieve that goal?

> Talk to Quin. He's the only one Max listens to cept Dad

> Q hjates nme

> Yeah. But you can corner him

> wherrreeeeee ??!!?!!!)

"She sent me an address," he announced suddenly to the room at large.

"Huh?" Mab asked.

"Nox. She gave me Quin's studio address." Ander then laid back down, curled up on his side, and promptly went to sleep.

His hangover was the thing of legends. And Mab woke him with the aggressively loud sound of a blender grinding and serrating. Ander pushed himself up with a groan, every part of him protesting having slept on the floor.

"What the *hell* is that noise?!"

"Oh good! You're up," Mab replied, sounding far too chipper for the way his head pounded.

She lifted the blender up off its base, which blessedly silenced the horrendous noise whirring about inside his head. But then she poured the green concoction into a glass and carried it around the island to him.

Ander stared at the green goop and shook his head. "No, ma'am. Nuh-uh. Nope."

"Ander." Her voice was stern. "Drink it. It'll help with the hangover and fill your body with something other than booze and whining."

"I'm not drinking that swamp water."

She glared. "When have I ever made you a bad drink?"

"That's not a drink. It's sludge."

"Drink it now, or I'm dumping it over your head."

Huffing, Ander took the glass. He sniffed it. Besides a faint scent of green, it smelled quite nice. He took a tentative sip, his nose wrinkling.

"Oh, stop it, it's not that bad."

It actually wasn't. He just didn't feel like admitting that to her. Not when his stomach lurched at the thought of anything in it and his head was threatening to split clean in two.

"Drink it. *All* of it. And no snapping it away when I'm not looking." She eyed him like an exasperated mother.

Sighing from the depths of his person, Ander tipped his head and the glass back and downed the contents quickly. When he was done, he pressed the back of his wrist to his lips, trying to hold it all in as his stomach protested and threatened to send it back up. When it settled, he dropped his hand and stared up at Mab.

"Happy now?"

"Overjoyed," she drawled and took the glass from him. "Now get ready, we're going to hunt down Quin."

Ander nodded but didn't move. At least, not right away. His body still protested being upright at all, and he wasn't quite sure how it would react if he stood. He took a deep breath and slowly climbed to his feet. His back spasmed in complaint. The floor was not meant to be used as a bed.

"I need to take a shower."

"Be my guest, you know where everything is." Mab nodded her head in the direction of the bathroom.

Once Ander had showered and dried off, brushed his teeth clean of the fuzzy feeling, and fully armored himself with makeup, he had to admit he felt a little more like himself. Snapping fresh clothing from his closets at home, he dressed in a wine-colored dress shirt made entirely of floral lace with delicate gold buttons lining the front. He paired this with charcoal dress pants fastened with a black leather belt.

He styled his hair into a fluffy half-mohawk, redefining his undercut with a quick buzz of magic, and placed a gold ear cuff on each upper lobe.

"Okay, I'm ready." He stepped out of the bathroom to find Mab dressed in a black Led Zepplin T-shirt and black stonewashed jeans.

"Why are you so dressed up?"

"Why are you dressed like a meth head?"

Mab rolled her eyes. "C'mon, let's just get this done. I've already googled the address." She brought her phone up to show him the location on the map.

He studied it to get his bearings of where they needed

to go, then pulled Mab into his side by the hip and snapped them both right outside the warehouse Quin Schields had his "studio" in.

Nox hadn't exactly told him what Quin *did* in this studio, only that this was where her brother spent most of his time when he wasn't on shift.

"What *is* this place?" Mab asked as they stared up at the two-story brick building. Many windows looked in on what had once been a factory of some kind. Now, it was abandoned, except for Quin Schields' purposes.

"I dunno. I'm assuming some sort of practice arena for his training? What else do ignis do on their days off?"

They looked at each other, shrugging in unison.

Together, they stepped up to the main door, and Ander knocked loudly on its surface. He waited to the beat of five before knocking again. There was no response.

"Maybe he's not here?" Ander suggested.

Mab grunted and reached for the handle. When the door opened, she pushed it all the way and stepped inside.

Ander hurried after her and was met with the sound of a violin cover of "Smooth Criminal". Mab turned to look at him, and their eyes met, mirroring the same question. What were they about to walk in on, and how would the ignis respond?

"Hello?" Ander called out, trying to shout over the music.

There was no response.

The old building was a wide-open space, the upper windows not leading to a second floor beyond a metal mezzanine that wrapped round the walls and had one metal bridge spanning from one side to the other. At one time, it had likely been used by the superiors to look down over their employees at work.

The building wasn't empty, however, but walled off by pallets nailed together in eight-foot-high walls made freestanding by two-by-four plank feet.

Slowly, Ander began walking past the first long stretch of pallets and realized they were covered in hanging art pieces. Gorgeous portraits that appeared to be hand-drawn in pencil or charcoal and painted sparingly to highlight certain aspects of the people they depicted. A splash of blue at the cheekbone, a touch of purple shading in the hair, a sparkle of crimson in the pupils.

They were breathtaking.

When he came to a partition in the pallets, he stepped through to find that the wider area of the building was set up with a series of smaller walls, also bearing portraits, almost like an art gallery. Except in the far right corner, where the sunlight currently streamed in through the windows, there were a number of easels, shelves of paints, brushes, and other items. A large canvas hung from the wall at proper height to be worked on from the floor, and an a-frame ladder sat beside it with a can of paint at the top—a piece in progress.

In his free time, it would seem, Quin Schields was an artist.

"What are you doing here?" The music had died suddenly, and the question came in a firm tone, the speaker thoroughly put out by the unrequested visit.

Ander spun to find Quin, a paint-splattered rag in his hands, bespeckled white shirt over his torso, and a brush of charcoal along one chiseled cheekbone. His vivid blue eyes were currently glaring at him and Mab like the proper intruders they were, his dark bangs doing nothing to conceal it, despite their attempts.

"We knocked . . ." Ander motioned behind him with his

thumb toward the door. Quin simply glared, stone-faced and silent. "I need to talk to you. Well, I need to talk to Max, but I need *you* to get him to listen to me."

Quin snorted. "Get out of here before I throw you out." His voice was a dark growl, and the look in his eyes promised to fulfill his threat.

"Please, you need to help me."

"Why would I help a *cheater* get back with my brother? Do you know what you've done to him?" Quin stepped forward, a menacing look on his face.

Ander held his ground but lifted a hand to try and pause him in his steps. "I didn't cheat on him—"

"Don't. Don't try to placate me with lies. You chose to go home with your ex-boyfriend over Max. You are exactly who everyone says you are. And I told Max not to get involved. You're not worth the heartbreak."

"Now, hold up." Mab stepped forward, a snarl in her voice. "Don't you dare talk about my brother that way! He didn't cheat. He risked everything to go undercover to save your brother's ass."

Quin blinked at Mab, staring at her for a moment, then he turned to look at Ander. "What do you mean 'undercover'?"

Ander sighed roughly, fingers rubbing at his forehead. "I ended up at Enrique's condo accidentally. Just went along with my friend, having no idea where we were headed. While we were there, before I got the *hell out* might I add, I saw a jar of feathers in Enrique's office. He's tortured ignis in the past. I saw it firsthand. It's part of the reason why I left his abusive ass."

Quin's shoulders tightened, and he looked between Ander and Mab. Mab nodded at him to confirm Ander's words.

"I wasn't sure if they were ignis feathers, but he had a set of ignis wings mounted on his wall, so I figured there was a pretty good chance they were. When Max told me about the missing ignis younglings . . . I figured there might be a connection there. Especially since Enrique went by the name Timoros in his early days."

"Why didn't you tell us?" Quin growled and took another step forward.

This time, it was Mab who stepped nearer to Ander, a glower on her face warning Quin to halt, angry about Enrique or not. Quin checked himself and remained where he was.

"I didn't say anything because Enrique is a *god*. Ignis were specifically made not to be able to take them down. I needed to be sure, before I brought this to you, that there would be enough evidence to get Indra and the other gods involved. So you would be prepared. I couldn't just send Max in to *die*."

Quin's jaw ticked, and Ander wondered if that was his tell, to show he was mulling over what was being said. "You could have at least told us what you were doing."

Ander quirked a brow. "Oh, really? Do you think Max would have let me face my abusive ex alone if he had known what I was up to?"

Quin sighed and shook his head. "No. He wouldn't have let you put yourself in danger."

Ander didn't need to have known Max very long to know that was the case.

"Why do you care?" Quin asked. "We're ignis, this is our job. Why risk yourself to help us?"

"Because I love him, you idiot!" Ander snapped.

His world spun on its axis, and he felt the air rush out of him. The pain in his chest that had been caused by the amare bond finally eased. Acceptance. Acknowledgement. That was what the bond had been seeking.

Ander shuddered out another breath, the weight of truth settling over him. He loved Max. In a way he had never loved Enrique or Estelle. In a way he had never loved anyone. He couldn't quite explain how or why it was different, not just yet. He simply could tell. This feeling inside him went so bone deep, it was now more a part of him than his own cells were. Truly losing Max, meaning the ignis was no longer in existence, would be an extinction-level event for Ander. And he would do anything required to make sure that didn't happen.

"And for Max to be safe, the ignis need to be safe. So, I will face Enrique as many times as needed to stand in the way of him hurting Maximus. I will stand against the entire ruling body of the gods, if that is what is necessary." His words rang out against the bare walls of the factory.

Silence surrounded them for a full count of ten seconds, and then Quin spoke.

"I'll take you to Max."

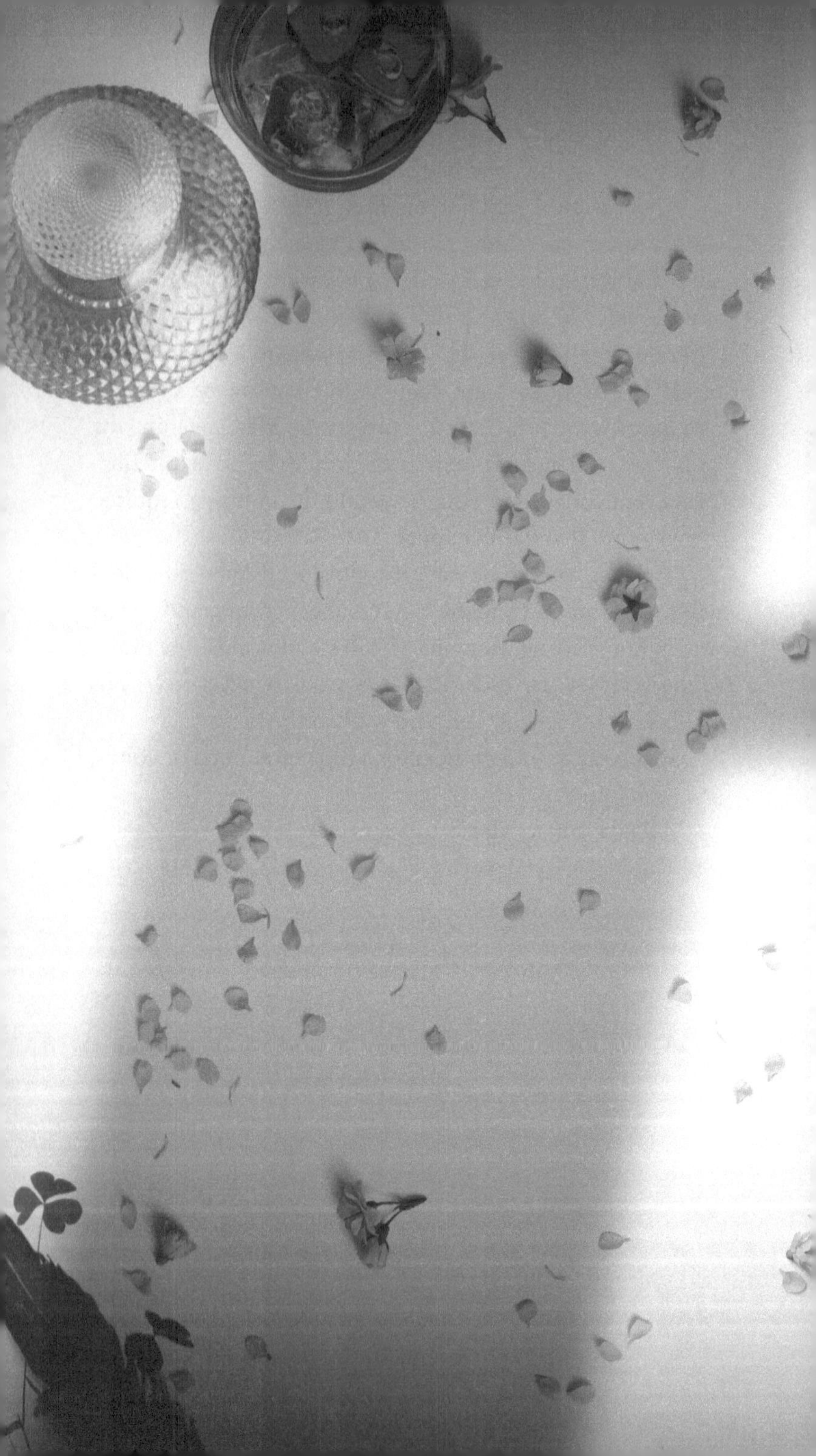

Chapter 34
Max

Focus lingered just out of reach, making Max stupid and slow. He couldn't believe he'd let this happen. Couldn't believe he was letting this affect his job. He was better than this, for fuck's sake. So much better. Had trained to be able to think through exhaustion, malnourishment, dehydration. Had pushed his body to the limits so he wouldn't ever have to worry about his siblings, his team getting hurt because of his own carelessness. But—

But here he was. Sitting at his desk, twirling the stylus for his tablet in his hand instead of filling out the paperwork he was supposed to be looking over, his mind running over anything and everything Ander had ever said to him on repeat. Because there had to have been some clue, right? Something he missed? Or maybe Max had just been reading Ander wrong all along. Maybe he'd been imagining feeling where there was none. He did that sometimes. Consequences of a soft heart, his Papa always told him. But knowing that about himself, knowing how he could see love when it wasn't there, didn't make him ache less.

The subtle pain had settled into every joint in his body,

and it lingered, even when he knew that it wasn't real. Heartbreak couldn't kill anyone, much less an ignis who wasn't supposed to know what heartbreak felt like to begin with. It couldn't cause physical pain, not really. But the psychological effects? Those could do a hell of a lot more than any knife wound ever would, at least in Max's experience, anyway.

The first time it happened, the first time he knew what it felt like to have his heart ripped out and trod on, he'd gone to the medic for it. Told them that there was something wrong with him, that he was injured in some way he couldn't explain. He thought—which was funny in hindsight, but also kind of sad—that he'd cracked his sternum. The medic had done a quick examination, and even a scan at his insistence, then looked at him with pitying eyes. Like he was intrinsically broken.

Maybe he was. Maybe he'd been built wrong. Come out wrong. It would explain a lot of things. Not the least of which why no one loved him the way he wanted them to, but also why he cared at all when the ignis around him seemed fine with it. Happy, even—if a person could call it that—to spend their lives alone, dedicating it to their mission.

Why couldn't Max be like that? His brother was. His sister was. Why couldn't he do it?

What was *wrong* with him?

Was he *greedy*?

Or was he just *broken*?

"Why not both?" Max muttered to himself, throwing his weight back into the little wheely chair behind his desk, making it slide and bump into the shelf set behind it. The shelf creaked a little from the impact and the weight of all the books stuffed onto it, crammed into every available space. It was a cheap, pressboard thing, bought at the local Walmart—because the whole Sanctum had gone digital, and no one understood why Max needed physical books— and put together one night over too much pizza and not nearly enough sleep. And sometimes it groaned like it'd give out under the weight of all the knowledge it held, just like Max might.

He slumped forward against his desk, pressing his forehead to his tablet where he'd no doubt leave a nice greasy smear, and tried to breathe through the catch and pull of something jagged lodged deep in his chest. It didn't do much. But it was better than looking at the paperwork for the investigation that had ground to a halt. Absolutely anything was better than that. The co-signer was somehow untraceable. Timoros knew how to cover his tracks.

Someone knocked on the door, and Max didn't even bother to lift his head before he grumbled, "Not now, Nash. I'm busy."

"You don't look busy," Quin deadpanned.

"Yeah, well, I am. So you can just—" The words died on Max's tongue when he lifted his head and found Ander lingering beside Quin in the doorway, shifting from foot to foot as if maybe he were trying to tuck himself behind Quin's wings where Max wouldn't be able to see him. Max's heart gave a sickening lurch, threatening to leap up his throat and land with a splat on his tablet. Everyone would see it then, all the broken bits and pieces, all the nastiness, all the ugliness. No one could ever possibly love it.

"Just hear him out," Quin said, heading off any of Max's protests before he'd even been able to get his mind to come up with them. "I promise, it's worth your time."

But was it worth the pain? Was it worth the way Max

had to hunch in on himself a little to relieve the catching of something jagged in his chest? Even if Max couldn't see how it would be, he trusted his brother. Always had. Quin wouldn't steer him wrong, not intentionally, anyway.

So he nodded and gestured to one of the chairs in front of his desk.

Ander waited a beat, seeming unsure as he looked between Max and the offered seat, his eyes bouncing like a ball on a sing-along video. The choice was taken from him when Mab pushed from behind them both and dropped into one of the chairs unceremoniously, then turned to lift a brow at Ander over her shoulder.

Hunching over with a sigh, Ander moved to settle into the other chair while Quin took a step inside, shutting the door behind him and taking up what little space was left in Max's office.

The clock ticked loudly, and nothing happened for a long minute—apart from Ander's jaw working as if he were chewing on his tongue—until Mab said, "Just show him."

Ander nodded. "I found this," he said, then waved his hand, and a jar stuffed full of feathers appeared on the desk in front of Max, "in Enrique's apartment."

"Are those . . . ?" Max's fingers twitched where he had pressed them into the top of his desk, an itch in his palms to reach for the jar even as his heart plummeted to his stomach, the shattered feeling forgotten for the moment in the face of this fresh atrocity. He all but begged Ander, "Tell me they're griffin feathers."

"Ignis. Every single one." Ander looked as physically ill as Max felt, and that didn't really make this any better. Because that was—That had to be at least fifty feathers, if not more.

"All different?" Bile rose in his throat even as he said the words, threatening to spill itself onto his desk.

"Yes."

"How many?" He didn't really want to know, but he felt he had to. If he was going to bear witness to the horror that was this new revelation, he had to know all of the facts. Had to be able to give his full report to his superiors.

"Fifty-seven." Ander's words were filled with a sorrow Max had never heard from him before.

Mab reached over to pat Ander's arm for a moment before her hands returned to gripping so hard at the arm rests of her chair that Max could see where her nails were leaving behind grooves in the wood.

"So this is why . . . ?" Hope swelled in Max's chest, warm and mending, putting the pieces back together with double-sided sticky tape and a little bit of Elmer's glue. How long that would hold, he didn't know. Maybe long enough for it to fix itself entirely. Maybe long enough for the pieces to grow back together like a broken bone or a sliced bit of skin. Did ignis's enhanced healing abilities extend to their hearts as well? One could only hope.

"It is," Ander was quick to agree. Maybe *too* quick to agree. "And there's more."

"All right," Max sighed, running his hands through his hair and sticking it up all over the place. "I'm listening."

And he did, while Ander rushed quickly through the whole sordid, terrible, dangerous ordeal. Every misstep, every conversation, every battle to fight Enrique—Timoros —off.

Breath whooshed out of Max. "Why didn't you just *tell* me? Or Quin?" He motioned to his brother. "Or *any* of us?"

"Because I had to be sure!"

"Ander—"

"No!" Ander was quick to cut him off, distress in his eyes. "You don't understand. I've seen it firsthand! I was there when Enrique tortured his first ignis just to see what he could withstand. I was forced—" Mab reached over to take his hand once more, squeezing strength into him. "I was forced to take part under threat of it being Mab it would happen to instead, if I didn't." His eyes fell, like he couldn't bear to meet Max's. "And it was me who mercy-killed a shattered warrior because living without his wings was too devastating to contemplate." Ander's voice broke, tears welling in his eyes. "I couldn't stand the thought of it being you!" He covered his face to hide the tears. To hide the shame.

Max was up out of his chair without thought, squeezing through the tight space of his office so he could pull Ander up into his arms, his wings wrapping protectively around Ander as if he could hide him from the world, protect him from it. They stood quietly for a moment, nothing said. There were no words. This tragedy spanned generations.

"Let's catch this asshole," Max said at last.

The powder sat heavy in the pouch strapped to Max's belt, the weight of it having nothing at all to do with actual physics and everything to do with what he knew it had cost Ander to get it, to test it, to bring it to Max.

"Are you going to forgive him?" Quin asked, his voice whisper-soft as they made their way through the sky toward the building where Enrique—Orcus, god of punishment —lived.

Max hadn't told his siblings the rest of it, the whole

amare-bound thing. It was too much. Too strange and disconcerting. Plus, there was the issue of consent. The issue of, did he love Ander because he had no *choice* or because he just *did*? Thinking about it made his head hurt, and honestly, he didn't want to hear his siblings' opinions on the matter. Not till he had the full story, at least.

"I don't know." Which was the truth, because how could he know? Everything was happening so fast, and there was so much, and now he was on his way to face down a literal god. What time had he had to find an answer to the question of if he forgave Ander? None.

Quin grunted, clearly disapproving. Which was kind of funny, considering he was the one who'd told Max not to get mixed up with Ander in the first place. How Max's siblings could all be so contradictory, he didn't know, but it was going to drive him to an early grave. Probably.

"There it is," Max said, pointing to the building looming tall on the Miami skyline instead of answering. Angling his body, he swooped down toward the roof, wings flapping once, twice, as he landed on his feet. "What floor did he say we need to go down to?"

"Penthouse." Quin moved to the door in the center of the roof. He glanced back at Max to make sure he was ready, and when Max nodded, he pulled the door open to reveal a short stairwell down to the floor below.

Max stopped in front of the door, pulling another packet of powder from his belt to blow into the open space. A ward check—it had saved them more times than he could count. When no alarm sounded, and the powder simply settled to the floor, he and Quin started down the stairs. There was another door at the bottom, with a little window in it that Max could just see a richly carpeted floor through.

Another little bit of the powder from his pouch to check

for wards, and Max wrinkled his nose. No wards. None at all. Maybe Enrique didn't think anyone would come from the roof, but still, it didn't sit right with Max. Most magical beings were more careful than that. Or maybe Orcus was just arrogant, confident in his power. Neither of which were very comforting.

A short inhale, a reprieve, as Max took hold of one of the daggers strapped to his thigh, then turned to check in with Quin. With a nod, they pushed through, trying to move as quietly as they could. If they could catch Enrique by surprise, then that would make life so much easier, especially since this mission was unsanctioned.

The door opened onto a short hallway, more alcove than corridor, which then dumped them into a huge foyer, complete with black and white marble tiles cut and designed into a compass rose, and a heavy looking crystal chandelier. Max didn't think he'd ever seen anything half as fancy in all his life, but there wasn't time to take it in. He gestured with two fingers toward the open living room area on the right of the foyer and took the first door in the hall to the left.

The hinges didn't even so much as creak, too well maintained for that, and Max opened first a half bath, then across from it, a study.

The study.

Streetlights streamed in through the windows, casting the room in glaring shadows, but the lamp on the desk lit the wings hung behind it perfectly.

They were pure white—so much like his own—they gleamed a million different shades, from electric blues to warm, coppery yellows, always reflecting what was around them. Taking what the world offered them and returning beauty. Was that how his wings looked from the outside?

For someone who didn't see them every day in the mirror? Was this why humans believed in angels?

But the angel was missing. These were just wings. Mounted and lifeless. The creature they had once been attached to long since returned to the fires of Prometheus. These were just signs of a fallen ignis. And Max didn't notice he was crying until he felt the tears cooling on his cheeks. He was quick to wipe them away, to hide the evidence of his weakness, and that's when he heard the soft creak of a shoe behind him.

"Beautiful, aren't they?" a low, dark, dangerous voice asked. Max didn't have to turn around to know that Enrique had snuck up behind him. He'd fucked up. And now he needed to think fast. "Yours will make a wonderful complement. A matched set."

The hilt of his dagger dug into his palm, and Max took a breath, steadying himself. Quin was still there, somewhere. Maybe he'd ducked into a room when he saw Enrique coming. Max just needed to blow the powder in Enrique's face and buy a little bit of time for Quin to get there and help Max cuff him. He turned slowly to face Enrique, silhouetted by the light of the foyer, and somehow looking larger than life. Max felt small, insignificant, when faced with the power of a god.

"Did my princeling send you?" Enrique tilted his head, dark hair falling artfully across his brow.

"Ander doesn't belong to you."

"Oh? And I suppose he belongs to you, does he?" A low, rumbling laugh left Enrique, and power began to fizzle at the tips of his fingers, popping and threatening.

"He doesn't belong to *anyone*."

Enrique snorted, soft, derisive, and opened his mouth to say "Now there's where you're wrong" just as Max scooped some of the powder from the other pouch and blew it into his face. There was a sharp inhale, followed by a sneeze, and Enrique stumbled a little on his feet.

"What the fuck was that? What did you jus—" He sneezed again, stumbling farther back into the wall. Max seized his chance and took a swing at Enrique's jaw, putting all of his weight behind it.

Enrique got ahold of himself in enough time to dodge the blow, sending Max stumbling. Quin came running into the room just in time to take up his position in the fight, but by then, Enrique had control of his magic again, and a sharp burst of power slammed Quin back into the wall, his head hitting hard enough to leave him dazed.

Max spun, using the momentum to lunge at Enrique, his arms wrapping around the god's waist and slamming him back into the desk, which slid dangerously toward the windows.

A snarl left Enrique, but even though he'd been disoriented, there was still strength behind the blows he landed to Max's back, his shoulders, his wings. Enough strength to leave Max bruised. To break bone. To rend flesh. That wasn't right. Ander had said the powder would make him weak, vulnerable. But Enrique wasn't even panting, wasn't bleeding.

Max took a knee to the stomach that cracked ribs and left him gasping for breath long enough that Enrique was able to throw him off. His knees hit the marble floor and left spiderweb fissures behind.

There was more fighting, more movement, Quin coming back for more, but it was hard to keep track of as Max stumbled, still trying to catch his breath. Max tried to push himself to his feet. To get enough air in his lungs.

Quin's body crashed through one of the windows

behind the desk, and he fell several feet, but Enrique didn't give Max time to see if Quin was all right, to make sure his brother got his head back on in enough time to not slam into the ground. He took hold of Max's wing, ruffling the feathers uncomfortably, and Max heard something snap just a moment before searing pain ripped through his entire body.

Darkness swam in his vision. Bile rose in his throat. But he wasn't done. He *couldn't* be done. Enrique was still there, and Max was going to cuff him. Going to take him back. He got his feet under him by some miracle, even as the room swam and the movement shifted his wing, making him cry out again.

He turned just in time to see Enrique grab something from his desk.

"Tell my princeling I'll be seeing him," Enrique hissed, a dark twist to his mouth, then magic sparked from his fingers, and he was gone.

Quin flew back through the window just as Max's knees gave out on him a second time. Or was it a third? It didn't matter. They'd failed.

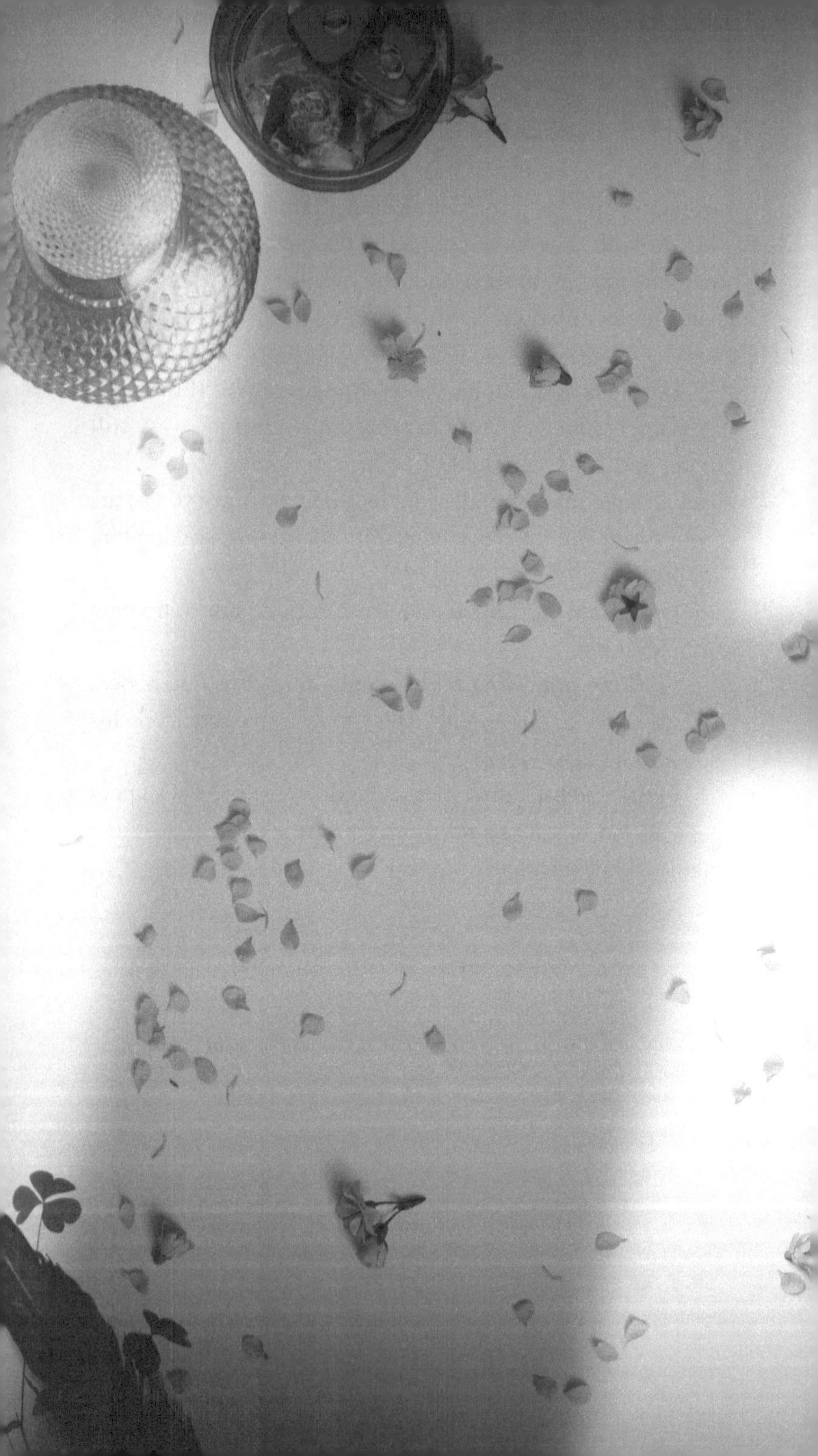

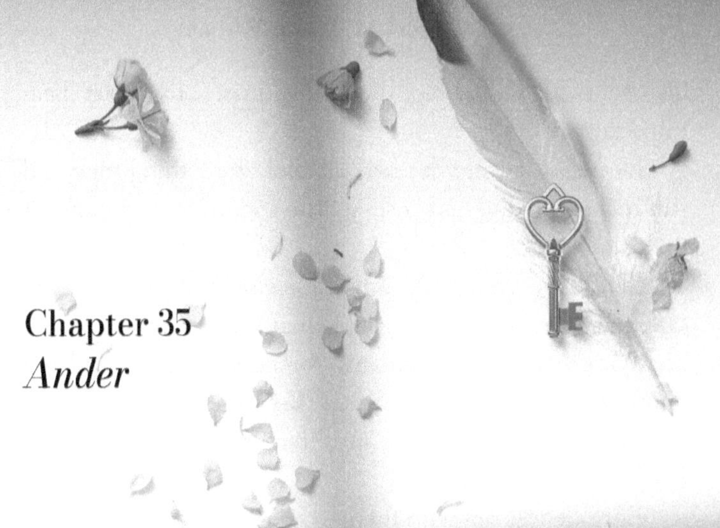

Chapter 35
Ander

Ander had sat in Max's office for as long as he could bear it. Then he began pacing the halls, hands ringing in front of him.

He hadn't expected them to head directly out to apprehend Enrique, and yet they had. As soon as Ander told Max about the powder he'd used to knock Enrique out, he'd asked for some, and they left.

It had given Ander no time to prepare. No time to ready himself for the fear and nerves that would fill him. What if something went wrong? What if it didn't work?

"Ander . . . you're going to wear a hole in the floor. Come sit down," Mab called from behind him.

He spun on his heel to face her. "Who can sit down at a time like this?!"

Mab sighed but nodded. "Okay, fine. But maybe calm down just a little?"

Ander took a deep breath, trying to steady himself, but he couldn't. It felt like a thousand beetles were scurrying beneath his skin, crawling up his neck, burrowing through his stomach, scratching down his legs. His heart beat frantically.

He really wished he had alcohol. Something nice and stiff that could dull his senses a little and drive away some of the anxiety.

Before he could say anything else, the doors to the sanctuary flew open, and a bloodied Quin stepped in. He had Max's arm slung over his shoulder, and he held the limping Max tightly to his side. Max looked battered. One of his wings was hanging at a terrifying angle that left Ander gasping in shock.

Enrique was not with them.

"Max!" he cried and rushed to his side.

He grabbed Max's other arm and slung it over his shoulders, wrapping his own around Max's waist. He looked at Quin. "Into his office."

Quin nodded, and together, they led Max down the hall.

"I'm fine," Max groaned as they rested him back against the desk.

Quin grunted at this and carefully extracted himself from under his arm.

"You're practically in pieces!" Ander roared, the beetles beneath his skin becoming flames of anger. He wanted to burn Enrique down to nothing but ashes. "What happened?" He looked from Max to Quin.

"The powder didn't work." Max winced.

Ander inhaled sharply, watching him. He hated seeing him in so much pain. Carefully, he began unstrapping his protective gear. "I don't understand. I just used it! It knocked him completely out. Were you at least able to hurt him?"

Quin shook his head. "Didn't even draw blood."

It didn't make any sense. "How much of the powder did he inhale?"

"Lots." Max winced more.

"Enough." Ander waved his hand before him, and Max's shirt disappeared. His torso was littered in dark bruises that turned his flesh black. "We've got to make this better first. Mab!"

"Yeah?" she hurried to say.

"I want you to look after Quin, he's got some deep gouges."

"I'll be fine. We heal fa—" Quin began.

"Did I ask?" Ander glared at him. "Take off your shirt so Mab can check for cuts and glass over your torso. Mab, wash the wounds carefully, and make sure to dig anything out so he doesn't heal with shards in him."

With a wave of his hand, hot water with mild soap, cloths, and tweezers appeared on the desk for Mab to use. Mab looked like she wanted to protest, but she must have seen the way he was barely clinging to his calm and simply gave a quick, "Mhm."

Ander turned back to Max, the sight of his injuries filling him with sickness and rage. He didn't know whether he was going to vomit everywhere or burn the world down.

"You don't have to do this," Max said softly.

"Yes. I do." He'd sent them after Enrique. A god. With faulty product. "This is my fault."

"Ander . . ."

He shook his head, a stern look telling Max not to finish that sentence. He didn't have time to be placated. Ander pressed his palm to Max's bruised and shattered ribs, careful not to push on the wounds. He hummed softly under his breath, using the music to draw on the healing properties of his muse magic. He could heal without the music, but for such wounds as these . . . it was better to use all the power he could.

Beneath his touch, he could feel the bones snapping back into place, and Max's breath hitched, then eased.

"That feels better."

"I'm glad." From the corner of his eye, he could see Mab methodically cleaning each of Quin's wounds, grumbling as he shifted and got in her way or didn't listen to what she told him to do.

Next, Ander cupped Max's face, gently brushing his thumbs over his lips and cheekbones as he hummed more, sending warm waves of magic through his skin. It was a relief to see the pain easing from Max's beloved features.

"Almost done, sweetheart," Ander murmured, their eyes meeting in something that felt tender yet taut with unspoken words. "Your wing next."

Max nodded.

"It might hurt a little . . . I have to put it back in position."

"I'm ready."

Ander moved to the side, gingerly reaching for the tip of his wing. He took a deep breath to steady himself, then lifted the wing back into proper placement. Max inhaled sharply, hissing breath through his teeth as the pain hit him. "I'm sorry! I'm sorry!"

"It's okay," he said through a clenched jaw.

Ander hated himself for every ounce of pain he was causing Max. He hated Enrique even more. Was it wrong to want him dead? To want to know the god of punishment had been wiped off the face of Earth and Underworld? "I'll be done really soon, I promise."

In order to repair the wing, Ander hummed louder than he had before, calling forth more magic from the well running deep within him. Pouring it into Max, telling his body to knit itself back together. He didn't stop until the feathers of his wings not only returned to position but gleamed with health.

Slumping a little in exhaustion, he looked Max over, making sure he hadn't missed anything.

"I'm good now, Ander. Thank you," Max said, reaching out to take his hand.

Ander accepted the touch gratefully, needing the contact with Max to reassure himself that he was okay. He could see him here, before him, in one piece, but he could also still picture the brokenness of before.

"So, what happened?"

Max shook his head. "I don't know. He got the jump on me. But even still, I managed to blow a whole bunch of powder into his face. I saw him inhale. He sneezed. He staggered, but that was it."

Ander frowned. "He went right out the minute I blew it in his face. I don't understand. It should have made him groggy at the very least, almost drunk like."

Waving his hand, Ander called the last of the powder to him. After studying it with his magic, he threw the container into the trash.

"Why did you do that?" Mab asked from her position beside Quin, washing the last of the blood off his face.

"There's barely any power left in it. It must not last as long in powder form." Ander swept his hand over his face. "I didn't even think about that. That changing it from a liquid to a powder could alter how long the substance was good for. Gods, Max, I'm sorry. This is all my fa—"

Max shut him up by pulling him in and placing a firm kiss to his lips. "I said to stop saying that."

Ander blinked up at him in surprise. He hadn't

expected a kiss. Just getting a hand to hold had seemed miraculous.

"So we need to make more of that stuff and take a fresh batch when we track Orcus down again," Quin said, pulling his bloodied shirt back over his head.

"*If* we can figure out where he's gone," Max responded.

Ander was having a hard time concentrating on anything they were saying when his heart was tripping along inside his chest like a wild rabbit thumping on a drum. Did the kiss mean Max forgave him? That he accepted the amare bond between them?

Did it mean he dared to hope again? Dared to dream of a time when there was nothing standing in the way of him being with Maximus?

Mab, being the darling best friend and little sister that she was, clearly read all that was going on inside his brain. "Hey, Q-tip, why don't we take this show on the road?"

Quin simply sat where he was, staring at her as if she'd lost her mind.

"Yeah, we could use a minute," Max interjected.

Quin nodded at this and stood up from his position slumped against the wall. "I'm not a fan of that one," he said to Mab.

"Oh, but Stink Eye is better?" she asked as they headed out the door, their voices disappearing down the hall.

Ander turned from watching them and looked at Max. "Are we . . . good? Have you had a chance to think about us and, well . . . everything?"

Max sighed. "Ander, when have I had a chance to think about *anything*?"

Ander's shoulders slumped. Of course he hadn't. He'd only just learned the truth about what Ander had been doing with Enrique, then he and his brother had swept off to try and bring him in. There had been no time to think on personal matters. Max had more important things to do than concern himself with Ander.

He took a step back to give Max some space, but a firm hand slipped around his once more and stopped him. Looking up at him, Ander paused. Max smiled ever so slightly and pulled Ander in against him.

Their lips connected in a sweet, gentle kiss that shook Ander down to his toes. Tingles spread through every nerve ending, making his cheeks heat and his muscles itch to respond. Max's lips tugged lightly on Ander's upper lip as he pulled away, and their eyes met in the slight space between them.

Ander's hands rested on his shoulders, rubbing gently at the tight muscles there. "Does this mean we're okay?" he whispered.

"It means . . . It means maybe we will be."

Ander nodded and slipped his arms around Max's neck, leaning in to hug him. Resting gratefully against his solid chest, Ander was simply glad to have him safe and near once more.

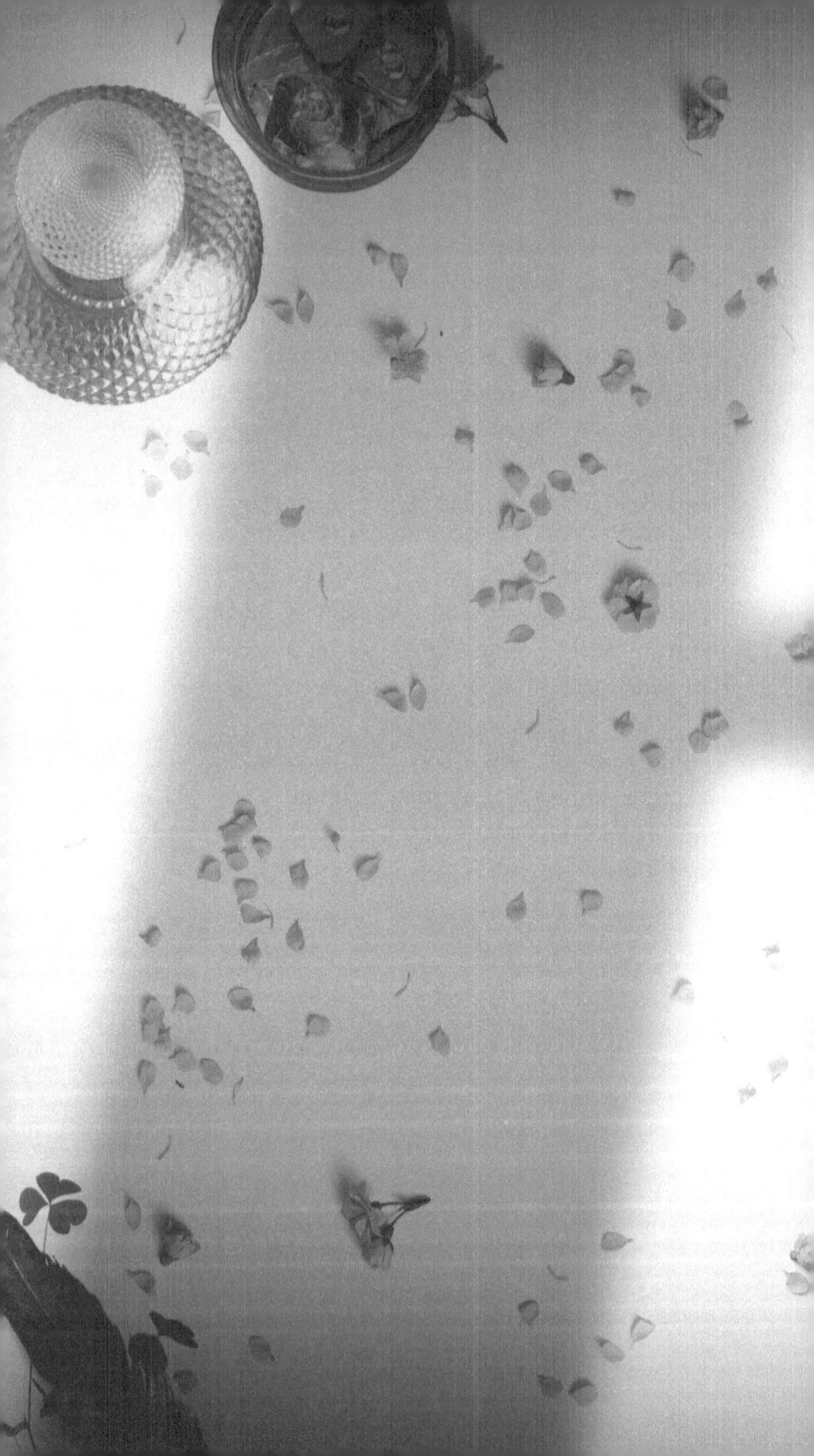

Chapter 36
Max

There was just so . . . so *much* now. So much warmth. So much color. So much vibrancy. Max didn't know if perhaps the world had always contained these multitudes and he'd been blind to them, or if loving Ander and accepting his love in return—even if Ander hadn't said it yet, Max *knew* without a shadow of a doubt that Ander loved him—made the world this way. Clearly, this was the kind of magic that ended wars and changed worlds. And yet . . .

And yet, here he was, his back straightened to the point of being ridiculous as he stood before Galeo's desk. His superior was watching him, eyes narrowed, blue wings spread out wide behind him, an intimidation tactic that had long stopped working on Max. He found it difficult to be intimidated by someone who he was fairly sure had seen less field time than his mortal father over the last decade. Still, he let Galeo think it worked, pulled his shoulders back, and leaned into something that the other man might mistake as false confidence.

"So, you're telling me," Galeo said, the words so slow that Max was sure they were supposed to land like a blow, "you went off without first clearing the mission through me, and managed to *lose* the suspect?"

"That is correct, sir." Max wished Quin were with him, if just for moral support. But he didn't actually want Galeo's displeasure to be turned on anyone else. This was his fault, his mistake; he should bear the brunt of the punishment for it.

"And now you want me to clear a second mission to retrieve the *same* suspect, using a mystery substance provided from a *prior* suspect." Galeo raised his blond brows, and—yeah, yeah, Max could admit, it sounded kind of bad when it was put that way. He could hear it now that someone else was saying it out loud. But he knew it was the right move. Could feel it in his gut. Just like he'd been able to feel that Ander wasn't their guy weeks ago. And look how that had turned out. He'd been right. "With a team of fifty, no less."

"I understand how this sounds, sir," Max said, his hands fidgeting where they were clenched behind his back, out of sight and out of mind. It was better not to let Galeo see that. Better not to let on how nervous he actually was. "And your skepticism—"

"*Skepticism,*" Galeo scoffed.

"—is completely valid. Warranted, even. But I know this is the right move. I can feel it in my gut. This thing with Orcus is never going to end until *we* put an end to it, and Ruin has provided us with a way to do that relatively safely. We won't get another chance like this one."

"Your gut." Galeo's bright blue eyes narrowed, and he licked his lips as he leaned back in his chair, his fingers steepling in front of his face. Which was not usually a good sign in Max's experience. It usually meant that he was gearing up to cut Max down and was thinking of how to do it in as few words as possible, for efficiency's sake.

So Max chewed on the inside of his cheek, already thinking of all the counterarguments or ways he could go behind Galeo's back. It wasn't a good plan, not really. Going behind his superior officer's back was a great way to get himself into trouble. But Max wasn't going to wait around for Enrique to make his move by stealing more younglings. And what was he even using them for, anyway? Was he just torturing and experimenting on them the way Ander said he had in Acheron? Or was there something else happening? Something more sinister? Another fighting ring or . . . ? No. There wasn't time to waste, to overthink, to find some other way to subdue—

"I'll allow it."

Max's spiraling thoughts screeched to a halt. He blinked once. Twice. "You will, sir?"

"I will. But I want to be clear about one thing, Schields." Galeo leaned forward again, meeting Max's eyes with a hard look that did actually make Max a little nervous. "Should this mission fail, that failure falls on your shoulders. I will not be held responsible."

"Yes, sir. Of—"

"Should this fail," Galeo continued, not allowing Max to say what he'd planned to, "you will be demoted, and the Schields family unit will be disbanded."

"Disbanded?" Max's stomach churned, bile eating away at him as he echoed the single word. A demotion he could take, would even expect. If Enrique got away again, if the powder didn't work, it would be definitive proof of his failure as a leader, and he would accept whatever consequences came with it. But he never thought those consequences would mean splitting up his family.

"Yes. Should this mission fail, it will be seen, not just by me but by the Princeps as well, as a failure of your Guardian's little experiment." Galeo's gaze hardened further, his mouth twisting a little. Max had never before realized just how much Galeo really hated Colton Schields' experimental ignis family. He'd known—it was hard not to—that most in the Sanctum didn't care for it. That they thought it was silly, idyllic in a world which didn't have room for such a thing. Too soft. Too gentle for a world that was happy enough to run through ignis like they were nothing more than tin soldiers. But he'd never realized the distaste his own superior held for it. Until now. "Is that a risk you're willing to take, Schields?"

Maybe he should have thought about it more. Maybe he should have taken a moment to consider the ramifications of what he was agreeing to. But Maximus Schields had always been, would always be, a man who acted on instinct. And those instincts, however others might look at him askance for following them, had saved his life and the lives of his family on more than one occasion. They would guide him in the right direction now.

Still, it felt a little like the words were being punched out of him when he said, "Yes, sir, it is."

Galeo nodded as if he hadn't expected anything else. "You'll have the fifty men you requested. I'll have the list sent to your command center as soon as possible. In the meantime, I suggest planning carefully. We wouldn't want to give the Princeps any more reason to disband your little *family* than they already have, would we?"

"No, sir," Max said, turning for the door, even though he knew the question was rhetorical, a taunt. That was fine. He could deal with that so long as Galeo provided them with what they needed to succeed. They would. The

Schields family had been in worse scrapes than this, and they would prove themselves again. He had faith in his siblings.

"And Schields," Galeo called just as Max reached the door. He didn't turn back around, but he tilted his head to let the other man know he was listening. "No civilians on the field."

"Of course, sir."

Quin was waiting outside the door when Max exited. He raised his dark brows in question, an invitation for Max to discuss what just happened. But he didn't have that in him, not right now, and they really didn't have the time for it anyway.

"You tell no one what was said," Max signed, his gaze pointed. It would only freak the twins out if they knew that this could be their last mission. And if Ander knew the gamble Max had just signed them all up for . . . well, he wasn't really sure what Ander would do, but it would probably be bad. He'd probably try to call the whole thing off. Or he'd insist on going with them, and that couldn't happen. Not after what Galeo said. He was right; Max didn't want to give Galeo or the Princeps another reason to pull the plug on his little family unit. And going against a direct order like that . . .

"We shouldn't keep this from them," Quin signed back, a frown marring his face. "They'd want to know."

"Would it help anything?" Max turned to his brother, fixing him with a look of pleading, because Quin knew, just like Max did, exactly what kind of strain that would put the entire group under. It was better that pressure stay on his and Quin's shoulders. If it were up to Max, Quin wouldn't know either.

Quin thought for a moment, a range of emotions

playing across his face, then he nodded and signed, "I'll follow your lead, as always."

Max's shoulders relaxed, and he nodded to himself, scrubbing at his face as they headed toward the conference room where all the others waited. The door was propped open, and when Max entered, he found Mab and Ander sitting on one side of the table staring down Nash. Nox was absent, likely gathering everything she needed for the presentation. Why Nash wasn't helping her with that, Max had no idea. He seemed to do everything in his power to skirt having to do work.

With a heavy sigh, Max settled into one of the open chairs on the side of the conference table next to Nash, because apparently someone was drawing lines between the Schields family and Mab and Ander. Which was silly. They were all on the same team. But Max was sure if he didn't play into Nash's dramatics, they'd just get worse, and that was another thing they didn't really have time for right now. He gave Ander a little wave as he sat, and Ander waved back, soft and tentative. Max wanted to hug him so badly, his muscles twitched with it, every single one burning to reach for Ander and pull him in close.

"Your girl over there looks like she eats grown men for breakfast," Nash signed to Quin, his fingers working carefully over the words as if to make sure Quin caught every one, a smug lilt to the way he moved them. Because he was a little shit, always had been.

Quin's bright gaze flicked from their brother over to Mab, and something shifted on his face. But Max didn't have time to decipher what the expression was or what it meant before Quin returned his glare to Nash. His long fingers moved slow and condescending over the words, "I don't think that's something you need to concern yourself with."

Max had to bite back a chuckle, covering it with a cough.

There was a beat where Nash looked pleased with himself, like he'd gotten one over one Quin, probably because Quin hadn't argued about Mab being *his* girl. Then the words registered, and he said, "Hey! I'm not—"

"Enough," Nox said, cutting her twin a pointed look from where she was smoothing her fingers over her ponytail to brush back invisible fly-aways, a nervous habit she'd picked up in her teen years and never grown out of. It made Max want nothing more than to stand and wrap her up in his arms. To hold her close to his chest and whisper into her hair that everything was going to be all right, that he was going to take care of everything, just as he'd done so many times when she and Nash were younger. But he couldn't promise that, and he'd always made a point not to lie to them, any of them. So he stayed in his seat and waited for her to straighten herself up and start the briefing. "What did Galeo say?"

"He's giving us a force of fifty. But it's up to us to find Enrique and figure out how to weaponize Ander's drug." Max turned his attention to the screen behind Nox, where she'd pulled up a diagram from her tablet.

"I have some ideas on that," Nox said, her teeth wearing on her lip as she zoomed in a little on the schematics in front of her. "This is a smoke bomb we already have in the armory. Nash says it should work with the powder Ander created. We had him make some fresh while you were dealing with Galeo. We just need to fit our own forces with some kind of gas mask."

"Won't be necessary." Ander shook his head. "It only

affects gods."

"Right, forgot about that," Nox muttered. She was tapping her fingers against the tablet, her nails clicking loudly, as she recalibrated her presentation in her mind. "All right then, all we've got left is to find this bastard."

"I can help with that," Ander said, raising his hand. Which was kind of adorable, if wholly unnecessary. "I know a tracking spell we can use to find him." He waved his hand over the table in front of him, and a crumpled piece of paper appeared. The edges were ragged, the color yellowed, the ink fading, but it was definitely a letter. Ander didn't explain what it was, or how he'd come by it, which might have been for the better. "I've used something like this before to find—" He paused, swallowing roughly, and shook himself even as Mab reached over to give his arm a squeeze. "Anyway, this will work. It'll take me right to him."

"You mean it'll take *us* right to him," Max corrected gently. "You can't go. It'll just be me, Quin, and the forces Galeo is giving us. All civilians have to stay here."

"But I—"

"Ander, I'm sorry. This is how it has to be." Ander looked like he wanted to argue, and Quin shifted in his seat next to Max. Max said with more firmness than he really felt, "I'm under orders."

Ander deflated. "All right. I'll need to alter the spell a little, to give us a map location instead." A map appeared on the table a second later, and before Max could even process what he was doing, Ander had focused his magic on the note.

Max's equipment was heavy, pressing down on skin that had healed over but was still tender, fresh and free of the callouses that he'd built up over the time he'd been an active ignis. He'd have to have a discussion with Ander about his healing abilities being a little too effective later.

Later.

Later.

After all of this was done. After Orcus was behind bars and Ander was well and truly safe from him.

"Ander . . ." Max called softly across the room full of clattering ignis readying for battle. He needed to see him, to hold him, in case it was the last time. In case he didn't come back from this. Because while Max had faith in his siblings, knew Quin had his back, he also knew the dangers here. Enrique—Orcus—was a god. A god who had already put a serious hurting on him. And Max had to be ready for more of the same violence.

"Hm?" Ander murmured. His long copper fingers fiddled with the dagger he had been in the middle of grabbing for Max to strap to his thigh.

He'd told Ander he didn't need the help getting ready, but he also understood better than anyone the need to feel useful when he couldn't do anything else. So there Ander was, fluttering about the soldiers, reinforcing armor and weapons with his magic. Max didn't doubt that if Ander had the power and the proximity, he'd try to place a bubble around all of them, to protect them from what was coming. Unnecessary, but beautiful just the same.

"I think I need to tell you something." His lips were suddenly dry, throat scratchy. Why was this so hard? It had never been hard to tell his family that he loved them. He said it every day, made sure they knew, so on the off chance that if he didn't come back, they'd never question. But this was the first *I love you* he'd say to someone who wasn't family. And the first one to Ander. It held more weight. "I think you need to know that—That I—"

Ander moved quickly, up onto his toes to close the slight distance their height difference provided, and silenced Max with his lips. Max stumbled a little under the force of it, his hands moving to brace Ander's waist as Ander threw his arms around Max's neck, holding him closer, firm but tender. When Ander pulled back, they were both breathless, but Ander's brow was pinched, his lips pursed in a serious line. His eyes were downcast, focused somewhere on Max's chin.

"We aren't going to talk like that. Not now." He sucked in a breath, tilting his head back to meet Max's eyes. "Because that makes it sound like you're not coming back. And you are. You're coming back to me. You have to."

What could Max say to that? Nothing. He couldn't argue against that logic. Couldn't tell Ander not to worry, because he should worry. He should be scared. *Max* was scared. So he just said "Okay" and pressed a kiss to Ander's temple.

"We'll talk about this, us, when you get back."

"Okay," Max said again, pressing a kiss to the opposite temple, inhaling deeply to try to memorize the smell of Ander's hair products: vanilla and something spicy, like citrus. "I'll hurry back."

"You do that." Ander pulled a wide, confident smile across his face, charming and gorgeous, even though Max saw it quiver at the edges in fear.

"You ready?" Quin asked from behind Max, and Max nodded once.

"Yeah. Let's go." He pressed a quick kiss to Ander's lips, then spun to follow his brother out.

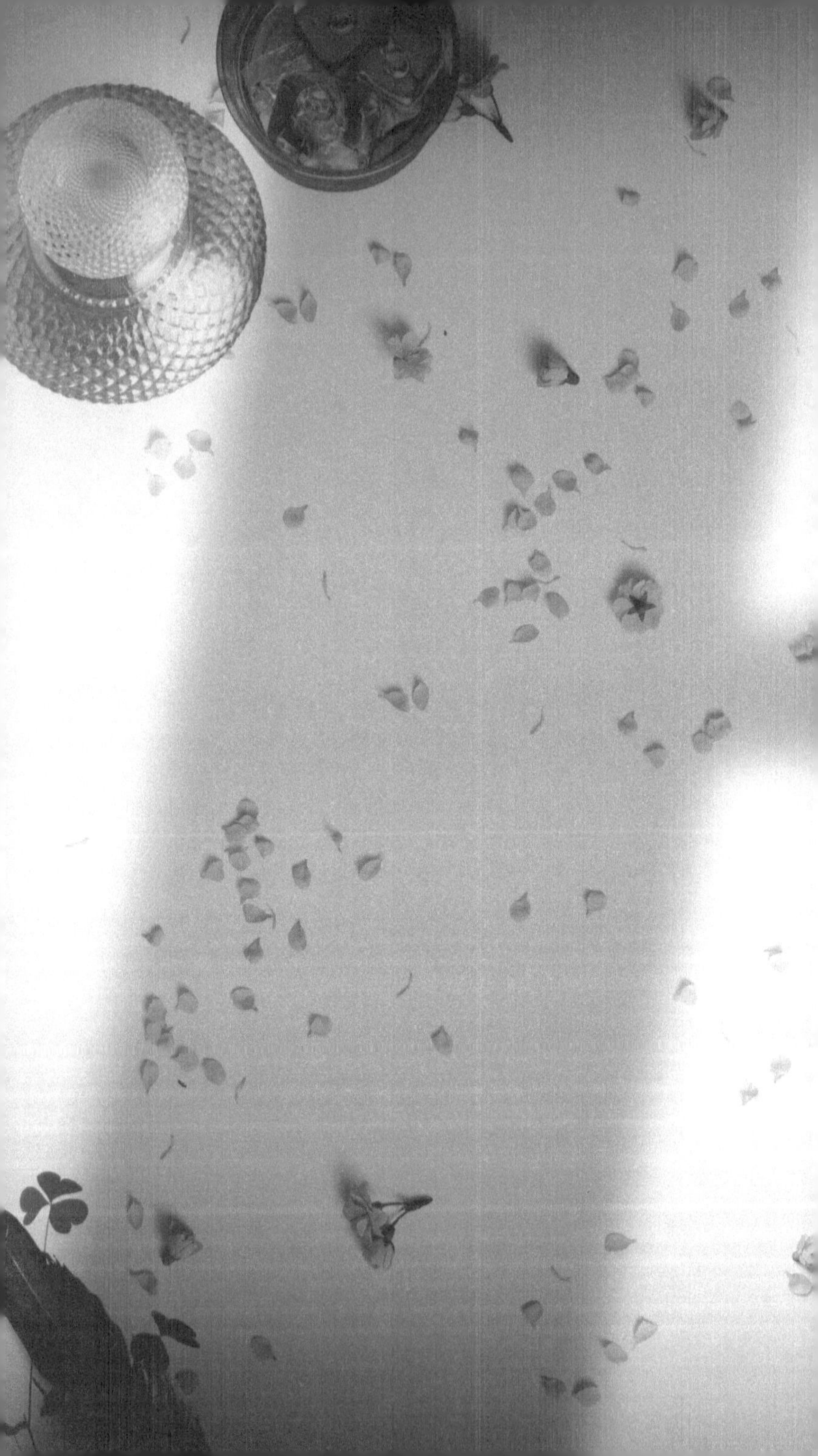

Chapter 37
Ander

All of the oxygen had gone out of the room. At least, that was what it felt like to Ander's screaming lungs that refused to take in new air. Terror was a living creature, racing through his blood stream. Slamming into his heart, lodging up beneath his ribcage, and squeezing tight around his lungs as it rampaged its way through his body.

Max had kissed him goodbye and left. Heading off in the direction Ander had pointed him. Sending him off to face the god of punishment. Who knew what Enrique had up his sleeve? The thought terrified Ander.

What had he done?

He should have figured out a way to kill Enrique on his own. A way to truly make him weak so that Ander could be rid of him instead of sending his sweet, tenderhearted ignis off to do it.

What if Max didn't come back?

What if he came back but he was so destroyed, all the magic in the world couldn't repair him?

"Ander." A soft hand slid into his, pulling him to a stop in his pacing.

Ander looked over his shoulder at Mab, who was eyeing him with a concerned look on her face. "Yeah?" he croaked.

"Let's go to Underworld."

"What?" Ander frowned. Now was not the time to party.

"Let's go to Underworld. We need to tell Indra and the others what Enrique is up to. And we promised Hades an update."

Ander just blinked, trying to put her words together through the haze of his fear.

"I don't—"

"For when they bring Enrique back. So there are gods waiting for him." He opened his mouth to start, but she cut him off again. "They need to know, Ander."

He grumbled but nodded. She was right. Indra needed to know. These were his soldiers after all, doing all his dirty work in the mortal realm. "Fine."

Mab squeezed his hand but didn't let go. Ander took a deep breath—or as deep as he could get with the vice grip around his chest—and centered himself so he didn't snap half of them to Olympia and half somewhere else. Fortunately, they were already in Feugo City, so they didn't need to hit up a portal.

"I know what you're doing."

"Oh?" Mab's brows went up. "And what is that?"

"Trying to distract me."

"And it's working, isn't it?"

Only a little. While his body was going through the motions of getting them to Olympia, his mind, his heart, were all back with Max and what he was about to face.

But Mab was right. It was much better that he go to the gods and tell them what was happening rather than standing around in the sanctuary losing his mind.

Ander squeezed Mab's hand and tugged her in against him. "To Olympia we go."

Mab nodded and held onto him. When his fingers snapped, they were taken from the Feugo City sanctuary and its linoleum floors to the very top of Mount Olympia, where Indra's palace sat.

While it was so high it felt like you could reach out your hand and skim your fingers across the sun, it did not in fact sit amongst the clouds. The palace itself was lovely and gilded, and glistened in the sunshine. It should have been a place of warmth and happiness.

But it was cold. And distant. Filled with gods who thought themselves better than everyone else in their perfection. In their ability to live forever and remain untouchable to the masses. Only another god could hurt them, and they all lived by a creed that you did not harm your own kind.

Mortals . . . they could be toyed with to one's heart's content. But other gods were to be left alone. Physically, anyway. Ander was well aware of the subterfuge poisoning the golden blood of the gods. Of the gossip and rumors that tore friendships and families apart.

Eternity was too long to hang on to all of one's morals.

The guards let them into the throne room without an issue. Indra was there, sprawled on the steps, sipping wine and being fanned by two young nymphs in sarongs.

"Ander! Mab!" He grinned as he sat up, then his eyes narrowed, and he pointed an accusing finger at Ander. "You knocked me out."

Ander offered an apologetic smile and bowed a touch. "I must apologize, but I had to test out the powder I was making on a god, and it was either you or your beautiful wife. You seemed the safer choice."

Indra chuckled a deep, booming laugh that echoed off the ceiling of the chamber. "That I must agree with. She has the fury of a thousand harpies and all the anger of a wild manticore." The king of gods looked between them. "Why do I feel you are not here to exchange pleasantries?"

"We're not." Mab was quick to get to the point. "Enri—Orcus was found to be collecting hordes of ignis, and we believe he may have hundreds more."

Indra frowned. "And doing what with them?"

Ander's shoulders were taut, his spine stiff. Tension coursed through him. "He's been capturing them as infants or younglings. Likely torturing some." He nearly spat the words out, Ikari at the forefront of his mind. "But I would say he's amassing an army."

"HERMAHAS!" Indra bellowed, climbing to his feet in one smooth motion.

The herald to the gods flew in through a window, landing quickly on the marble floor. Ander wasn't sure where they had been posted, but they had clearly heard Indra's call.

Hermahas bowed, then straightened. They wore a lovely lavender loincloth that fell in glorious folds over front and bottom, attached by a gold belt low on their hips. Golden cuffs clasped both biceps lovingly, and a gold barbell pierced one nipple. Ander could remember capturing that barbell between his teeth and tugging on it just firmly enough to bring moans out of the messenger god's mouth.

Hermahas' curly blond hair framed their face and cascaded, long and glorious, in a thick braid over one shoulder. Gold glitter coated their bare flesh and left the god glinting in the sunlight. Spotting Ander, they winked at him.

"Yes, Your Majesty, you beckoned?" Hermahas' voice was soft and elegant, like a lazy, winding brook.

"Go and fetch Prometheus at *once*. Tell him there is a matter of grave importance concerning the ignis."

Hermahas nodded and curtsied. "Of course." The long, elegant white wings attached to both heels fluttered, and then the slender god was gone, darting back out through the open window.

Ander, who had been watching Hermahas leave, suddenly found Indra standing before him.

"Is this what you thought Orcus was up to? What you wanted to know about *dues somnum* for?" His eyes were fierce and intent, and Ander recognized the power residing within the god.

For all his dramatics and sexual exploits, Ander now saw how this being had taken command of Olympia and all of Underworld.

"Yes," Ander practically squeaked out.

"Why didn't you tell me it was this severe? That he was amassing an army?" Indra leaned in closer, the heat of his breath wafting over Ander's face.

"I didn't want to cause a stir if it were for nothing." He swallowed, his mouth parched.

"He wanted to be sure, so he didn't bring false information to you!" Mab growled, seeming undisturbed by the king's ire. "Why force you into action if there was nothing to be worried about?"

Indra scoffed but stepped back.

"And we weren't sure you would care." Ander finally found his backbone. Thinking of Max. His dear sweet Max. Thinking of all the times he'd heard of, or seen for himself, Indra brushing off the fatalities of the ignis. How their deaths meant as little to him as an ant farm smashed on the floor by a child. "The ignis are just toys to you."

Indra's brows shot up.

"While our dear king may not care about the lives of the ignis, I do," a smoky voice announced from behind them.

Spinning on his heel, Ander found Prometheus, the titan who had created the ignis within the flames of his forge, standing in the doorway to the throne room.

"They are my children, after all."

"Cousin." There was a dark glint in Indra's eyes.

"Indra," Prometheus responded, coming toward them all.

"Have your little younglings been going missing?"

As Prometheus stopped beside him, Ander couldn't help but look him over. The titan looked as if he were carved from stone itself, each sinew of flesh and tendon clearly defined. His shoulders were broad, his waist thick, and his thighs like the trunks of trees.

Titans were a different breed. While Indra had been born to titan parents, there was something softer looking about him than the being standing beside Ander now, whose bearing was like something wild and unkempt. How Indra had managed to subdue the titans under his control was beyond him.

"Yes, they have been," Prometheus snarled. "Since the beginning when you first begged me to create them, they've gone missing. That's what happens when you create weapons and drop them into the mortal realm without preparation." His features were pinched, his forehead creased with anger lines.

Indra shifted, but his own anger did not soften under the subtle finger-pointing.

"But *hundreds*? Why did you not speak to me about such matters?"

"What is wrong, *cousin*?" Prometheus threw the term back at him. "Are you worried about your toy soldiers disappearing, or that someone else may be using your own weapons against you?"

Indra scoffed and waved a hand. "I am a god. Your ignis cannot kill me."

"No, but they could destroy your kingdom and every other kingdom within Underworld if raised to do so," Ander spoke up, the words suddenly leaving him, unbidden. "Orcus wants to rule. It's why he wanted me. He wanted us to take over Helicon together. He hungers for power."

Ander shuddered, a chill of fear and foreboding coursing through him. It suddenly made sense. Beyond Enrique wanting new toys to torture. Beyond him wanting some twisted underground network.

He wanted power.

He wanted to rule.

He would use Indra's own soldiers against him to take over Underworld.

Gods. He had to be stopped.

Mab's hand was suddenly in his once more, her fingers sliding carefully through his, offering a squeeze of solidarity. He turned his head to look at her, and she gave him a little smile of reassurance.

"He's going to be okay," she whispered.

Ander took a deep breath and squeezed her hand back. Gods bless Mab for always sensing what was going on inside him, even sometimes before his own thoughts caught up.

When he focused on the room at large once more, he

found that both Indra and Prometheus were staring at him. Ander fought the urge to squirm. "What?"

"Do you believe that is what he is amassing an army for?" Indra questioned.

Mab snorted. "Well, what else do you think he'd be doing? Teaching them to tap dance in an ensemble?"

Ander couldn't hold back a little snicker. Perhaps it was the stressful situation he found himself in now or the deep-seated worry holding his body hostage. But he couldn't keep it in.

Prometheus looked like his lips wanted to form into a smirk. Instead, he looked at Indra. "I will go to Earth. Someone should be there to help apprehend Orcus and bring him to you for sentencing."

"We will both go," Indra announced, fury settling behind his eyes. "If overthrowing me is his plan, I will be there to let him know *no one* unseats me from my throne."

"Hades needs to be told as well," Ander stated. "Orcus is his right hand."

Indra huffed but nodded. His finger scrawled a message in the air, leaving gleaming letters, then he blew on them. The letters disappeared, the message sent.

"There," Indra announced, then stormed through them, forcing Mab and Ander to step out of the way. They looked at each other, then at Prometheus.

"To the sanctuary," he muttered, then followed after the king.

Ander and Mab shared another glance. "Back to Feugo we go, I guess."

Mab nodded at him, and together, they followed after the two gods, watching as first Indra then Prometheus snapped themselves away.

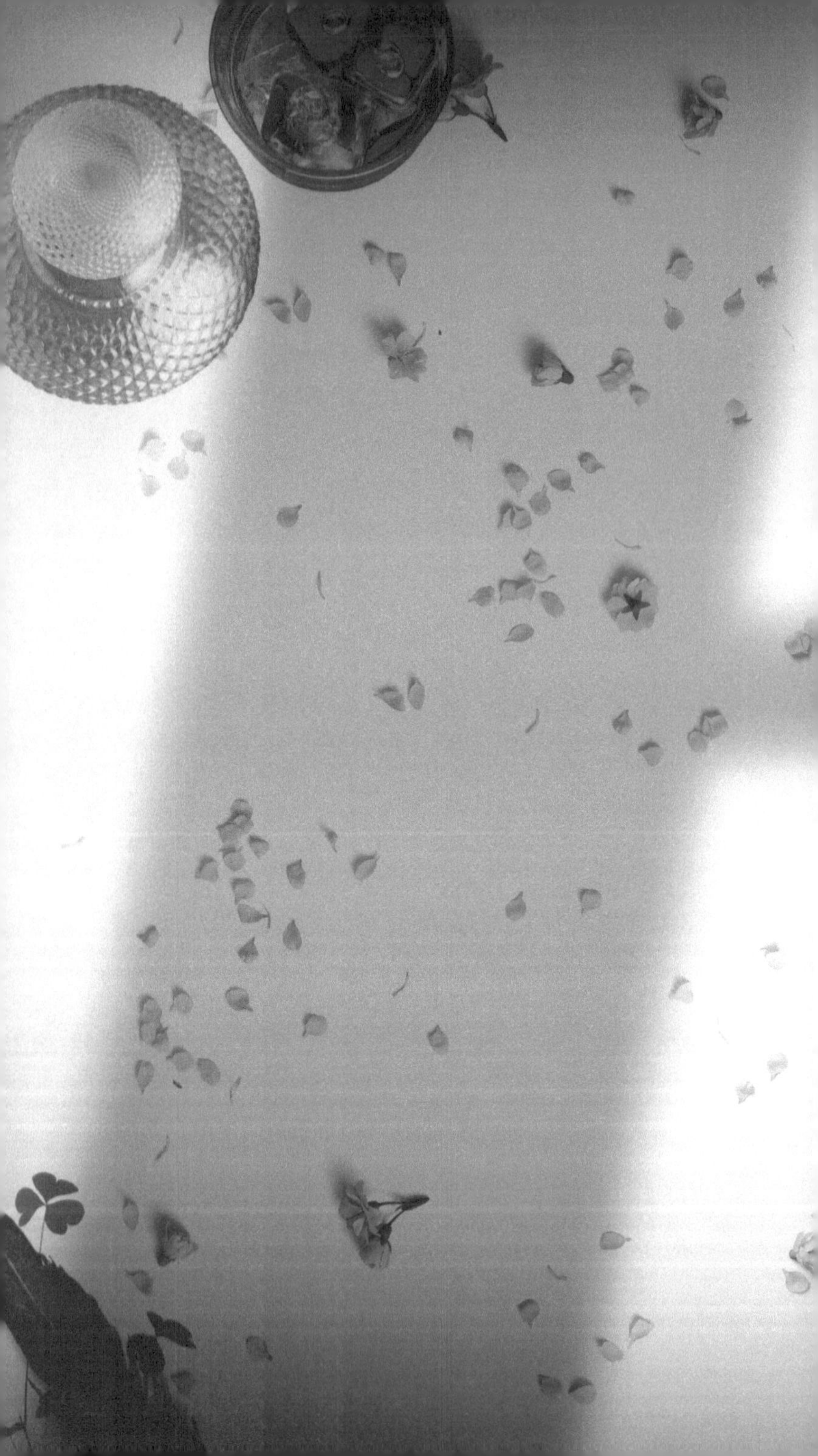

Chapter 38
Mab

Mab didn't exactly love traveling by snap. It was like being locked in that cell again for a moment, only to be thrust into the first rays of dawn. It left behind a ringing in her ears and a burn in her eyes that would cling for what seemed like weeks. In reality, there was absolutely nothing left behind from the travel. It was probably neurosis. Leftovers from spending so many years in the dark and the dirt of the asylum before being forced into the light. Even now, hundreds of years later. *Some things you just never get over.*

And then there was the fact that, even once they snapped to the sanctuary, there still was nothing for Mab and Ander to do to help. They weren't gods. They weren't soldiers, even though they had both spent as much time—if not more—learning to defend themselves as any ignis. That didn't mean they were built for battle. Didn't mean the ignis would even let them fight. So, there they were, benched, again.

Mab liked it about as much as Ander did. It was like that nightmare where she ran and ran and ran and still couldn't escape the mobs that were after her, looked around, and found that she'd been running in place the whole time. A scream had clawed its way up her throat and made a home for itself at the back of her tongue, scraping raw and jagged any time she tried to swallow around it. And she knew that the only way to handle it, the only way to not spend all of the time that they sat and waited screaming, was to distract herself.

She grabbed Ander, her fingers closing hard around his wrist and giving it a tug. He tugged back, as if to try to break her hold and return to his pacing of the Sanctum lobby, which was just making both of them crazy. He looked too much like a man in a cage. Tightening her hold, she tugged again.

"Mab," Ander hissed.

"Ander," she hissed back, and even though he dug his heels into the floor, she was able to pull him along behind her toward Max's office. No one stopped them, which was probably because all of the ignis left in the Sanctum were a little busy trying to support those who had gone out into the field, and she managed to make it to the door of the Schields command center without too much fuss. The little room was empty, echoing with the sounds of fans kicking on to keep the computers and screens cool but devoid of the Schields twins. Hopefully because they had moved to a bigger room where they could monitor their brothers' team along with other techs and not because something had gone wrong.

Oh gods, what if something had gone wrong?

No. She couldn't think like that. They were fine. They were going to be fine. They were going to stop Enrique, and that rat bastard would finally see the justice he should have seen a hundred years ago. It was fine. Telling herself that didn't make her hands any less clammy as she nudged the door to Max's office shut and guided Ander to a chair, but it made breathing past the scream a little easier. The chair legs screeched against the floor, too loud in the quiet of the office, as Mab turned her chair completely to face his.

Ander wasn't looking at her, though; his eyes were flicking around the space, seemingly to take in anything and everything of Max that he could while the other male wasn't right in front of him. She hoped he found comfort in being surrounded by Max's things, and if the way the skin around his eyes had softened a little meant anything, maybe he had.

The office was tiny and chaotic, stuffed to the brim with books and rolled up blueprints. At least five cardigans hung over the back of Max's chair in layers, like someone might wear when they were too cold. Mab counted the different colors of the collars to make sure she was seeing right in a fit of near hysteria as she tried to think of a distraction.

A distraction. A distraction.

Oh!

With a loud *thunk*, she pulled her purse from her lap and sat it on the desk, then proceeded to dig through it, unloading pens and mascaras and even a couple of snack bars onto the surface before she crowed in victory, "Found it!"

"Found what?" Ander asked. He had been oddly quiet up until that point, watching Mab as if she'd suddenly turned into someone he didn't recognize. Or maybe he wasn't watching her at all. Maybe he was just staring. His eyes unfocused. His mind off somewhere else. And that was the whole problem she was trying to solve here! She was trying to keep him from thinking about everything that could possibly be going wrong with Max as they spoke.

She took his hands again to place the napkin into them.

They were still shaking, likely hadn't stopped from when he'd had to heal Max what felt like a lifetime and only seconds ago. Gods, everything was happening so fast. Speeding past them in a race toward the end. She was going to throw up if she didn't get her mind off all of this soon.

"It looks familiar, doesn't it?" she asked by way of explanation as his fingers smoothed over the edges of the drawing, careful not to wrinkle or soil it.

She'd stored it in the little notebook she kept in her purse to preserve the drawing itself, but the edges still looked a little ragged. She should probably stop carrying it around like she was. But . . . but every time she went to take it out and leave it at home or, gods, even throw it away like she knew she ought, something stayed her hand. Something refused to let her fingers unclench from where they held tightly to this little drawing—not much more than a sketch— of herself. It had probably taken, what? Twenty minutes to draw? It wasn't even that detailed. But there was something in the softness of the lines, in the shadows, that reminded her so much of the portraits Edward had . . .

No. That was then. This was now. Whoever this was, they were not Edward. Edward was long gone, and even before then, he hadn't deserved her. Hadn't cared for her. Had hurt her in the most profound way imaginable. A betrayal. Not cheating, no, that would have been forgivable compared to him standing by and letting those men lock her away.

She shook herself.

"Mab," Ander said, his tone gentle as he smoothed the napkin over his lap, working a little magic into it to shore up the edges and repair any damage from wear. "I'm sure a lot of artists have a similar style. Quin is—You don't really think this was him, do you?"

"Maybe? He was there that night. He sat at the bar." Why was she pushing so hard for this? Was she this hard up for answers that she was going to latch on to the first available person with graphite on their hand and call them her mysterious artist? And why did she care, anyway? It was just a drawing. Just a doodle. It didn't mean anything. It couldn't mean anything. For so many reasons, none of which she could really put a name to.

"Do you want it to be him?" Ander tilted his head to one side, his focus now homed in on their discussion instead of the what ifs of the battlefield. Which was better, probably. But also made Mab squirm in her seat. He saw too much. Knew too much. "I thought you hated him. You're always calling him names."

Mab shrugged, the chair creaking beneath her as she shifted around some more. That was the question, wasn't it? Did she want it to be Quin? Or did she just want an answer, any answer? Her mind flashed back to those few scant minutes in this very office after they'd returned from Enrique's.

"Hold still," Mab chided, the tweezers Ander had conjured shaking a little in her hands. It had been a really long time since she'd had to patch anyone up after a battle. Not since World War II, probably. And then it had been humans. Humans that would die sooner rather than later. Every treatment like slapping a Band-Aid on a fatal wound. Even if some of them weren't, in fact, life threatening, she was still patching the men up to send them back out onto the field to die. But she'd been a surer hand at it then, used to it after only having twenty-odd years in between one war and the next. Now it had been closer to a hundred years, and much of them she'd spent as bartender, not nursemaid for the dying. Plus, her current patient

wasn't unconscious from shock, and he was fucking squirming.

"I am holding still," Quin hissed back, his wings shifting behind him, catching the light and sending off rainbows in every direction. Black. "Not the absence of color but the presence of too much of it," Edward had once said.

"Are you? Because you look like you're wriggling around like a toddler. I've treated children who were better patients than you."

Quin went completely still for a moment, allowing Mab to pick the last of the glass from his left arm and drop it into the tray, where it tinked softly against the metal. Then, in a voice that was very low, like he wasn't sure he actually wanted an answer to the question, "You've treated children before?"

"Yeah." Mab shrugged and moved on to pick the glass from his shoulder, his dark feathers brushing against her arm as she worked. "They hit a couple of orphanages during the blitz. What? Did you think only adults were hurt in war?"

He reached back to take ahold of her wrist for a brief moment, long enough to pull her around to face him, then dropped it a second later like he had been burned. "I didn't know you were a nurse during World War II."

"Bird brain, the things you know about me could fill a thimble." Another shrug. "Being immortal isn't all fun and games. Sometimes it's also a fuckload of pain and sorrow. We had friends who fought. We lost friends who fought."

"Oh," Quin replied, blinking at her for a moment, his brows creased together. She couldn't make out exactly what the expression meant, but when he didn't say anything else right away, she returned to her work. To the methodical, repetitive tink, tink, tink of glass being dropped into the tray. He didn't squirm or fuss anymore, but he did wait until she *couldn't see his face before he said, "That was really good of you."*

"It was really necessary of me, is what it was." Still, something warm and bubbling curled up in her chest, spreading out to her fingers, cutting through the cold of her anxiety.

"No. No, it wasn't."

The silence that followed felt comfortable, warm, but also heavy, like curling up under that weighted blanket Ander had gotten her for Christmas a few years back.

She didn't hate it. She didn't hate him.

"I mean . . . he doesn't suck? Or at least, not like I thought." Which was perhaps an understatement. There was a lot more to Quin than she'd originally seen, and maybe there was a lot more to her than he'd originally seen too. Maybe they could be . . . friends? Yeah, friends would be nice. Especially with what was happening with Max and Ander.

"I see," Ander said, his gaze narrowed on her, inspecting.

"You see?" Mab didn't think she liked the way he was looking at her. "You see what?"

"Oh. Nothing." But the small, secretive smirk on his face could only spell trouble. Damn it. Maybe she'd distracted him a little *too* well.

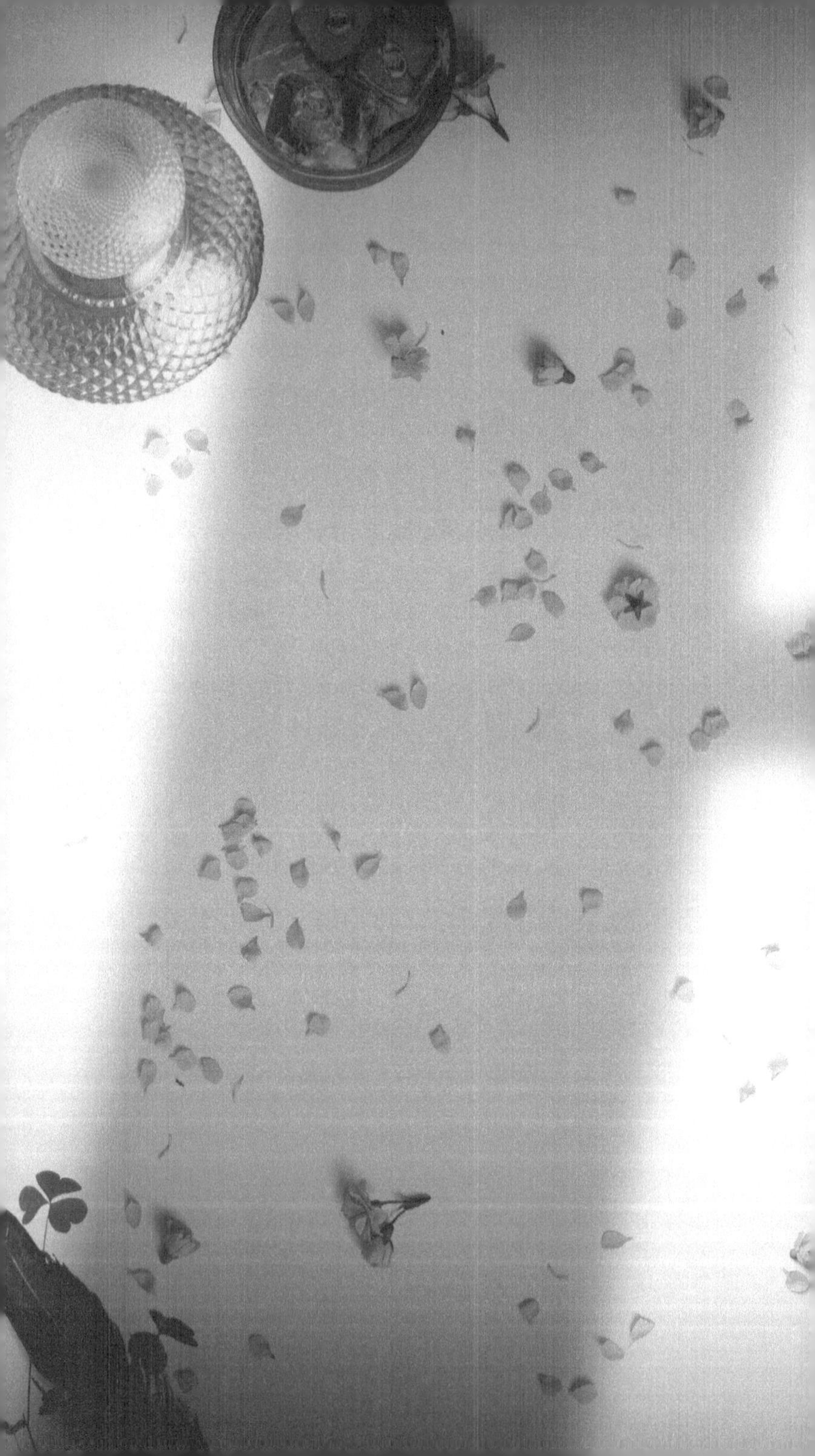

Chapter 39
Quin

Ruin had directed them to a warehouse in Sarasota, right on the coastline. An old, decrepit building with broken windows and one crumbling wall on the north side. It seemed that the more a place was falling down, the more Orcus liked it.

The warehouse itself sat against a rickety looking wharf with a large ship bobbing on the water attached to it.

Riding the air current with his wings spread wide behind him, Quin glided in toward the structure.

Max spoke through his earpiece. "Land soft and easy on the roof, we'll find access there."

"Roger that." Quin shifted his body, angling sharply to the right so that he could head to the safer south side of the warehouse.

His black combat boots touched down on the roof, and he folded his wings in against his back. Max followed shortly behind him, landing just a few feet away. Beyond them, other ignis were landing. Some in the shadows of the street, some along the wharf, others on top of the ship.

"B Team is on the ground and in position. We have the

building surrounded. Over," Marcellus sounded off in Quin's ear.

"A Team is in position on the roof," Max whispered beside him, notifying the remainder of their squad. "C Team, what is your location? Over."

While Max fulfilled his leadership responsibilities, Quin knelt down on the roof near the skylight. Pulling a small crowbar from the pouch secured to his side, he began prying the windowpane free of the frame. With a soft grunt, he worked his way around it.

"C Team has dropped the cargo and is now falling into position. Over," Albina responded. That meant that Nash and Nox had been safely, but closely, stowed away in their tactical trailer: a large shipping container that the ignis themselves carried through the air and dropped into each mission location. It gave them the ability to continue to monitor the situation with computers, satellites, and whatever other technological aid the twins could provide.

"Team Awesome is set and ready to proceed. Over," Nash announced.

Quin couldn't help rolling his eyes at the call sign Nash had assigned himself and their sister.

"C Team, let us know when you have a body count. Over." Max knelt across from him, helping to lift the pane of glass up and out of the frame. Together, they set it down on the roof.

"We've got heat signatures for twenty inanimi and one god." There was a pause in Albina's report, and Quin wondered if something had happened to her. He looked over at Max, a brow lifting, but then the radio crackled in his ear once more. "We've got six ignis inside. All younglings." Her voice was strained, hard.

Quin's shoulders tightened, and heat swirled inside of

him. He clenched his hand around the crowbar and contemplated how much damage he could actually do to a god before they recovered and bashed him in instead.

Could he manage to draw a little of that gold blood? See just a touch of it flow before he died?

"We're going to get him, Q. You have my word."

Quin looked over at Max, their eyes meeting in the moonlight. His brother had read him like a very open book. He didn't respond, he just nodded and pointed at the hole. "Ready?" he signed.

Max nodded. "A Team is entering. Over."

Gripping the frame on either end, Quin lifted all of his weight up onto his arms and, curling upward, settled himself over the hole, then slowly lowered himself through the skylight. Once he was hanging from the frame and fully inside the building, he gave his eyes a moment to adjust.

They were over a mezzanine, which would give them the perfect position to set up the powder bomb for release. With a soft *phewt*, his wings unfurled, and he let go of the skylight, using his wings to create enough resistance that he dropped slowly and silently onto the metal mezzanine.

"Traveling down the west side of the building to set the powder bomb. Over." Quin took just enough time to see Max follow in after him, then moved down the opposite side of the building.

Below him, satyrs, demogorgons, and minotaurs were shifting crates into position near a large bay door. Scanning quickly, Quin frowned. He didn't see any ignis.

"Be quick. I want this shipment on its way to Texas by midnight." The voice was elegant, controlled, with an underlying note of power. Quin knelt down, hiding himself more thoroughly in the darkness.

Orcus—or Enrique, as Ruin referred to him—exited an

office on the other side of the building. He wore an expensive looking suit and had perfectly coiffed hair. Quin couldn't wait to see him in cuffs as well.

"We've got one last one to crate up, Boss, then we'll be ready to take 'em out to the ship." A satyr came up to Orcus, no clothes on his body, just his bare chest and his lower fur-covered goat half.

Quin grit his teeth and pulled his powder bomb out of his side satchel. Carefully, he used a black cable tie to attach it to the railing of the mezzanine, situating it so that it faced out over the room.

"My powder bomb is ready. Over," Quin said into the mic attached to his collar.

"As is mine," Max said. "B & C Team, are you ready? Over."

Both Marcellus and Albina replied with a quick "ready".

"B and C, enter ten seconds after detonation. Nox, cut power to the building, and Quin, detonate on the count of three. One. Two. Three."

As Max said "three", Quin pressed the detonation switch on his powder bomb. It beeped, then a giant cloud of powder erupted from it. Across the warehouse, a second powder bomb released. At the same time, the overhead lights went out.

"What the hell?!" came shouts from below.

Quin waited long enough to see the powder fill the entire warehouse below, then spread his wings and leaped into the open air.

The powder only added to the darkness, making it difficult to see, but he didn't care. He swooped down into the thick of things, drawing his bo staff from his back. As his feet touched down on the cement floor, a minotaur appeared before him, coughing up powder and looking as pissed as a bull in a slaughter shop.

Quin struck out with his staff. The minotaur blocked with a thick, muscular forearm. Quin pushed against his arm, forcing the beast back, and drove a knee up into his side. The bull grunted and drove one meaty fist into Quin's face.

It hurt, but it was nothing he wasn't used to. Shaking it off, Quin spun, twirling the staff around his form to protect himself, then jabbed forward. This time, he was fast enough to catch the minotaur by surprise, and the tip landed directly in his abs. He gasped and doubled over.

The sides of the warehouse exploded open as ignis burst through doors and created holes for themselves. Further shouts rang out from Enrique's minions as the ignis swarmed them with blazing swords.

Shots from an assault rifle rang out, flashes from the bullets lighting up the darkness of the warehouse. Quin wasn't distracted. As his minotaur lurched forward, he swung the bo staff around swiftly and let it connect with the side of the minotaur's head. The impact ricocheted through his arm, and the minotaur staggered.

Not allowing him a moment to recover, Quin flapped down with his wings to lift into the air and kicked forward, planting his boot squarely in the minotaur's face.

The beast flew backward, skidding a little on the ground, and did not get up.

Landing back on the ground, Quin brought his bo staff in against his side. Sensing motion, he spun on his heel but wasn't fast enough to avoid the butt of a rifle coming for his head.

The blow rocked him back, but he deflected a second with his staff as he dropped down to one knee. Blinking blood from his eyes, he braced the end of his staff on the floor and, using his grip on it as momentum, swung his body around low on the ground to sweep his leg against the satyr's ankles.

The male went down onto his back, and Quin was upon him, the bo staff pressed to his windpipe, cutting off his oxygen until he passed out.

All around Quin, guns fired, creatures shouted, and bodies clashed in hand-to-hand combat.

Quin climbed off the unconscious satyr and looked up in time to see Cyprian slam the hilt of his sword down on the head of a fellow ignis. Quin blinked away dust, uncertain that he'd seen correctly. But the smirk Cyprian gave him when he turned and saw Quin watching told him everything he needed to know.

They advanced on each other, Cyprian's sword glowing with fire and Quin's staff crossed protectively in front of him.

"Why?" Quin growled, disgust filling him. To betray his own kind?

Cyprian only shrugged. "I have my reasons, you mindless slave."

Quin bristled and lunged at Cyprian, who managed to parry his bo with a swipe of his sword. The flames licked along his staff but did not ignite. Their arms locked, Cyprian landed a kick to Quin's shin, causing his knee to buckle.

Recovering quickly, Quin put all of his strength into his rise back up and forced Cyprian to take a step back. Spinning around, he used the momentum to bring the bo staff down hard on Cyprian's shoulder. He cried out, and his stance buckled just a fraction. It was enough for Quin to get in under his guard and thrust the butt of the bo into his abdomen.

Cyprian bent forward, air whooshing out of him in a deep grunt. But he recovered quickly, his free hand clamping down on the bo so Quin couldn't pull it away in time to avoid Cyprian cutting it in half.

Quin growled, looking at what was left of his bo staff in his hand, then tossed it aside. Pulling the large dagger from the strap on his thigh, he brought his other hand up to protect his face. "I can still beat you."

Cyprian smirked. "Is that so?" He advanced aggressively with slices of the burning sword that Quin was forced to duck beneath, hitting the ground to tumble sideways.

The sword swung through the air, and Quin rolled out of the way just in time for it to smash into the concrete, embedding in the floor itself. Spinning, Quin swept a leg out at Cyprian's ankles, knocking him to the floor.

Throwing himself down on top of Cyprian, he pressed the edge of his dagger to his throat. "I'm taking you in, and I'm going to personally make certain you spill everything."

Cyprian's smirk did not fade. "Long live Orcus," he rasped out. Something in his jaw clicked, and then foam began spewing from his mouth.

"Blast!" Quin shouted, and he watched as the light in Cyprian's eyes faded.

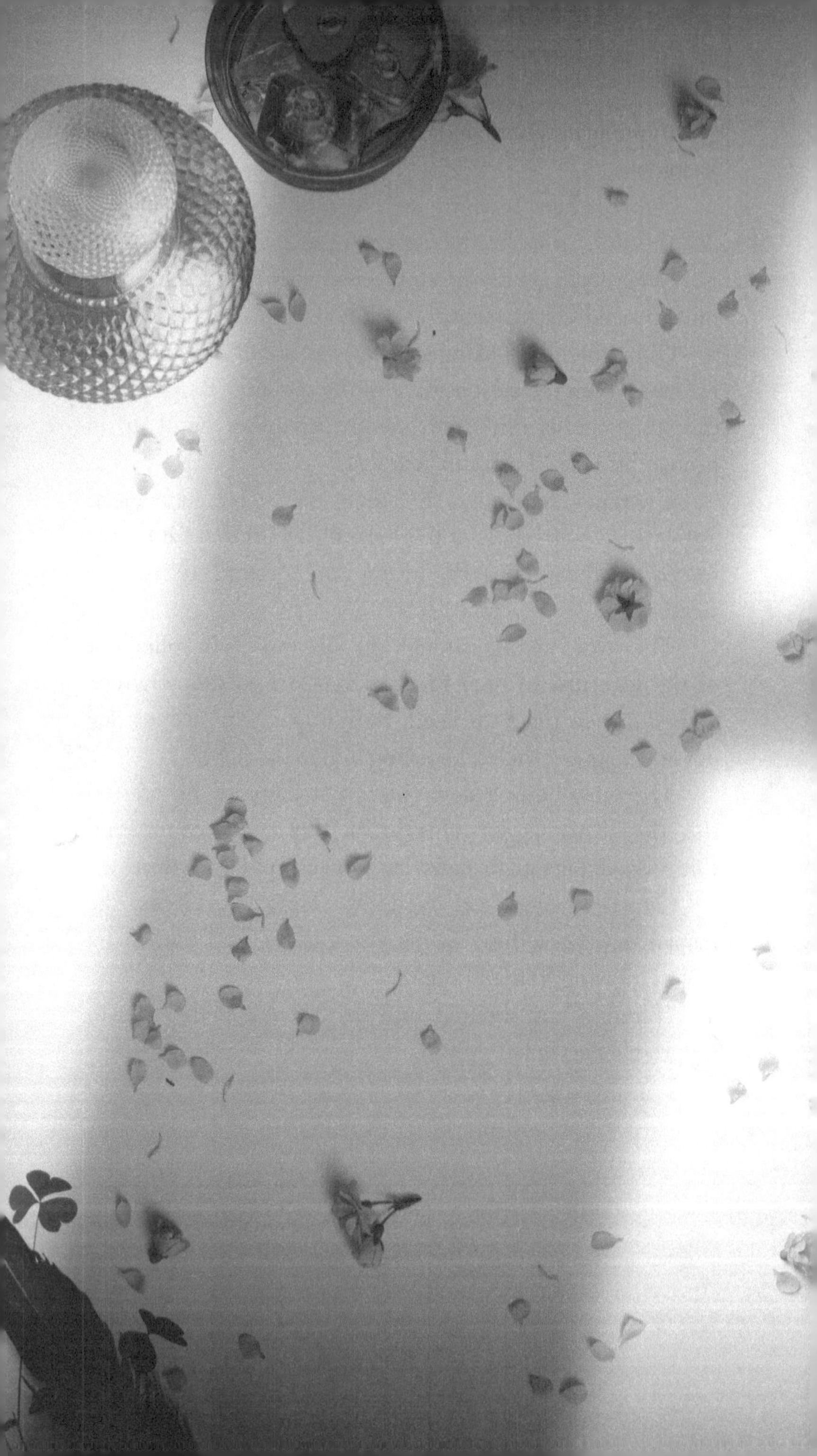

Chapter 40
Max

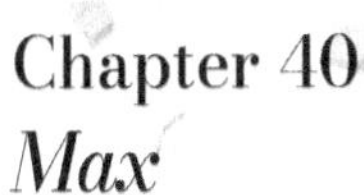

His family wouldn't approve, Max knew that. Ignis weren't supposed to seek out vengeance. Weren't supposed to even feel the things required to hold a grudge, at least not a personal one. But watching Enrique—Orcus—whatever he was calling himself this week—strut around like a little emperor commanding his army was enough to make Max's blood boil. Rage was not a feeling Max was accustomed to. He lived on a more even keel than that, as was expected of his race. But Enrique had hurt someone Max loved. *Loved.* He could think that now, could acknowledge it. He loved Ander Ruin. And the moment he got back to the Sanctum, he was going to tell him so.

But first, he was going to bring the abusive asshole who had hurt the one he loved down a peg or two. Hopefully ten.

Max cracked his knuckles the moment before the smoke bombs detonated, sending the room into a haze that even his enhanced ignis vision struggled to see through. But he'd clocked where Enrique was standing when the bomb went off, and he couldn't have gotten too far in the ensuing commotion. So Max took one breath, steadying himself, pulled his daggers from their holsters on his thighs, then dove over the railing into the fray. Straight toward where he had seen Enrique last.

His hip hit something in the haze, maybe the corner of a table, and he winced a little but stayed on his feet, kept hold of his weapons. Maximus Schields was trained for this, built for it. He gave his eyes a moment to adjust, blinking through the haze of powder as it settled.

Then there was a sneeze—a recognizable sneeze—off to his right, and Max didn't have time to focus on the way the powder burned his eyes anymore. He lurched in that direction, sending another table skidding across the room loudly just as Enrique came into view.

Enrique's eyes widened for a moment, then narrowed when recognition set in. "Of course it's you. I should have known the princeling would send his pet ignis after me."

There was no time to deny the accusation. No time to trade banter, quips, or barbs. The battle raged around them, the sound of Max's ignis brethren fighting for the lives of their own, and there Enrique stood, throwing shade at Ander like he had any right.

"Orcus, god of punishment, you are under arrest for the trafficking of magical creatures. Come quietly, or risk making this harder for yourself." It was a warning Max honestly hoped he didn't heed. He'd love to dole out even half of the pain Enrique had inflicted on those around him.

"Oh, you stupid boy," Enrique said after another sneeze. His hand reached out, a blazing sword appearing in his grasp as he set his feet. "You're going to regret ever setting eyes on what is mine."

Max wouldn't. Not even if it cost him his life. Ander was worth all of this. But this fight, it wasn't just about

Ander. So Max steadied himself, raised his daggers, and met the first slash of Enrique's sword with all the strength that he possessed. The metal burned hot, scorching too close to Max's face where Enrique pushed his advantage, making Max take a step back to brace himself.

Enrique was stronger. Yes. He was a god. And the powder hadn't done its job, not yet. But there was no way he was angrier or more determined than Max to see this thing through. To end it on his own terms. And his terms included Enrique locked up for a thousand years, preferably in a tiny cage the way those ignis had been.

Another sneeze, and Max pushed back, shoving Enrique off him long enough to frown down at where the god's sword had left indents in his daggers. Melted metal dribbled down toward the hilts. That shouldn't have been possible, not with the way his blades were built to withstand an ignis's heat.

Damn it.

"This weapon was forged in the pits of Acheron," Enrique said, tone almost conversational as he shoved a crate out of the way, making space for him to circle Max like a shark. Max's skin crawled under that gaze. Every instinct in his body told him to run, to flee. He was not meant to take on gods. It went against his nature. But he stood his ground, his feet moving slowly as he tracked Enrique's movements, waiting for the next attack. He could see the battle raging out of the corner of his eye. An ignis squaring up with a demogorgon off to his right. Another behind Enrique had already cuffed a pair of satyrs. "Its fire burns hotter than any Ignis flame in existence."

"Do you always talk this much when you're about to kill someone?" Max asked through his teeth, a tight smile crawling across his face. Enrique was unsettled, he could see it. They'd caught him by surprise, and now he was blustering, trying to make himself seem larger than life, when really, he was just a god who'd gotten caught doing something he shouldn't. Just another criminal. "Or am I just special?"

He didn't wait for Enrique to lunge again, to find a weakness. As Enrique circled around to his left, likely thinking he could attack Max on his non-dominant side, Max spun. His wings flared out, forcing yet more powder toward Enrique, who sneezed, wobbled—and Max struck. One dagger slashed across his abdomen, drawing a pinprick of golden blood from his skin. The other caught the sword Enrique raised to counter.

The heat of the sword singed Max's skin, too hot even for an ignis, where Enrique pressed it in closer to his face, using the fact that Max was holding him off with one arm. Flames snapped and sizzled, popping off toward Max's skin and dancing against his cheek. If he weren't made of fire himself, he would have been burned by now. Nothing but ash and stardust. And maybe if he let Enrique push closer, maybe if he let this go on for much longer, he would be.

Max lifted a foot and kicked Enrique's stomach, shoving him away to give Max more breathing room. Enrique used the momentum and spun, slashing out with his sword again and catching Max in the bicep. There wasn't even blood left behind; the wound cauterized the moment it'd happened. Max didn't so much as hiss at the bite of the blade and the sting of the fire. There was too much else to focus on. Like how Enrique had pulled a dagger from nowhere and used the opening created by his wild swing to thrust the blade at Max. It glanced to the left as Max shifted but still dug in deep beneath his ribs.

Max dropped one of his own daggers to grab Enrique's

wrist in a grip so tight that, on anything but a god, it would've cracked bone.

With a wince, Enrique tried to pull his arm free, jiggling the dagger where it was still buried deep in Max's side. But Max wasn't going to let go. Not now that he had him. And he felt the god's strength waning. His pulse became erratic in the delicate veins beneath Max's tight hold. The sword sputtered once, then went out, then disappeared entirely, as if Enrique couldn't keep the magic that was needed to maintain its existence on the mortal plane going.

"You've drugged me." Enrique gasped, struggling uselessly against Max's grip, every tug, every shift opening the wound at Max's side up further and further. But he didn't care, couldn't. Because there was fear in Enrique's eyes now, and he relished it. "You and that little bint drugged me."

"Sucks to be at the mercy of someone bigger and stronger, doesn't it?" Max asked, finally forcing Enrique to release the dagger and grabbing his other wrist, which had taken to swatting at Max's face, nails digging in, the only line of defense left to him in his weakened state.

"You'll die for this," Enrique spat. His face was twisted, furious, but his eyes were starting to look glassy and distant. Each breath he took had him swallowing down more of Ander's powder, the magic doing its work as he sagged against Max.

"After what you've done? You'll be lucky if you see sunlight before the dawn of a new century," Max whispered, his tone dark and cutting, so unlike the man he usually was. Unlike the man Ander had fallen in love with. There wasn't room for that man, not here, not facing this enemy. If Max wanted to make sure Enrique never came for him or Ander again, he had to make it clear there would be consequences. He had to strike fear into the heart of the god. Even if he didn't know that he could back it up. "Look me up in 3010."

Enrique snarled, and with one last blast of hate, summoning reserves of strength Max was sure he didn't really have, he grabbed Max around the throat, his grip crushing and strong enough to leave behind a bruise. Max's breath caught in his throat, unable to get out of his lungs, as Enrique lifted him from the ground, the pressure only relieved by the fluttering of his wings. "I'm going to fucking *burn* you and that little mutt."

Max did nothing more than smile, his lips curled back in something sarcastic and cutting, and waited one beat, two, for Enrique to swallow down another lungful of the powder in his rage and sag. His grip released, dropping Max to his feet, before Enrique's eyes rolled back into his head, and he fell, head cracking against one of the tables on his way to the floor.

Sucking in a breath that burned all the way down, Max pulled the cuffs from his belt and moved to nudge Enrique over onto his stomach, pulling his arms behind his back and restraining them. Satisfaction rippled through him, curling his toes in his boots as he gave Enrique one solid kick to the ribs just for the sheer pettiness of it.

"That our guy?" Chiron—an ignis with dusty gray wings—asked.

"Yup." Max replied, resisting the urge to give Enrique another kick. It was usually frowned upon to beat the living shit out of a suspect after they'd been cuffed, but he didn't think anyone would begrudge him this small bit of vengeance considering all Enrique had done to their kind.

"You've still got a little something—" They pointed to the dagger still hanging from Max's side. Blood had dribbled down from the wound and was now cooling against his skin.

The adrenaline burned away. Max swayed on his feet as the pain hit him full force. "Shit."

"Yeah. Shit." Chiron moved to shore up Max's side, helping remove the dagger. It dropped to the floor with a hollow *clang*, making Max realize for the first time that the sounds of battle had subsided. He looked around, his vision still swimming, to take in the scene.

There was blood spilled, yes.

Ignis blood, yes.

But there was also the blood of their enemies. And while his people looked worse for wear, the battle was won. Enrique and his henchmen were all on the floor, bound.

"Report," Max said, tapping on the piece in his ear. The twins had been eerily silent through the whole fight, which, honestly, was probably for the best. He couldn't have dealt with their bickering when he was trying to subdue someone as strong as Enrique.

"All of ours are present and accounted for aside from Cyprian. Over," Nash replied. His tone was a little stilted, a little strained, like maybe he was shaken up by everything that had just gone down. Or maybe he'd heard what Max said to Enrique? Heard the threats?

"Cyprian?" Max frowned. "What happened to Cyprian?"

"He, uh—" Max thought he heard Nash shifting in his chair through the comm.

"He killed himself, Max," Nox murmured softly. "We— We'll give you a full report later."

Max swallowed around the bile rising in his throat and nodded. "And the other side?" Max pushed past the gnawing feeling in his belly. His eyes fixed on Quin over in one corner, a tiny ignis wrapped tight around his leg, little green wings—like a hummingbird's—fluttering too fast behind them. "C Team, report. Did anyone escape? Over."

"No escapes, sir. Our reinforcements held the line. Over," the leader of C Team reported, her voice sharp and curt. Max liked her well enough, but he wished sometimes that she weren't quite so to the point.

He glanced down at the wound in his side again. It was deep. Would likely need stitches. Might even scar. But it wasn't life-threatening. One of the other members of A Team returned with some bandages, and between Chiron, Max, and them, they managed to get his torso wrapped up to at least staunch the bleeding until he could get back to the sanctuary and be seen by a medic.

"Send in the cleanup crew," he ordered Nox and Nash, and didn't wait for a reply before he made his way across the ruined warehouse to where Quin was looking increasingly uncomfortable with the child holding fast to his leg.

When Quin looked up to see Max approaching, he signed a slow, "Approach carefully. They're very scared."

Max nodded, measured his steps out more, and made sure to telegraph his movements so the child saw him coming. He tucked his wings in close to his back, to make himself smaller, and squatted down to the child's level even though it pulled on his injuries. "Hi there. I'm Quin's brother, Max."

The child squeaked, hiding their face behind Quin's thigh.

"It's okay. Max isn't going to hurt you." Quin's voice was the softest Max thought he'd ever heard it, and he'd been there for Quin's first words after coming home from Syria.

The child trembled, their tiny fists tightening in Quin's cargo pants, knuckles turning pale with the pressure.

Quin lifted his head to look at Max helplessly, asking with nothing more than his eyes, *What do I do?* Max had never been able to leave Quin hanging when he looked that lost. It was the foundation of their whole relationship. Quin was lost, and Max found him. He'd always had Quin's back that way; now would be no different.

Max glanced around. The other children all seemed calmer, less afraid of the ignis who had come to rescue them, and he wasn't sure exactly what that meant. Had they been with Enrique longer? Were they going to need to go through testing to ensure they weren't sleeper agents? Or was it that they hadn't been with him as long? Had they not yet given up hope that someone would save them, while the child clinging to Quin looked like they believed if they released their hold on Quin, the safety he offered might disappear.

"Why don't you stick with me and Q for a bit?" Max asked the child, not really expecting an answer. "We're going to head back to the sanctuary and get patched up. Then maybe grab a bite to eat. Are you hungry?"

"Max," Quin signed, the movement small, unsure. Max wanted to hug him so tight. But any sudden movement would probably have made the child uncomfortable, so he just shook his head.

"They can hang out with us until we find them a Guardian," Max signed back, making sure that his own fingers moved confidently to put Quin at ease. He wasn't sure how he knew it—maybe he could just read his brother that well—but it didn't look like Quin actually *wanted* to hand the child off to anyone else. Maybe he saw too much of himself in them. Or maybe it was just that Quin was feeling a little vulnerable himself after what just happened. Maybe it was some combination of the two. Max didn't think it mattered. "It'll be fine."

"Hungy," a small voice squeaked, half muffled by the fabric of Quin's pants, and tentative, like they thought maybe they'd be punished for voicing a complaint.

"Well, that's great, so am I." Max fixed them with a small smile, and his fingers worked over the words, "You got them?"

Quin nodded, seeming to relax, then bent down to scoop the child up into his arms, careful of their delicate wings. "We need to get them all back to the medic." His gaze flicked down to Max's injury as if just noticing it, and he was clearly no happy about it. "Is that a stab wound?"

"Tis but a scratch." Max chuckled. "C'mon, let's go home."

Quin just snorted and hitched the child up higher and more securely in his arms.

Chapter 41
Ander

After separating from Mab and Ander at the palace, Indra and Prometheus finally appeared at the sanctuary with a small contingent of guards alongside them and a scowling Hades following not long behind. Indra filled the space with his self-importance and command, making the sanctuary seem smaller than it actually was. Rather than hiding away in Galeo's office, like the captain seemed to want to happen, Indra settled down at the reception desk, leaning back in the chair with his feet propped up on the edge of the desk itself.

While he appeared casual and comfortable, Ander could see the fury that resided just below the surface. The king of the gods was ready to snap someone in half if they sneezed the wrong way, but he wasn't going to show it. Better to let it simmer just out of sight, leaving the space around them all feeling strained.

Prometheus and Hades stood behind Indra, two wild and stormy bodyguards emitting their own equally terrifying fury.

Ander likely should have stayed at Indra's side—it was

what any proper, loyal citizen of Underworld would have done. But he couldn't stomach Indra's energy with his own anxiety running rampant. Instead, he cloistered himself away in Max's office once more. Pulling one of Max's sweaters around him, he buried his nose in the smell and remembered the feel of his strong arms.

Mab had followed him around the sanctuary as was needed, continuing to distract him. Nothing had worked quite as well as her comment about Quin being the one who had sketched the picture of her on the napkin. A napkin she had kept with her. He'd seen the way she looked at it even if she didn't want to admit it.

That information Ander was going to store away for a later date.

At last, a young ignis who wasn't ready for the field poked his head into the office and let them know the tactical team was on their way back home. Ander felt like he was going to jump out of his skin but did not need to be told twice.

He raced down the hall, almost skidding to a stop when he came to the reception desk. Indra himself sat up, his feet back on the ground and an official look on his face.

When the sanctuary doors finally burst open, a number of dirty, bruised, and bloody ignis entered. They looked weary but triumphant. A good sign for the mission. None of them, however, were Max.

Ander brushed his hands along his thighs, feeling his impatience and worry mount. He needed to see him. Needed to know that he was okay.

The first group parted, and behind them was Max, his hands on a handcuffed Enrique, whose face was twisted in a sullen pout. Just behind them came Quin, who carried a small ignis youngling in his arms. Ander didn't have eyes for anyone else but Max, and he bit his lip harshly to keep from squealing in pure joy.

He was alive.

Ander's eyes dropped to the bloodstained bandage around his waist. He was alive, but he had been badly injured.

Fury filled Ander's vision, and without thought, he glided forward and punched Enrique square in the jaw. The god's head went sideways, and Ander's knuckles screamed in pain, but a little part of him felt validated.

"Ander!" Max squawked in surprise.

Enrique, however, slowly turned his head back around to face him, a glint of contempt but also amusement in his eyes. His tongue licked away the spot of gold at the corner of his lips. "Hello to you too, princeling."

Ander lifted his hand and pointed his finger in Enrique's face. "Shut up. Just. Shut. Up. It's over, Enrique. You're through. Do you understand me? They all know what you've been up to, I made sure of it."

He laughed darkly, bitterly. "Do you think this is enough to stop me? A few ignis?"

"Perhaps they aren't," came a deep, angry voice from behind Ander. "But I am." Indra stepped forward.

"*We* are," Hades corrected. He and Prometheus fell in line with Indra, their furious eyes pinned on Enrique.

Enrique's face faltered.

"Galeo, have him placed in an interrogation room. Prometheus will aid you. He's brought some chains specially made for our prisoner."

Indra's eyes were dark. Darker than Ander had ever seen them. He didn't think he'd actually ever seen Indra so angry. One did not mess with the king of Olympia's playthings and amass an army right under his nose.

Max passed Enrique off to a stern looking ignis with bluebird-like wings and Prometheus, who kicked Enrique's feet out from under him so he was left hanging awkwardly by his bound arms behind his back. From that position, the two males dragged him away,

Ander felt a sense of peace watching him be carted away. This was strike two for Enrique. Hopefully, they would lock him away in Tartarus and never let him out.

"Were you the one responsible for bringing him in?" Indra asked Max.

"I led the team, Your Majesty." Max bowed to the god. "But we couldn't have done it without Ander's help."

Indra threw an arm around Ander's shoulders, pulling him in for a brief side-hug. "He did well this time. I'm more used to this one getting himself into trouble rather than getting others out of it." He ruffled Ander's hair, which he grumbled at, throwing his hands up to try and stop the mussing. "But well done on your behalf as well. What is your name, ignis?"

"Maximus Schields." Max seemed to stand up taller, his shoulders a little broader.

"Maximus Schields," Indra echoed. He nodded his head, eyes shifting between the two of them. "I'll be keeping an eye on you." He then turned on his heel and walked away.

"Thank you, Ander, for bringing this to my attention," said Hades. "And I'm sorry for all of the pain Orcus has caused you." He looked solemn and sincere.

Too shocked to say anything, never having had a god apologize to him before, Ander simply nodded. Hades seemed to read his shocked expression and took it for what it was. With a tip of his head to Max, he turned to follow after his brother.

Shaking off the surprise, Ander didn't wait. He flung himself into Max's arms, which brought a grunt of pain out of him. "Oh, gods, you're injured!" Ander cried, pulling back.

Max didn't let him go far but pulled him back into his chest. "It's fine. I'm fine." He held Ander tight, burying his face in his hair. "And you're safe. You don't ever have to deal with him again."

"Oh, Max, I don't care about that!" He pulled back, cupping Max's face in his hands. "I don't care about him at all. I would face him down as many times as I had to if it meant keeping you safe. Gods, can't you see it?"

Max blinked. "See what?"

"How foolishly and completely in love with you I am! Gods, I can't think because of it. Because of *you*. And it's not because of stupid Erotes and his stupid arrow and that stupid amare bond. I love you to the point that it's maddening. You're the sweetest, most precious being I've ever met, and you might not want to be with me, but I want to be with you. Until the end of time! And if you say no, I'll accept it. I'll walk away and leave you be. But know this: I may just *die* if you do."

The entire time, Max had been staring at him with wide eyes. Ander wasn't sure if he was going to scoff, protest, or just back away from the slew of words that had come at him.

Instead, he laughed.

He laughed, and he grabbed Ander's face and pulled him in for a kiss.

Ander moved into it willingly, throwing his arms around his neck and pressing his body to Max's. Their lips melded together tightly, fitting as if they had been molded to connect. The taste of him was sweet but also not enough. Ander wanted all of him, completely and without reserve.

When Max pulled back, they both took a much-needed deep breath.

"I don't care what brought us together, Ander, I'm just so happy that we found each other. I don't want to live without you either."

Happiness bubbled up inside Ander, making him unable to do anything but pull Max in for another kiss. Desire, hot and heady, swelled within him. He wanted nothing more than to drag Max home and finally show him how much he meant to him, through every soft kiss and gentle caress.

He was pulled from the kiss when Max winced. Ander stepped back, panting a little, and frowned. "Gods . . . I'm sorry. We need to get you fixed up."

"I'm okay." Ander narrowed his gaze at him. "Okay, fine. I was stabbed. I could use some help."

"Maximus!" Ander squawked. "*Stabbed?!* Oh my gods! Why didn't you say something?!"

From nearby, Quin grunted. "He's good at avoiding it. Max, go let Ander heal you, then go home."

Max shook his head. "I can't. I have all my pap—"

Quin cut him off. "I'll take care of your paperwork."

"No, you don't have to do that." This time it was Quin who narrowed his eyes on Max. Something passed silently between the brothers that Ander wasn't privy to, but eventually, Max sighed and nodded. "Okay. Thanks."

Ander reached out to take Max's hand, which he accepted quickly. "Can I just take you back to my place now?" he asked hopefully. "I'd rather not let you out of my sight tonight if I can avoid it."

Max grinned a little goofily and nodded. "Okay. Sure."

Unable to help himself, Ander leaned in to kiss Max

quickly on the cheek. Then he turned to find Mab not too far behind him. "I'm sorry to just abandon you—"

"Go." She shoved him a little, a smirk on her lips and tenderness in her eyes. "Go take care of Wonderboy and call me in the morning."

Ander pulled her into a hug, hoping that his tight squeeze would tell her everything he needed her to know. "Thanks, Mabbers." He kissed her cheek and released her. Winking, he spun back around to Max and carefully pulled him into his arms. "Let's get you back to my place, sweetheart."

Max blushed and nodded.

In his condo, Monnie began to yip excitedly at their appearance. She scurried from her soft, plush bed in the living room to prance around them, yipping more.

"Monnie! Hush!"

Max laughed a little, pressing a hand to his side as he winced. "She's just happy to see us."

"Yes, well, her bark is a tad too high-pitched for my liking." Ander bent down and scooped up the small dog. "Listen here, miss, you're a bit much right now." She yipped once more and lapped at his nose. Grinning at her, he kissed the top of her head, then set her on the island. With a snap of his fingers, her food and water were refilled. "Now that she's settled, let's get you taken care of."

Taking Max's hand, he brought him over to the island as well so he could sit on one of the stools. With careful movements, Ander unwrapped the bandage from around Max's waist, frowning when he saw the gouge in his side.

"Gods, baby," he rasped. "This wasn't just a little wound." He pressed his hand gently over the red and bloody spot and began to pour magic into it.

Max shrugged a little. "Injuries happen on the job. It's why we were given fast healing abilities. If you left that be, I'd be fine in a couple days."

Ander glanced up at him. "Yes, but if we left it, I wouldn't be able to do to you what I'm planning on doing."

Max's cheeks flushed a deep red, and he licked his lips. "What are you . . . what are you planning on doing?" His voice was soft and husky.

Ander smirked up at him. "Well, darling, that's something you'll have to experience. I wouldn't want to ruin the surprise by filling you in just yet. But I can promise it will be terribly naughty."

If possible, Max's cheeks flushed even more as he looked down at Ander. "Then, please, heal me fast."

Ander's brows shot up, and his smirk widened. "Is that so? Well, who am I to keep the beautiful ignis waiting?"

Focusing all of his energy on healing the wound in his side, Ander pushed more magic into Max's flesh until each fine thread had stitched itself back together. When there was nothing but a fine red line to indicate the gash that had been there, Ander leaned down and pressed a soft kiss to the spot.

"How do you feel?" Ander looked up at Max, who was gazing down at him as if he were the most desirable thing he'd ever laid eyes on.

Ander blushed in response, his heart tripping faster and his stomach tightening. No one had ever looked at him like that before. As if they couldn't imagine anything ever being better.

He stepped between Max's spread thighs and ran his

hands along his shoulders, then slowly up along the back of his neck and into his hair. Max sighed, his eyes sliding shut. "How do you feel?"

"Wonderful," Max breathed out.

Ander smiled to himself and gently tipped Max's head back. "I'm so glad to hear that." He dipped his head down and claimed Max's lips. Max sighed happily into the kiss.

It was easy to melt into him. To let go of any doubts and worries and just lose himself in the feel of Max's lips against his own.

When his strong hands tightened on Ander's hips, Ander groaned happily and climbed onto Max's lap. Wrapping his legs around his waist, he deepened the kiss and dropped his hands to brush his fingers up over the silken wings at Max's back. The action wrung shudders out of Max, whose fingers bit into Ander's waist.

"Never stop touching me," Max breathed against his lips.

"Your wish is my command," Ander purred back, sliding his fingers between his feathers.

Beneath him, he could feel the telltale hardness of Max's pleasure and need, and it fueled Ander's own desire. Heated his blood and brought all the longing he'd been shutting away so that they could take this slow to the forefront.

Their lips met once more, the kiss hungry and demanding. The gentleness disappeared in favor of a building frenzy. Max stood, and Ander wrapped himself around him more tightly.

The journey to the bedroom was not smooth. They collided with a stool, had to lean against the wall to gain their bearings, and got caught on the doorframe. Eventually, they made it to Ander's room. Even in his need, Max was gentle laying Ander down on his back on the bed, kissing tenderly over his jaw and down his neck, making Ander wiggle in pleasure.

He took ahold of Max's shoulders and smoothly rolled him onto his back on the large bed, the long white wings spread out beneath him and Ander straddling him from above. With a snap of his fingers, Max's dirty and torn shirt was gone, leaving him bare. Ander brushed his hands down over Max's taught chest and leaned forward to trail kisses and nips over each sloping muscle and plane of flesh.

"I'm going to make you feel better than you've ever felt before," Ander rasped against the skin of his stomach while his fingers quickly undid the belt at his waist.

Max flushed brightly, gazing down at him with heated hazel eyes. "You already do."

Ander's heart swelled nearly to bursting, and he stretched up to kiss Max once more. He thought he had loved before, but nothing he had ever experienced before felt quite like this. So complete. So full.

Ander's kisses didn't stop until both of them were panting. His touches didn't stop until Max was a writhing mess beneath him and their bodies at last were joined. Sex had always been a pleasure, but as he looked into Max's eyes as they came together, he felt the connection that had been missing with everyone else. Felt the way his entire body came alive from the mere contact of his soulmate. Felt Max's love deep down to the core of himself and felt that broken part of himself begin to heal.

When at last stars erupted before his eyes and he collapsed back down to the mattress, Max pulled him in against his sweat-slicked chest and held him, pressing soft kisses to his forehead. Ander murmured contentedly and pressed a kiss to his shoulder.

"You are perfect," Ander muttered.

"Mm, no. That's you."

Ander shook his head. "No, definitely you."

Max pressed a fingertip against his lips. "Sh. You."

Giggling sleepily, he nipped at the fingertip and looked up into the adoring features of his love. Max grinned back, happiness shining on his face.

"Move in with me?" Ander asked suddenly, without any prior thought or intention. But there was no regret or hesitation in the question, only certainty.

Max's eyes widened in surprise, and he pressed their foreheads together. "Okay." He grinned, the sweetest grin that Ander had ever seen. It made his heart hurt with happiness.

"Yeah?" Ander was sure his heart was going to explode. Was this much joy even physically possible?

"Yeah," Max whispered. Everything Ander felt he could see reflected in Max's eyes. How he'd managed to earn this kind of love he would never know, but it was too amazing to let go of.

"We should call our siblings!" Ander snapped their phones to his hands, holding Max's out to him.

Max took the phone, chuckling a little. "Okay." His grin didn't seem capable of slipping from his lips, and Ander wondered if his own face looked like that.

Together, Ander and Max pressed the Call buttons for Mab and Quin respectively. When the two answered, and their faces popped up on their phone screens, Max and Ander pressed their heads together and held the phones so they could both be seen in each.

"Guess what?" Max asked excitedly.

Neither Quin nor Mab seemed too enthused. Quin just

stared, his expression blank, and Mab rolled her eyes, clicking her tongue at their theatrics.

"I asked Max to move in with me!" Ander cried.

Mab's mouth fell open a little and Quin's brows went up a fraction.

"And I said yes!"

The two on the other side were quiet. If they had been in the same room, Ander swore they would have shared a silent look of disapproval between them.

"Um . . . I hate to put a damper on this happy moment . . . but I feel like I need to be the voice of reason, *as usual*," Mab said through the phone.

Both Ander and Max gazed at each other quickly before looking back at the screen.

"Don't you think it's a bit too soon to move in with each other?"

Quin nodded. "I have to agree, Max. Maybe give it a little more time?"

Ander rolled his eyes at them. "Well, we don't think so. This feels right to us." He looked at Max, who he found was already looking back at him. There was such joy in the depths of Max's hazel eyes. Joy, comfort, acceptance. Ander didn't know what it was exactly, but when he looked into Max's eyes, he was sure he had found home.

"I love you," Ander whispered.

"I love you too," Max whispered back.

Ander's hand tightened lightly where it rested on top of Max's thigh, and Max's arm tugged him in a little closer. Their lips met without hesitation, despite the sound of disgust coming from Mab.

"Really, guys . . . I'm leaving if you're going to just make out in front of us."

From somewhere in the background behind Quin,

Ander could hear Nox and Nash exclaiming happily, "Leave them alone, you two!"

"Really, though, it's about freaking time!"

Max giggled against his lips, and Ander couldn't help but respond in kind.

The rest of the conversation disappeared around them as they tossed their phones down to the bed. Let the others hang up. None of it mattered. Not their families' concerns. Not the protests or the support. Not even what the Sanctum would say when they realized one of their ignis was in a committed relationship—with an inanimi, no less.

All that mattered was that the pain in Ander's chest had finally gone away. The fierce tug pulling him toward Max had settled.

He was where he was meant to be.

At long last, Ander had found true and honest love.

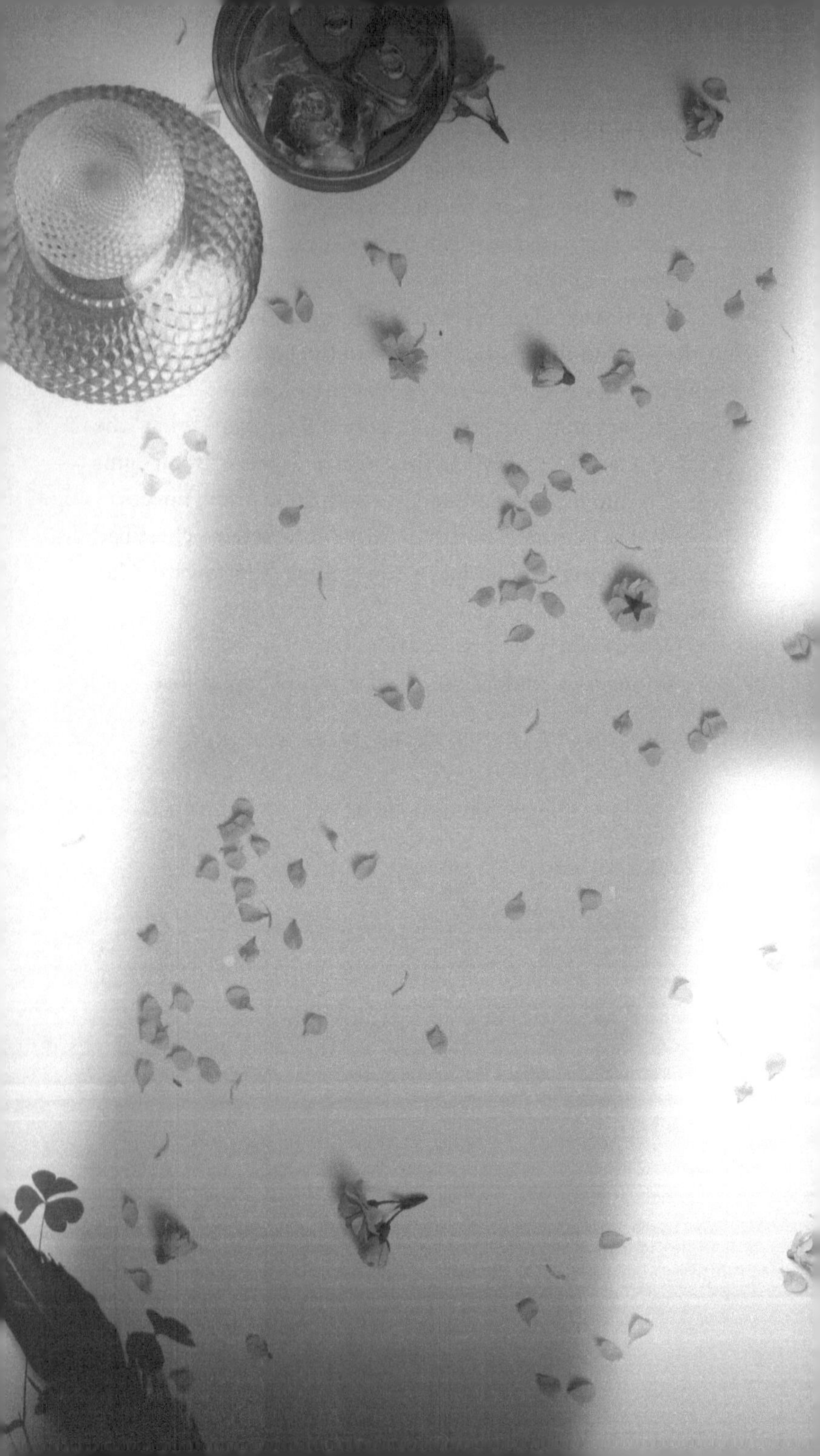

Epilogue
Mab

It hadn't been more than a couple of weeks—a month, maximum. Mab wasn't really sure, time was kind of hazy when a person was fighting for the lives of the people they loved, sorta liked, didn't hate, etc. And yet, there she was, carting boxes up in the elevator of Ander's ridiculously glitzy building. Why did he have a condo and not a house? She still didn't understand. Maybe it was something about the community that surrounded such a thing. Or maybe it was because the building was only a few blocks from Inferno, and Ander felt like he was inside the beating heart of Miami. Either way, she'd never get it. Mab liked her little house. Liked her privacy and her quiet. Liked knowing she could go there, and people couldn't find her unless she wanted them to.

What was more surprising still was the fact that Max had agreed to move in there with Ander. He wasn't *exactly* the clubbing type. So, she had to wonder—

"Why didn't they just get a place somewhere else? Together?" Mab asked no one in particular as the elevator dinged its way past floor after floor.

"Why didn't Ander just snap the boxes to his place?" Quin countered. He was still quiet around her, his words always careful and measured, but she could see how he was opening up. How they were sort of becoming friends. She had to wonder if it had anything to do with the youngling wrapped around his shoulders like an octopus, the little ignis's green wings flapping behind her. Whatever the reason, it was nice. And probably for the best since they were going to be spending a shit ton of time together now that Ander and Max were pretty much inseparable. Gods, Ander was going to be insufferable, wasn't he?

"Oh, but then we wouldn't have the spectacular experience of carrying boxes containing—" She jiggled the box to get the lid open enough for her to peek inside, but it remained stubbornly closed. "What the he—" She cleared her throat, her eyes darting up to the little girl—Octavia, Tavi, Max had said her name was—who was watching Mab through wide brown eyes. She was so tiny, her dark curls falling into even darker eyes, and thin brown fingers twisted in Quin's own black locks, giving him a disheveled look that made him almost seem approachable. *Almost.* "Heck is in this, anyways?"

"That's probably Max's popcorn buckets." Quin tilted his head to read the label on the side of the box, his brows raised a little. Tavi clung harder to Quin's neck, her wings fluttering to maintain her balance. "Yup. Popcorn buckets."

"Popcorn buckets? Like those ugly, chintzy, plastic things you get from the amusement park? The ones that usually have the same design on them as the souvenir cups?"

Quin raised a brow at her, and Mab wasn't very well versed in Quin facial expressions yet, but she thought this one might mean *How do you know so much about souvenir cups?*

"What? I go places." It had been a long time since she'd been to an amusement park, actually, and she and Ander had been *way* too drunk for it. Ander had thrown up after riding the teacups, and Mab had thrown up after riding one of the smaller coasters. She was honestly surprised they hadn't been blacklisted from the place.

"They're *Disney*," Quin said, as if this explained everything, though really it didn't. But Mab didn't actually care that much, so she just shrugged as they lapsed into comfortable silence, broken only by the soft ding of the elevator when they reached Ander's floor. Someone had propped the door to the condo open, and Max and Ander were milling about in the kitchen, already moving around each other as if in an eerily coordinated dance. She frowned as she watched Ander duck under one of Max's wings to get to the cabinet with the glasses, then snap his fingers, making room for Max's collection of coffee mugs.

"Do all you Schields collect random junk?" Mab asked loudly enough to earn her a glare from Ander and Max. And probably Quin and Tavi too, since she was an honorary Schields, at least for the time being.

Quin made a strange choking sound, and when Mab spun around to make sure he hadn't somehow managed to suffocate himself on his own spit, she found him clutching the box in his arms so hard that it was dented, and a small smile split his lips.

And, wow. Okay. So what the hell was with the Schields family and being unfairly attractive?

He made the sound again.

It took Mab a full thirty seconds to realize the sound was a laugh, a choking chortle that was echoed approximately twenty seconds later by Max from across the room. Mab looked over at Ander, making eye contact, and mouthed, "What'd I say?"

Ander shrugged, but he was grinning. One of those stupidly sappy ear-to-ear affairs, his eyes flicking back to Max with an expression so soft, it made Mab feel like she was intruding.

"You think that's funny, do you, Stink Eye?" Mab asked, her tone dry. She wondered if she could make Quin laugh more. Maybe make him laugh so hard it actually *sounded* like a laugh. A full-bellied thing that made him bend over, holding his stomach. Wouldn't that be interesting?

Quin shook his head, his lips still twitching involuntarily even as the laugh died away. "You know, I think I'm getting used to the Stink Eye thing?"

"You are?"

Quin nodded, but there was a sparkle in his eyes, something like mischief or gentle teasing.

"You know that means I'm going to have to come up with something else, right?" Mab tilted her head, a lock of curly white hair falling free from the braid Ander had helped her wrangle it into.

"Do your worst."

Something thrilled along Mab's nerves. A challenge. It'd been a while since she'd had one of those. Then Tavi leaned forward, pressing her stomach into the back of Quin's head so she could sign something in his face, and the mood was broken.

"Do you want water, milk, or juice?" Quin responded, already moving to pull her carefully from his shoulders.

Tavi scrunched her little upturned nose for a moment, considering, then held up two fingers.

When Mab turned back to the kitchen, because

watching Tavi and Quin interact like that also felt weirdly like intruding, she found Max throwing a wadded-up piece of tape into the bin on his way to the fridge.

"One point," Quin called from over her shoulder.

"One and a half," Max countered. "It didn't have as much weight to it as you think it did."

Quin grunted in response.

"Fine. One." Max rolled his eyes and pulled out his phone with one hand while tugging open the fridge with the other, recording something in an app Mab had never seen before.

"Points?" Ander asked, leaning over Max's shoulder to get a look at what he was doing.

"The Schields Family Scorecard." Max passed his phone to Ander while he grabbed a sippy cup from the diaper bag on the counter and filled it with milk. "Keeps things interesting."

Ander hummed, scrolling for a moment with his tongue between his teeth. "What do you win?"

"Honor," Quin called gravely.

Mab choked back a laugh, glad he couldn't see her face as she met Ander's eyes across the island, mirth dancing between them. With a raised brow, Ander tucked Max's phone back into his pocket. Mab shook her head. Now was not the time to continue their discussion about Quin and his drawing. Hopefully, that time would never come. Looking the strange warmth in the face would only upset the delicate balance Mab had found in her life.

"We should make a toast!" Ander called, cutting through the weird tension that had settled between them. He snapped his fingers, and a little bucket of ice appeared, a bottle of champagne already sweating inside of it.

"What to?" Max asked. He grabbed the bottle and

wrangled it open with only minimal trouble, then poured each of them a glass while Quin collected the little sippy cup from the counter and handed it to Tavi, who was now comfortably on his hip.

Mab picked her way across the living room to take one of the flutes between her fingers and hold it up to the light so she could watch the bubbles rise to the top. When she looked back at Max and Ander, how they leaned into each other, caught in each other's orbit, there was only one toast that felt appropriate.

"To family," she declared.

"To family," Ander echoed and clinked his glass with hers.

Acknowledgments

The Sanctuary of the Lost was a passion project for us. Mab and Ander are characters we created years ago on a RPG site, and never in our wildest dreams did we think they'd ever see the light of day. When we first began discussing the notion of co-authoring something together, there was never any question about what story we should do. The characters were there already, begging to be let out into the world. For this reason, we want to say a big thank you to everyone who stumbled upon this novella and decided to give Mab and Ander a chance. We hope their story speaks to you, just like it continues to speak to us.

There is something special about the found family a person chooses to surround themselves with, and we would be nothing without our fabulous family of fellow authors at Midnight Tide Publishing. Thank you all for your continued support through all aspects of the writing process! To our mutual bestie, Elle, thank you for being the push that got us both into this publishing game in the first place.

To our betas: Elle, Jordan, Candace, Jalessa, and Tanya you are all amazing! Your comments and insights helped Of Loyalties & Wreckage become the book it is today and we can't thank you enough.

Meg. Oh, Meg. We have nothing but praise for our grammar queen! (And we write ALL the suspicion just for you) You never bemoan our comma use, be it excessive or lacking, and you help make each sentence shine. Thank you.

Lastly, we want to thank the friends who support, encourage and maintain. Life is nothing without our besties, and it's because of them that we laugh, boast more confidence than we have on our own, and sometimes make truly terrible (but also amazing) decisions.

Give your bestie a tight hug for us!
XO

About Christis Christie

 Christis Christie was born and raised in a small town in New Brunswick, Canada where she spent most of her time either reading someone else's book, or dreaming of writing her own. Her favourite thing to dive into is an epic fantasy, or anything else magical and wondrous that really allows her imagination to take her away.

She now lives on the East Coast in Halifax, Nova Scotia where she works as an event designer, putting her interior decorating degree to wonderful use. Whenever she's not busy magically transforming venues for her clients, Christis is working on her own writing.

Her other dreams consist of one day visiting Ireland so she can frolic over the hills, and owning a teacup Pomeranian she can cart around everywhere with her.

Also By Christis Christie

Spun Gold: A Rumpelstiltskin Origin Story

Reaping Book One: Epheus

Sanctuary of the Lost
    Of Loyalties and Wreckage
    Of Love and Ruin

Anthologies
    Cirque de vol Mystique
    Something in the Shadows: A Halloween Anthology
    Emporium of Superstition - An Old Wives' Tale Anthology

Co-Authored with Elle Beaumont:
    The Dragon's Bride
    Seeds of Sorrow (Immortal Realms Book 1)
    Tides of Torment (Immortal Realms Book 2)

About Lou Wilham

Born and raised in a small town near the Chesapeake Bay, Lou Wilham grew up on a steady diet of fiction, arts and crafts, and Old Bay. After years of absorbing everything, there was to absorb of fiction, fantasy, and sci-fi she's left with a serious writing/drawing habit that just won't quit. These days, she spends much of her time writing, drawing, and chasing a very short Basset Hound named Sherlock.

When not, daydreaming up new characters to write and draw she can be found crocheting, making cute bookmarks, and binge-watching whatever happens to catch her eye.

Learn more about Lou and her future projects on her website: http://louinprogress.com/ or join her mailing list at: http://subscribepage.com/mailermailer

facebook.com/LouWilham

instagram.com/lou.wilham

Also By Lou Wilham

The Witches of Moondale
   The Hex Next Door
   The Ghost of Hexes Past

The Hunters of Ironport
   Overkill

The Heir To Moondust
   The Prince of Starlight
   The Prince of Daybreak
   The Crown of Night

Sanctuary of the Lost
   Of Loyalties and Wreckage
   Of Love and Ruin

The Curse Collection
   The Curse of The Black Cat
   The Curse of Ash and Blood
   The Curse of Flour and Feeling

Completed Series
   The Tales of the Sea Trilogy
   Villainous Heroics
   The Clockwork Chronicles

More Books You'll Love

If you enjoyed this story, please consider leaving a review.

Then check out more books from Midnight Tide
Publishing!

Of Flames and Curses by Whitney L. Spradling

Do fairies exist?

This is the question Lainey asks herself after her sister's brutal murder in Central Park. Armed with her sister's diary and the mysterious entries within, Lainey's quest for answers leads her to Phoenix, a surly but handsome fae.

The answer to Lainey's question reveals a truth that will change everything she thought she knew about herself and the world she lives in. A sacrifice must be made to break a curse that locked the gate between the human and faerie realms.

Leaving the only world she has known, Lainey finds

herself surrounded by evil queens, curses, and magical creatures. Together, Lainey and Phoenix must find a way to break the curse that doesn't result in Lainey's death—like her sister's.

Do fairies exist? The answer will change Lainey's life in ways she never imagined.

Available Now

Maiden of the Hollow Path by Shar Khan

Something dark has shaped the Marizad Palace and pulled Shahina Rukhezzi from exile. After spending eight years amongst the dwarven regime, the Paragon and Fifth Raja to the Lotus Throne has returned. A curse has touched the royal family, leaving the Great and Immortal Maharaj to stray upon his death bed.

In the seaport city of Stonegrave, Crogan Takahashi stands as the King of Lords. He rules over the War Table in a place forsaken and left to rot. With magicks that run rampant through his veins, he finds himself at the mercy of Shahina who searches for answers he's not willing to give so easily.

Yet as her presence pulls dark entities from their resting place in the Northern Province, Crogan learns there are things worse than death. As an ancient evil struggles to take the throne, he realizes Shahina might not be as bad as she seems.

Or so he thinks.

Available Soon

www.ingramcontent.com/pod-product-compliance
Lightning Source LLC
Chambersburg PA
CBHW030836190726
48285CB00004B/1242